BOOKS BY KAREN M. McMANUS

One of Us Is Lying

Two Can Keep a Secret

One of Us Is Next

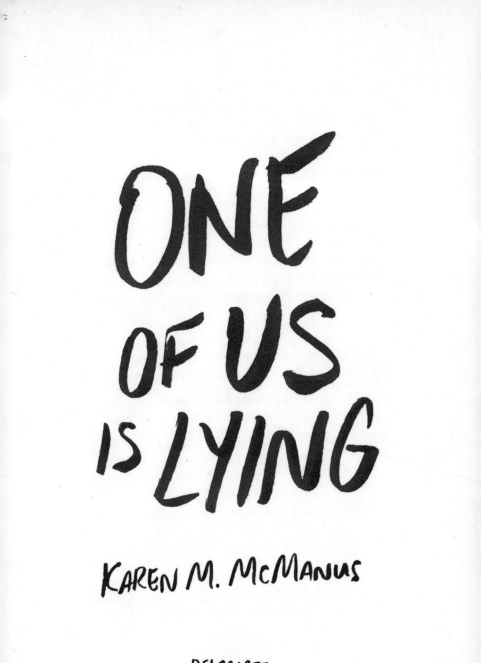

ONE
OF US
IS LYING

KAREN M. McMANUS

DELACORTE
PRESS

Text copyright © 2017 by Karen M. McManus, LLC.
Jacket art copyright © 2021 by Peacock TV LLC

All rights reserved. Published in the United States by Delacorte Press, an imprint of Random House Children's Books, a division of Penguin Random House LLC, New York.

Delacorte Press is a registered trademark and the colophon is a trademark of Penguin Random House LLC.

Visit us on the Web! GetUnderlined.com

Educators and librarians, for a variety of teaching tools, visit us at RHTeachersLibrarians.com

Library of Congress Cataloging-in-Publication Data
Names: McManus, Karen M., author.
Title: One of us is lying / Karen M. McManus.
Description: First edition. | New York : Delacorte Press, [2017] |
Summary: "When the creator of a high school gossip app mysteriously dies in front of four high-profile students all four become suspects. It's up to them to solve the case"— Provided by publisher.
Identifiers: LCCN 2016032495 | ISBN 978-1-5247-1468-0 (hc) |
ISBN 978-1-5247-1470-3 (ebook)
Subjects: | CYAC: Mystery and detective stories. | Murder—Fiction. |
High schools—Fiction. | Schools—Fiction.
Classification: LCC PZ7.1.M4637 On 2017 | DDC [Fic]—dc23

ISBN 978-0-593-56537-7 (Peacock edition)

The text of this book is set in 12-point Adobe Garamond Pro.
Interior design by Ken Crossland

Printed in the United States of America
10 9 8 7 6 5 4 3 2 1
First Edition

For Jack,
who always makes me laugh

PART ONE

SIMON SAYS

CHAPTER ONE

Bronwyn
Monday, September 24, 2:55 p.m.

A sex tape. A pregnancy scare. Two cheating scandals. And that's just this week's update. If all you knew of Bayview High was Simon Kelleher's gossip app, you'd wonder how anyone found time to go to class.

"Old news, Bronwyn," says a voice over my shoulder. "Wait till you see tomorrow's post."

Damn. I hate getting caught reading About That, especially by its creator. I lower my phone and slam my locker shut. "Whose lives are you ruining next, Simon?"

Simon falls into step beside me as I move against the flow of students heading for the exit. "It's a public service," he says with a dismissive wave. "You tutor Reggie Crawley, don't you? Wouldn't you rather know he has a camera in his bedroom?"

I don't bother answering. Me getting anywhere near the

3

bedroom of perpetual stoner Reggie Crawley is about as likely as Simon growing a conscience.

"Anyway, they bring it on themselves. If people didn't lie and cheat, I'd be out of business." Simon's cold blue eyes take in my lengthening strides. "Where are you rushing off to? Covering yourself in extracurricular glory?"

I wish. As if to taunt me, an alert crosses my phone: *Mathlete practice, 3 p.m., Epoch Coffee.* Followed by a text from one of my teammates: *Evan's here.*

Of course he is. The cute Mathlete—less of an oxymoron than you might think—seems to only ever show up when I can't.

"Not exactly," I say. As a general rule, and especially lately, I try to give Simon as little information as possible. We push through green metal doors to the back stairwell, a dividing line between the dinginess of the original Bayview High and its bright, airy new wing. Every year more wealthy families get priced out of San Diego and come fifteen miles east to Bayview, expecting that their tax dollars will buy them a nicer school experience than popcorn ceilings and scarred linoleum.

Simon's still on my heels when I reach Mr. Avery's lab on the third floor, and I half turn with my arms crossed. "Don't you have someplace to be?"

"Yeah. Detention," Simon says, and waits for me to keep walking. When I grasp the knob instead, he bursts out laughing. "You're kidding me. You too? What's your crime?"

"I'm wrongfully accused," I mutter, and yank the door open. Three other students are already seated, and I pause to take them in. Not the group I would have predicted. Except one.

Nate Macauley tips his chair back and smirks at me. "You make a wrong turn? This is detention, not student council."

He should know. Nate's been in trouble since fifth grade, which is right around the time we last spoke. The gossip mill tells me he's on probation with Bayview's finest for . . . something. It might be a DUI; it might be drug dealing. He's a notorious supplier, but my knowledge is purely theoretical.

"Save the commentary." Mr. Avery checks something off on a clipboard and closes the door behind Simon. High arched windows lining the back wall send triangles of afternoon sun splashing across the floor, and faint sounds of football practice float from the field behind the parking lot below.

I take a seat as Cooper Clay, who's palming a crumpled piece of paper like a baseball, whispers "Heads up, Addy" and tosses it toward the girl across from him. Addy Prentiss blinks, smiles uncertainly, and lets the ball drop to the floor.

The classroom clock inches toward three, and I follow its progress with a helpless feeling of injustice. I shouldn't even *be* here. I should be at Epoch Coffee, flirting awkwardly with Evan Neiman over differential equations.

Mr. Avery is a give-detention-first, ask-questions-never kind of guy, but maybe there's still time to change his mind. I clear my throat and start to raise my hand until I notice Nate's smirk broadening. "Mr. Avery, that wasn't my phone you found. I don't know how it got into my bag. *This* is mine," I say, brandishing my iPhone in its melon-striped case.

Honestly, you'd have to be clueless to bring a phone to Mr. Avery's lab. He has a strict no-phone policy and spends the first ten minutes of every class rooting through backpacks like

5

he's head of airline security and we're all on the watch list. My phone was in my locker, like always.

"You too?" Addy turns to me so quickly, her blond shampoo-ad hair swirls around her shoulders. She must have been surgically removed from her boyfriend in order to show up alone. "That wasn't my phone either."

"Me three," Cooper chimes in. His Southern accent makes it sound like *thray*. He and Addy exchange surprised looks, and I wonder how this is news to them when they're part of the same clique. Maybe überpopular people have better things to talk about than unfair detentions.

"Somebody punked us!" Simon leans forward with his elbows on the desk, looking spring-loaded and ready to pounce on fresh gossip. His gaze darts over all four of us, clustered in the middle of the otherwise empty classroom, before settling on Nate. "Why would anybody want to trap a bunch of students with mostly spotless records in detention? Seems like the sort of thing that, oh, I don't know, a guy who's here all the time might do for fun."

I look at Nate, but can't picture it. Rigging detention sounds like work, and everything about Nate—from his messy dark hair to his ratty leather jacket—screams *Can't be bothered.* Or yawns it, maybe. He meets my eyes but doesn't say a word, just tips his chair back even farther. Another millimeter and he'll fall right over.

Cooper sits up straighter, a frown crossing his Captain America face. "Hang on. I thought this was just a mix-up, but if the same thing happened to all of us, it's somebody's stupid idea of a prank. And I'm missing *baseball practice* because of it." He

6

says it like he's a heart surgeon being detained from a lifesaving operation.

Mr. Avery rolls his eyes. "Save the conspiracy theories for another teacher. I'm not buying it. You all know the rules against bringing phones to class, and you broke them." He gives Simon an especially sour glance. Teachers know About That exists, but there's not much they can do to stop it. Simon only uses initials to identify people and never talks openly about school. "Now listen up. You're here until four. I want each of you to write a five-hundred-word essay on how technology is ruining American high schools. Anyone who can't follow the rules gets another detention tomorrow."

"What do we write with?" Addy asks. "There aren't any computers here." Most classrooms have Chromebooks, but Mr. Avery, who looks like he should have retired a decade ago, is a holdout.

Mr. Avery crosses to Addy's desk and taps the corner of a lined yellow notepad. We all have one. "Explore the magic of longhand writing. It's a lost art."

Addy's pretty, heart-shaped face is a mask of confusion. "But how do we know when we've reached five hundred words?"

"Count," Mr. Avery replies. His eyes drop to the phone I'm still holding. "And hand that over, Miss Rojas."

"Doesn't the fact that you're confiscating my phone *twice* give you pause? Who has two phones?" I ask. Nate grins, so quick I almost miss it. "Seriously, Mr. Avery, somebody was playing a joke on us."

Mr. Avery's snowy mustache twitches in annoyance, and he extends his hand with a beckoning motion. "*Phone*, Miss Rojas.

Unless you want a return visit." I give it over with a sigh as he looks disapprovingly at the others. "The phones I took from the rest of you earlier are in my desk. You'll get them back after detention." Addy and Cooper exchange amused glances, probably because their actual phones are safe in their backpacks.

Mr. Avery tosses my phone into a drawer and sits behind the teacher's desk, opening a book as he prepares to ignore us for the next hour. I pull out a pen, tap it against my yellow notepad, and contemplate the assignment. Does Mr. Avery really believe technology is ruining schools? That's a pretty sweeping statement to make over a few contraband phones. Maybe it's a trap and he's looking for us to contradict him instead of agree.

I glance at Nate, who's bent over his notepad writing *computers suck* over and over in block letters.

It's possible I'm overthinking this.

Cooper
Monday, September 24, 3:05 p.m.

My hand hurts within minutes. It's pathetic, I guess, but I can't remember the last time I wrote anything longhand. Plus I'm using my right hand, which never feels natural no matter how many years I've done it. My father insisted I learn to write right-handed in second grade after he first saw me pitch. *Your left arm's gold,* he told me. *Don't waste it on crap that don't matter.* Which is anything but pitching as far as he's concerned.

That was when he started calling me Cooperstown, like the

8

baseball hall of fame. Nothing like putting a little pressure on an eight-year-old.

Simon reaches for his backpack and roots around, unzipping every section. He hoists it onto his lap and peers inside. "Where the hell's my water bottle?"

"No talking, Mr. Kelleher," Mr. Avery says without looking up.

"I know, but—my water bottle's missing. And I'm thirsty."

Mr. Avery points toward the sink at the back of the room, its counter crowded with beakers and petri dishes. "Get yourself a drink. *Quietly.*"

Simon gets up and grabs a cup from a stack on the counter, filling it with water from the tap. He heads back to his seat and puts the cup on his desk, but seems distracted by Nate's methodical writing. "Dude," he says, kicking his sneaker against the leg of Nate's desk. "Seriously. Did you put those phones in our backpacks to mess with us?"

Now Mr. Avery looks up, frowning. "I said *quietly,* Mr. Kelleher."

Nate leans back and crosses his arms. "Why would I do that?"

Simon shrugs. "Why do you do anything? So you'll have company for whatever your screw-up of the day was?"

"One more word out of either of you and it's detention tomorrow," Mr. Avery warns.

Simon opens his mouth anyway, but before he can speak there's the sound of tires squealing and then the crash of two cars hitting each other. Addy gasps and I brace myself against my desk like somebody just rear-ended me. Nate, who looks glad for the interruption, is the first on his feet toward the window. "Who gets into a fender bender in the school parking lot?" he asks.

Bronwyn looks at Mr. Avery like she's asking for permission, and when he gets up from his desk she heads for the window as well. Addy follows her, and I finally unfold myself from my seat. Might as well see what's going on. I lean against the ledge to look outside, and Simon comes up beside me with a disparaging laugh as he surveys the scene below.

Two cars, an old red one and a nondescript gray one, are smashed into each other at a right angle. We all stare at them in silence until Mr. Avery lets out an exasperated sigh. "I'd better make sure no one was hurt." He runs his eyes over all of us and zeroes in on Bronwyn as the most responsible of the bunch. "Miss Rojas, keep this room contained until I get back."

"Okay," Bronwyn says, casting a nervous glance toward Nate. We stay at the window, watching the scene below, but before Mr. Avery or another teacher appears outside, both cars start their engines and drive out of the parking lot.

"Well, that was anticlimactic," Simon says. He heads back to his desk and picks up his cup, but instead of sitting he wanders to the front of the room and scans the periodic table of elements poster. He leans out into the hallway like he's about to leave, but then he turns and raises his cup like he's toasting us. "Anyone else want some water?"

"I do," Addy says, slipping into her chair.

"Get it yourself, princess." Simon smirks. Addy rolls her eyes and stays put while Simon leans against Mr. Avery's desk. "Literally, huh? What'll you do with yourself now that homecoming's over? Big gap between now and senior prom."

Addy looks at me without answering. I don't blame her. Simon's train of thought almost never goes anywhere good when it comes to our friends. He acts like he's above caring whether he's popular, but he was pretty smug when he wound up on the junior prom court last spring. I'm still not sure how he pulled that off, unless he traded keeping secrets for votes.

Simon was nowhere to be found on homecoming court last week, though. I was voted king, so maybe I'm next on his list to harass, or whatever the hell he's doing.

"What's your point, Simon?" I ask, taking a seat next to Addy. Addy and I aren't close, exactly, but I kind of feel protective of her. She's been dating my best friend since freshman year, and she's a sweet girl. Also not the kind of person who knows how to stand up to a guy like Simon who just won't quit.

"She's a princess and you're a jock," he says. He thrusts his chin toward Bronwyn, then at Nate. "And you're a brain. And you're a criminal. You're all walking teen-movie stereotypes."

"What about you?" Bronwyn asks. She's been hovering near the window, but now goes to her desk and perches on top of it. She crosses her legs and pulls her dark ponytail over one shoulder. Something about her is cuter this year. New glasses, maybe? Longer hair? All of a sudden, she's kind of working this sexy-nerd thing.

"I'm the omniscient narrator," Simon says.

Bronwyn's brows rise above her black frames. "There's no such thing in teen movies."

"Ah, but Bronwyn." Simon winks and chugs his water in one long gulp. "There *is* such a thing in life."

He says it like a threat, and I wonder if he's got something on Bronwyn for that stupid app of his. I hate that thing. Almost all my friends have been on it at one point or another, and sometimes it causes real problems. My buddy Luis and his girlfriend broke up because of something Simon wrote. Though it *was* a true story about Luis hooking up with his girlfriend's cousin. But still. That stuff doesn't have to be published. Hallway gossip is bad enough.

And if I'm being honest, I'm pretty freaked at what Simon could write about me if he put his mind to it.

Simon holds his cup up, grimacing. "This tastes like crap." He drops the cup, and I roll my eyes at his attempt at drama. Even when he falls to the floor, I still think he's messing around. But then the wheezing starts.

Bronwyn's on her feet first, then kneeling beside him. "Simon," she says, shaking his shoulder. "Are you okay? What happened? Can you talk?" Her voice goes from concerned to panicky, and that's enough to get me moving. But Nate's faster, shoving past me and crouching next to Bronwyn.

"A pen," he says, his eyes scanning Simon's brick-red face. "You have a pen?" Simon nods wildly, his hand clawing at his throat. I grab the pen off my desk and try to hand it to Nate, thinking he's about to do an emergency tracheotomy or something. Nate just stares at me like I have two heads. "An *epinephrine* pen," he says, searching for Simon's backpack. "He's having an allergic reaction."

Addy stands and wraps her arms around her body, not saying a word. Bronwyn turns to me, face flushed. "I'm going to find a teacher and call nine-one-one. Stay with him, okay?" She grabs her phone out of Mr. Avery's drawer and runs into the hallway.

I kneel next to Simon. His eyes are bugging out of his head, his lips are blue, and he's making horrible choking noises. Nate dumps the entire contents of Simon's backpack on the floor and scrabbles through the mess of books, papers, and clothes. "Simon, where do you keep it?" he asks, tearing open the small front compartment and yanking out two regular pens and a set of keys.

Simon's way past talking, though. I put one sweaty palm on his shoulder, like that'll do any good. "You're okay, you're gonna be okay. We're gettin' help." I can hear my voice slowing, thickening like molasses. My accent always comes out hard when I'm stressed. I turn to Nate and ask, "You sure he's not chokin' on somethin'?" Maybe he needs the Heimlich maneuver, not a freaking medical pen.

Nate ignores me, tossing Simon's empty backpack aside. "Fuck!" he yells, slamming a fist on the floor. "Do you keep it on you, Simon? Simon!" Simon's eyes roll back in his head as Nate digs around in Simon's pockets. But he doesn't find anything except a wrinkled Kleenex.

Sirens blare in the distance as Mr. Avery and two other teachers race in with Bronwyn trailing behind them on her phone. "We can't find his EpiPen," Nate says tersely, gesturing to the pile of Simon's things.

Mr. Avery stares at Simon in slack-jawed horror for a second, then turns to me. "Cooper, the nurse's office has EpiPens. They should be labeled in plain sight. *Hurry!*"

I run into the hallway, hearing footsteps behind me that fade as I quickly reach the back stairwell and yank the door open. I take the stairs three at a time until I'm on the first floor, and weave through a few straggling students until I get to the nurse's office. The door's ajar, but nobody's there.

It's a cramped little space with the exam table up against the windows and a big gray storage cabinet looming to my left. I scan the room, my eyes landing on two wall-mounted white boxes with red block lettering. One reads EMERGENCY DEFIBRILLATOR, the other EMERGENCY EPINEPHRINE. I fumble at the latch on the second one and pull it open.

There's nothing inside.

I open the other box, which has a plastic device with a picture of a heart. I'm pretty sure that's not it, so I start rummaging through the gray storage cabinet, pulling out boxes of bandages and aspirin. I don't see anything that looks like a pen.

"Cooper, did you find them?" Ms. Grayson, one of the teachers who'd entered the lab with Mr. Avery and Bronwyn, barrels into the room. She's panting hard and clutching her side.

I gesture toward the empty wall-mounted box. "They should be there, right? But they're not."

"Check the supply cabinet," Ms. Grayson says, ignoring the Band-Aid boxes scattered across the floor that prove I've already tried. Another teacher joins us, and we tear the office apart as the sound of sirens gets closer. When we've opened the last cabinet, Ms. Grayson wipes a trickle of sweat from her forehead with the back of her hand. "Cooper, let Mr. Avery know we haven't found anything yet. Mr. Contos and I will keep looking."

I get to Mr. Avery's lab the same time the paramedics do.

There are three of them in navy uniforms, two pushing a long white stretcher, one racing ahead to clear the small crowd that's gathered around the door. I wait until they're all inside and slip in behind them. Mr. Avery's slumped next to the chalkboard, his yellow dress shirt untucked. "We couldn't find the pens," I tell him.

He runs a shaking hand through his thin white hair as one of the paramedics stabs Simon with a syringe and the other two lift him onto the stretcher. "God help that boy," he whispers. More to himself than to me, I think.

Addy's standing off to the side by herself, tears rolling down her cheeks. I cross over to her and put an arm around her shoulders as the paramedics maneuver Simon's stretcher into the hallway. "Can you come along?" one asks Mr. Avery. He nods and follows, leaving the room empty except for a few shell-shocked teachers and the four of us who started detention with Simon.

Barely fifteen minutes ago, by my guess, but it feels like hours.

"Is he okay now?" Addy asks in a strangled voice. Bronwyn clasps her phone between her palms like she's using it to pray. Nate stands with his hands on his hips, staring at the door as more teachers and students start trickling inside.

"I'm gonna go out on a limb and say no," he says.

CHAPTER TWO

Addy
Monday, September 24, 3:25 p.m.

Bronwyn, Nate, and Cooper are all talking to the teachers, but I can't. I need Jake. I pull my phone out of my bag to text him but my hands are shaking too bad. So I call instead.

"Baby?" He picks up on the second ring, sounding surprised. We're not big callers. None of our friends are. Sometimes when I'm with Jake and his phone rings, he holds it up and jokes, "What does 'incoming call' mean?" It's usually his mom.

"Jake" is all I can get out before I start bawling. Cooper's arm is still around my shoulders, and it's the only thing keeping me up. I'm crying too hard to talk, and Cooper takes the phone from me.

"Hey, man. 'S Cooper," he says, his accent thicker than normal. "Where you at?" He listens for a few seconds. "Can you meet us outside? There's been . . . Somethin' happened. Addy's

16

real upset. Naw, she's fine, but . . . Simon Kelleher got hurt bad in detention. Ambulance took him an' we dunno if he's gon' be okay." Cooper's words melt into one another like ice cream, and I can hardly understand him.

Bronwyn turns to the closest teacher, Ms. Grayson. "Should we stay? Do you need us?"

Ms. Grayson's hands flutter around her throat. "Goodness, I don't suppose so. You told the paramedics everything? Simon . . . took a drink of water and collapsed?" Bronwyn and Cooper both nod. "It's so strange. He has a peanut allergy, of course, but . . . you're sure he didn't eat anything?"

Cooper gives me my phone and runs a hand through his neatly cropped sandy hair. "I don't think so. He just drank a cup of water an' fell over."

"Maybe it was something he had with lunch," Ms. Grayson says. "It's possible he had a delayed reaction." She looks around the room, her eyes settling on Simon's discarded cup on the floor. "I suppose we should put this aside," she says, brushing past Bronwyn to pick it up. "Somebody might want to look at it."

"I want to go," I burst out, swiping at the tears on my cheeks. I can't stand being in this room another second.

"Okay if I help her?" Cooper asks, and Ms. Grayson nods. "Should I come back?"

"No, that's all right, Cooper. I'm sure they'll call you if they need you. Go home and try to get back to normal. Simon's in good hands now." She leans in a little closer, her tone softening. "I am so sorry. That must have been awful."

She's mostly looking at Cooper, though. There's not a female teacher at Bayview who can resist his all-American charm.

17

Cooper keeps an arm around me on the way out. It's nice. I don't have brothers, but if I did, I imagine this is how they'd prop you up when you felt sick. Jake wouldn't like most of his friends being this close to me, but Cooper's fine. He's a gentleman. I lean into him as we pass posters for last week's homecoming dance that haven't been taken down yet. Cooper pushes the front door open, and there, thank God, is Jake.

I collapse into his arms, and for a second, everything's okay. I'll never forget seeing Jake for the first time, freshman year: he had a mouth full of braces and hadn't gotten tall or broad-shouldered yet, but I took one look at his dimples and summer sky–blue eyes and *knew*. He was the one for me. It's just a bonus he turned out beautiful.

He strokes my hair while Cooper explains in a low voice what happened. "God, Ads," Jake says. "That's awful. Let's get you home."

Cooper leaves on his own, and I'm suddenly sorry I didn't do more for him. I can tell by his voice he's as freaked out as I am, just hiding it better. But Cooper's so golden, he can handle anything. His girlfriend, Keely, is one of my best friends, and the kind of girl who does everything right. She'll know exactly how to help. Way better than me.

I settle myself into Jake's car and watch the town blur past as he drives a little too fast. I live only a mile from school, and the drive is short, but I'm bracing myself for my mother's reaction because I'm positive she'll have heard. Her communication channels are mysterious but foolproof, and sure enough she's standing on our front porch as Jake pulls into the driveway.

I can read her mood even though the Botox froze her expressions long ago.

I wait until Jake opens my door to climb out of the car, fitting myself under his arm like always. My older sister, Ashton, likes to joke that I'm one of those barnacles that would die without its host. It's not actually so funny.

"Adelaide!" My mother's concern is theatrical. She stretches out a hand as we make our way up the steps and strokes my free arm. "Tell me what happened."

I don't want to. Especially not with Mom's boyfriend lurking in the doorway behind her, pretending his curiosity is actual concern. Justin is twelve years younger than my mother, which makes him five years younger than her second husband, and fifteen years younger than my dad. At the rate she's going, she'll date Jake next.

"It's fine," I mutter, ducking past them. "I'm fine."

"Hey, Mrs. Calloway," Jake says. Mom uses her second husband's last name, not my dad's. "I'm going to take Addy to her room. The whole thing was awful. I can tell you about it after I get her settled." It always amazes me how Jake talks to my mother, like they're peers.

And she lets him get away with it. *Likes* it. "Of course," she simpers.

My mother thinks Jake's too good for me. She's been telling me that since sophomore year when he got super hot and I stayed the same. Mom used to enter Ashton and me into beauty pageants when we were little, always with the same results for both of us: second runner-up. Homecoming princess, not queen. Not bad, but not good enough to attract and keep the kind of man who can take care of you for life.

I'm not sure if that's ever been stated as a *goal* or anything, but it's what we're supposed to do. My mother failed. Ashton's failing in her two-year marriage with a husband who's dropped out of law school and barely spends any time with her. Something about the Prentiss girls doesn't stick.

"Sorry," I murmur to Jake as we head upstairs. "I didn't handle this well. You should've seen Bronwyn and Cooper. They were great. And Nate—my God. I never thought I'd see Nate Macauley take charge that way. I was the only one who was useless."

"Shhh, don't talk like that," Jake says into my hair. "It's not true."

He says it with a note of finality, because he refuses to see anything but the best in me. If that ever changed, I honestly don't know what I'd do.

Nate
Monday, September 24, 4:00 p.m.

When Bronwyn and I get to the parking lot it's nearly empty, and we hesitate once we're outside the door. I've known Bronwyn since kindergarten, give or take a few middle-school years, but we don't exactly hang out. Still, it's not weird having her next to me. Almost comfortable after that disaster upstairs.

She looks around like she just woke up. "I didn't drive," she mutters. "I was supposed to get a ride. To *Epoch Coffee*." Something about the way she says it sounds significant, as if there's more to the story she's not sharing.

I have business to transact, but now probably isn't the time. "You want a ride?"

Bronwyn follows my gaze to my motorcycle. "Seriously? I wouldn't get on that deathtrap if you paid me. Do you know the fatality rates? They're no joke." She looks ready to pull out a spread sheet and show me.

"Suit yourself." I should leave her and go home, but I'm not ready to face *that* yet. I lean against the building and pull a flask of Jim Beam out of my jacket pocket, unscrewing the top and holding it toward Bronwyn. "Drink?"

She folds her arms tightly across her chest. "Are you kidding? That's your brilliant idea before climbing onto your machine of destruction? And on school property?"

"You're a lot of fun, you know that?" I don't actually drink much; I'd grabbed the flask from my father this morning and forgotten about it. But there's something satisfying about annoying Bronwyn.

I'm about to put it back in my pocket when Bronwyn furrows her brow and holds out her hand. "What the hell." She slumps against the redbrick wall beside me, inching down until she's sitting on the ground. For some reason I flash back to elementary school, when Bronwyn and I went to the same Catholic school. Before life went completely to hell. All the girls wore plaid uniform skirts, and she's got a similar skirt on now that hikes up her thighs as she crosses her ankles. The view's not bad.

She drinks for a surprisingly long time. "What. Just. Happened?"

I sit next to her and take the flask, putting it on the ground between us. "I have no idea."

"He looked like he was going to die." Bronwyn's hand shakes so hard when she picks up the flask again that it clatters against the ground. "Don't you think?"

"Yeah," I say as Bronwyn takes another swig and makes a face.

"Poor Cooper," she says. "He sounded like he left Ole Miss yesterday. He always gets that way when he's nervous."

"I wouldn't know. But what's-her-name was useless."

"Addy." Bronwyn's shoulder briefly nudges mine. "You should know her name."

"Why?" I can't think of a good reason. That girl and I have barely crossed paths before today and probably won't again. I'm pretty sure that's fine with both of us. I know her type. Not a thought in her head except her boyfriend and whatever petty power play's happening with her friends this week. Hot enough, I guess, but other than that she's got nothing to offer.

"Because we've all been through a huge trauma together," Bronwyn says, like that settles things.

"You have a lot of rules, don't you?"

I forgot how *tiring* Bronwyn is. Even in grade school, the amount of crap she cared about on a daily basis would wear down a normal person. She was always trying to join things, or start things for other people to join. Then be in charge of all the things she joined or started.

She's not boring, though. I'll give her that.

We sit in silence, watching the last of the cars leave the parking lot, while Bronwyn sips occasionally from the flask. When I finally take it from her, I'm surprised at how light it is. I doubt Bronwyn's used to hard liquor. She seems more a wine cooler girl. If that.

I put the flask back in my pocket as she plucks lightly at my sleeve. "You know, I meant to tell you, back when it happened—I was really sorry to hear about your mom," she says haltingly. "My uncle died in a car accident too, right around the same time. I wanted to say something to you, but . . . you and I, you know, we didn't really . . ." She trails off, her hand still resting on my arm.

"Talk," I say. "It's fine. Sorry about your uncle."

"You must miss her a lot."

I don't want to talk about my mother. "Ambulance came pretty fast today, huh?"

Bronwyn gets a little red and pulls her hand back, but rolls with the quick-change conversation. "How did you know what to do? For Simon?"

I shrug. "Everybody knows he has a peanut allergy. That's what you do."

"I didn't know about the pen." She snorts out a laugh. "Cooper gave you an actual pen! Like you were going to write him a note or something. Oh my God." She bangs her head so hard against the wall she might've cracked something. "I should go home. This is unproductive at best."

"Offer of a ride stands."

I don't expect her to take it, but she says "Sure, why not" and holds out her hand. She stumbles a little as I help her up. I didn't

23

think alcohol could kick in after fifteen minutes, but I might've underestimated the Bronwyn Rojas lightweight factor. Probably should have taken the flask away sooner.

"Where do you live?" I ask, straddling the seat and fitting the key in the ignition.

"Thorndike Street. A couple miles from here. Past the center of town, turn left onto Stone Valley Terrace after Starbucks." The rich part of town. Of course.

I don't usually take anybody on my bike and don't have a second helmet, so I give her mine. She takes it and I have to will myself to pull my eyes away from the bare skin of her thigh as she hops on behind me, tucking her skirt between her legs. She clamps her arms around my waist too tightly, but I don't say anything.

"Go slow, okay?" she asks nervously as I start the engine. I'd like to irritate her more, but I leave the parking lot at half my normal speed. And though I didn't think it was possible, she squeezes me even tighter. We ride like that, her helmeted head pressed up against my back, and I'd bet a thousand dollars, if I had it, that her eyes are shut tight until we reach her driveway.

Her house is about what you'd expect—a huge Victorian with a big lawn and lots of complicated trees and flowers. There's a Volvo SUV in the driveway, and my bike—which you could call a classic if you were feeling generous—looks as ridiculous next to it as Bronwyn must look behind me. Talk about things that don't go together.

Bronwyn climbs off and fumbles at the helmet. I unhook it and help her pull it off, loosening a strand of hair that catches on the strap. She takes a deep breath and straightens her skirt.

"That was terrifying," she says, then jumps as a phone rings. "Where's my backpack?"

"Your back."

She shrugs it off and yanks her phone from the front pocket. "Hello? Yes, I can. . . . Yes, this is Bronwyn. Did you— Oh God. Are you sure?" Her backpack slips out of her hand and falls at her feet. "Thank you for calling." She lowers the phone and stares at me, her eyes wide and glassy.

"Nate, he's gone," she says. "Simon's dead."

CHAPTER THREE

Bronwyn
Tuesday, September 25, 8:50 a.m.

I can't stop doing the math in my head. It's eight-fifty a.m. on Tuesday, and twenty-four hours ago Simon was going to homeroom for the last time. Six hours and five minutes from then we were heading to detention. An hour later, he died.

Seventeen years, gone just like that.

I slide down into my chair in the back corner of homeroom, feeling twenty-five heads swivel my way as I sit. Even without About That to provide an update, news of Simon's death was everywhere by dinnertime last night. I got multiple texts from everyone I've ever given my phone number to.

"You all right?" My friend Yumiko reaches over and squeezes my hand. I nod, but the gesture makes the pounding in my head even worse. Turns out half a flask of bourbon on an empty stomach is a *terrible* idea. Luckily both my parents were still at work when Nate dropped me off, and my sister, Maeve, poured enough black coffee down my throat that I was semicoherent by the time they got home. Any lingering effects they chalked up to trauma.

The first bell rings, but the speaker crackle that usually signals morning announcements never comes. Instead, our homeroom teacher, Mrs. Park, clears her throat and gets up from behind her desk. She's clutching a sheet of paper that trembles in her hand as she starts to read. "The following is an official announcement from Bayview High's administration. I'm so sorry to have to share this terrible news. Yesterday afternoon one of your classmates, Simon Kelleher, suffered a massive allergic reaction. Medical help was called immediately and arrived quickly, but unfortunately, it was too late to help Simon. He died at the hospital shortly after arrival."

A low whispering buzz runs through the room as somebody chokes out a sob. Half the class already has their phones out. Rules be damned today, I guess. Before I can stop myself, I pull my phone from my backpack and swipe to About That. I half expect a notification for the juicy new update Simon bragged about before detention yesterday, but of course there's nothing except last week's news.

Our favorite stoner drummer's trying his hand at film. RC's installed a camera in the light fixture in his bedroom, and he's been holding premieres for all his friends. You've been warned, girls. (Too late for KL, though.)

Everyone's seen the flirting between manic pixie dream girl TC and new rich boy GR, but who knew it might be something more? Apparently not her boyfriend, who sat oblivious in the bleachers at Saturday's game while T&G got hot and heavy right underneath him. Sorry, JD. Always the last to know.

The thing with About That was . . . you could pretty much guarantee every word was true. Simon built it sophomore year, after he spent spring break at some expensive coding camp in Silicon Valley, and nobody except him was allowed to post there. He had sources all over school, and he was choosy and careful about what he reported. People usually denied it or ignored it, but he was never wrong.

I'd never been featured; I'm too squeaky-clean for that. There's only one thing Simon might have written about me, but it would have been almost impossible for him to find out.

Now I guess he never will.

Mrs. Park is still talking. "There will be grief counseling provided in the auditorium all day. You may leave class any time you feel the need to speak with someone about this tragedy. The school is planning a memorial service for Simon after Saturday's football game, and we'll provide those details as soon as they're available. We'll also be sure to keep you up to date on his family's arrangements once we know them."

The bell rings and we all get up to leave, but Mrs. Park calls my name before I've even collected my backpack. "Bronwyn, can you hold back a moment?"

Yumiko shoots me a sympathetic look as she stands, tucking a strand of her choppy black hair behind her ear. "Kate and I'll wait for you in the hallway, okay?"

I nod and grab my bag. Mrs. Park is still dangling the announcement from one hand as I approach her desk. "Bronwyn, Principal Gupta wants all of you who were in the room with Simon to receive one-on-one counseling today. She's asked me to let you know that you're scheduled for eleven o'clock in Mr. O'Farrell's office."

Mr. O'Farrell is my guidance counselor, and I'm very familiar with his office. I've spent a lot of time there over the past six months, strategizing college admissions. "Is Mr. O'Farrell doing the counseling?" I ask. I guess that wouldn't be so bad.

Mrs. Park's forehead creases. "Oh, no. The school's bringing in a professional."

Great. I'd spent half the night trying to convince my parents I didn't need to see anybody. They'll be thrilled it was forced on me anyway. "Okay," I say, and wait in case she has anything else to tell me, but she just pats my arm awkwardly.

As promised, Kate and Yumiko are hovering outside the door. They flank me as we walk to first-period calculus, like they're shielding me from intrusive paparazzi. Yumiko steps aside, though, when she sees Evan Neiman waiting outside our classroom door.

"Bronwyn, hey." Evan's wearing one of his usual monogrammed polo shirts with EWN embroidered in script above his heart. I've always wondered what the *W* stands for. Walter? Wendell? William? I hope for his sake it's William. "Did you get my text last night?"

I did. *Need anything? Want some company?* Since that's the only time Evan Neiman has ever texted me, my cynical side decided he was angling for a front-row seat to the most shocking thing that's ever happened at Bayview. "I did, thanks. I was really tired, though."

"Well, if you ever feel like talking, let me know." Evan glances around the emptying hallway. He's a stickler for punctuality. "We should probably get inside, huh?"

Yumiko grins at me as we take our seats and whispers, "Evan kept asking where you were at Mathlete practice yesterday."

I wish I could match her enthusiasm, but at some point between detention and calculus I lost all interest in Evan Neiman. Maybe it's posttraumatic stress from the Simon situation, but right now I can't remember what attracted me in the first place. Not that I was ever head over heels. Mostly I thought Evan and I had potential to be a solid couple until graduation, at which point we'd break up amicably and head to our different colleges. Which I realize is pretty uninspiring, but so is high school dating. For me, anyway.

I sit through calculus, my mind far, far away from math, and then suddenly it's over and I'm walking to AP English with Kate and Yumiko. My head's still so full of what happened yesterday that when we pass Nate in the hallway it seems perfectly natural to call out, "Hi, Nate." I stop, surprising us both, and he does too.

"Hey," he replies. His dark hair is more disheveled than ever, and I'm pretty sure he's wearing the same T-shirt as yesterday. Somehow, though, it works on him. A little too well. Everything from his tall, rangy build to his angular cheekbones and wide-set, dark-fringed eyes is making me lose my train of thought.

Kate and Yumiko are staring at him too, but in a different way. More like he's an unpredictable zoo animal in a flimsy cage.

Hallway conversations with Nate Macauley aren't exactly part of our routine. "Have you had your counseling session yet?" I ask.

His face is a total blank. "My what?"

"Grief counseling. Because of Simon. Didn't your homeroom teacher tell you?"

"I just got here," he says, and my eyes widen. I never expected Nate to win any attendance awards, but it's almost ten o'clock.

"Oh. Well, all of us who were there are supposed to have one-on-one sessions. Mine's at eleven."

"Jesus Christ," Nate mutters, raking a hand through his hair.

The gesture pulls my eyes to his arm, where they remain until Kate clears her throat. My face heats as I snap back to attention, too late to register whatever she said. "Anyway. See you around," I mumble.

Yumiko bends her head toward mine as soon as we're out of earshot. "He looks like he just rolled out of bed," she whispers. "And *not alone*."

"I hope you doused yourself in Lysol after getting off his motorcycle," Kate adds. "He's a total man-whore."

I glare at her. "You realize it's sexist to say *man*-whore, right? If you have to use the term you should at least be gender-neutral about it."

"Whatever," Kate says dismissively. "Point is, he's a walking STD."

I don't answer. That's Nate's reputation, sure, but we don't really know anything about him. I almost tell her how carefully he drove me home yesterday, except I'm not sure what point I'd be trying to make.

After English I head for Mr. O'Farrell's office, and he waves me inside when I knock on his open door. "Have a seat, Bronwyn. Dr. Resnick is running a little late, but she'll be here shortly." I sit down across from him and spy my name scrawled across the manila folder placed neatly in the middle of his desk. I move to pick it up, then hesitate, not sure if it's confidential, but he pushes it toward me. "Your recommendation from the Model UN organizer. In plenty of time for Yale's early-action deadline."

I exhale, letting out a small sigh of relief. "Oh, thanks!" I say, and pick up the folder. It's the last one I've been waiting for. Yale's a family tradition—my grandfather was a visiting scholar there and moved his whole family from Colombia to New Haven when he got tenure. All his kids, including my dad, went to undergrad there, and it's where my parents met. They always say our family wouldn't exist if it weren't for Yale.

"You're very welcome." Mr. O'Farrell leans back and adjusts his glasses. "Were your ears burning earlier? Mr. Camino stopped by to ask if you'd be interested in tutoring for chemistry this semester. A bunch of bright juniors are struggling the way you did last year. They'd love to learn strategies from someone who ended up acing the course."

I have to swallow a couple of times before I can answer. "I would," I say, as brightly as I can manage, "but I might be overcommitted already." My smile stretches too tightly over my teeth.

"No worries. You have a lot on your plate."

Chemistry was the only class I'd ever struggled with, so much so that I had a D average at midterm. With every quiz I bombed, I could feel the Ivy League slipping out of reach. Even

Mr. O'Farrell started gently suggesting that any top-tier school would do.

So I brought my grades up, and got an A by the end of the year. But I'm pretty sure nobody wants me sharing my strategies with the other students.

Cooper
Thursday, September 27, 12:45 p.m.

"Will I see you tonight?"

Keely takes my hand as we walk to our lockers after lunch, looking up at me with huge dark eyes. Her mom is Swedish and her dad's Filipino, and the combination makes Keely the most beautiful girl in school by a lot. I haven't seen her much this week between baseball and family stuff, and I can tell she's getting antsy. Keely's not a clinger, exactly, but she needs regular couple time.

"Not sure," I say. "I'm pretty behind on homework."

Her perfect lips curve down and I can tell she's about to protest when a voice floats over the loudspeaker. *"Attention, please. Would Cooper Clay, Nate Macauley, Adelaide Prentiss, and Bronwyn Rojas please report to the main office. Cooper Clay, Nate Macauley, Adelaide Prentiss, and Bronwyn Rojas to the main office."*

Keely looks around like she's expecting an explanation. "What's that about? Something to do with Simon?"

"I guess." I shrug. I already answered questions from Principal Gupta a couple of days ago about what happened during detention, but maybe she's gearing up for another round. My father says Simon's parents are pretty connected around town, and the school should be worried about a lawsuit if it turns out they were negligent in any way. "Better go. I'll talk to you later, okay?" I give Keely a quick kiss on the cheek, shoulder my backpack, and head down the hall.

When I get to the principal's office, the receptionist points me toward a small conference room that's already crowded with people: Principal Gupta, Addy, Bronwyn, Nate, and a police officer. My throat gets a little dry as I take the last empty chair.

"Cooper, good. Now we can get started." Principal Gupta folds her hands in front of her and looks around the table. "I'd like to introduce Officer Hank Budapest with the Bayview Police Department. He has some questions about what you witnessed on Monday."

Officer Budapest shakes each of our hands in turn. He's young but already balding, with sandy hair and freckles. Not very intimidating, authority-wise. "Nice to meet you all. This shouldn't take long, but after speaking with the Kelleher family we want to take a closer look at Simon's death. Autopsy results came back this morning, and—"

"Already?" Bronwyn interrupts, earning a look from Principal Gupta that she doesn't notice. "Don't those usually take longer?"

"Preliminary results can be available within a couple days," Officer Budapest says. "These were fairly conclusive, showing that Simon died from a large dose of peanut oil ingested shortly before death. Which his parents found strange, considering how careful he always was with his food and drink. All of you told Principal Gupta that Simon drank a cup of water just before he collapsed, is that right?"

We all nod, and Officer Budapest continues, "The cup contained traces of peanut oil, so it seems clear Simon died from that drink. What we're trying to figure out now is how peanut oil could have gotten into his cup."

Nobody speaks. Addy meets my eyes and then cuts hers away, a small frown creasing her forehead. "Does anyone remember where Simon got the cup from?" Officer Budapest prompts, poising his pen over a blank notebook in front of him.

"I wasn't paying attention," Bronwyn says. "I was writing my assignment."

"Me too," Addy says, although I could've sworn she hadn't even started. Nate stretches and stares at the ceiling.

"I remember," I volunteer. "He got the cup from a stack next to the sink."

"Was the stack upside down, or right-side up?"

"Upside down," I say. "Simon pulled the top one off."

"Did you notice any liquid leave the cup when he did that? Did he shake it?"

I think back. "No. He just filled it with water."

"And then he drank it?"

"Yeah," I say, but Bronwyn corrects me.

"No," she says. "Not right away. He talked for a while. Remember?" She turns to Nate. "He asked you if you put the cell phones in our backpacks. The ones that got us in trouble with Mr. Avery."

"The cell phones. Right." Officer Budapest scratches something down in his notebook. He doesn't say it like a question, but Bronwyn explains anyway.

"Somebody played a prank on us," she says. "It's why we were in detention. Mr. Avery found phones in our backpacks that didn't belong to us." She turns to Principal Gupta with an injured expression. "It really wasn't fair. I've been meaning to ask, is that something that goes on your permanent record?"

Nate rolls his eyes. "It wasn't me. Someone stuck a phone in my backpack too."

Principal Gupta furrows her brow. "This is the first I'm hearing about this."

I shrug when she meets my eyes. Those phones were the last thing on my mind these past few days.

Officer Budapest doesn't look surprised. "Mr. Avery mentioned that when I met with him earlier. He said none of the kids ever claimed the phones, so he thought it must've been a prank after all." He slides his pen between his index and middle finger and taps it rhythmically against the table. "Is that the sort of joke Simon might have played on you all?"

"I don't see why," Addy says. "There was a phone in his backpack too. Besides, I barely knew him."

"You were on junior prom court with him," Bronwyn points out. Addy blinks, like she's only just remembering that's true.

"Any of you kids ever have trouble with Simon?" Officer Budapest asks. "I've heard about the app he made—About That, right?" He's looking at me, so I nod. "You guys ever been on it?"

Everyone shakes their head except Nate. "Lots of times," he says.

"What for?" Officer Budapest asks.

Nate smirks. "Stupid shit—" he starts, but Principal Gupta cuts him off.

"Language, Mr. Macauley."

"Stupid stuff," Nate amends. "Hooking up, mostly."

"Did that bother you? Being gossiped about?"

"Not really." He looks like he means it. I guess being on a gossip app isn't a big deal compared to getting arrested. If that's true. Simon never posted it, so nobody seems to know exactly what Nate's deal is.

Kinda pathetic, how Simon was our most trusted news source.

Officer Budapest looks at the rest of us. "But not you three?" We all shake our heads again. "Did you ever worry about ending up on Simon's app? Feel like you had something hanging over your heads, or anything like that?"

"Not me," I say, but my voice isn't as confident as I would have liked. I glance away from Officer Budapest and catch Addy and Bronwyn looking like polar opposites: Addy's gone pale as a ghost, and Bronwyn's flushed brick red. Nate watches them for a few seconds, tilts his chair back, and looks at Officer Budapest.

"Everybody's got secrets," he says. "Right?"

My workout routine goes long that night, but my dad makes everyone wait till I'm done so we can eat dinner together. My brother, Lucas, clutches his stomach and staggers to the table with a long-suffering look when we finally sit down at seven.

The topic of conversation's the same as it's been all week:

Simon. "You had to figure the police'd get involved at some point," Pop says, spooning a small mountain of mashed potatoes onto his plate. "Something's not right about how that boy died." He snorts. "Peanut oil in the water system, maybe? Lawyers are gonna have a field day with that."

"Were his eyes bugging out of his head like *this*?" asks Lucas, making a face. He's twelve, and Simon's death is nothing but video-game gore to him.

My grandmother reaches over and swats Lucas on the back of his hand. Nonny's barely five feet tall with a head full of tight white curls, but she means business. "Hush your mouth unless you can speak of that poor young man with respect."

Nonny's lived with us since we moved here from Mississippi five years ago. It surprised me then that she came along; our grandfather had been dead for years, but she had plenty of friends and clubs that kept her busy. Now that we've lived here for a while, I get it. Our basic colonial costs three times what our house in Mississippi did, and there's no way we could afford it without Nonny's money. But you can play baseball year-round in Bayview, and it's got one of the best high school programs in the country. At some point, Pop expects I'll make this gigantic mortgage and the job he hates worthwhile.

I might. After my fastball improved by five miles an hour over the summer, I ended up fourth on ESPN's predictions for the June MLB draft next year. I'm getting scouted by a lot of colleges too, and wouldn't mind heading there first. But baseball's not the same as football or basketball. If a guy can head for the minors right out of high school, he usually does.

Pop points at me with his knife. "You got a showcase game Saturday. Don't forget."

As if I could. The schedule's posted around the whole house.

"Kevin, maybe one weekend off?" my mother murmurs, but her heart's not in it. She knows it's a losing battle.

"Best thing Cooperstown can do is business as usual," Pop says. "Slacking off won't bring that boy back. God rest his soul."

Nonny's small, bright eyes settle on me. "I hope you realize none of you kids could've done anything for Simon, Cooper. The police have to dot their i's and cross their t's, that's all."

I don't know about that. Officer Budapest kept asking me about the missing EpiPens and how long I was by myself in the nurse's office. Almost like he thought I might've done something with them before Ms. Grayson got there. But he didn't come out and say it. If he thinks someone messed with Simon, I'm not sure why he isn't looking at Nate. If anybody asked me—which they didn't—I'd wonder how a guy like Nate even knew about EpiPens in the first place.

We've just finished clearing the table when the doorbell rings, and Lucas sprints for the door, hollering, "I'll get it!" A few seconds later he yells again. "It's Keely!"

Nonny rises to her feet with difficulty, using the skull-topped cane Lucas picked out last year when she faced up to the fact that she couldn't walk on her own anymore. "Thought you said you two didn't have plans tonight, Cooper."

"We didn't," I mutter as Keely enters the kitchen with a smile, wrapping her arms around my neck in a tight hug.

"How are you?" she murmurs in my ear, her soft lips brushing my cheek. "I've been thinking about you all day."

"Okay," I say. She pulls back and reaches into her pocket, briefly flashing a cellophane packet and a smile. Red Vines, which are definitely not part of my nutritional regimen, but my favorite candy in the world. The girl gets me. And my parents, who require a few minutes of polite conversation before they head out for their bowling league.

My phone chimes, and I pull it out of my pocket. *Hey, handsome.*

I duck my head to hide the grin that's suddenly tugging at my mouth, and text back: *Hey.*

Can I see you tonight?

Bad time. Call you later?

OK miss you.

Keely's talking to my mother, her eyes bright with interest. She's not faking it. Keely isn't only beautiful; she's what Nonny calls "sugar all the way through." A genuinely sweet girl. Every guy at Bayview wishes he were me.

Miss you too.

CHAPTER FOUR

Addy
Thursday, September 27, 7:30 p.m.

I should be doing homework before Jake stops by, but instead I'm sitting at the vanity in my bedroom, pressing fingers to the skin at my hairline. The tenderness on my left temple feels as though it's going to turn into one of those horrible oversized pimples I get every few months or so. Whenever I have one I know it's all anyone can see.

I'll have to wear my hair down for a while, which is how Jake likes it anyway. My hair is the only thing I feel one hundred percent confident about all the time. I was at Glenn's Diner last week with my girlfriends, sitting next to Keely across from the big mirror, and she reached over and ran a hand through my hair while grinning at our reflections. *Can we please trade? Just for a week?* she said.

I smiled at her, but wished I were sitting on the other side of the table. I hate seeing Keely and me side by side. She's so beautiful, all tawny skin and long eyelashes and Angelina Jolie lips. She's the lead character in a movie and I'm the generic best friend whose name you forget before the credits even start rolling.

The doorbell rings, but I know better than to expect Jake upstairs right away. Mom's going to capture him for at least ten minutes. She can't hear enough about the Simon situation, and she'd talk about today's meeting with Officer Budapest all night if I let her.

I separate my hair into sections and run a brush along each length. My mind keeps going back to Simon. He'd been a constant presence around our group since freshman year, but he was never one of us. He had only one real friend, a sorta-Goth girl named Janae. I used to think they were together until Simon started asking out all my friends. Of course, none of them ever said yes. Although last year, before she started dating Cooper, Keely got super drunk at a party and let Simon kiss her for five minutes in a closet. It took her ages to shake him after that.

I'm not sure what Simon was thinking, to be honest. Keely has one type: jock. He should have gone for someone like Bronwyn. She's cute enough, in a quiet kind of way, with interesting gray eyes and hair that would probably look great if she ever wore it down. Plus she and Simon must've tripped over each other in honors classes all the time.

Except I got the impression today that Bronwyn didn't like Simon much. Or at all. When Officer Budapest talked about how Simon died, Bronwyn looked . . . I don't know. Not sad.

A knock sounds at the door and I watch it open in the

mirror. I keep brushing my hair as Jake comes in. He pulls off his sneakers and flops on my bed with exaggerated exhaustion, arms splayed at his sides. "Your mom's wrung me dry, Ads. I've never met anyone who can ask the same question so many ways."

"Tell me about it," I say, getting up to join him. He puts an arm around me and I curl into his side, my head on his shoulder and my hand on his chest. We know exactly how to fit together, and I relax for the first time since I got called into Principal Gupta's office.

I trail my fingers along his bicep. Jake's not as defined as Cooper, who's practically a superhero with all the professional-level working out he does, but to me he's the perfect balance of muscular and lean. And he's fast, the best running back Bayview High's seen in years. There's not the same feeding frenzy around him as Cooper, but a few colleges are interested and he's got a good shot at a scholarship.

"Mrs. Kelleher called me," Jake says.

My hand halts its progress up his arm as I stare at the crisp blue cotton of his T-shirt. "Simon's mother? Why?"

"She asked if I'd be a pallbearer at the funeral. It's gonna be Sunday," Jake says, his shoulders lifting in a shrug. "I told her sure. Can't really say no, can I?"

I forget sometimes that Simon and Jake used to be friends in grade school and middle school, before Jake turned into a jock and Simon turned into . . . whatever he was. Freshman year Jake made the varsity football team and started hanging out with Cooper, who was already a Bayview legend after almost pitching his middle school team to the Little League World Series. By sophomore year the two of them were basically the kings of our class, and Simon was just some weird guy Jake used to know.

I half think Simon started About That to impress Jake. Simon found out one of Jake's football rivals was behind the anonymous sexting harassment of a bunch of junior girls and posted it on this app called After School. It got tons of attention for a couple of weeks, and so did Simon. That might've been the first time anyone at Bayview noticed him.

Jake probably patted him on the back once and forgot about it, and Simon moved on to bigger and better things by building his own app. Gossip as a public service doesn't go very far, so Simon started posting things a lot pettier and more personal than the sexting scandal. Nobody thought he was a hero anymore, but by then they were getting scared of him, and I guess for Simon that was almost as good.

Jake usually defended Simon, though, when our friends got down on him for About That. *It's not like he's lying,* he'd point out. *Stop doing sneaky shit and it won't be a problem.*

Jake can be pretty black-and-white in his thinking sometimes. Easy when you never make a mistake.

"We're still headed for the beach tomorrow night, if that's okay," he tells me now, winding my hair around his fingers. He says it like it's up to me, but we both know Jake's in charge of our social life.

"Of course," I murmur. "Who's going?" *Don't say TJ.*

"Cooper and Keely are supposed to, although she's not sure he's up for it. Luis and Olivia. Vanessa, Tyler, Noah, Sarah . . ."

Don't say TJ.

". . . and TJ."

Argh. I'm not sure if it's my imagination or if TJ, who used to be on the outskirts of our group as the new kid, has started working his way into the center right when I wish he'd disappear altogether. "Great," I say blandly, reaching up and kissing Jake's jawline. It's the time of day when it's a little scratchy, which is new this year.

"Adelaide!" My mother's voice floats up the stairs. "We're heading out." She and Justin go somewhere downtown almost every night, usually restaurants but sometimes clubs. Justin's only thirty and still into that whole scene. My mother enjoys it almost as much, especially when people mistake her for being Justin's age.

"Okay!" I call, and the door slams. After a minute Jake leans down to kiss me, his hand sliding under my shirt.

A lot of people think Jake and I have been sleeping together since freshman year, but that's not true. He wanted to wait until after junior prom. It was a big deal; Jake rented a fancy hotel room that he filled with candles and flowers, and bought me amazing lingerie from Victoria's Secret. I wouldn't have minded something a little more spontaneous, I guess, but I know I'm beyond lucky to have a boyfriend who cares enough to plan every last detail.

"Is this okay?" Jake's eyes scan my face. "Or would you rather just hang out?" His brows rise like it's a real question, but his hand keeps inching lower.

I never turn Jake down. It's like my mother said when she first took me to get birth control: if you say no too much, pretty

45

soon someone else will say yes. Anyway, I want it as much as he does. I live for these moments of closeness with Jake; I'd crawl inside him if I could.

"More than okay," I say, and pull him on top of me.

Nate
Thursday, September 27, 8:00 p.m.

I live in *that* house. The one people drive past and say, *I can't believe someone actually lives there.* We do, although "living" might be a stretch. I'm gone as much as possible and my dad's half-dead.

Our house is on the far edge of Bayview, the kind of shitty ranch rich people buy to tear down. Small and ugly, with only one window in front. The chimney's been crumbling since I was ten. Seven years later everything else is joining it: the paint's peeling, shutters are hanging off, the concrete steps in front are cracked wide open. The yard's just as bad. The grass is almost knee-high and yellow after the summer drought. I used to mow it, sometimes, until it hit me that yard work is a waste of time that never ends.

My father's passed out on the couch when I get inside, an empty bottle of Seagram's in front of him. Dad considers it a stroke of luck that he fell off a ladder during a roofing job a few years ago, while he was still a functioning alcoholic. He got a workman's comp settlement and wound up disabled enough to collect social security, which is like winning the lottery for a guy like him. Now he can drink without interruption while the checks roll in.

The money's not much, though. I like having cable, keeping my bike on the road, and occasionally eating more than mac and cheese. Which is how I came to my part-time job, and why I spent four hours after school today distributing plastic bags full of painkillers around San Diego County. Obviously not something I should be doing, especially since I was picked up for dealing weed over the summer and I'm on probation. But nothing else pays as well and takes so little effort.

I head for the kitchen, open the refrigerator door, and pull out some leftover Chinese. There's a picture curling under a magnet, cracked like a broken window. My dad, my mother, and me when I was eleven, right before she took off.

She was bipolar and not great about taking her meds, so it's not as though I had some fantastic childhood while she was around. My earliest memory is her dropping a plate, then sitting on the floor in the middle of the pieces, crying her eyes out. Once I got off the bus to her throwing all our stuff out the window. Lots of times she'd curl up in a corner of her bed and not move for days.

Her manic phases were a trip, though. For my eighth birthday she took me to a department store, handed me a cart, and told me to fill it with whatever I wanted. When I was nine and into reptiles she surprised me by setting up a terrarium in the living room with a bearded dragon. We called it Stan after Stan Lee, and I still have it. Those things live forever.

My father didn't drink as much then, so between the two of them they managed to get me to school and sports. Then my mother went totally off her meds and started getting into other mind-altering substances. Yeah, I'm the asshole who deals drugs after they wrecked his mother. But to be clear: I don't sell anything except weed and painkillers. My mother would've been fine if she'd stayed away from cocaine.

For a while she came back every few months or so. Then once a year. The last time I saw her was when I was fourteen and my dad started falling apart. She kept talking about this farm commune she'd moved to in Oregon and how great it was, that she'd take me and I could go to school there with all the hippie kids and grow organic berries or whatever the hell they did.

She bought me a giant ice cream sundae at Glenn's Diner, like I was eight years old, and told me all about it. *You'll love it, Nathaniel. Everyone is so accepting. Nobody labels you the way they do here.*

It sounded like bullshit even then, but better than Bayview. So I packed a bag, put Stan in his carrier, and waited for her on our front steps. I must have sat there half the night, like a complete fucking loser, before it finally dawned on me she wasn't going to show.

Turned out that trip to Glenn's Diner was the last time I ever saw her.

While the Chinese heats up I check on Stan, who's still got a pile of wilted vegetables and a few live crickets from this morning. I lift the cover from his terrarium and he blinks up at me from his rock. Stan is pretty chill and low maintenance, which is the only reason he's managed to stay alive in this house for eight years.

"What's up, Stan?" I put him on my shoulder, grab my food, and flop into an armchair across from my comatose father. He has a baseball game on, which I turn off because (a) I hate baseball and (b) it reminds me of Cooper Clay, which reminds me of Simon Kelleher and that whole sick scene in detention. I'd never liked the kid, but that was horrible. And Cooper was almost as useless as the blond girl when you come right down to it. Bronwyn was the only one who did anything except babble like an idiot.

My mother used to like Bronwyn. She'd always notice her at school things. Like the Nativity play in fourth grade when I was a shepherd and Bronwyn was the Virgin Mary. Someone stole baby Jesus before we were supposed to go on, probably to mess with Bronwyn because she took everything way too seriously even then. Bronwyn went into the audience, borrowed a bag, wrapped a blanket around it, and carried it around as if nothing had happened. *That girl doesn't take crap from anyone,* my mother had said approvingly.

Okay. In the interest of full disclosure, *I* stole baby Jesus, and it was definitely to mess with Bronwyn. It would've been funnier if she'd freaked out.

My jacket beeps, and I dig in my pockets for the right phone. I almost laughed in detention on Monday when Bronwyn said nobody has two cell phones. I have three: one for people I know, one for suppliers, and one for customers. Plus extras so I can switch them out. But I wouldn't be stupid enough to take any of them into Avery's class.

My work phones are always set to vibrate, so I know it's a personal message. I pull out my ancient iPhone and see a text from Amber, a girl I met at a party last month. *U up?*

I hesitate. Amber's hot and never tries to hang out too long, but she was just here a few nights ago. Things get messy when I let casual hookups happen more than once a week. But I'm restless and could use a distraction.

Come over, I write back.

I'm about to put my phone away when another text comes through. It's from Chad Posner, a guy at Bayview I hang out with sometimes. *You see this?* I click on the link in the message and it opens a Tumblr page with the headline "About This."

I got the idea for killing Simon while watching *Dateline.*

I'd been thinking about it for a while, obviously. That's not the kind of thing you pluck out of thin air. But the *how* of getting away with it always stopped me. I don't kid myself that I'm a criminal mastermind. And I'm much too good-looking for prison.

On the show, a guy killed his wife. Standard *Dateline* stuff, right? It's always the husband. But turns out lots of people were happy to see her gone. She'd gotten a coworker fired, screwed over people on city council, and had an affair with a friend's husband. She was a nightmare, basically.

The guy on *Dateline* wasn't too bright. Hired someone to murder his wife and the cell phone records were easy to trace. But before those came out he had a decent smoke screen because of all the other suspects. That's the kind of person you can get away with killing: someone everybody else wants dead.

Let's face it: everyone at Bayview High hated
Simon. I was just the only one with enough guts to
do something about it.

You're welcome.

The phone almost slips out of my hand. Another text from
Chad Posner came through while I was reading. *People r fucked up.*

I text back, *Where'd you get this?*

Posner writes *Some rando emailed a link,* with the laughing-
so-hard-I'm-crying emoji. He thinks it's somebody's idea of a
sick joke. Which is what most people would think, if they hadn't
spent an hour with a police officer asking ten different ways how
peanut oil got into Simon Kelleher's cup. Along with three other
people who looked guilty as hell.

None of them have as much experience as I do keeping a
straight face when shit's falling apart around them. At least,
none of them are as good at it as me.

CHAPTER FIVE

Bronwyn
Friday, September 28, 6:45 p.m.

Friday evening is a relief. Maeve and I are settled into her room for a *Buffy the Vampire Slayer* marathon on Netflix. It's our latest obsession, and I've been looking forward to it all week, but tonight we only half pay attention. Maeve's curled up on the window seat, tapping away on her laptop, and I'm sprawled across her bed with my Kindle open to *Ulysses* by James Joyce. It's number one on the Modern Library's 100 Best Novels and I'm determined to finish it before the semester's over, but it's pretty slow going. And I can't concentrate.

All anybody could talk about at school today was that Tumblr post. A bunch of kids had the link emailed to them last night from some "About This" Gmail address, and by lunchtime everyone had read it. Yumiko helps out in the principal's office on Fridays, and she heard them talking about trying to track whoever did it by IP address.

I doubt they'll have any luck. Nobody with half a brain would send something like that from their own technology.

Since detention on Monday people have been careful and overly nice to me, but today was different. Conversations kept stopping when I approached. Yumiko finally said, "It's not like people think *you* sent it. They just think it's weird, how you guys got questioned by the police yesterday and then this pops up." Like that was supposed to make me feel better.

"Just imagine." Maeve's voice startles me back to her bedroom. She puts aside her laptop and raps her fingers lightly on the window. "This time next year, you'll be at Yale. What do you think you'll do there on a Friday night? Frat party?"

I roll my eyes at her. "Right, because you get a personality transplant along with your acceptance letter. Anyway, I still have to get in."

"You will. How could you not?"

I shift restlessly on the bed. *Lots of ways.* "You never know."

Maeve keeps tapping her fingers against the glass. "If you're being modest on my account, you can give it a rest. I'm quite comfortable in my role as the family slacker."

"You're not a slacker," I protest. She just grins and flutters a hand. Maeve's one of the smartest people I know, but until her freshman year she was too sick to go to school consistently. She was diagnosed with leukemia when she was seven, and wasn't fully disease-free until two years ago, when she was fourteen.

We almost lost her a couple of times. Once when I was

in fourth grade, I overheard a priest at the hospital asking my parents if they'd considered starting to make "arrangements." I knew what he meant. I bowed my head and prayed: *Please don't take her. I'll do everything right if you let her stay. I'll be perfect. I promise.*

After so many years in and out of the hospital, Maeve never really learned how to participate in life. I do that for both of us: join the clubs, win the awards, and get the grades so I can go to Yale like our parents did. It makes them happy, and keeps Maeve from extending herself too much.

Maeve goes back to staring out the window with her usual faraway expression. She looks like a daydream herself: pale and ethereal, with dark-brown hair like mine but startling amber eyes. I'm about to ask what she's thinking when she suddenly sits up straight and cups her hands around her eyes, pressing her face against the window. "Is that Nate Macauley?" I snort without moving, and she says, "I'm serious. Check it out."

I get up and lean in next to her. I can just about make out the faint outline of a motorcycle in our driveway. "What the hell?" Maeve and I exchange glances, and she shoots me a wicked grin. *"What?"* I ask. My voice comes out more snappish than I intended.

"What?" she mimics. "You think I don't remember you mooning over him in elementary school? I was sick, not dead."

"Don't joke about that. *God.* And that was light-years ago." Nate's motorcycle is still in our driveway, not moving. "What do you suppose he's doing here?"

"Only one way to find out." Maeve's voice is annoyingly singsongy, and she ignores the dirty look I give her as I stand up.

My heart thumps all the way downstairs. Nate and I have talked more at school this week than we have since fifth grade, which admittedly still isn't much. Every time I see him I get the impression he can't wait to be someplace else. But I keep running into him.

Opening the front door triggers a floodlight in front of our garage that makes Nate look as though he's on center stage. As I walk toward him my nerves are jangling, and I'm acutely conscious of the fact that I'm in my usual hanging-out-with-Maeve ensemble: flip-flops, a hoodie, and athletic shorts. Not that *he's* making an effort. I've seen that Guinness T-shirt at least twice this week.

"Hi, Nate," I say. "What's up?"

Nate takes his helmet off, and his dark-blue eyes flick past me to our front door. "Hey." He doesn't say anything else for an uncomfortably long time. I cross my arms and wait him out. Finally he meets my gaze with a wry smile that makes my stomach do a slow somersault. "I don't have a good reason for being here."

"Do you want to come in?" I blurt out.

He hesitates. "I bet your parents would love that."

He doesn't know the half of it. Dad's least favorite stereotype is that of the Colombian drug dealer, and he wouldn't appreciate even a hint of association from me. But I find myself saying, "They're not home." Then I hastily add, "I'm hanging out with my sister," before he thinks that was some sort of come-on.

"Yeah, okay." Nate gets off his bike and follows me like it's no big deal, so I try to act equally nonchalant. Maeve's leaning against the kitchen counter when we get inside, even though I'm sure she was staring out her bedroom window ten seconds ago. "Have you met my sister, Maeve?"

Nate shakes his head. "No. How's it going?"

"All right," Maeve answers, eyeing him with frank interest.

I have no idea what to do next as he shrugs off his jacket and tosses it over a kitchen chair. How am I supposed to . . . *entertain* Nate Macauley? It's not even my responsibility, right? He's the one who showed up out of the blue. I should do what I normally do. Except that's sit in my sister's room and watch retro vampire shows while half reading *Ulysses*.

I'm completely out of my depth here.

Nate doesn't notice my discomfort, wandering past the french doors that open into our living room. Maeve elbows me as we follow him and murmurs, *"Que boca tan hermosa."*

"Shut up," I hiss. Dad encourages us to speak Spanish around the house, but I doubt this is what he had in mind. Besides, for all we know, Nate's fluent.

He stops at the grand piano and looks back at us. "Who plays?"

"Bronwyn," Maeve says before I can even open my mouth. I stay near the doorway, arms folded, as she settles into Dad's favorite leather armchair in front of the sliding door leading to our deck. "She's really good."

"Oh yeah?" Nate asks at the same time I say, "No, I'm not."

"You are," Maeve insists. I narrow my eyes and she widens hers in fake innocence.

Nate crosses to the large walnut bookcase covering one wall, picking up a picture of Maeve and me with identical gap-toothed smiles in front of Sleeping Beauty's castle at Disneyland. It was taken six months before Maeve was diagnosed, and for a long time it was the only vacation picture we had. He studies it, then glances my way with a small smile. Maeve was right about his mouth—it is sexy. "You should play something."

Well, it's easier than talking to him.

I shuffle to the bench and sit, adjusting the sheet music in front of me. It's "Variations on the Canon," which I've been practicing for months now. I've taken lessons since I was eight and I'm pretty competent, technically. But I've never made people *feel* anything. "Variations on the Canon" is the first piece that made me want to try. There's something about the way it builds, starting soft and sweet but gaining in volume and intensity until it's almost angry. That's the hard part, because at a certain point the notes grow harsh, verging on discordant, and I can't muster the force to pull it off.

I haven't played it in over a week. The last time I tried I hit so many wrong notes, even Maeve winced. She seems to remember, glancing toward Nate and saying, "This is a really hard song." As if she suddenly regrets setting me up for embarrassment. But what the hell. This whole situation is too surreal to take seriously. If I woke up tomorrow and Maeve told me I'd dreamed it all, I'd fully accept that.

So I start, and right away it feels different. Looser and less of a reach for the harder parts. For a few minutes I forget anyone's in the room, and enjoy how notes that usually trip me up flow easily. Even the crescendo—I don't attack it as hard as I need to, but I'm faster and surer than I normally am, and don't hit a single wrong note. When I finish I smile triumphantly at Maeve, and it's only when her eyes drift toward Nate that I remember I have an audience of two.

He's leaning against our bookcase, arms crossed, and for once he doesn't look bored or about to make fun of me. "That's the best thing I've ever heard," he says.

Addy
Friday, September 28, 7:00 p.m.

God, my mother. She's actually *flirting* with Officer Budapest, of the pink freckled face and receding hairline. "Of course Adelaide will do anything to help," she says in a husky voice, trailing one finger around the rim of her wineglass. Justin's having dinner with his parents, who hate Mom and never invite her. This is his punishment whether he knows it or not.

Officer Budapest stopped by just as we finished the vegetable pad Thai Mom always orders when my sister, Ashton, comes to visit. Now he doesn't know where to look, so he's got his eyes fixed on a dried flower arrangement on the living room wall. My mother redecorates every six months, and her latest theme is shabby chic with a weird beachy edge. Cabbage roses and seashells as far as the eye can see.

"Just a few follow-up points, if you don't mind, Addy," he says.

"Okay," I say. I'm surprised he's here, since I thought we'd already answered all his questions. But I guess the investigation's still going strong. Today Mr. Avery's lab was blocked off with yellow tape, and police officers were in and out of school all day. Cooper said Bayview High's probably going to get into trouble for having peanut oil in the water or something.

I glance at my mother. Her eyes are fixed on Officer Budapest, but with that distant expression I know well. She's already mentally checked out, probably planning her wardrobe for the weekend. Ashton comes into the living room and settles herself in an armchair across from me. "Are you talking to all the kids who were in detention that day?" she asks.

Officer Budapest clears his throat. "The investigation is ongoing, but I'm here because I had a particular question for Addy. You were in the nurse's office the day Simon died, is that right?"

I hesitate and dart a glance toward Ashton, then look back at Officer Budapest. "No."

"You were," Officer Budapest says. "It's in the nurse's log."

I'm looking at the fireplace, but I can feel Ashton's eyes boring into me. I wind a strand of hair around my finger and tug nervously. "I don't remember that."

"You don't remember going to the nurse's office on Monday?"

"Well, I go a lot," I say quickly. "For headaches and stuff. It was probably for that." I scrunch my forehead like I'm thinking hard, and finally meet Officer Budapest's eyes. "Oh, right. I had my period and I was cramping really bad, so yeah. I needed Tylenol."

Officer Budapest is a blusher. He turns red as I smile politely and release my hair. "And you got what you needed there? Just the Tylenol?"

"Why do you want to know?" Ashton asks. She rearranges

a throw pillow behind her so the starfish pattern, made out of actual seashells, isn't digging into her back.

"Well, one of the things we're looking into is why there appeared to be no EpiPens in the nurse's office during Simon's allergy attack. The nurse swears she had several pens that morning. But they were gone that afternoon."

Ashton stiffens and says, "You can't possibly think Addy took them!" Mom turns to me with a faintly surprised air, but doesn't speak.

If Officer Budapest notices that my sister has stepped into the parenting role here, he doesn't mention it. "Nobody's saying that. But did you happen to see whether the pens were in the office then, Addy? According to the nurse's log, you were there at one o'clock."

My heart's beating uncomfortably fast, but I keep my tone even. "I don't even know what an EpiPen looks like."

He makes me tell him everything I remember about detention, *again*, then asks a bunch of questions about the Tumblr post. Ashton's all alert and interested, leaning forward and interrupting the whole time, while Mom goes into the kitchen twice to refill her wineglass. I keep looking at the clock, because Jake and I are supposed to be going to the beach soon and I haven't even started touching up my makeup. My pimple's not going to cover itself.

When Officer Budapest finally gets ready to leave, he hands me a card. "Call if you remember anything else, Addy," he says. "You never know what might be important."

"Okay," I say, sliding the card into the back pocket of my jeans. Officer Budapest says good-bye to Mom and Ashton as I open the door for him. Ashton leans against the doorframe next to me and we watch Officer Budapest get into his squad wagon and start slowly backing out of our driveway.

I spy Justin's car waiting to pull in behind Officer Budapest, and that gets me moving again. I don't want to have to talk to him and I *still* haven't fixed my makeup, so I escape upstairs with Ashton following behind me. My bedroom is the biggest one in our house except the master, and used to be Ashton's until I took it over when she got married. She still makes herself at home there as if she'd never left.

"You didn't tell me about that Tumblr thing," she says, sprawling across my white eyelet bedspread and opening the latest issue of *Us Weekly*. Ashton is even blonder than me, but her hair is cut in chin-length layers that our mother hates. I think it's cute, though. If Jake didn't love my hair so much, I'd consider a cut like that.

I sit at my vanity and dab concealer on my hairline pimple. "Somebody's being a creep, that's all."

"Did you really not remember being in the nurse's office? Or did you just not want to answer?" Ashton asks. I fumble with the concealer cap, but I'm saved from answering when my phone blares its Rihanna "Only Girl" text tone from the bedside table. Ashton picks it up and reports, "Jake's almost here."

"God, Ash." I glare at her in the mirror. "You shouldn't look at my phone like that. What if it was private?"

"Sorry," she says in a completely not-sorry tone. "Everything okay with Jake?"

I twist in my chair to face her, frowning. "Why wouldn't it be?"

Ashton holds a palm up at me. "Just a question, Addy. I'm not implying anything." Her tone darkens. "No reason to think you'll turn out like me. It's not as though Charlie and I were high school sweethearts."

I blink at her in surprise. I mean, I've thought for a while that things weren't going well between Ashton and Charlie—for one thing, she's suddenly here a lot, and for another, he was hard-core flirting with a slutty bridesmaid at our cousin's wedding last month—but Ashton's never come out and admitted a problem before. "Are things . . . uh, really bad?"

She shrugs, dropping the magazine and picking at her nails. "It's complicated. Marriage is way harder than anyone tells you. Be thankful you don't have to make life decisions yet." Her mouth tightens. "Don't let Mom get in your ear and twist everything. Just enjoy being seventeen."

I can't. I'm too afraid it's all going to be ruined. That it's already ruined.

I wish I could tell Ashton that. It would be such a relief to get it out. I usually tell Jake everything, but I can't tell him *this*. And after him, there's literally not one other person in the world I trust. Not any of my friends, certainly not my mother, and not my sister. Because even though she probably means well, she can be awfully passive-aggressive about Jake.

The doorbell rings, and Ashton's mouth twists into a half smile. "Must be Mr. Perfect," she says. Sarcastic, right on schedule.

I ignore her and bound down the stairs, opening the door with the big smile I can't help when I'm about to see Jake. And there he is, in his football jacket with his chestnut hair tousled by the wind, giving me the exact same smile back. "Hey, baby."

I'm about to kiss him when I catch sight of another figure behind him and freeze. "You don't mind if we give TJ a ride, do you?"

A nervous laugh bubbles up in my throat and I push it down. "Of course not." I go in for my kiss, but the moment's ruined.

TJ flicks his eyes toward me, then at the ground. "Sorry about this. My car broke down and I was gonna stay home, but Jake insisted. . . ."

Jake shrugs. "You were on the way. No reason to miss a night out because of car trouble." His eyes travel from my face to my canvas sneakers as he asks, "You wearing that, Ads?"

It's not a criticism, exactly, but I'm in Ashton's college sweatshirt and Jake's never liked me in shapeless clothes. "It'll be cold at the beach," I say tentatively, and he grins.

"I'll keep you warm. Put on something a little cuter, huh?"

I give him a strained smile and go back inside, mounting the stairs with dragging steps because I know I haven't been gone long enough for Ashton to have left my room. Sure enough she's still flipping through *Us Weekly* on my bed, and she knits her brows together as I head for my closet. "Back so soon?"

I pull out a pair of leggings and unbutton my jeans. "I'm changing."

Ashton closes the magazine and watches me in silence until I exchange her sweatshirt for a formfitting sweater. "You won't be warm enough in that. It's chilly tonight." She snorts out a disbelieving laugh when I slip off my sneakers and step into a pair of strappy sandals with kitten heels. "You're wearing those to the *beach*? Is this wardrobe change Jake's idea?"

I toss my discarded clothes into the hamper, ignoring her. "Bye, Ash."

"Addy, wait." The snarky tone's gone from Ashton's voice, but I don't care. I'm down the stairs and out the door before she can stop me, stepping into a breeze that chills me instantly. But Jake gives me an approving smile and wraps an arm around my shoulders for the short walk to the car.

I hate the entire ride. Hate sitting there acting normal when I want to throw up. Hate listening to Jake and TJ talk about tomorrow's game. Hate when the latest Fall Out Boy song comes on and TJ says, "I love this song," because now I can't like it anymore. But mostly, I hate the fact that barely a month after my and Jake's momentous first time, I got blind drunk and slept with TJ Forrester.

When we get to the beach Cooper and Luis are already building a bonfire, and Jake heaves a frustrated grunt as he shifts into park. "They do it wrong every time," he complains, launching himself out of the car toward them. "You guys. You're too close to the water!"

TJ and I get out of the car more slowly, not looking at each other. I'm already freezing, and wrap my arms around my body for warmth. "Do you want my jack—" TJ starts, but I don't let him finish.

"No." I cut him off and stalk toward the beach, almost tripping in my stupid shoes when I reach the sand.

TJ's at my side, arm out to steady me. "Addy, hey." His voice is low, his minty breath briefly on my cheek. "It doesn't have to be this awkward, you know? I'm not going to say anything."

I shouldn't be mad at him. It's not his fault. I'm the one who got insecure after Jake and I slept together, and started thinking he was losing interest every time he took too long to answer a text. I'm the one who flirted with TJ when we ran into each other on this exact same beach over the summer while Jake was on vacation. I'm the one who dared TJ to get a bottle of rum, and drank almost half of it with a Diet Coke chaser.

At one point that day I laughed so hard I snorted soda out of my nose, which would have disgusted Jake. TJ just said in this dry way, "Wow, Addy, that was attractive. I'm very turned on by you right now."

That was when I kissed him. And suggested we go back to his place.

So really, none of this is his fault.

We reach the edge of the beach and watch Jake douse the fire so he can rebuild it where he wants. I sneak a glance at TJ and see dimples flash as he waves to the guys. "Just forget it ever happened," he says under his breath.

He sounds sincere, and hope sparks in my chest. Maybe we really can keep this to ourselves. Bayview's a gossipy school, but at least About That isn't hanging over everybody's heads anymore.

And if I'm being one hundred percent honest, I have to admit—that's a relief.

CHAPTER SIX

Cooper
Saturday, September 29, 4:15 p.m.

I squint at the batter. We're at full count and he's fouled off the last two pitches. He's making me work, which isn't good. In a showcase game like this, facing a right-handed second baseman with so-so stats, I should've mowed him down already.

Problem is, I'm distracted. It's been a hell of a week.

Pop's in the stands, and I can picture exactly what he's doing. He'll have taken his cap off, knotting it between his hands as he stares at the mound. Like burning a hole into me with his eyes is going to help.

I bring the ball into my glove and glance at Luis, who catches for me during regular season. He's on the Bayview High football team too but got permission to miss today's game so he could be here. He signals a fastball, but I shake my head. I've thrown five already and this guy's figured every one out. I keep shaking Luis off until he gives me the signal I want. Luis adjusts his crouch slightly, and we've played together long enough that I can read his thoughts in the movement. *Your funeral, man.*

I position my fingers on the ball, tensing myself in preparation to throw. It's not my most consistent pitch. If I miss, it'll be a big fat softball and this guy'll crush it.

I draw back and hurl as hard as I can. My pitch heads straight for the middle of the plate, and the batter takes an eager, triumphant swing. Then the ball breaks, dropping out of the strike zone and into Luis's glove. The stadium explodes in cheers, and the batter shakes his head like he has no idea what happened.

I adjust my cap and try not to look pleased. I've been working on that slider all year.

I strike the next hitter out on three straight fastballs. The last one hits ninety-three, the fastest I've ever pitched. Lights-out for a lefty. My stats through two innings are three strikeouts, two groundouts, and a long fly that would've been a double if the right fielder hadn't made a diving catch. I wish I could have that pitch back—my curveball didn't curve—but other than that I feel pretty good about the game.

I'm at Petco—the Padres' stadium—for an invitation-only showcase event, which my father insisted I go to even though Simon's memorial service is in an hour. The organizers agreed to let me pitch first and leave early, so I skip my usual postgame routine, take a shower, and head out of the locker room with Luis to find Pop.

I spot him as someone calls my name. "Cooper Clay?" The man approaching me looks successful. That's the only way I can think to describe him. Sharp clothes, sharp haircut, just the right amount of a tan, and a confident smile as he holds his hand out to me. "Josh Langley with the Padres. I've spoken to your coach a few times."

"Yes, sir. Pleased to meet you," I say. My father grins like somebody just handed him the keys to a Lamborghini. He manages to introduce himself to Josh without drooling, but barely.

"Hell of a slider you threw there," Josh says to me. "Fell right off the plate."

"Thank you, sir."

"Good velocity on your fastball too. You've really brought that up since the spring, haven't you?"

"I've been working out a lot," I say. "Building up arm strength."

"Big jump in a short time," Josh observes, and for a second the statement hangs in the air between us like a question. Then he claps a hand on my shoulder. "Well, keep it up, son. Nice to have a local boy on our radar. Makes my job easy. Less travel." He flashes a smile, nods good-bye to my dad and Luis, and takes off.

Big jump in a short time. It's true. Eighty-eight miles per hour to ninety-three in a few months is unusual.

Pop won't shut up on the way home, alternating between complaining about what I did wrong and crowing about Josh Langley. He winds up in a good mood, though, more happy about the Padres scout than upset about someone almost getting a hit off me. "Simon's family gonna be there?" he asks as he pulls up to Bayview High. "Pay our respects if they are."

"I dunno," I answer him. "It might just be a school thing."

"Hat off, boys," Pop says. Luis crams his into the pocket of his football jacket, and Pop raps the steering wheel impatiently when I hesitate. "Come on, Cooper, it might be outside but this is still a service. Leave it in the car."

I do as I'm told and get out, but as I run a hand through my hat-hair and close the passenger door, I wish I had it back. I feel exposed, and people have already been staring at me enough this week. If it were up to me I'd go home and spend a quiet evening watching baseball with my brother and Nonny, but there's no way I can miss Simon's memorial service when I was one of the last people to see him alive.

We start toward the crowd on the football field, and I text Keely to find out where our friends are. She tells me they're near the front, so we duck under the bleachers and try to spot them from the sidelines. I have my eyes on the crowd, and don't see the girl in front of me until I almost bump into her. She's leaning against a post, watching the football field with her hands stuffed into the pockets of her oversized jacket.

"Sorry," I say, and realize who it is. "Oh, hey, Leah. You heading out to the field?" Then I wish I could swallow my words, because there's no way in hell Leah Jackson's here to mourn Simon. She actually tried to kill herself last year because of him. After he wrote about her sleeping with a bunch of freshmen, she was harassed on social media for months. She slit her wrists in her bathroom and was out of school for the rest of the year.

Leah snorts. "Yeah, right. Good riddance." She stares at the scene in front of us, kicking the toe of her boot into the dirt. "Nobody could stand him, but they're all holding candles like he's some kind of martyr instead of a gossipy douchebag."

She's not wrong, but now doesn't seem like the time to be that honest. Still, I'm not going to try defending Simon to Leah. "I guess people want to pay their respects," I hedge.

"Hypocrites," she mutters, cramming her hands deeper into her pockets. Her expression shifts, and she pulls out her phone with a sly look. "You guys see the latest?"

"Latest what?" I ask with a sinking feeling. Sometimes the best thing about baseball is the fact that you can't check your phone while you're playing.

"There's another email with a Tumblr update." Leah swipes a few times at her phone and hands it to me. I take it reluctantly and look at the screen as Luis reads over my shoulder.

> Time to clarify a few things.
>
> Simon had a severe peanut allergy—so why not stick a Planters into his sandwich and be done with it?
>
> I'd been watching Simon Kelleher for months. Everything he ate was wrapped in an inch of cellophane. He carried that goddamn water bottle everywhere and it was all he drank.
>
> But he couldn't go ten minutes without swigging from that bottle. I figured if it wasn't there, he'd default to plain old tap water. So yeah, I took it.
>
> I spent a long time figuring out where I could slip peanut oil into one of Simon's drinks. Someplace contained, without a water fountain. Mr. Avery's detention seemed like the ideal spot.

I did feel bad watching Simon die. I'm not a sociopath. In that moment, as he turned that horrible color and fought for air—if I could have stopped it, I would have.

I couldn't, though. Because, you see, I'd taken his EpiPen. And every last one in the nurse's office.

My heart starts hammering and my stomach clenches. The first post was bad enough, but this one—this one's written like the person was actually in the room when Simon had his attack. Like it was one of us.

Luis snorts. "That's fucked up."

Leah's watching me closely, and I grimace as I hand back the phone. "Hope they figure out who's writing this stuff. It's pretty sick."

She lifts one shoulder in a shrug. "I guess." She starts to back away. "Have a blast *mourning*, guys. I'm outta here."

"Bye, Leah." I squelch the urge to follow her, and we trudge forward until we hit the ten-yard line. I start shouldering through the crowd and finally find Keely and the rest of our friends. When I reach her, she hands me a candle she lights with her own, and loops her arm through mine.

Principal Gupta steps up to the microphone and taps against it. "What a terrible week for our school," she says. "But how inspiring to see all of you gathered here tonight."

I should be thinking about Simon, but my head's too full of other stuff. Keely, who's gripping my arm a little too tight. Leah, saying the kind of things most people only think. The new Tumblr—posted right before Simon's memorial service. And Josh Langley with his flashy smile: *Big jump in a short time.*

That's the thing about competitive edges. Sometimes they're too good to be true.

Nate
Sunday, September 30, 12:30 p.m.

My probation officer isn't the worst. She's in her thirties, not bad-looking, and has a sense of humor. But she's a pain in my ass about school.

"How did your history exam go?" We're sitting in the kitchen for our usual Sunday meeting. Stan's hanging out on the table, which she's fine with since she likes him. My dad is upstairs, something I always arrange before Officer Lopez comes over. Part of her job is to make sure I'm being adequately supervised. She knew his deal the first time she saw him, but she also knows I've got nowhere else to go and state care can be way worse than alcoholic neglect. It's easier to pretend he's a fit guardian when he's not passed out in the living room.

"It went," I say.

She waits patiently for more. When it doesn't come, she asks, "Did you study?"

"I've been kind of distracted," I remind her. She'd heard the Simon story from her cop pals, and we spent the first half hour after she got here talking about what happened.

"I understand. But keeping up with school is important, Nate. It's part of the deal."

She brings up The Deal every week. San Diego County is getting tougher on juvenile drug offenses, and she thinks I was lucky to get probation. A bad report from her could put me back in front of a pissed-off judge. Another drug bust could land me in juvie. So every Sunday morning before she shows up, I gather up all my unsold drugs and burner phones and stick them in our senile neighbor's shed. Just in case.

Officer Lopez holds out her palm to Stan, who crawls halfway toward it before he loses interest. She picks him up and lays him across her arm. "How has your week been otherwise? Tell me something positive that happened." She always says that, as if life is full of great shit I can store up and report every Sunday.

"I got to three thousand in *Grand Theft Auto.*"

She rolls her eyes. She does that a lot at my house. "Something else. What progress have you made toward your goals?"

Jesus. My *goals.* She made me write a list at our first appointment. There's not anything I actually care about on there, just stuff I know she wants to hear about school and jobs. And friends, which she's figured by now I don't have. I have people I go to parties with, sell to, and screw, but I wouldn't call any of them friends.

"It's been a slow week, goal-wise."

"Did you look at that Alateen literature I left you?"

Nope. I didn't. I don't need a brochure to tell me how bad it sucks when your only parent's a drunk, and I definitely don't need to talk about it with a bunch of whiners in a church basement somewhere. "Yeah," I lie. "I'm thinking about it."

I'm sure she sees right through me, since she's not stupid. But she doesn't push it. "That's good to hear. Sharing experiences with other kids whose parents are struggling would be transformative for you."

Officer Lopez doesn't let up. You have to give her that. We could be surrounded by walking dead in the zombie apocalypse and she'd look for the bright side. *Your brains are still in your head, right? Way to beat the odds!* She'd love, just once, to hear an actual positive thing from me. Like how I spent Friday night with Ivy League–bound Bronwyn Rojas and didn't disgrace myself. But that's not a conversation I need to open up with Officer Lopez.

I don't know why I showed up there. I was restless, staring at the Vicodin I had left over after drop-off and wondering if I should take a few and see what all the fuss is about. I've never gone down that road, because I'm pretty sure it'd end with me comatose in the living room alongside my dad until someone kicked us out for not paying the mortgage.

So I went to Bronwyn's instead. I didn't expect her to come outside. Or invite me in. Listening to her play the piano had a strange effect on me. I almost felt . . . peaceful.

"How is everyone coping with Simon's death? Have they held the funeral yet?"

"It's today. The school sent an email." I glance at the clock on our microwave. "In about half an hour."

Her brows shoot up. "Nate. You should go. That would be a positive thing to do. Pay your respects, gain some closure after a traumatic event."

"No thanks."

She clears her throat and gives me a shrewd look. "Let me

put it another way. Go to that goddamn funeral, Nate Macauley, or I won't overlook your spotty school attendance the next time I file an update report. I'll come with you."

Which is how I end up at Simon Kelleher's funeral with my probation officer.

We're late and St. Anthony's Church is packed, so we barely find space in the last pew. The service hasn't started but no one's talking, and when the old guy in front of us coughs it echoes through the room. The smell of incense brings me back to grade school, when my mother used to take me to Mass every Sunday. I haven't been to church since then, but it looks almost exactly the same: red carpet, shiny dark wood, tall stained-glass windows.

The only thing that's different is the place is crawling with cops.

Not in uniform. But I can tell, and Officer Lopez can too. After a while some of them look my way, and I get paranoid she's led me into some kind of trap. But I don't have anything on me. So why do they keep staring at me?

Not only me. I follow their gazes to Bronwyn, who's near the front with her parents, and to Cooper and the blond girl, sitting in the middle with their friends. The back of my neck tingles, and not in a good way. My body tenses, ready to bolt until Officer Lopez puts a hand on my arm. She doesn't say anything, but I stay put.

A bunch of people talk—nobody I know except that Goth girl who used to follow Simon everywhere. She reads a weird, rambling poem and her voice shakes the whole time.

The past and present wilt—I have fill'd them,
    emptied them,
And proceed to fill my next fold of the future.

Listener up there! what have you to confide to me?
Look in my face while I snuff the sidle of evening,
(Talk honestly, no one else hears you, and I stay
    only a minute longer.)

Do I contradict myself?
Very well then I contradict myself,
(I am large, I contain multitudes.) . . .

Will you speak before I am gone? will you prove
    already too late? . . .

I depart as air, I shake my white locks at the
    runaway sun,
I effuse my flesh in eddies, and drift it in lacy jags.

I bequeath myself to the dirt to grow from the
    grass I love,
If you want me again look for me under
    your boot-soles.

You will hardly know who I am or what I mean,
But I shall be good health to you nevertheless,
And filter and fiber your blood.

Failing to fetch me at first keep encouraged,
Missing me one place search another,
I stop somewhere waiting for you.

"Song of Myself," Officer Lopez murmurs when the girl finishes. "Interesting choice."

There's music, more readings, and it's finally over. The priest tells us the burial's going to be private, family only. Fine by me. I've never wanted to leave anyplace so bad in my life and I'm ready to take off before the funeral procession comes down the aisle, but Officer Lopez has her hand on my arm again.

A bunch of senior guys carry Simon's casket out the door. A couple dozen people dressed in dark colors file out after them, ending with a man and a woman holding hands. The woman has a thin, angular face like Simon. She's staring at the floor, but as she passes our pew she looks up, catches my eye, and chokes out a furious sob.

More people crowd the aisles, and someone edges into the pew with Officer Lopez and me. It's one of the plainclothes cops, an older guy with a buzz cut. I can tell right away he's not bushleague like Officer Budapest. He smiles like we've met before.

"Nate Macauley?" he asks. "You got a few minutes, son?"

CHAPTER SEVEN

Addy
Sunday, September 30, 2:05 p.m.

I shade my eyes against the sun outside the church, scanning the crowd until I spot Jake. He and the other pallbearers put Simon's casket onto some kind of metal stretcher, then step aside as the funeral directors angle it toward the hearse. I look down, not wanting to watch Simon's body get loaded into the back of a car like an oversized suitcase, and somebody taps me on the shoulder.

"Addy Prentiss?" An older woman dressed in a boxy blue suit gives me a polite, professional smile. "I'm Detective Laura Wheeler with the Bayview Police. I want to follow up on the discussion you had last week with Officer Budapest about Simon Kelleher's death. Could you come to the station with me for a few minutes?"

I stare at her and lick my lips. I want to ask why, but she's so calm and assured, like it's the most natural thing in the world to pull me aside after a funeral, that it seems rude to question her. Jake comes up beside me then, handsome in his suit, and gives Detective Wheeler a friendly, curious smile. My eyes dart between them and I stammer, "Isn't it—I mean—can't we talk here?"

Detective Wheeler winces. "So crowded, don't you think? And we're right around the corner." She gives Jake a half smile. "Detective Laura Wheeler, Bayview Police. I'm looking to borrow Addy for a little while and get clarification on a few points related to Simon Kelleher's death."

"Sure," he says, like that settles things. "Text me if you need a ride after, Ads. Luis and I will stick around downtown. We're starving and we gotta talk offensive strategy for next Saturday's game. Going to Glenn's, probably."

So that's it, I guess. I follow Detective Wheeler down the cobblestone path behind the church that leads to the sidewalk, even though I don't want to. Maybe this is what Ashton means when she says I don't think for myself. It's three blocks to the police station, and we walk in silence past a hardware store, the post office, and an ice cream parlor where a little girl out front is having a meltdown about getting chocolate sprinkles instead of rainbow. I keep thinking I should tell Detective Wheeler that my mother will worry if I don't come straight home, but I'm not sure I could say it without laughing.

We pass through metal detectors in the front of the police station and Detective Wheeler leads me straight to the back and into a small, overheated room. I've never been inside a police station before, and I thought it would be more . . . I don't know.

Official-looking. It reminds me of the conference room in Principal Gupta's office, with worse lighting. The flickering fluorescent tube above us deepens every line on Detective Wheeler's face and turns her skin an unattractive yellow. I wonder what it does to mine.

She offers me a drink, and when I decline she leaves the room for a few minutes, returning with a messenger bag slung over one shoulder and a small, dark-haired woman trailing behind her. Both of them sit across from me at the squat metal table, and Detective Wheeler lowers her bag onto the floor. "Addy, this is Lorna Shaloub, a family liaison for the Bayview School District. She's here as an interested adult on your behalf. Now, this is not a custodial interrogation. You don't have to answer my questions and you are free to leave at any time. Do you understand?"

Not really. She lost me at "interested adult." But I say "Sure," even though I wish more than ever I'd just gone home. Or that Jake had come with me.

"Good. I hope you'll hang in here with me. My sense is, of all the kids involved, you're the most likely to have gotten in over your head with no ill intent."

I blink at her. "No ill what?"

"No ill intent. I want to show you something." She reaches into the bag next to her and pulls out a laptop. Ms. Shaloub and I wait as she opens it and presses a few keys. I suck in my cheeks, wondering if she's going to show me the Tumblr posts. Maybe the police think one of us wrote them as some kind of awful joke. If they ask me who, I guess I'd have to say Bronwyn. Because the whole thing sounds like it's written by somebody who thinks they're ten times smarter than everyone else.

Detective Wheeler turns the laptop so it's facing me. I'm not sure what I'm looking at, but it seems like some kind of blog, with the About That logo front and center. I give her a questioning look, and she says, "This is the admin panel Simon used to manage content for About That. The text below last Monday's date stamp are his latest posts."

I lean forward and start to read.

First time this app has ever featured good-girl BR, possessor of school's most perfect academic record. Except she didn't get that A in chemistry through plain old hard work, unless that's how you define stealing tests from Mr. C's Google Drive. Someone call Yale. . . .

On the opposite end of the spectrum, our favorite criminal NM's back to doing what he does best: making sure the entire school is as high as it wants to be. Pretty sure that's a probation violation there, N.

MLB plus CC equals a whole lot of green next June, right? Seems inevitable Bayview's southpaw will make a splash in the major leagues . . . but don't they have some pretty strict antijuicing rules? Because CC's performance was most definitely enhanced during showcase season.

AP and JR are the perfect couple. Homecoming princess and star running back, in love for three years straight. Except for that intimate detour A took over the summer with TF at his beach house. Even more awkward now that the guys are friends. Think they compare notes?

I can't breathe. It's out there for everyone to see. How? Simon's dead; he can't have published this. Has someone else taken over for him? The Tumblr poster? But it doesn't even matter: the how, the why, the when—all that matters is that it *is*. Jake will see it, if he hasn't already. All the things I read before I got to my initials, that shocked me as I realized who they were about and what they meant, fall out of my brain. Nothing exists except my stupid, horrible mistake in black and white on the screen for the whole world to read.

Jake will *know*. And he'll never forgive me.

I'm almost folded in half with my head on the table, and can't make out Detective Wheeler's words at first. Then some start breaking through. ". . . can understand how you felt trapped . . . keep this from being published . . . If you tell us what happened we can help you, Addy. . . ."

Only one phrase sinks in. "Is this not published?"

"It was queued up the day Simon died, but he never got the chance to post it," Detective Wheeler says calmly.

Salvation. Jake hasn't seen this. Nobody has. Except . . . this police officer, and maybe other police officers. What I'm focused on and what she's focused on are two different things.

Detective Wheeler leans forward, her lips stretched in a smile that doesn't reach her eyes. "You may already have recognized the initials, but those other stories were about Bronwyn Rojas, Nate Macauley, and Cooper Clay. The four of you who were in the room with Simon when he died."

"That's . . . a weird coincidence," I manage.

"Isn't it?" Detective Wheeler agrees. "Addy, you already know how Simon died. We've analyzed Mr. Avery's room and can't see any way that peanut oil could have gotten into Simon's cup unless someone put it there after he filled it from the tap. There were only six people in the room, one of whom is dead. Your teacher left for a long period of time. The four of you who remained with Simon all had reasons for wanting to keep him quiet." Her voice doesn't get any louder, but it fills my ears like buzzing from a hive. "Do you see where I'm heading with this? This might have been carried out as a group, but it doesn't mean you share equal responsibility. There's a big difference between coming up with an idea and going along with it."

I look at Ms. Shaloub. She does look *interested,* I have to say, but not like she's on my side. "I don't understand what you mean."

"You lied about being in the nurse's office, Addy. Did someone put you up to that? To removing the EpiPens so Simon couldn't be helped later?"

My heart pounds as I pull a strand of hair off my shoulders and twist it around my fingers. "I didn't lie. I forgot." God, what if she makes me take a lie detector test? I'll never pass.

"Kids your age are under a lot of pressure today," Detective Wheeler says. Her tone is almost friendly, but her eyes are as flat as ever. "The social media alone—it's like you can't make a mistake anymore, can you? It follows you everywhere. The court is very forgiving toward impressionable young people who act hastily when they have a lot to lose, especially when they help us uncover the truth. Simon's family deserves the truth, don't you think?"

I hunch my shoulders and tug at my hair. I don't know what to do. Jake would know—but Jake's not here. I look at Ms. Shaloub tucking her short hair behind her ears, and suddenly Ashton's voice pops into my head. *You don't have to answer any questions.*

Right. Detective Wheeler said that at the beginning, and the words push everything else out of my brain with startling relief and clarity.

"I'm going to leave now."

I say it with confidence, but I'm still not one hundred percent sure I can do that. I stand and wait for her to stop me, but she doesn't. She just narrows her eyes and says, "Of course. As I told you, this isn't a custodial interrogation. But please understand, the help I can give you now won't be the same once you leave this room."

"I don't need your help," I tell her, and walk out the door, then out of the police station. Nobody stops me. Once I'm outside, though, I don't know where to go or what to do.

I sit on a bench and pull out my phone, my hands shaking. I can't call Jake, not for this. But who does that leave? My mind's as blank as if Detective Wheeler took an eraser and wiped it clean. I've built my entire world around Jake and now that it's shattered I realize, way too late, that I should have cultivated some other people who'd care that a police officer with mom hair and a sensible suit just accused me of murder. And when I say "care," I don't mean in an *oh-my-God-did-you-hear-what-happened-to-Addy* kind of way.

My mother would care, but I can't face that much scorn and judgment right now.

I scroll to the *As* in my contact list and press a name. It's my only option, and I say a silent prayer of thanks when she picks up.

"Ash?" Somehow I manage not to cry at my sister's voice. "I need help."

Cooper
Sunday, September 30, 2:30 p.m.

When Detective Chang shows me Simon's unpublished About That page, I read everyone else's entry first. Bronwyn's shocks me, Nate's doesn't, I have no idea who the hell this "TF" Addy supposedly hooked up with is—and I'm almost positive I know what's coming for me. My heart pounds as I spy my initials: *Because CC's performance was most definitely enhanced during showcase season.*

Huh. My pulse slows as I lean back in my chair. That's not what I expected.

Although I guess I shouldn't be surprised. I improved too much, too quickly—even the Padres scout said something.

Detective Chang dances around the subject for a while, dropping hints until I understand he thinks the four of us who were in the room planned the whole thing to keep Simon from posting his update. I try to picture it—me, Nate, and the two girls plotting murder by peanut oil in Mr. Avery's detention. It's so stupid it wouldn't even make a good movie.

I know I'm quiet for too long. "Nate and I never even spoke before last week," I finally say. "And I sure as heck never talked to the girls about this."

Detective Chang leans almost halfway across the table. "You're a good kid, Cooper. Your record's spotless till now, and you've got a bright future. You made one mistake and you got caught. That's scary. I get that. But it's not too late to do the right thing."

I'm not sure which mistake he's referring to: my alleged juicing, my alleged murdering, or something we haven't talked about yet. But as far as I know, I haven't been *caught* at anything. Just accused. Bronwyn and Addy are probably getting the exact same speech somewhere. I guess Nate would get a different one.

"I didn't cheat," I tell Detective Chang. "And I didn't hurt Simon." *Ah didn't.* I can hear my accent coming back.

He tries a different tack. "Whose idea was it to use the planted cell phones to get all of you into detention together?"

I lean forward, palms pressed on the black wool of my good pants. I hardly ever wear them, and they're making me hot and itchy. My heart's banging against my chest again. "Listen. I don't know who did that, but . . . isn't it something you should look into? Like, were there fingerprints on the phones? Because it feels to me like maybe we were framed." The other guy in the room, some representative from the Bayview School District who hasn't said a word, nods like I've said something profound. But Detective Chang's expression doesn't change.

"Cooper, we examined those phones as soon as we started to suspect foul play. There's no forensic evidence to suggest anyone else was involved. Our focus is on the four of you, and that's where I expect it to remain."

Which finally gets me to say, "I want to call my parents."

The "want" part isn't true, but I'm in over my head. Detective Chang heaves a sigh like I've disappointed him but says, "All right. You have your cell phone with you?" When I nod, he says, "You can make the call here." He stays in the room while I call Pop, who catches on a lot faster than I did.

"Give me that detective you're talking to," he spits. "Right now. And Cooperstown—wait, Cooper! Hold up. Don't you say another goddamn word to *anyone.*"

I hand Detective Chang my phone and he puts it to his ear. I can't hear everything Pop's saying, but he's loud enough that I get the basic idea. Detective Chang tries to insert a few words—along the lines of how it's perfectly legal to question minors in California without their parents present—but mostly he lets Pop rant. At one point he says, "No. He's free to go," and my ears prick up. It hadn't occurred to me that I could *leave.*

Detective Chang gives my phone back, and Pop's voice crackles in my ear. "Cooper, you there? Get your ass home. They're not charging you with anything, and you're not gonna answer any more questions without me and a lawyer."

A lawyer. Do I actually need one of those? I hang up and face Detective Chang. "My father told me to leave."

"You have that right," Detective Chang says, and I wish I'd known that from the beginning. Maybe he told me. I honestly don't remember. "But, Cooper, these conversations are happening all over the station with your friends. One of them is going to agree to work with us, and that person will be treated very differently from the rest of you. I think it should be you. I'd like you to have that chance."

I want to tell him he's got it all wrong, but Pop told me to stop talking. I can't bring myself to leave without saying anything, though. So I end up shaking Detective Chang's hand and saying, "Thank you for your time, sir."

I sound like the ass-kisser of the century. It's years of conditioning kicking in.

CHAPTER EIGHT

Bronwyn
Sunday, September 30, 3:07 p.m.

I'm beyond grateful my parents were with me at church when Detective Mendoza pulled me aside and asked me to come to the police station. I thought I'd just get a few follow-up questions from Officer Budapest. I wasn't prepared for what came next and wouldn't have known what to do. My parents took over and refused to let me answer his questions. They got tons of information out of the detective and didn't give up anything in return. It was pretty masterful.

But. Now they know what I've done.

Well. Not yet. They know the rumor. At the moment, driving home from the police station, they're still ranting against the injustice of it all. My mother is, anyway. My father's keeping his attention on the road, but even his turn signals are unusually aggressive.

"I mean," my mother says, in an urgent voice that indicates she's barely warming up, "it's horrible what happened to Simon. Of course his parents want answers. But to take a high school gossip post and turn it into an accusation like that is just ludicrous. I can't fathom how anyone could think Bronwyn would *kill* a boy because he was about to post a lie."

"It's not a lie," I say, but too quietly for her to hear me.

"The police have nothing." My father sounds like he's judging a company he's thinking of acquiring and finds it lacking. "Flimsy circumstantial evidence. Obviously no real forensics or they wouldn't be reaching this way. That was a Hail Mary." The car in front of us stops short at a yellow light, and Dad swears softly in Spanish as he brakes. "Bronwyn, I don't want you to worry about this. We'll hire an outstanding lawyer, but it's purely a formality. I may sue the police department when it's all over. Especially if any of this goes public and harms your reputation."

My throat feels like I'm getting ready to push words through sludge. "I did." I'm barely audible. I press the palm of my hand to my burning cheek and force my voice higher. "I did cheat. I'm sorry."

Mom rotates in her seat. "I can't hear you, honey. What was that?"

"I cheated." The words tumble out of me: how I'd used a computer in the lab right after Mr. Camino, and realized he hadn't logged out of his Google Drive. A file with all our chemistry test questions for the rest of the year was right there. I downloaded it onto a flash drive almost without thinking about it. And I used it to get perfect scores for the rest of the year.

I have no idea how Simon found out. But as usual, he was right.

The next few minutes in the car are horrible. Mom turns in her seat and stares at me with betrayal in her eyes. Dad can't do the same, but he keeps glancing into the rearview mirror like he's hoping to see something different. I can read the hurt in both their expressions: *You're not who we thought you were.*

My parents are all about merit-based achievement. Dad was one of the youngest CFOs in California before we were even born, and Mom's dermatology practice is so successful she hasn't been able to take on any new patients in years. They've been drumming the same message into me since kindergarten: *Work hard, do your best, and the rest will follow.* And it always had, until chemistry.

I guess I didn't know what to do about that.

"Bronwyn." Mom's still staring at me, her voice low and tight. "My God. I never would have imagined you'd do something like that. This is terrible on so many levels, but most important, it gives you a motive."

"I didn't do anything to Simon!" I burst out.

The hard lines of her mouth soften slightly as she shakes her head at me. "I'm disappointed in you, Bronwyn, but I didn't make *that* leap. I'm just stating fact. If you can't unequivocally say that Simon was lying, this could get very messy." She rubs a hand over her eyes. "How did he know you cheated? Does he have proof?"

"I don't know. Simon didn't . . ." I pause, thinking about all the About That updates I'd read over the years. "Simon never really *proved* anything. It's just . . . everybody believed him because he was never wrong. Things always came out eventually."

And here I'd thought I was in the clear, since I'd taken Mr. Camino's files last March. What I just don't get is, if Simon had known, why hadn't he pounced on it right away?

I knew what I did was wrong, obviously. I even thought it might be illegal, although technically I didn't break into Mr. Camino's account since it was already open. But that part hardly seemed real. Maeve uses her mad computer skills to hack into stuff for fun all the time, and if I'd thought of it I probably could have asked her to get Mr. Camino's files for me. Or even change my grade. But it wasn't premeditated. The file was in front of me in that moment, and I took it.

Then I chose to use it for months afterward, telling myself it was okay because one hard class shouldn't ruin my whole future. Which is kind of horribly ironic, given what just happened at the police station.

I wonder if everything Simon wrote about Cooper and Addy is true too. Detective Mendoza showed us all the entries, implying that somebody else might already be confessing and cutting a deal. I always thought Cooper's talent was God-given and that Addy was too Jake-obsessed to even look at another guy, but they probably never imagined me as a cheater, either.

With Nate, I don't wonder. He's never pretended to be anything other than exactly who he is.

Dad pulls into our driveway and cuts the engine, slipping the keys from the ignition and turning to face me. "Is there anything else you haven't told us?"

I think back to the claustrophobic little room at the police station, my parents on either side of me as Detective Mendoza lobbed questions like grenades. *Were you competitive with Simon?*

Have you ever been to his house? Did you know he was writing a post about you?

Did you have any reason, beyond this, to dislike or resent Simon?

My parents said I didn't have to respond to any of his questions, but I did answer that one. *No,* I said then.

"No," I say now, meeting my father's eyes.

If he knows I'm lying, he doesn't show it.

Nate
Sunday, September 30, 5:15 p.m.

Calling my ride home with Officer Lopez after Simon's funeral "tense" would be an understatement.

It was hours later, for one thing. After Officer Buzz Cut had brought me to the station and asked me a half-dozen different ways whether I'd killed Simon. Officer Lopez had asked if she could be present during questioning, and he agreed, which was fine with me. Although things got a little awkward when he pulled up Simon's drug-dealing accusation.

Which, although true, he can't prove. Even I know that. I stayed calm when he told me the circumstances surrounding Simon's death gave the police probable cause to search my house for drugs, and that they already had a warrant. I'd cleared everything out this morning, so I knew they wouldn't find anything.

Thank God Officer Lopez and I meet on Sundays. I'd probably be in jail otherwise. I owe her big-time for that, although she doesn't know it. And for having my back during questioning, which I didn't expect. I've lied to her face every time we've met and I'm pretty sure she knows that. But when Officer Buzz Cut started getting heated, she'd dial him back. I got the sense, eventually, that all they have is some flimsy circumstantial evidence and a theory they were hoping to pressure someone into admitting.

I answered a few of their questions. The ones I knew couldn't get me into trouble. Everything else was some variation of *I don't know* and *I don't remember.* Sometimes it was even true.

Officer Lopez didn't say a word from the time we left the police station until she pulled into my driveway. Now she gives me a look that makes it clear even she can't find a bright side to what just happened.

"Nate. I won't ask if what I saw on that site is true. That's a conversation for you and a lawyer if it ever comes to that. But you need to understand something. If, from this day forward, you deal drugs in any way, shape, or form—*I can't help you.* Nobody can. This is no joke. You're dealing with a potential capital offense. There are four kids involved in this investigation and every single one of them *except you* is backed by parents who are materially comfortable and present in their children's lives. If not outright wealthy and influential. You're the obvious outlier and scapegoat. Am I making myself clear?"

Jesus. She's not pulling any punches. "Yeah." I got it. I'd been thinking about it all the way home.

"All right. I'll see you next Sunday. Call me if you need me before then."

I climb out of the car without thanking her. It's a bullshit move, but I don't have it in me to be grateful. I step inside our low-ceilinged kitchen and the smell hits me right away: stale vomit seeps into my nose and throat, making me gag. I look around for the source, and I guess today's my lucky day because my father managed to make it to the sink. He just didn't bother rinsing it afterward. I put one hand over my face and use the other to aim a spray of water, but it's no good. The stuff's caked on by now and it won't come off unless I scrub it.

We have a sponge somewhere. Probably in the cabinet under the sink. Instead of looking, though, I kick it. Which is pretty satisfying, so I do it another five or ten times, harder and harder until the cheap wood splinters and cracks. I'm panting, breathing in lungsful of puke-infested air, and I'm so fucking sick of it all, I could kill somebody.

Some people are too toxic to live. They just are.

A familiar scratching sound comes from the living room—Stan, clawing at the glass of his terrarium, looking for food. I squirt half a bottle of dish detergent in the sink and aim another blast of water over it. I'll deal with the rest later.

I get a container of live crickets from the refrigerator and drop them into Stan's cage, watching them hop around with no clue what's in store for them. My breathing slows and my head clears, but that's not exactly good news. If I'm not thinking about one shit storm, I have to think about another.

Group murder. It's an interesting theory. I guess I should be grateful the cops didn't try to pin the whole thing on me. Ask the other three to nod and get out of jail free. I'm sure Cooper and the blond girl would have been more than happy to play along.

Maybe Bronwyn wouldn't, though.

I close my eyes and brace my hands on the top of Stan's terrarium, thinking about Bronwyn's house. How clean and bright it was, and how she and her sister talked to each other like all the interesting parts of their conversation were the things they didn't say. It must be nice, after getting accused of murder, to come home to a place like that.

When I leave the house and get on my bike, I tell myself I don't know where I'm going, and drive aimlessly for almost an hour. By the time I end up in Bronwyn's driveway, it's dinnertime for normal people, and I don't expect anyone to come outside.

I'm wrong, though. Someone does. It's a tall man in a fleece vest and a checked shirt, with short dark hair and glasses. He looks like a guy who's used to giving orders, and he approaches me with a calm, measured tread.

"Nate, right?" His hands are on his hips, a big watch glinting on one wrist. "I'm Javier Rojas, Bronwyn's father. I'm afraid you can't be here."

He doesn't sound mad, just matter-of-fact. But he also sounds like he's never meant anything more in his life.

I take my helmet off so I can meet his eyes. "Is Bronwyn home?" It's the most pointless question ever. Obviously she is, and obviously he's not going to let me see her. I don't even know why I want to, except that I can't. And because I want to ask her: *What's true? What did you do? What didn't you do?*

"You can't be here," Javier Rojas says again. "I'm sure you don't want police involvement any more than I do." He's doing a decent job of pretending I wouldn't be his worst nightmare even if I weren't involved in a murder investigation with his daughter.

That's it, I guess. Lines are drawn. I'm the obvious outlier and scapegoat. There isn't much else to say, so I reverse out of his driveway and head home.

CHAPTER NINE

Addy
Sunday, September 30, 5:30 p.m.

Ashton unlocks the door to her condo in downtown San Diego. It's a one-bedroom, because she and Charlie can't afford anything bigger. Especially with a year's worth of law school debt that'll be hard to repay now that Ashton's graphic design business hasn't taken off and Charlie's decided to make nature documentaries instead of being a lawyer.

But that's not what we're here to talk about.

Ashton brews coffee in her kitchen, which is tiny but cute: white cabinets, glossy black granite countertops, stainless steel appliances, and retro light fixtures. "Where's Charlie?" I ask as she doctors mine with cream and sugar, pale and sweet the way I like it.

"Rock climbing," Ashton says, pressing her lips into a thin line as she hands me the mug. Charlie has lots of hobbies Ashton doesn't share, and they're all expensive. "I'll call him about finding you a lawyer. Maybe one of his old professors knows someone."

Ashton insisted on taking me to get something to eat after we left the police station, and I told her everything at the restaurant—well, almost everything. The truth about Simon's rumor, anyway. She tried calling Mom on the way here, but got voice mail and left a cryptic *call-me-as-soon-as-you-get-this* message.

Which Mom has ignored. Or not seen. Maybe I should give her the benefit of the doubt.

We take our coffee to Ashton's balcony and settle ourselves into bright-red chairs on either side of a tiny table. I close my eyes and swallow a mouthful of hot, sweet liquid, willing myself to relax. It doesn't work, but I keep sipping slowly until I'm done. Ashton pulls out her phone and leaves a terse message for Charlie, then tries our mother again. "Still voice mail," she sighs, draining the last of her coffee.

"Nobody's home except us," I say, and for some reason that makes me laugh. A little hysterically. I might be losing it.

Ashton rests her elbows on the table and clasps her hands together under her chin. "Addy, you've got to tell Jake what happened."

"Simon's update isn't live," I say weakly, but Ashton shakes her head.

"It'll get out. Maybe gossip, maybe the police talking to him to put pressure on you. But it's something you need to deal with in your relationship no matter what." She hesitates, tucking her hair behind her ears. "Addy, is there some part of you that's been *wanting* Jake to find out?"

Resentment surges through me. Ashton can't stop her anti-Jake crusade even in the middle of a crisis. "Why would I ever want that?"

"He calls the shots on everything, doesn't he? Maybe you got tired of that. I would."

"*Right*, because you're the relationship expert," I snap. "I haven't seen you and Charlie together in over a month."

Ashton purses her lips. "This isn't about me. You need to tell Jake, and soon. You don't want him to hear this from someone else."

All the fight goes out of me, because I know she's right. Waiting will only make things worse. And since Mom's not calling us back, I might as well rip off the Band-Aid. "Will you take me to his house?"

I have a bunch of texts from Jake anyway, asking how things went at the station. I should probably be focusing on the whole criminal aspect of this, but as usual, my mind's consumed with Jake. I take out my phone, open my messages, and text, *Can I tell you in person?*

Jake responds right away. "Only Girl" blares, which seems inappropriate for the conversation that's about to follow.

Of course.

I rinse out our mugs while Ashton collects her keys and purse. We step into the hallway and Ashton shuts the door behind us, tugging the knob to make sure it's locked. I follow her to the elevator, my nerves buzzing. I shouldn't have had that coffee. Even if it *was* mostly milk.

We're more than halfway to Bayview when Charlie calls. I try to tune out Ashton's tense, clipped conversation, but it's impossible in such close quarters. "I'm not asking for *me*," she says at one point. "Can you be the bigger person for once?"

I scrunch in my seat and take out my phone, scrolling through messages. Keely's sent half a dozen texts about Halloween costumes, and Olivia's agonizing about whether she should get back together with Luis. Again. Ashton finally hangs up and says with forced brightness, "Charlie's going to make a few calls about a lawyer."

"Great. Tell him thanks." I feel like I should say more, but I'm not sure what, and we lapse into silence. Still, I'd rather spend hours in my sister's quiet car than five minutes in Jake's house, which looms in front of us all too quickly. "I'm not sure how long this will take," I tell Ashton as she pulls into the driveway. "And I might need a ride home." Nausea rolls through my stomach. If I hadn't done what I did with TJ, Jake would insist on being a part of whatever comes next. The whole situation would still be terrifying, but I wouldn't have to face it on my own.

"I'll be at the Starbucks on Clarendon Street," Ashton says as I climb out of the car. "Text me when you're done."

I feel sorry, then, for snapping at her and goading her about Charlie. If she hadn't picked me up from the police station, I don't know what I would have done. But she backs out of the driveway before I can say anything, and I start my slow march to Jake's front door.

His mom answers when I ring the bell, smiling so normally that I almost think everything's going to be okay. I've always liked Mrs. Riordan. She used to be a hotshot advertising executive till right before Jake started high school, when she decided to downshift and focus on her family. I think my mother secretly wishes she were Mrs. Riordan, with a glamorous career she doesn't have to do anymore and a handsome, successful husband.

Mr. Riordan can be intimidating, though. He's a my-way-or-nothing sort of man. Whenever I mention that, Ashton starts muttering about apples not falling far from trees.

"Hi, Addy. I'm on my way out, but Jake's waiting for you downstairs."

"Thanks," I say, stepping past her into the foyer.

I can hear her lock the door behind her and her car door slam as I take the stairs down to Jake. The Riordans have a finished basement that's basically Jake's domain. It's huge, and they have a pool table and a giant TV and lots of overstuffed chairs and couches down there, so our friends hang out here more than anywhere else. As usual, Jake is sprawled on the biggest couch with an Xbox controller in hand.

"Hey, baby." He pauses the game and sits up when he sees me. "How'd everything go?"

"Not good," I say, and start shaking all over. Jake's face is full of concern I don't deserve. He gets to his feet, trying to pull me down next to him, but I resist for once. I take a seat in the armchair beside the couch. "I think I should sit over here while I tell you this."

A frown creases Jake's forehead. He sits back down, on the edge of the couch this time, his elbows resting on his knees as he gazes at me intently. "You're scaring me, Ads."

"It's been a scary day," I say, twisting a strand of hair around my finger. My throat feels as dry as dust. "The detective wanted to talk to me because she thinks I . . . She thinks all of us who were in detention with Simon that day . . . killed him. They think we deliberately put peanut oil in his water so he'd die." It occurs to me as the words slip out that maybe I wasn't supposed to talk about this part. But I'm used to telling Jake everything.

Jake stares at me, blinks, and barks out a short laugh. "Jesus. That's not funny, Addy." He almost never calls me by my actual name.

"I'm not joking. She thinks we did it because he was about to publish an update of About That featuring the four of us. Reporting awful things we'd never want to get out." I'm tempted to tell him the other gossip first—*See, I'm not the only horrible person!*—but I don't. "There was something about me on there, something true, that I have to tell you. I should have told you when it happened but I was too scared." I stare at the floor, my eyes focusing on a loose thread in the plush blue carpet. If I pulled it I bet the whole section would unravel.

"Go on," Jake says. I can't read his tone at all.

God. How can my heart be hammering this hard and I still be alive? It should have burst out of my chest by now. "At the end of school last year, when you were in Cozumel with your parents, I ran into TJ at the beach. We got a bottle of rum and ended up getting really drunk. And I went to TJ's house and, um, I hooked up with him." Tears slide down my cheeks and drip onto my collarbone.

"Hooked up how?" Jake asks flatly. I hesitate, wondering if there's any possible way I can make this sound less awful than it is. But then Jake repeats himself—"Hooked up *how?*"—so forcefully that the words spring out of me.

"We slept together." I'm crying so hard I can barely get more words out. "I'm sorry, Jake. I made a stupid, horrible mistake and I'm so, so sorry."

Jake doesn't say anything for a minute, and when he speaks his voice is icy cold. "You're sorry, huh? That's great. That's all right, then. As long as you're *sorry.*"

"I really am," I start, but before I can continue he springs up and rams his fist into the wall behind him. I can't help the startled cry that escapes me. The plaster cracks, raining white dust across the blue rug. Jake shakes his fist and hits the wall harder.

"*Fuck,* Addy. You screw my friend months ago, you've been lying to me ever since, and you're *sorry?* What the hell is wrong with you? I treat you like a *queen.*"

"I know," I sob, staring at the bloody smears his knuckles left on the wall.

"You let me hang out with a guy who's laughing his ass off behind my back while you jump out of his bed and into mine like nothing happened. Pretending you give a shit about me." Jake almost never swears in my presence, or if he does, he apologizes afterward.

"I do! Jake, I love you. I've always loved you, since the first time I saw you."

"So why'd you do it? *Why?*"

I've asked myself that question for months and can't come up with anything except weak excuses. *I was drunk, I was stupid, I was insecure.* I guess that last one's closest to the truth; years of being not enough finally catching up with me. "I made a mistake. I'd do anything to fix it. If I could take it back I would."

"But you can't, can you?" Jake asks. He's silent for a minute, breathing hard. I don't dare say another word. "Look at me." I keep my head in my hands as long as I can. "*Look* at me, Addy. You fucking owe me that."

So I do, but I wish I hadn't. His face—that beautiful face I've loved since before it ever looked as good as it does now—is twisted with rage. "You ruined everything. You know that, right?"

"I know." It comes out as a moan, like I'm a trapped animal. If I could gnaw my own limb off to escape this situation, I would.

"Get out. Get the hell out of my house. I can't stand the sight of you."

I'm not sure how I manage to get up the stairs, never mind out the door. Once I'm in the driveway I scramble through my bag trying to find my phone. There's no way I can stand in Jake's driveway sobbing while I wait for Ashton. I need to walk to Clarendon Street and find her. Then a car across the street beeps softly, and through a haze of tears I watch my sister lower her window.

Her mouth droops as I approach. "I thought it might go like this. Come on, get in. Mom's waiting for us."

PART TWO

HIDE-AND-SEEK

CHAPTER TEN

Bronwyn
Monday, October 1, 7:30 a.m.

I get ready for school on Monday the way I always do. Up at six so I can run for half an hour. Oatmeal with berries and orange juice at six-thirty, a shower ten minutes later. Dry my hair, pick out clothes, put on sunscreen. Scan the *New York Times* for ten minutes. Check my email, pack my books, make sure my phone's fully charged.

The only thing that's different is the seven-thirty meeting with my lawyer.

Her name is Robin Stafford, and according to my father she's a brilliant, highly successful criminal defense attorney. But not *overly* high-profile. Not the kind of lawyer automatically associated with guilty rich people trying to buy their way out of trouble. She's right on time and gives me a wide, warm smile when Maeve leads her into the kitchen.

I wouldn't be able to guess her age by looking at her, but the bio my father showed me last night says she's forty-one. She's wearing a cream-colored suit that's striking against her dark skin, subtle gold jewelry, and shoes that look expensive but not Jimmy Choo level.

She takes a seat at our kitchen island across from my parents and me. "Bronwyn, it's a pleasure. Let's talk about what you might expect today and how you should handle school."

Sure. Because that's my life now. School is something to be *handled.*

She folds her hands in front of her. "I'm not sure the police truly believed the four of you planned this together, but I do think they hoped to shock and pressure one of you into giving up useful information. That indicates their evidence is flimsy at best. If none of you point fingers and your stories line up, they don't have anywhere to take this investigation, and it's my belief it will ultimately be closed out as an accidental death."

The vise that's been gripping my chest all morning loosens a little. "Even though Simon was about to post those awful things about us? And there's that whole Tumblr thing going on?"

Robin gives an elegant little shrug. "At the end of the day, that's nothing but gossip and trolling. I know you kids take it seriously, but in the legal world it's meaningless unless hard proof emerges to back it up. The best thing you can do is not talk about the case. Certainly not with the police, but not with school administrators either."

"What if they ask?"

"Tell them you've retained counsel and can't answer questions without your lawyer present."

I try to imagine having that conversation with Principal Gupta. I don't know what the school's heard about this, but me pleading the Fifth would be a major red flag.

"Are you friendly with the other kids who were in detention that day?" Robin asks.

"Not exactly. Cooper and I have some classes together, but—"

"Bronwyn." My mother interrupts with a chill in her voice. "You're friendly enough with Nate Macauley that he showed up here last night. For the *third* time."

Robin sits straighter in her chair, and I flush. That was a big topic of discussion last night after my dad made Nate leave. Dad thought he'd stalked our address in a creepy way, so I had some explaining to do.

"Why has Nate been here three times, Bronwyn?" Robin asks with a polite, interested air.

"It's no big deal. He gave me a ride home after Simon died. Then he stopped by last Friday to hang out for a while. And I don't know what he was doing here last night, since nobody would let me talk to him."

"It's the 'hanging out' while your parents aren't home that disturbs me—" my mother starts, but Robin interrupts her.

"Bronwyn, what's the nature of your relationship with Nate?"

I have no idea. Maybe you could help me analyze it? Is that part of your retainer? "I hardly know him. I hadn't talked to him in years before last week. We're both in this weird situation and . . . it helps to be around other people going through the same thing."

"I recommend maintaining distance from the others," Robin says, ignoring my mother's evil eye in my direction. "No need to give the police further ammunition for their theories. If your cell phone and email are examined, will they show recent communication with those three students?"

"No," I say truthfully.

"That's good news." She glances at her watch, a slim gold Rolex. "That's all we can address now if you're going to get to school on time, which you should. Business as usual." She flashes me that warm smile again. "We'll talk more in depth later."

I say good-bye to my parents, not quite able to look them in the eye, and call for Maeve as I grab the keys to the Volvo. I spend the whole drive steeling myself for something awful to happen once we get to school, but it's weirdly normal. No police lying in wait for me. Nobody's looking at me any differently than they have since the first Tumblr post came out.

Still, I'm only half paying attention to Kate and Yumiko's chatter after homeroom, my eyes roaming the hallway. There's only one person I want to talk to, even though it's exactly who I'm supposed to stay away from. "Catch you guys later, okay?" I murmur, and intercept Nate after he ducks into the back stairwell.

If he's surprised to see me, he doesn't show it. "Bronwyn. How's the family?"

I lean against the wall next to him and lower my voice. "I wanted to apologize for my dad making you leave last night. He's kind of freaked out by all this."

"Wonder why." Nate drops his voice as well. "You been searched yet?" My eyes widen, and he laughs darkly. "Didn't think so. I was. You're probably not supposed to be talking to me, right?"

I can't help but glance around the empty stairwell. I'm already paranoid and Nate's not helping. I have to keep reminding myself that we did not, in fact, conspire to commit murder. "Why did you stop by?"

His eyes search mine as though he's about to say something profound about life and death and the presumption of innocence. "I was going to apologize for stealing Jesus from you."

I recoil a little. I have no idea what he's talking about. Is he making some kind of religious allegory? "What?"

"In the fourth-grade Nativity play at St. Pius. I stole Jesus and you had to carry a bag wrapped in a blanket. Sorry about that."

I stare at him for a second as the tension flows out of me, leaving me limp and slightly giddy. I punch him in the shoulder, startling him so much he actually laughs. "I *knew* it was you. Why'd you do that?"

"To get a rise out of you." He grins at me, and for a second I forget everything except the fact that Nate Macauley still has an adorable smile. "Also, I wanted to talk to you about—all this. But I guess it's too late. You must be lawyered up by now, right?" His smile disappears.

"Yes, but . . . I want to talk to you too." The bell rings, and I pull out my phone. Then I remember Robin asking about communication records between the four of us and stuff it back into my bag. Nate catches the gesture and snorts another humorless laugh.

"Yeah, exchanging numbers is a shit idea. Unless you want

to use this." He reaches into his backpack and hands me a flip phone.

I take it gingerly. "What is it?"

"An extra phone. I have a few." I run my thumb across the cover with a dawning idea of what it might be for, and he adds hastily, "It's new. Nobody's going to call it or anything. But I have the number. I'll call you. You can answer, or not. Up to you." He pauses, and adds, "Just don't, you know, leave it lying around. They get a warrant for your phone and computer, that's all they can touch. They can't go through your whole house."

I'm pretty sure my expensive lawyer would tell me not to take legal advice from Nate Macauley. And she'd probably have something to say about the fact that he has an apparently inexhaustible supply of the same cheap phones that corralled us all in detention last week. I watch him head up the stairs, knowing I should drop the phone into the nearest trash can. But I put it in my backpack instead.

Cooper
Monday, October 1, 11:00 a.m.

It's almost a relief to be at school. Better than home, where Pop spent hours ranting about how Simon's a liar and the police are incompetent and the school should be on the hook for this and lawyers will cost a fortune we don't have.

He didn't ask if any of it was true.

We're in a weird limbo now. Everything's different but it all looks the same. Except Jake and Addy, who're walking around like they want to kill and die, respectively. Bronwyn gives me the least convincing smile ever in the hallway, her lips pressed so tight they almost disappear. Nate's nowhere in sight.

We're all waiting for something to happen, I guess.

After gym something does, but it doesn't have anything to do with me. My friends and I are heading for the locker room after playing soccer, lagging behind everyone else, and Luis is going on about some new junior girl he's got his eye on. Our gym teacher opens the door to let a bunch of kids inside when Jake suddenly whirls around, grabs TJ by the shoulder, and punches him in the face.

Of course. "TF" from About That is TJ Forrester. The lack of a *J* confused me.

I grab Jake's arms, pulling him back before he can throw another punch, but he's so furious he almost gets away from me before Luis steps in to help. Even then, two of us can barely hold him. "You *asshole*," Jake spits at TJ, who staggers but doesn't fall. TJ puts a hand to his bloody, probably broken mess of a nose. He doesn't make any effort to go after Jake.

"Jake, come on, man," I say as the gym teacher races toward us. "You're gonna get suspended."

"Worth it," Jake says bitterly.

So instead of today's big story being Simon, it's about how Jake Riordan got sent home for punching TJ Forrester after gym class. And since Jake refused to speak to Addy before he left and she's practically in tears, everyone's pretty sure they know why.

"How could she?" Keely murmurs in the lunch line as Addy shuffles around like a sleepwalker.

"We don't know the whole story," I remind her.

I guess it's good Jake's not here since Addy sits with us at lunch like usual. I'm not sure she'd have the nerve otherwise. But she doesn't talk to anybody, and nobody talks to her. They're pretty obvious about it. Vanessa, who's always been the bitchiest girl in our group, physically turns away when Addy takes the chair next to her. Even Keely doesn't make any effort to include Addy in the conversation.

Bunch of hypocrites. Luis was on Simon's app for the same damn thing and Vanessa tried to give me a hand job at a pool party last month, so they shouldn't be judging anyone.

"How's it goin', Addy?" I ask, ignoring the stares of the rest of the table.

"Don't be nice, Cooper." She keeps her head down, her voice so low I can hardly hear it. "It's worse if you're nice."

"Addy." All the frustration and fear I've been feeling finds its way into my voice, and when Addy looks up a jolt of understanding passes between us. There're a million things we should be talking about, but we can't say any of them. "It'll be all right."

Keely puts her hand on my arm, asking, "What do *you* think?" and I realize I've missed an entire conversation.

"About what?"

She gives me a little shake. "About Halloween! What should we be for Vanessa's party?"

I'm disoriented, like I just got yanked into some shiny video-game version of the world where everything's too bright and I don't understand the rules. "God, Keely, I don't know. Whatever. That's almost a month away."

Olivia clucks her tongue disapprovingly. "Typical guy. You

have no idea how hard it is to find a costume that's sexy but not slutty."

Luis waggles his brows at her. "Just be slutty, then," he suggests, and Olivia smacks his arm. The cafeteria's too warm, almost hot, and I wipe my damp brow as Addy and I exchange another look.

Keely pokes me. "Give me your phone."

"What?"

"I want to look at that picture we took last week, at Seaport Village? That woman in the flapper dress. She looked amazing. Maybe I could do something like that." I shrug and pull out my phone, unlocking it and handing it over. She squeezes my arm as she opens my photos. "You'd look totally hot in one of those gangster suits."

She hands the phone to Vanessa, who gives an exaggerated, breathless "Ohhh!" Addy pushes food around on her plate without ever lifting her fork to her mouth, and I'm about to ask her if she wants me to get her something else when my phone rings.

Vanessa keeps hold of it and snorts, "Who calls during *lunch*? Everybody you know is already here!" She looks at the screen, then at me. "Ooh, Cooper. Who's *Kris*? Should Keely be jealous?"

I don't answer for a few seconds too long, then too fast. "Just, um, a guy I know. From baseball." My whole face feels hot and prickly as I take the phone from Vanessa and send it to voice mail. I wish like hell I could take that call, but now's not the time.

Vanessa raises an eyebrow. "A boy who spells *Chris* with a *K*?"

"Yeah. He's . . . German." *God. Stop talking.* I put my phone in my pocket and turn to Keely, whose lips are slightly parted like she's about to ask a question. "I'll call him back later. So. A flapper, huh?"

I'm about to head home after the last bell when Coach Ruffalo stops me in the hall. "You didn't forget about our meeting, did you?"

I exhale in frustration because yeah, I did. Pop's leaving work early so we can meet with a lawyer, but Coach Ruffalo wants to talk college recruiting. I'm torn, because I'm pretty sure Pop would want me to do both at the same time. Since that's not possible, I follow Coach Ruffalo and figure I'll make it quick. His office is next to the gym and smells like twenty years' worth of student athletes passing through. In other words, not good.

"My phone's ringing off the hook for you, Cooper," he says as I sit across from him in a lopsided metal chair that creaks under my weight. "UCLA, Louisville, and Illinois are putting together full-scholarship offers. They're all pushing for a November commitment even though I told them there's no way you'll make a decision before spring." He catches my expression and adds, "It's good to keep your options open. Obviously the draft's a real possibility but the more interest there is on the college level, the better you'll look to the majors."

"Yes, sir." It's not draft strategy I'm worried about. It's how these colleges will react if the stuff on Simon's app gets out. Or if this whole thing spirals and I keep getting investigated by the police. Are all these offers gonna dry up, or am I innocent until proven guilty? I'm not sure if I should be telling any of this to Coach Ruffalo. "It's just . . . hard to keep 'em all straight."

He picks up a thin sheaf of stapled-together papers, waving them at me. "I've done it for you. Here's a list of every college I've been in touch with and their current offer. I've highlighted the ones I think are the best fit or will be most impressive to the majors. I wouldn't necessarily put Cal State or UC Santa Barbara on the short list, but they're both local and offering facility tours. You want to schedule those some weekend, let me know."

"Okay. I . . . I have some family stuff coming up, so I might be kinda busy for a while."

"Sure, sure. No rush, no pressure. It's entirely up to you, Cooper."

People always say that but it doesn't feel true. About anything.

I thank Coach Ruffalo and head into the almost-empty hallway. I have my phone in one hand and Coach's list in the other, and I'm so lost in thought as I look between them that I almost mow someone over in my path.

"Sorry," I say, taking in a slight figure with his arms wrapped around a box. "Uh . . . hey, Mr. Avery. You need help carrying that?"

"No thank you, Cooper." I'm a lot taller than he is, and when I look down I don't see anything but folders in the box. I guess he can manage those. Mr. Avery's watery eyes narrow when he sees my phone. "I wouldn't want to interrupt your *texting*."

"I was just . . ." I trail off, since explaining the lawyer appointment I'm almost late for won't win me any points.

Mr. Avery sniffs and adjusts his grip on the box. "I don't understand you kids. So obsessed with your screens and your *gossip.*" He grimaces like the word tastes bad, and I'm not sure what to say. Is he making a reference to Simon? I wonder if the police bothered questioning Mr. Avery this weekend, or if he's been disqualified by virtue of not having a motive. That they know of, anyway.

He shakes himself, like he doesn't know what he's talking about either. "Anyway. If you'll excuse me, Cooper."

All he'd have to do to get past me is step aside, but I guess that's my job. "Right," I say, moving out of his way. I watch him shuffle down the hall and decide to leave my stuff in my locker and head for the car. I'm late enough as it is.

I'm stopped at the last red light before my house when my phone beeps. I look down expecting a text from Keely, because somehow I ended up promising we'd get together tonight to plan Halloween costumes. But it's from my mom.

Meet us at the hospital. Nonny had a heart attack.

CHAPTER ELEVEN

Nate
Monday, October 1, 11:50 p.m.

I made a round of calls to my suppliers this morning to tell them I'm out of commission for a while. Then I threw away that phone. I still have a couple of others. I usually pay cash for a bunch at Walmart and rotate them for a few months before replacing them.

So after I've watched as many Japanese horror movies as I can stand and it's almost midnight, I take a new phone out and call the one I gave Bronwyn. It rings six times before she picks up, and she sounds nervous as hell. "Hello?"

I'm tempted to disguise my voice and ask if I can buy a bag of heroin to mess with her, but she'd probably throw the phone out and never talk to me again. "Hey."

"It's late," she says accusingly.

"Were you sleeping?"

"No," she admits. "I can't."

"Me either." Neither of us says anything for a minute. I'm stretched out on my bed with a couple of thin pillows behind me, staring at paused screen credits in Japanese. I click off the movie and scroll through the channel guide.

"Nate, do you remember Olivia Kendrick's birthday party in fifth grade?"

I do, actually. It was the last birthday party I ever went to at St. Pius, before my dad withdrew me because we couldn't pay the tuition anymore. Olivia invited the whole class and had a scavenger hunt in her yard and the woods behind it. Bronwyn and I were on the same team, and she tore through those clues like it was her job and she was up for a promotion. We won and all five of us got twenty-dollar iTunes gift cards. "Yeah."

"I think that's the last time you and I spoke before all this."

"Maybe." I remember better than she probably realizes. In fifth grade my friends started noticing girls and at one point they all had girlfriends for, like, a week. Stupid kid stuff where they asked a girl out, the girl said yes, and then they ignored each other. While we were walking through Olivia's woods I watched Bronwyn's ponytail swing in front of me and wondered what she'd say if I asked her to be my girlfriend. I didn't do it, though.

"Where'd you go after St. Pi?" she asks.

"Granger." St. Pius went up to eighth grade, so I wasn't in school with Bronwyn again until high school. By then she was in full-on overachiever mode.

She pauses, as though she's waiting for me to continue, and

laughs a little. "Nate, why'd you call me if you're only going to give one-word answers to everything?"

"Maybe you're not asking the right questions."

"Okay." Another pause. "Did you do it?"

I don't have to ask what she means. "Yes and no."

"You'll have to be more specific."

"Yes, I sold drugs while on probation *for* selling drugs. No, I didn't dump peanut oil in Simon Kelleher's cup. You?"

"Same," she says quietly. "Yes and no."

"So you cheated?"

"Yes." Her voice wavers, and if she starts crying I don't know what I'll do. Pretend the call dropped, maybe. But she pulls herself together. "I'm really ashamed. And I'm so afraid of people finding out."

She's all worried-sounding, so I probably shouldn't laugh, but I can't help it. "So you're not perfect. So what? Welcome to the real world."

"I'm familiar with the real world." Bronwyn's voice is cool. "I don't live in a bubble. I'm sorry for what I did, that's all."

She probably is, but it's not the whole truth. Reality's messier than that. She had months to confess if it was really eating at her, and she didn't. I don't know why it's so hard for people to admit that sometimes they're just assholes who screw up because they don't expect to get caught. "You sound more worried about what people are gonna think," I say.

"There's nothing wrong with worrying about what people think. It keeps you off *probation*."

My main phone beeps. It's next to my bed on the scarred side table that lurches every time I touch it, because it's missing a leg tip and I'm too lazy to fix it. I roll over to read a text from Amber: *U up?* I'm about to tell Bronwyn I have to go when she heaves a sigh.

"Sorry. Low blow. It's just . . . it's more complicated than that, for me. I've disappointed both my parents, but it's worse for my dad. He's always pushing against stereotypes because he's not from here. He built this great reputation, and I could tarnish the whole thing with one stupid move."

I'm about to tell her nobody thinks that way. Her family looks pretty untouchable from where I sit. But I guess everyone has shit to deal with, and I don't know hers. "Where's your dad from?" I ask instead.

"He was born in Colombia, but moved here when he was ten."

"What about your mom?"

"Oh, her family's been here forever. Fourth-generation Irish or something."

"Mine too," I say. "But let's just say my fall from grace won't surprise anyone."

She sighs. "This is all so surreal, isn't it? That anybody could think either one of us would actually *kill* Simon."

"You're taking me at my word?" I ask. "I'm on *probation*, remember?"

"Yeah, but I was there when you tried to help Simon. You'd have to be a pretty good actor to fake that."

"If I'm enough of a sociopath to kill Simon I can fake anything, right?"

"You're not a sociopath."

"How do you know?" I say it like I'm making fun, but I

really want to know the answer. I'm the guy who got searched. *The obvious outlier and scapegoat*, as Officer Lopez said. Someone who lies whenever it's convenient and would do it in a heartbeat to save his own ass. I'm not sure how all that adds up to trust for someone I hadn't talked to in six years.

Bronwyn doesn't answer right away, and I stop channel surfing at the Cartoon Network to watch a snippet of some new show with a kid and a snake. It doesn't look promising. "I remember how you used to look out for your mom," she finally says. "When she'd show up at school and act . . . you know. Like she was sick or something."

Like she was sick or something. I guess Bronwyn could be referring to the time my mother screamed at Sister Flynn during parent-teacher conferences and ended up ripping all our artwork off the walls. Or the way she'd cry on the curb while she was waiting to pick me up from soccer practice. There's a lot to choose from.

"I really liked your mom," Bronwyn says tentatively when I don't answer. "She used to talk to me like I was a grown-up."

"She'd swear at you, you mean," I say, and Bronwyn laughs.

"I always thought it was more like she was swearing *with* me."

Something about the way she says that gets to me. Like she could see the person under all the other crap. "She liked you." I think about Bronwyn in the stairwell today, her hair still in that shiny ponytail and her face bright. As if everything is interesting and worth her time. *If she were around, she'd like you now.*

"She used to tell me . . ." Bronwyn pauses. "She said you only teased me so much because you had a crush on me."

I glance at Amber's text, still unanswered. "I might have. I don't remember."

Like I said. I lie whenever it's convenient.

Bronwyn's quiet for a minute. "I should go. At least try to sleep."

"Yeah. Me too."

"I guess we'll see what happens tomorrow, huh?"

"Guess so."

"Well, bye. And, um, Nate?" She speaks quickly, in a rush. "I had a crush on *you* back then. For whatever that's worth. Nothing, probably. But anyway. FYI. So, good night."

After she hangs up I put the phone on my bedside table and pick up the other one. I read Amber's message again, then type, *Come over.*

Bronwyn's naïve if she thinks there's more to me than that.

Addy
Wednesday, October 3, 7:50 a.m.

Ashton keeps making me go to school. My mother couldn't care less. As far as she's concerned I've ruined all our lives, so it doesn't much matter what I do anymore. She doesn't say those exact words, but they're etched across her face every time she looks at me.

"Five thousand dollars just to talk to a lawyer, Adelaide," she hisses at me over breakfast Wednesday morning. "I hope you know that's coming out of your college fund."

I'd roll my eyes if I had the energy. We both know I don't

have a college fund. She's been on the phone to my father in Chicago for days, hassling him for the money. He doesn't have much to spare, thanks to his second, younger family, but he'll probably send at least half to shut her up and feel good about what an involved parent he is.

Jake still won't talk to me, and I miss him so much, it's like I've been hollowed out by a nuclear blast and there's nothing left but ashes fluttering inside brittle bones. I've sent him dozens of texts that aren't only unanswered; they're unread. He unfriended me on Facebook and unfollowed me on Instagram and Snapchat. He's pretending I don't exist and I'm starting to think he's right. If I'm not Jake's girlfriend, who am I?

He was supposed to be suspended all week for hitting TJ, but his parents raised a fuss about how Simon's death has put everyone on edge, so I guess he's back today. The thought of seeing him makes me sick enough that I decided to stay home. Ashton had to drag me out of bed. She's staying with us indefinitely, for now.

"You're not going to wither up and die from this, Addy," Ashton lectures as she shoves me toward the shower. "He doesn't get to erase you from the world. God, you made a stupid mistake. It's not like you murdered someone.

"Well," she adds with a short, sarcastic laugh, "I guess the jury's still out on that one."

Oh, the gallows humor in our household now. Who knew Prentiss girls had it in them to be even a little bit funny?

Ashton drives me to Bayview and drops me off out front. "Keep your chin up," she advises. "Don't let that sanctimonious control freak get you down."

"*God,* Ash. I did cheat on him, you know. He's not unprovoked."

She purses her lips in a hard line. "Still."

I get out of the car and try to steel myself for the day. School used to be so easy. I belonged to everything without even trying. Now I'm barely hanging on to the edges of who I used to be, and when I catch my reflection in a window I hardly recognize the girl staring back at me. She's in my clothes—the kind of form-fitting top and tight jeans that Jake likes—but her hollow cheeks and dead eyes don't match the outfit.

My hair looks tremendous, though. At least I have that going for me.

There's only one person who looks worse than me at school, and that's Janae. She must have lost ten pounds since Simon died, and her skin's a mess. Her mascara's running all the time, so I guess she cries in the bathroom between classes as much as I do. It's surprising we haven't run into each other yet.

I see Jake at his locker almost as soon as I enter the hallway. All the blood rushes out of my head, making me so light-headed I actually sway as I walk toward him. His expression is calm and preoccupied as he twirls his combination. For a second I hope everything's going to be fine, that his time away from school has helped him cool off and forgive me. "Hi, Jake," I say.

His face changes in an instant from neutral to livid. He yanks his locker open with a scowl and pulls out an armful of books, stuffing them into his backpack. He slams his locker, shoulders his backpack, and turns away.

"Are you ever going to talk to me again?" I ask. My voice is tiny, breathless. Pathetic.

He turns and gives me such a hate-filled look that I step backward. "Not if I can help it."

Don't cry. Don't cry. Everyone's staring at me as Jake stalks away. I catch Vanessa smirking from a few lockers over. She's *loving* this. How did I ever think she was my friend? She'll probably go after Jake soon, if she hasn't already. I stumble in front of my own locker, my hand stretching toward the lock. It takes a few seconds for the word written in thick black Sharpie to sink in.

WHORE.

Muffled laughter surrounds me as my eyes trace the two *V*s that make up the *W.* They cross each other in a distinctive, loopy scrawl. I've made dozens of pep rally posters for the Bayview Wildcats with Vanessa, and teased her for her funny-looking *W*s. She didn't even try to hide it. I guess she wanted me to know.

I force myself to walk, not run, to the nearest bathroom. Two girls stand at the mirror, fixing their makeup, and I duck past them into the farthest stall. I collapse onto the toilet seat and cry silently, burying my head in my hands.

The first bell rings but I stay where I am, tears rolling down my cheeks until I'm cried out. I fold my arms onto my knees and lower my head, immobile as the second bell rings and girls come in and out of the bathroom again. Snatches of conversation float through the room and, yeah, some of it's about me. I plug my ears and try not to listen.

It's the middle of third period by the time I uncoil myself and stand. I unlock the stall door and head for the mirror, pushing my hair away from my face. My mascara's washed away, but I've been here long enough that my eyes aren't puffy. I stare at my reflection and try to collect my scattered thoughts. I can't deal with classes today. I'd go to the nurse's office and claim a headache, but I don't feel comfortable there now that I'm a suspected EpiPen thief. That leaves only one option: getting out of here and going home.

I'm in the back stairwell with my hand on the door when heavy footsteps pound the stairs. I turn to see TJ Forrester coming down; his nose is still swollen and framed by a black eye. He stops when he sees me, one hand gripping the banister. "Hey, Addy."

"Shouldn't you be in class?"

"I have a doctor's appointment." He puts a hand to his nose and grimaces. "I might have a deviated septum."

"Serves you right." The bitter words burst out before I can stop them.

TJ's mouth falls open, then closes, and his Adam's apple bobs up and down. "I didn't say anything to Jake, Addy. I swear to God. I didn't want this to come out any more than you did. It's messed things up for me too." He touches his nose again gingerly.

I wasn't actually thinking about Jake; I was thinking about Simon. But of course TJ wouldn't know anything about the unpublished posts. How did Simon know, though? "We were the only two people there," I hedge. "You must have told *somebody*."

TJ shakes his head, wincing as though the movement hurts. "We were kissing on a public beach before we got to my house, remember? Anyone could have seen us."

"But they wouldn't have known—" I stop, realizing Simon's site never said TJ and I slept together. He *implied* it, pretty heavily, but that was it. Maybe I'd overconfessed. The thought sickens me, although I'm not sure I could have managed to tell Jake only a half-truth anyway. He'd have gotten it out of me eventually.

TJ looks at me with regret in his eyes. "I'm sorry this sucks so bad for you. For what it's worth, I think Jake's being a jerk. But I didn't tell anybody." He puts a hand over his heart. "Swear on my granddad's grave. I know that doesn't mean anything to you but it does to me." I finally nod, and he lets out a deep breath. "Where are you going?"

"Home. I can't stand being here. All my friends hate me." I'm not sure why I'm telling him this, other than the fact that I don't have anyone else to tell. "I doubt they'll even let me sit with them now that Jake's back." It's true. Cooper's out today, visiting his sick grandmother and probably, although he didn't say so, meeting with his lawyer. With him gone nobody will dare stand up to Jake's anger. Or want to.

"Screw them." TJ gives me a lopsided grin. "If they're still being assholes tomorrow, come sit with me. They wanna talk, let's give them something to talk about."

It shouldn't make me smile, but it almost does.

CHAPTER TWELVE

Bronwyn
Thursday, October 4, 12:20 p.m.

I got lulled into a false sense of complacency.

It happens, I guess, even during the worst week of your life. Horrible, earth-shattering stuff piles on top of you until you're about to suffocate and then—it stops. And nothing else happens, so you start to relax and think you're in the clear.

That's a rookie mistake that smacks me in the face Thursday during lunch when the usual low-grade cafeteria buzz suddenly grows and swells. At first I look around, interested, like anyone would be, and wondering why everyone's suddenly pulled out their phones. But before I can take mine out, I notice the heads swiveling in my direction.

"Oh." Maeve is quicker than me, and her soft exhalation as she scans her phone is loaded with so much regret that my heart sinks. She catches her bottom lip between her teeth and wrinkles her forehead. "Bronwyn. It's, um, another Tumblr. About . . . well. Here."

I take her phone, heart pounding, and read the exact same words Detective Mendoza showed me on Sunday after Simon's funeral. *First time this app has ever featured good-girl BR, possessor of school's most perfect academic record . . .*

It's all there. Simon's unpublished entries for each of us, with an added note at the bottom:

Did you think I was joking about killing Simon? Read it and weep, kids. Everyone in detention with Simon last week had an extraspecial reason for wanting him gone. Exhibit A: the posts above, which he was about to publish on About That.

Now here's your assignment: connect the dots. Is everybody in it together, or is somebody pulling strings? Who's the puppet master and who's the puppet?

I'll give you a hint to get you started: everyone's lying.

GO!

I raise my eyes and lock on Maeve's. She knows the truth, all of it, but I haven't told Yumiko or Kate. Because I thought maybe this could stay contained, quiet, while the police ran their investigation in the background and then closed it out from lack of evidence.

I'm pathetically naïve. Obviously.

"Bronwyn?" I can barely hear Yumiko over the roaring in my ears. "Is this for real?"

"*Fuck* this Tumblr bullshit." I'd be startled at Maeve's language if I hadn't vaulted over my surprise threshold two minutes ago. "I bet I could hack that stupid thing and figure out who's behind it."

"Maeve, no!" My voice is so *loud*. I lower it and switch to Spanish. "No lo hagas . . . No queremos . . ."

I force myself to stop talking as Kate and Yumiko keep staring at me. *You can't. We don't want.* That should be enough, for now.

But Maeve won't shut up. "I don't care," she says furiously. "*You* might, but I—"

Saved by the loudspeaker. Sort of. Déjà vu seizes me as a disembodied voice floats through the room: *"Attention, please. Would Cooper Clay, Nate Macauley, Adelaide Prentiss, and Bronwyn Rojas please report to the main office. Cooper Clay, Nate Macauley, Adelaide Prentiss, and Bronwyn Rojas to the main office."*

I don't remember getting to my feet, but I must have, because here I am, moving. Shuffling like a zombie past the stares and whispers, weaving through tables until I get to the cafeteria exit. Down the hallway, past homecoming posters that are three weeks old now. Our planning committee is slacking, which would inspire more disdain if I weren't on it.

When I get to the main office, the receptionist gestures toward the conference room with the weary wave of someone who thinks I should know the drill by now. I'm the last to arrive—at least, I think I am, unless Bayview Police or school committee members are joining us. "Close the door, Bronwyn," Principal Gupta says. I comply and sidle past her to take a seat between Nate and Addy, across from Cooper.

Principal Gupta steeples her fingers under her chin. "I'm

sure I don't have to tell you why you're here. We've been keeping an eye on that repulsive Tumblr site and got today's update as soon as you did. At the same time, we've had a request from the Bayview Police Department to make the student body available for interviews starting tomorrow. My understanding, based on conversations with police, is that today's Tumblr is an accurate reflection of posts Simon wrote before he died. I realize most of you now have legal representation, which of course the school respects. But this is a safe space. If there's anything you'd like to tell me that might help the school better understand the pressures you were facing, now is the time."

I stare at her as my knees start to tremble. Is she for real? Now is most definitely *not* the time. Still, I feel this almost irresistible urge to answer her, to explain myself, until a hand under the table grasps mine. Nate doesn't look at me, but his fingers thread through mine, warm and strong, resting against my shaking leg. He's in his Guinness T-shirt again, and the material stretches thin and soft across his shoulders, as though it's been through hundreds of washes. I glance at him and he gives a tiny, almost imperceptible shake of his head.

"Ah got nothin' more to say than what ah told ya last week," Cooper drawls.

"Me either," Addy says quickly. Her eyes are red-rimmed and she looks exhausted, her pixie features pinched. She's so pale, I notice the light dusting of freckles across her nose for the first time. Or maybe she's just not wearing makeup. I think with a stab of sympathy that she's been the hardest hit of anyone so far.

"I hardly think—" Principal Gupta begins, when the door opens and the receptionist sticks her head in.

"Bayview Police on line one," she says, and Principal Gupta gets to her feet.

"Excuse me for a moment."

She closes the door behind her and the four of us sit in strained silence, listening to the hum of the air conditioner. It's the first time we've all been in one room together since Officer Budapest questioned us last week. I almost laugh when I remember how clueless we were then, arguing about unfair detentions and junior prom court.

Although to be fair, that was mostly me.

Nate lets go of my hand and tips his chair back, surveying the room. "Well. This is awkward."

"Are you guys all right?" My words come out in a rush, surprising me. I'm not sure what I intended to say, but that wasn't it. "This is unreal. That they—suspect us."

"It was an accident," Addy says immediately. Not like she's positive, though. More like she's testing a theory.

Cooper slides his eyes over to Nate. "Weird kind of accident. How does peanut oil get in a cup all by itself?"

"Maybe someone came into the room at some point and we didn't notice," I say, and Nate rolls his eyes at me. "I know it sounds ridiculous, but—you have to consider everything, right? It's not impossible."

"Lots of people hated Simon," Addy says. From the hard set of her jaw, she's one of them. "He ruined plenty of lives. You guys remember Aiden Wu? In our class, transferred sophomore year?" I'm the only one who nods, so Addy turns her gaze on me. "My sister knows his sister from college. Aiden didn't transfer for

134

the hell of it. He had a breakdown after Simon posted about his cross-dressing."

"Seriously?" Nate asks. Cooper runs a hand back and forth over his hair.

"You remember those spotlight posts Simon used to do when he first launched the app?" Addy asks. "More in-depth stuff, like a blog, almost?"

My throat gets tight. "I remember."

"Well, he did that with Aiden," Addy says. "It was straight-up evil." Something about her tone makes me uneasy. I never thought I'd hear shallow little Addy Prentiss speak with such venom in her voice. Or have an opinion of her own.

Cooper jumps in hastily, like he's worried she's going to go off on a rant. "That's what Leah Jackson said at the memorial service. I ran into her under the bleachers. She said we were all hypocrites for treating him like some kind of martyr."

"Well, there you go," Nate says. "You were right, Bronwyn. The entire school's probably been walking around with bottles of peanut oil in their backpacks, waiting for their chance."

"Not just any peanut oil," Addy says, and we all turn to her. "It would have to be cold-pressed for a person with allergies to react to it. The gourmet type, basically."

Nate stares at her, brow creased. "How would you know that?"

Addy shrugs. "I saw it on the Food Network once."

"Maybe that's the sort of thing you keep to yourself when Gupta comes back," Nate suggests, and the ghost of a grin flits across Addy's face.

Cooper glares at Nate. "This isn't a joke."

Nate yawns, unperturbed. "Feels like it sometimes."

I swallow hard, my mind still churning through the conversation. Leah and I were friendly once—we partnered in a Model United Nations competition that brought us to the state finals at the beginning of junior year. Simon had wanted to participate too, but we told him the wrong application deadline and he missed the cutoff. It wasn't on purpose, but he never believed that and was furious with both of us. A few weeks later he started writing about Leah's sex life on About That. Usually Simon posted something once and let it go, but with Leah, he kept the updates coming. It was personal. I'm sure he'd have done the same to me if there had been anything to find back then.

When Leah started sliding off the rails, she asked me if I'd misled Simon on purpose. I hadn't but still felt guilty, especially once she slit her wrists. Nothing was the same for her after Simon started his campaign against her.

I don't know what going through something like that does to a person.

Principal Gupta comes back into the room, shutting the door behind her and settling into her seat. "My apologies, but that couldn't wait. Where were we?"

Silence falls for a few seconds, until Cooper clears his throat. "With all due respect, ma'am, I think we were agreeing we can't have this conversation." There's a steel in his voice that wasn't there before, and in an instant I feel the energy of the room coalesce and shift. We don't trust one another, that's pretty obvious—but we trust Principal Gupta and the Bayview Police Department even less. She sees it too and pushes her chair back.

"It's important you know this door is always open to you," she says, but we're already getting to our feet and opening the door ourselves.

I'm out of sorts and anxious for the rest of the day, going through the motions of everything I'm supposed to do at school and at home. But I can't relax, not really, until the clock inches past midnight and the phone Nate gave me rings.

He's called me every night since Monday, always around the same time. He's told me things I couldn't have imagined about his mother's illness and his father's drinking. I've told him about Maeve's cancer and the nameless pressure I've always felt to be twice as good at everything. Sometimes we don't talk at all. Last night he suggested we watch a movie, and we both logged in to Netflix and watched a god-awful horror movie he picked until two in the morning. I fell asleep with my earbuds still in, and might have snored in his ear at some point.

"Your turn to pick a movie," he says by way of greeting. I've noticed that about Nate; he doesn't do pleasantries. Just starts with whatever's on his mind.

My mind's elsewhere, though. "I'm looking," I say, and we're silent for a minute as I scroll through Netflix titles without really seeing them. It's no good; I can't go straight into movie mode. "Nate, are you in trouble because of how everything came out at school today?" After I left Principal Gupta's office, the rest of the afternoon was a blur of stares, whispers, and uncomfortable conversations with Kate and Yumiko once I finally explained what had been going on for the past few days.

He snorts a short laugh. "I was in trouble before. Nothing's changed."

"My friends are mad at me for not telling them."

"About cheating? Or being investigated by the police?"

"Both. I hadn't said anything about either. I thought maybe it would all go away and they'd never have to know." Robin had said not to answer any questions about the case, but I didn't see how I could apply that to my two best friends. When the whole school's starting to turn against you, you need *somebody* on your side. "I wish I could remember more about that day. What class were you in when Mr. Avery found the phone in your backpack?"

"Physical science," Nate says. "Science for dummies, in other words. You?"

"Independent study," I say, chewing the sides of my cheeks. Ironically enough, my stellar grades in chemistry let me construct my own science course senior year. "I suppose Simon would've been in AP physics. I don't know what classes Addy and Cooper have with Mr. Avery, but in detention they acted surprised to see each other."

"So?" Nate asks.

"Well, they're friends, right? You'd think they'd have talked about it. Or even been in the same class when it happened."

"Who knows. Could've been homeroom or study period for one of them. Avery's a jack-of-all-trades," Nate says. When I don't reply, he adds, "What, you think those two masterminded the whole thing?"

"Just following a train of thought," I say. "I feel like the police are barely paying attention to how weird that phone situation is, because they're so sure we're all in it together. I mean, when you think about it, Mr. Avery knows better than anyone what classes we have with him. Maybe *he* did it. Planted phones in all our backpacks and coated the cups with peanut oil before we got there. He's a science teacher; he'd know how to do that."

Even as I say it, though, the mental image of our frail, mousy teacher manically doctoring cups before detention doesn't ring true. Neither does Cooper making off with the school's EpiPens, or Addy hatching a murder scheme while watching the Food Network.

But I don't really know any of them. Including Nate. Even though it feels like I do.

"Anything's possible," Nate says. "You pick a movie yet?"

I'm tempted to choose something cool and art house-y to impress him, except he'd probably see right through it. Plus he picked a crap horror movie, so there's not a lot to live up to. "Have you seen *Divergent*?"

"No." His tone is wary. "And I don't want to."

"Tough. I didn't want to watch a bunch of people get killed by a mist created from an alien tear in the space-time continuum, but I did."

"Damn it." Nate sounds resigned. He pauses, then asks, "You have it buffered?"

"Yes. Hit Play." And we do.

CHAPTER THIRTEEN

Cooper
Friday, October 5, 3:30 p.m.

I pick Lucas up after school and stop by Nonny's hospital room before our parents get there. She'd been asleep most of the time we visited all week, but today she's sitting up in bed with the TV remote in hand. "This television only gets three channels," she complains as Lucas and I hover in the doorway. "We might as well be in 1985. And the food is terrible. Lucas, do you have any candy?"

"No, ma'am," Lucas says, flipping his too-long hair out of his eyes. Nonny turns a hopeful face to me, and I'm struck by how *old* she looks. I mean, sure, she's well into her eighties, but she's always had so much energy that I never really noticed. It hits me now that even though her doctor says she's recovering well, we'll be lucky to go a few years before something like this happens again.

And then at some point, she's not gonna be around at all.

"I got nothin'. Sorry," I say, dropping my head to hide my stinging eyes.

Nonny lets out a theatrical sigh. "Well, goddamn. You boys are pretty, but not helpful from a practical standpoint." She rummages on the side table next to her bed and finds a rumpled twenty-dollar bill. "Lucas, go downstairs to the gift shop and buy three Snickers bars. One for each of us. Keep the change and take your time."

"Yes, ma'am." Lucas's eyes gleam as he calculates his profit. He's out the door in a flash, and Nonny settles back against a stack of hospital pillows.

"Off he goes to pad his pockets, bless his mercenary little heart," she says fondly.

"Are you supposed to be eating candy right now?" I ask.

"Of course not. But I want to hear how you're doing, darlin'. Nobody tells me anything but I hear things."

I lower myself into the side chair next to her bed, eyes on the floor. I don't trust myself to look at her yet. "You should rest, Nonny."

"Cooper, this was the least dangerous heart attack in cardiac history. A blip on the monitor. Too much bacon, that's all. Catch me up on the Simon Kelleher situation. I promise you it will not cause a relapse."

I blink a few times and imagine myself getting ready to throw a slider: straightening my wrist, placing my fingers on the outer portion of the baseball, letting the ball roll off my thumb and index finger. It works; my eyes dry and my breathing evens out, and I can finally meet Nonny's eyes. "It's a goddamn mess."

She sighs and pats my hand. "Oh, darlin'. Of course it is."

I tell her everything: How Simon's rumors about us are all over school now, and how the police set up shop in the administrative offices today and interviewed everybody we know. Plus lots of people we don't know. How Coach Ruffalo hasn't pulled me aside yet to ask whether I'm on the juice but I'm sure he will soon. How we had a sub for astronomy because Mr. Avery was holed up in another room with two police officers. Whether he was being questioned like we'd been or giving some kind of evidence against us, I couldn't tell.

Nonny shakes her head when I finish. She can't set her hair here the way she does at home, and it bobs around like loose cotton. "I could not be sorrier you got pulled into this, Cooper. You of all people. It's not right."

I wait for her to ask me, but she doesn't. So I finally say—tentatively, because after spending days with lawyers it feels wrong to state anything like an actual fact—"I didn't do what they say, Nonny. I didn't use steroids and I didn't hurt Simon."

"Well, for goodness' sake, Cooper." Nonny brushes impatiently at her hospital blanket. "You don't have to tell *me* that."

I swallow hard. Somehow, the fact that Nonny accepts my word without question makes me feel guilty. "The lawyer's costing a fortune and she's not helping. Nothing's getting better."

"Things'll get worse before they get better," Nonny says placidly. "That's how it goes. And don't you worry about the cost. I'm payin' for it."

A fresh wave of guilt hits me. "Can you afford that?"

"Course I can. Your grandfather and I bought a lot of Apple stock in the nineties. Just because I didn't hand it all over to your father to buy a McMansion in this overpriced town doesn't mean I couldn't have. Now. Tell me something I *don't* know."

I'm not sure what she means. I could mention how Jake is freezing out Addy and all our friends are joining in, but that's too depressing. "Not much else to tell, Nonny."

"How's Keely handling all this?"

"Like a vine. Clingy," I say before I can stop myself. Then I feel horrible. Keely's been nothing but supportive, and it's not her fault that makes me feel suffocated.

"Cooper." Nonny takes my hand in both of hers. They're small and light, threaded with thick blue veins. "Keely is a beautiful, sweet girl. But if she's not who you love, she's just *not*. And that's fine."

My throat goes dry and I stare at the game show on the screen. Somebody's about to win a new washer/dryer set and they're pretty happy about it. Nonny doesn't say anything else, just keeps holding my hand. "I dunno whatcha mean," I say.

If Nonny notices my good ol' boy accent coming and going, she doesn't mention it. "I mean, Cooper Clay, I've been in the room when that girl calls or texts you, and you always look like you're trying to escape. Then someone else calls and your face lights up like a Christmas tree. I don't know what's holding you back, darlin', but I wish you'd stop letting it. It's not fair to you *or* to Keely." She squeezes my hand and releases it. "We don't have to talk about it now. In fact, could you please hunt down that brother of yours? It may not have been the best idea I ever had to let a twelve-year-old wander the hospital with money burning a hole in his pocket."

"Yeah, sure." She's letting me off the hook and we both know

143

it. I stand up and ease out of the room into a hallway crowded with nurses in brightly colored scrubs. Every one of them stops what they're doing and smiles at me. "You need help, hon?" the one closest to me asks.

It's been that way my whole life. People see me and immediately think the best of me. Once they know me, they like me even more.

If it ever came out that I'd actually done something to Simon, plenty of people would hate me. But there'd also be people who'd make excuses for me, and say there must be more to my story than just getting accused of using steroids.

The thing is, they'd be right.

Nate
Friday, October 5, 11:30 p.m.

My father's awake for a change when I get home Friday from a party at Amber's house. It was still going strong when I left, but I'd had enough. I've got ramen noodles on the stove and toss some vegetables into Stan's cage. As usual he just blinks at them like an ingrate.

"You're home early," my father says. He looks the same as ever—like hell. Bloated and wrinkled with a pasty, yellow tinge to his skin. His hand shakes when he lifts his glass. A couple of months ago I came home one night and he was barely breathing, so I called an ambulance. He spent a few days in the hospital, where doctors told him his liver was so damaged

144

he could drop dead at any time. He nodded and acted like he gave a shit, then came home and cracked another bottle of Seagram's.

I've been ignoring that ambulance bill for weeks. It's almost a thousand dollars thanks to our crap insurance, and now that I have zero income there's even less chance we can pay it.

"I have things to do." I dump the noodles into a bowl and head for my room with them.

"Seen my phone?" my father calls after me. "Kept ringing today but I couldn't find it."

"That's 'cause it's not on the couch," I mutter, and shut my door behind me. He was probably hallucinating. His phone hasn't rung in months.

I scarf down my noodles in five minutes, then settle back onto my pillows and put in my earbuds so I can call Bronwyn. It's my turn to pick a movie, thank God, but we're barely half an hour into *Ringu* when Bronwyn decides she's had enough.

"I can't watch this alone. It's too scary," she says.

"You're not alone. I'm watching it with you."

"Not *with* me. I need a person in the room for something like this. Let's watch something else instead. My turn to pick."

"I'm not watching another goddamn Divergent movie, Bronwyn." I wait a beat before adding, "You should come over and watch *Ringu* with me. Climb out your window and drive here." I say it like it's a joke, and it mostly is. Unless she says yes.

Bronwyn pauses, and I can tell she's thinking about it as a not-joke. "My window's a fifteen-foot drop to the ground," she says. *Joke.*

"So use a door. You've got, like, ten of them in that house."
Joke.

"My parents would kill me if they found out." *Not-joke.*
Which means she's considering it. I picture her sitting next to
me in those little shorts she had on when I was at her house, her
leg pressed against mine, and my breathing gets shallow.

"Why would they?" I ask. "You said they can sleep through
anything." *Not-joke.* "Come on, just for an hour till we finish the
movie. You can meet my lizard." It takes a few seconds of silence
for me to realize how that might be interpreted. "That's not a
line. I have an actual lizard. A bearded dragon named Stan."

Bronwyn laughs so hard she almost chokes. "Oh my God.
That would have been completely out of character and yet . . .
for a second I really did think you meant something else."

I can't help laughing too. "Hey, girl. You were into that
smooth talk. Admit it."

"At least it's not an anaconda," Bronwyn sputters. I laugh
harder, but I'm still kind of turned on. Weird combination.

"Come over," I say. *Not-joke.*

I listen to her breathe for a while, until she says, "I can't."

"Okay." I'm not disappointed. I never really thought she
would. "But you need to pick a different movie."

We agree on the last Bourne movie and I'm watching it with
my eyes half-closed, listening to increasingly frequent texts from
Amber chime in the background. She might be starting to think
we're something we're not. I reach for that phone to shut it down
when Bronwyn says, "Nate. Your phone."

"What?"

"Someone keeps texting you."

146

"So?"

"So it's really late."

"And?" I ask, annoyed. I hadn't pegged Bronwyn as the possessive type, especially when all we ever do is talk on the phone and she just turned down my joke-not-joke invitation.

"It's not . . . customers, is it?"

I exhale and shut the other phone off. "No. I told you, I'm not doing that anymore. I'm not stupid."

"All right." She sounds relieved, but tired. Her voice is starting to drag. "I might go to sleep now."

"Okay. Do you want to hang up?"

"No." She laughs thickly, already half-asleep. "I'm running out of minutes, though. I just got a warning. I have half an hour left."

Those prepaid phones have hundreds of minutes on them, and she's had it less than a week. I didn't realize we'd been talking that much. "I'll give you another phone tomorrow," I tell her, before I remember tomorrow's Saturday and we don't have school. "Bronwyn, wait. You need to hang up."

I think she's already asleep until she mutters, "What?"

"Hang up, okay? So your minutes don't run out and I can call you tomorrow about getting you another phone."

"Oh. Right. Okay. Good night, Nate."

"Good night." I hang up and place the two phones side by side, pick up the remote, and shut off the TV. Might as well go to sleep.

CHAPTER FOURTEEN

Addy
Saturday, October 6, 9:30 a.m.

I'm at home with Ashton and we're trying to figure out something to do. But we keep getting stuck on the fact that nothing interests me.

"Come on, Addy." I'm lying across an armchair, and Ashton nudges me with her foot from the couch. "What would you normally do on a weekend? And don't say hang out with Jake," she adds quickly.

"But that *is* what I'd do," I whine. Pathetic, but I can't help it. I've had this awful sickening lurch in my stomach all week, as though I'd been walking along a sturdy bridge and it vanished under my feet.

"Can you honestly not come up with a single, non-Jake-related thing you like?"

I shift in my seat and consider the question. What did I do

before Jake? I was fourteen when we started dating, still partly a kid. My best friend was Rowan Flaherty, a girl I'd grown up with who moved to Texas later that year. We'd drifted apart in ninth grade when she had zero interest in boys, but the summer before high school we'd still ridden our bikes all over town together. "I like riding my bike," I say uncertainly, even though I haven't been on one in years.

Ashton claps her hands as if I'm a reluctant toddler she's trying to get excited about a new activity. "Let's do that! Ride bikes somewhere."

Ugh, no. I don't want to move. I don't have the energy. "I gave mine away years ago. It was half-rusted under the porch. And you don't have one anyway."

"We'll use those rental bikes—what are they called? Hub Bikes or something? They're all over town. Let's find some."

I sigh. "Ash, you can't babysit me forever. I appreciate you keeping me from falling apart all week, but you've got a life. You should get back to Charlie."

Ashton doesn't answer right away. She goes into the kitchen, and I hear the refrigerator door opening and the faint clink of bottles. When she returns she's holding a Corona and a San Pellegrino, which she hands to me. She ignores my raised eyebrows—it's not even ten o'clock in the morning—and takes a long sip of beer as she sits down, crossing her legs beneath her. "Charlie's happy as can be. I'm guessing he's moved his girlfriend in by now."

"*What?*" I forget how tired I am and sit up straight.

"I caught them when I went home to get more clothes last weekend. It was all so horribly clichéd. I even threw a vase at his head."

"Did you hit him?" I ask hopefully. And hypocritically, I guess. After all, I'm the Charlie in my and Jake's relationship. She shakes her head and takes another gulp of her beer.

"Ash." I move from my armchair and sit next to her on the couch. She's not crying, but her eyes are shiny, and when I put my hand on her arm she swallows hard. "I'm so sorry. Why didn't you say something?"

"You had enough to worry about."

"But it's your marriage!" I can't help looking at Ashton and Charlie's wedding photo from two years ago, which sits next to my junior prom picture on our mantel. They were such a perfect couple, people used to joke that they looked as though they came with the frame. Ashton had been so happy that day, gorgeous and glowing and giddy.

And relieved. I'd tried to squash the idea because I knew it was catty, but I couldn't help thinking Ashton had feared losing Charlie right up till the day she married him. He was *tremendous* on paper—handsome, good family, headed to Stanford Law— and our mother had been thrilled. It wasn't until they'd been married a year that I noticed Ashton almost never laughed when Charlie was around.

"It's been over for a while, Addy. I should have left six months ago, but I was too much of a coward. I didn't want to be alone, I guess. Or admit I'd failed. I'll find my own place eventually, but I'll be here for a while." She shoots me a wry look. "All right. I've made my true confession. Now you tell me something. Why did you lie when Officer Budapest asked about being in the nurse's office the day Simon died?"

I let go of her arm. "I didn't—"

"Addy. Come on. You started playing with your hair as soon as he brought it up. You always do that when you're nervous." Her tone's matter-of-fact, not accusing. "I don't believe for one second you took those EpiPens, so what are you hiding?"

Tears prick my eyes. I'm so tired, suddenly, of all the half-truths I've piled up over the past days and weeks. Months. *Years.* "It's so stupid, Ash."

"Tell me."

"I didn't go for myself. I went to get Tylenol for Jake, because he had a headache. And I didn't want to say so in front of you because I knew you'd give me that *look.*"

"What look?"

"*You* know. That whole *Addy-you're-such-a-doormat* look."

"I don't think that," Ashton says quietly. A fat tear rolls down my cheek, and she reaches over to brush it away.

"You should. I am."

"Not anymore," Ashton says, and that does it. I start flat-out bawling, curled in the fetal position in a corner of the couch with Ashton's arms around me. I don't even know who or what I'm crying for: Jake, Simon, my friends, my mother, my sister, myself. All of the above, I guess.

When the tears finally stop I'm raw and exhausted, my eyelids hot and my shoulders sore from shaking for so long. But I feel lighter and cleaner too, like I've purged something that's been making me sick. Ashton gets me a pile of Kleenex and gives me a minute to wipe my eyes and blow my nose. When I've finally wadded up all the damp tissues and tossed them into a corner wastebasket, she takes a small sip of her beer and wrinkles her nose. "This doesn't taste as good as I thought it would. Come on, let's ride bikes."

I can't say no to her now. So I trail after her to the park a half mile from our house, where there's a whole row of rental bikes. Ashton figures out the sign-up deal, swiping her credit card to release two bikes. We don't have helmets, but we're just going around the park so it doesn't really matter.

I haven't ridden a bike in years but I guess it's true what they say: you don't forget how. After a wobbly start we take off on the wide path through the park and I have to admit, it's kind of fun. The breeze flutters through my hair as my legs pump and my heart rate accelerates. It's the first time in a week I haven't felt half-dead. I'm surprised when Ashton stops and says, "Hour's up." She catches sight of my face and asks, "Should we rent for another hour?"

I grin at her. "Yeah, okay." We get tired about halfway through, though, and return the bikes so we can go to a café and rehydrate. Ashton gets our drinks while I find seats, and I scroll through my messages while I wait for her. It takes a lot less time than it used to—I only have a couple from Cooper, asking if I'm going to Olivia's party tonight.

Olivia and I have been friends since freshman year, but she hasn't spoken to me all week. *Pretty sure I'm not invited,* I text.

"Only Girl" trills out with Cooper's response. I make a mental note that when all this is over and I have a minute to think straight, I'm going to change my text tone to something less annoying. *That's BS. They're your friends too.*

Sitting this one out, I write. *Have fun.* At this point, I'm not even sad about being excluded. It's just one more thing.

Cooper doesn't get it. I guess I should thank him; if he'd dropped me like everyone else, Vanessa would have gone nuclear on me by now. But she doesn't dare cross the homecoming king, even when he's been accused of steroid use. School opinion is split down the middle about whether he did it or not, but he's not saying either way.

I wonder if I could have done the same—bluffed and brazened my way through this whole nightmare without telling Jake the truth. Then I look at my sister, chuckling with the guy behind the coffee counter in a way she never did with Charlie, and remember how careful and contained I always had to be around Jake. If I was going to the party tonight I'd have to wear something he picked out, stay as late as he wanted, and not talk to anyone who might make him mad.

I miss him still. I do. But I don't miss that.

Bronwyn
Saturday, October 6, 10:30 a.m.

My feet fly over the familiar path as my arms and legs match the rhythm of the music blaring in my ears. My heart accelerates and the fears that have been crowding my brain all week recede, replaced by pure physical effort. When I finish my run I'm drained but pumped full of endorphins, and feel almost cheerful as I head for the library to pick up Maeve. It's our usual

Saturday-morning routine, but I can't find her in any of her typical spots and have to text her.

Fourth floor, she replies, so I head for the children's room.

She's sitting on a tiny chair near the window, tapping away at one of the computers. "Revisiting your childhood?" I ask, sinking to the floor beside her.

"No," Maeve says, her eyes on the screen. She lowers her voice to almost a whisper. "I'm in the admin panel for About That."

It takes a second for what she said to register, and when it does my heart takes a panicky leap. "Maeve, what the hell? What are you doing?"

"Looking around. Don't freak out," she adds with a sideways glance at me. "I'm not disturbing anything, but even if I were, nobody would know it's me. I'm at a public computer."

"Using your library card!" I hiss. You can't get online here without entering your account number.

"No. Using his." Maeve inclines her head toward a small boy a few tables over with a stack of picture books in front of him. I stare at her incredulously, and she shrugs. "I didn't *take* it from him. He left it lying out and I wrote down the numbers."

The little boy's mother joins him then, smiling as she catches Maeve's eye. She'd never guess my sweet-faced sister just committed identity theft against her six-year-old.

I can't think of anything to say except "Why?"

"I wanted to see what the police are seeing," Maeve says. "If there were any other draft posts, other people who might've wanted to keep Simon quiet."

I inch forward in spite of myself. "Were there?"

154

"No, but there *is* something odd. About Cooper's post. It's date-stamped days after everyone else's, for the night before Simon died. There's an earlier file with his name on it, but it's encrypted and I can't open it."

"So?"

"I don't know. But it's different, which makes it interesting. I need to come back with a thumb drive and download it." I blink at her, trying to pinpoint the exact moment when she morphed into a hacker-investigator. "There's something else. Simon's user name for the site is AnarchiSK. I Googled it and came up with a bunch of 4chan threads he posted to constantly. I didn't have time to read them, but we should."

"Why?" I ask as she loops her backpack over her shoulder and gets to her feet.

"Because something's weird about all this," Maeve says matter-of-factly, leading me out the door and down the stairs. "Don't you think?"

"Understatement of the year," I mutter. I stop in the empty stairwell, so she does too, half turning with a questioning look. "Maeve, how'd you even get into Simon's admin panel? How did you know where to look?"

A small smile tugs at the corners of her mouth. "You're not the only one who grabs confidential information off computers other people were using."

I gape at her. "So you—so Simon was posting About That at school? And left it open?"

"Of course not. Simon was smart. He did it here. Not sure if it was a one-time thing or if he posted from the library all the time, but I saw him one weekend last month when you were running. He didn't see me. I logged in to the computer after him and got the address from the browser history. I didn't do anything with it at first," she says, meeting my incredulous look with a calm gaze. "Just put it aside for future reference. I started trying to get in after you came back from the police station. Don't worry," she adds, patting me on the arm. "Not from home. Nobody can trace it."

"Okay, but . . . why the interest in the app? Before Simon even died? What were you going to do?"

Maeve purses her lips thoughtfully. "I hadn't figured that part out. I thought maybe I'd start wiping it clean right after he posted, or switch all the text to Russian. Or dismantle the whole thing."

I shift my feet and stumble a little, grabbing the railing for support. "Maeve, is this because of what happened freshman year?"

"No." Maeve's amber eyes get hard. "Bronwyn, you're the one who still thinks about that. Not me. I just wanted the stupid hold he had over the entire school to stop. And, well"—she lets out a short, humorless laugh that echoes against the concrete walls of the stairwell—"I guess it did." She starts back down the stairs with long strides and pushes hard on the exit when she gets to the bottom. I follow her silently, trying to wrap my brain around the fact that my sister was keeping a secret from me similar to the one I kept from her. And that both of them tie back to Simon.

Maeve gives me a sunny smile when we get outside, as if the conversation we just had never happened. "Bayview Estates is on our way home. Should we pick up your forbidden technology?"

"We could try." I've told Maeve all about Nate, who called

this morning to say he'd leave a phone in the mailbox of 5 Bay-view Estate Road. It's part of a new development of half-built houses, and the area tends to be deserted on weekends. "I'm not sure how early Nate gets moving on a Saturday, though."

We reach Bayview Estates in less than fifteen minutes, turning into a street filled with boxy, half-finished houses. Maeve puts a hand on my arm as we approach number 5. "Let me go," she says with a forbidding air, eyes darting around dramatically as though the Bayview Police could descend with sirens blaring at any minute. *"Just in case."*

"Have at it," I mutter. We're probably too early anyway. It's barely eleven.

But Maeve returns waving a small black device with a triumphant flourish, laughing when I yank it from her. "Eager much, nerd?" When I power it up there's one message, and I open it to a picture of a yellow-brown lizard sitting placidly on a rock in the middle of a large cage. *Actual lizard,* reads the caption, and I laugh out loud.

"Oh my God," Maeve mutters, peering over my shoulder. "Private jokes. You're *soooo* into him, aren't you?"

I don't have to answer her. It's a rhetorical question.

Cooper
Saturday, October 6, 9:20 p.m.

By the time I get to Olivia's party, nearly everyone's out of it. Somebody's puking in the bushes as I push open the front door. I spot Keely huddled next to the stairs with Olivia, having one of those intense conversations girls get into when they're wasted. A few juniors are toking up on the couch. Vanessa's in a corner trying to paw at Nate, who couldn't look less interested as he scans the room behind her. If Vanessa were a guy, somebody would've reported her by now for all the unsolicited groping she does. My eyes briefly meet Nate's, and we both look away without acknowledging each other.

I finally find Jake on the patio with Luis, who's headed inside for more drinks. "Whaddya want?" Luis asks, clapping me on the shoulder.

"Whatever you're getting." I take a seat next to Jake, who's listing sideways in his chair.

"Whassup, killer?" he slurs, and sputters out a laugh. "Are you getting tired of murder jokes yet? 'Cause I'm not."

I'm surprised Jake is this drunk; he usually holds back during football season. But I guess his week's been almost as bad as mine. That's what I came to talk to him about, although as I watch him swat hazily at a bug, I'm not sure I should bother.

I try anyway. "How're you doing? Been a lousy few days, huh?"

Jake laughs again, but this time not as though he finds anything funny. "That's so *Cooper* of you, man. Don't talk about your shit week, just check in on mine. You're a goddamn saint, Coop. You really are."

The edge in his voice warns me I shouldn't take the bait, but I do. "You mad at me for something, Jake?"

"Why would I be? It's not like you're defending my whore ex-girlfriend to anybody who'll listen. Oh, wait. That's exactly what you're doing."

Jake narrows his eyes at me, and I realize I can't have the conversation I came to have. He's in no frame of mind to talk about easing up on Addy at school. "Jake, I know Addy's in the wrong. Everybody knows it. She made a stupid mistake."

"Cheating isn't a mistake. It's a choice," Jake says furiously, and for a second he sounds stone-cold sober. He drops his empty beer bottle on the ground and cocks his head with an accusing glare. "Where the hell is Luis? Hey." He grabs the arm of a passing sophomore and plucks an unopened beer out of his hand, twisting the cap off and taking a long sip. "What was I saying? Oh yeah. Cheating. That's a choice, Coop. You know, my mom cheated on my dad when I was in junior high. Screwed up our whole family. Threw a grenade right in the middle and—" He flings an arm, spilling half his beer, and makes a whoosh sound. "Everything exploded."

"I didn't know that." I'd met Jake when I moved to Bayview in eighth grade, but we didn't start hanging out till high school. "Sorry, man. That makes it even worse, huh?"

Jake shakes his head, eyes glittering. "Addy has no clue what she's done. Ruined everything."

"But your dad . . . forgave your mom, right? They're still together?" It's a stupid question. I was at his house a month ago for a cookout before all this started. His dad was grilling hamburgers and his mom was talking to Addy and Keely about a new manicure place that opened in Bayview Center. Like normal. Like always.

"Yeah, they're together. Nothing's the same, though. It's never been the same." Jake's staring in front of him with such disgust that I don't know what to say. I feel like a jerk for telling Addy she should come, and I'm glad she didn't listen to me.

Luis returns and hands us both a beer. "You going to Simon's tomorrow?" he asks Jake.

I think I can't possibly have heard Luis right, but Jake says, "I guess."

Luis catches my confused look. "His mom asked a bunch of us to come over and, like, take something to remember him by before they pack his stuff. Creeps me out since I barely knew the guy, but she seems to think we were friends so what can you say, right?" He takes a sip of his beer and cocks an eyebrow at me. "Guess you're not invited?"

"Nope," I say, feeling a little sick. The last thing I want to do is pick through Simon's things in front of his grieving parents, but if all my friends are going, the slight's pretty clear. I'm under suspicion, and not welcome.

"Simon, man." Jake shakes his head solemnly. "He was freaking brilliant." He holds his beer up and for a second I think he's going to pour it onto the patio in a homeboy salute, but he refrains and drinks it instead.

Olivia joins us, wrapping one arm around Luis's waist. Guess those two are back on again. She pokes me with her free hand and holds up her phone, her face bright with that excited look she gets when she's about to share a great piece of gossip. "Cooper, did you know you're in the *Bayview Blade*?"

The way she says it, I'm pretty sure they're not covering baseball. This night keeps getting better. "Had no idea."

"Sunday edition, online tonight. All about Simon. They're

not . . . accusing you, exactly, but the four of you are named as persons of interest, and they mention that stuff Simon was gonna post about you. There're pictures of you all. And, um, it's been shared a few hundred times already. So." Olivia hands me her phone. "It's out there now, I guess."

CHAPTER FIFTEEN

Nate
Monday, October 8, 2:50 p.m.

I hear the rumors before I see the news vans. Three of them parked out front of the school with reporters and camera crews waiting for last bell to ring. They're not allowed on school property, but they're as close as they can get.

Bayview High is *loving* this. Chad Posner finds me after last period to tell me people are practically lining up to be interviewed outside. "They're asking about you, man," he warns. "You might wanna head out the back. They're not allowed in the parking lot, so you can cut through the woods on your bike."

"Thanks." I take off and scan the hallway for Bronwyn. We don't talk much at school to avoid—as she says in her lawyer voice—*the appearance of collusion.* But I'll bet this will freak her out. I spot her at her locker with Maeve and one of her friends, and sure enough she looks ready to throw up. When she sees me she waves me closer, not even trying to pretend she hardly knows me.

"Did you hear?" she asks, and I nod. "I don't know what to do." A horrified realization crosses her face. "I guess we have to drive past them, don't we?"

"I'll drive," Maeve volunteers. "You can, like, hide in the back or something."

"Or we can stay here till they leave," her friend suggests. "Wait them out."

"I hate this," Bronwyn says. Maybe it's the wrong time to notice, but I like how her face floods with color whenever she feels strongly about something. It makes her look twice as alive as most people, and more distracting than she already does in a short dress and boots.

"Come with me," I say. "I'm taking my bike out back to Boden Street. I'll bring you to the mall. Maeve can pick you up later."

Bronwyn brightens as Maeve says, "That'll work. I'll come find you in half an hour at the food court."

"Are you sure that's a good idea?" mutters the other girl, giving me a hard look. "If they catch you together it'll be ten times worse."

"They won't catch us," I say shortly.

I'm not positive Bronwyn's on board, but she nods and tells Maeve she'll see her soon, meeting her friend's annoyed glance with a calm smile. I feel this stupid rush of triumph, like she chose me, even though she basically chose not winding up on the five o'clock news. But she walks close to me as we head out the back door to the parking lot, not seeming to care about the stares. At least they're the kind we've gotten used to. No microphones or cameras involved.

I hand her my helmet and wait for her to settle herself on my bike and loop her arms around me. Too tight again, but I don't mind. Her death grip, along with how her legs look in that dress, is why I engineered this escape in the first place.

We're not in the woods long before the narrow trail I'm taking widens into a dirt path that runs past a row of houses behind the school. I take back roads for a couple of miles until we make it to the mall, and ease my bike into a parking spot as far from the entrance as I can get. Bronwyn takes the helmet off and hands it to me, squeezing my arm as she does. She swings her legs onto the pavement, her cheeks flushed and her hair tousled. "Thanks, Nate. That was nice of you."

I didn't do it to be nice. My hand reaches out and catches her around the waist, pulling her toward me. And then I stop, not sure what to do next. I'm off my game. If anyone had asked me ten minutes ago, I would have said I don't have game. But now it occurs to me that I probably do, and it's not giving a shit.

When I'm still sitting and she's standing we're almost the same height. She's close enough for me to notice that her hair smells like green apples. I can't stop looking at her lips while I wait for her to back away. She doesn't, and when I raise my eyes to hers it feels like the breath is yanked right out of my lungs.

Two thoughts run through my head. One, I want to kiss her more than I want air. And two, if I do I'm bound to screw everything up and she'll stop looking at me that way.

A van screeches into the spot next to us and we both jump, bracing for the Channel 7 News camera crew. But it's an ordinary soccer-mom van filled with screaming kids. When they tumble out Bronwyn blinks and moves off to the side. "Now what?" she asks.

Now wait till they're gone and get back here. But she's already walking toward the entrance. "Buy me a giant pretzel for saving your ass," I say instead. She laughs and I wonder if she's thankful for the interruption.

We walk past the potted palms that frame the front entrance, and I pull the door open for a stressed-looking mother with two screaming toddlers in a double stroller. Bronwyn flashes her a sympathetic smile but as soon as we're inside it disappears and she ducks her head. "Everyone's staring at me. You were smart not to have your class picture taken. That photo in the *Bayview Blade* didn't even look like you."

"Nobody's staring," I tell her, but it's not true. The girl folding sweaters at Abercrombie & Fitch widens her eyes and pulls out her phone when we pass by. "Even if they were, all you'd have to do is take your glasses off. Instant disguise."

I'm kidding, but she pulls them off and reaches into her bag for a bright-blue case she snaps them into. "Good idea, except I'm blind without them." I've seen Bronwyn without glasses only once before, when they got knocked off by a volleyball in fifth-grade gym class. It was the first time I'd noticed her eyes weren't blue like I always thought, but a clear, bright gray.

"I'll guide you," I tell her. "That's a fountain. Don't walk into it."

Bronwyn wants to go to the Apple store, where she squints at iPod Nanos for her sister. "Maeve's starting to run now. She keeps borrowing mine and forgetting to charge it."

"You know that's a rich-girl problem nobody else cares about, right?"

She grins, unoffended. "I need to make a playlist to keep her motivated. Any recommendations?"

"I doubt we like the same music."

"Maeve and I have varied musical taste. You'd be surprised. Let me see your library." I shrug and unlock my phone, and she scrolls through iTunes with an increasingly furrowed brow. "What *is* all this? Why don't I recognize anything?" Then she glances at me. "You have 'Variations on the Canon'?"

I take the phone from her and put it back in my pocket. I forgot I'd downloaded that. "I like your version better," I say, and her lips curve into a smile.

We head for the food court, making small talk about stupid stuff like we're a couple of ordinary teenagers. Bronwyn insists on actually buying me a pretzel, although I have to help her since she can't see two feet in front of her face. We sit by the fountain to wait for Maeve, and Bronwyn leans across the table so she can meet my eyes. "There's something I've been meaning to talk to you about." I raise my brows, interested, until she says, "I'm worried about the fact that you don't have a lawyer."

I swallow a hunk of pretzel and avoid her eyes. "Why?"

"Because this whole thing's starting to implode. My lawyer thinks the news coverage is going to go viral. She made me set all my social media accounts to private yesterday. You should do that too, by the way. If you have any. I couldn't find you anywhere. Not that I was stalking you. Just curious." She gives herself a little shake, like she's trying to get her thoughts back on track. "Anyway. The pressure's on, and you're already on probation, so you . . . you need somebody good in your corner."

You're the obvious outlier and scapegoat. That's what she means; she's just too polite to say it. I push my chair away from the table and tip it backward on two legs. "That's good news for you, right? If they focus on me."

"No!" She's so loud, people at the next table look over, and she lowers her voice. "No, it's awful. But I was thinking. Have you heard of Until Proven?"

"What?"

"Until Proven. It's that pro bono legal group that started at California Western. Remember, they got that homeless guy who was convicted of murder released because of mishandled DNA evidence that led them to the real killer?"

I'm not sure I'm hearing her correctly. "Are you comparing me to a homeless guy on death row?"

"That's only one example of a high-profile case. They do other stuff too. I thought it might be worth checking them out."

She and Officer Lopez would really get along. They're both positive you can fix any problem with the right support group. "Sounds pointless."

"Would you mind if I called them?"

I return my chair to the floor with a bang, my temper rising. "You can't run this like it's student council, Bronwyn."

"And you can't just wait to be railroaded!" She puts her palms flat on the table and leans forward, eyes blazing.

Jesus. She's a pain in my ass and I can't remember why I

wanted to kiss her so badly a few minutes ago. She'd probably turn it into a *project*. "Mind your own business." It comes out harsher than I intended, but I mean it. I've made it through most of high school without Bronwyn Rojas running my life, and I don't need her to start now.

She crosses her arms and glares at me. "I'm trying to *help* you."

That's when I realize Maeve is standing there, looking back and forth between us like she's watching the world's least entertaining ping-pong game. "Um. Is this a bad time?" she says.

"It's a *great* time," I say.

Bronwyn stands abruptly, putting her glasses on and hiking her bag over her shoulder. "Thanks for the ride." Her voice is as cold as mine.

Whatever. I get up and head for the exit without answering, feeling a dangerous combination of pissed off and restless. I need a distraction but never know what the hell to do with myself now that I'm out of the drug business. Maybe stopping was just delaying the inevitable.

I'm almost outside when someone tugs on my jacket. When I turn, arms wrap around my neck and the clean, bright scent of green apples drifts around me as Bronwyn kisses my cheek. "You're right," she whispers, her breath warm in my ear. "I'm sorry. It's not my business. Don't be mad, okay? I can't get through this if you stop talking to me."

"I'm not mad." I try to unfreeze so I can hug her back instead of standing there like a block of wood, but she's already gone, hurrying after her sister.

Addy

Somehow Bronwyn and Nate managed to dodge the cameras. Cooper and I weren't as lucky. We were both on the five o'clock news on all the major San Diego channels: Cooper behind the wheel of his Jeep Wrangler, me climbing into Ashton's car after I'd abandoned my brand-new bike at school and sent her a panicked text begging for a ride. Channel 7 News ended up with a pretty clear shot of me, which they put side by side with an old picture of eight-year-old me at the Little Miss Southeast San Diego pageant. Where, naturally, I was second runner-up.

At least there aren't any vans when Ashton pulls up to drop me off at school the next day. "Call me if you need a ride again," she says, and I give her a quick, stranglehold hug. I thought I'd be more comfortable showing sisterly affection after last weekend's cryfest, but it's still awkward and I manage to snag my bracelet on her sweater. "Sorry," I mutter, and she gives me a pained grin.

"We'll get better at that eventually."

I've gotten used to stares, so the fact that they've intensified since yesterday doesn't faze me. When I leave class in the middle of history, it's because I feel my period coming on and not because I have to cry.

But when I arrive in the girls' room, someone else is. Muffled sounds come from the last stall before whoever's there gets control of herself. I take care of my business—false alarm—and wash my hands, staring at my tired eyes and surprisingly bouncy hair. No matter how awful the rest of my life is, my hair still manages to look good.

I'm about to leave, but hesitate and head for the other end of the restroom. I lean down and see scuffed black combat boots under the last stall door.

"Janae?"

No answer. I rap my knuckles against the door. "It's Addy. Do you need anything?"

"Jesus, Addy," Janae says in a strangled voice. "*No.* Go away."

"Okay," I say, but I don't. "You know, I'm usually the one in that stall bawling my eyes out. So I have a lot of Kleenex if you need some. Also Visine." Janae doesn't say anything. "I'm sorry about Simon. I don't suppose it means much given everything you've heard, but . . . I was shocked by what happened. You must miss him a lot."

Janae stays silent, and I wonder if I've stuck my foot in my mouth again. I'd always thought Janae was in love with Simon and he was oblivious. Maybe she'd finally told him the truth before he died, and got rejected. That would make this whole thing even worse.

I'm about to leave when Janae heaves a deep sigh. The door opens, revealing her blotchy face and black-on-black clothing. "I'll take that Visine," she says, wiping at her raccoon eyes.

"You should take the Kleenex, too," I suggest, pressing both into her hand.

She snorts out something like a laugh. "How the mighty have fallen, Addy. You've never talked to me before."

"Did that bother you?" I ask, genuinely curious. Janae never struck me as someone who wanted to be part of our group.

Unlike Simon, who was always prowling around the edges, looking for a way in.

Janae wets a Kleenex under the sink and dabs at her eyes, glaring at me in the mirror the whole time. "Screw you, Addy. Seriously. What kind of question is that?"

I'm not as offended as I'd normally be. "I don't know. A stupid one, I guess? I'm only just realizing I suck at social cues."

Janae squirts a stream of Visine into both eyes and her raccoon circles reappear. I hand her another Kleenex so she can repeat the wiping process. "Why?"

"Turns out Jake's the one who was popular, not me. I was riding coattails."

Janae takes a step back from the mirror. "I never thought I'd hear you say that."

"'I am large, I contain multitudes,'" I tell her, and her eyes widen. "*Song of Myself*, right? Walt Whitman. I've been reading it since Simon's funeral. I don't understand most of it, but it's comforting in a weird way."

Janae keeps dabbing at her eyes. "That's what I thought. It was Simon's favorite poem."

I think about Ashton and how she's kept me sane over the past couple of weeks. And Cooper, who's defended me at school even though there's no real friendship between us. "Do you have anybody to talk to?"

"No," Janae mutters, and her eyes fill again.

I know from experience she won't thank me for continuing the conversation. At some point we need to suck it up and get to class. "Well, if you want to talk to me—I have a lot of time.

171

And space next to me in the cafeteria. So, open invitation or whatever. Anyway, I really am sorry about Simon. See you."

All things considered, I think that went pretty well. She stopped insulting me toward the end, anyway.

I return to history but it's almost over, and after the bell rings it's time for lunch—my least favorite part of the day. I've told Cooper to stop sitting with me, because I can't stand the hard time everyone else gives him, but I hate eating alone. I'm about to skip and go to the library when a hand plucks at my sleeve.

"Hey." It's Bronwyn, looking surprisingly fashionable in a fitted blazer and striped flats. Her hair's down, spilling over her shoulders in glossy dark layers, and I notice with a stab of envy how clear her skin is. No giant pimples for her, I'll bet. I'm not sure I've ever seen Bronwyn looking this good, and I'm so distracted that I almost miss her next words. "Do you want to eat lunch with us?"

"Ah . . ." I tilt my head at her. I've spent more time with Bronwyn in the past two weeks than I have the last three years at school, but it hasn't exactly been social. "Really?"

"Yeah. Well. We have some stuff in common now, so . . ." Bronwyn trails off, her eyes flicking away from mine, and I wonder if she ever thinks I might be the one behind all this. She must, because I think it about her sometimes. But in an evil-genius, cartoon-villain sort of way. Now that she's standing in front of me with cute shoes and a tentative smile, it seems impossible.

"All right," I say, and follow Bronwyn to a table with her sister, Yumiko Mori, and some tall, sullen-looking girl I don't know. It's better than skipping lunch at the library.

When I get out front after the last bell, there's nothing—no news vans, no reporters—so I text Ashton that she doesn't have to pick me up, and take the opportunity to ride my bike home. I stop at the extralong red light on Hurley Street, resting my feet on the pavement as I look at the stores in the strip mall to my right: cheap clothes, cheap jewelry, cheap cellular. And cheap haircuts. Nothing like my usual salon in downtown San Diego, which charges sixty dollars every six weeks to keep split ends at bay.

My hair feels hot and heavy under my helmet, weighing me down. Before the light changes I angle my bike off the road and over the sidewalk into the mall parking lot. I lock my bike on the rack outside Supercuts, pull off my helmet, and go inside.

"Hi!" The girl behind the register is only a few years older than me, wearing a flimsy black tank top that exposes colorful flower tattoos covering her arms and shoulders. "Are you here for a trim?"

"A cut."

"Okay. We're not super busy, so I can take you right now."

She directs me to a cheap black chair that's losing its stuffing, and we both gaze at my reflection in the mirror as she runs her hands through my hair. "This is so pretty."

I stare at the shining locks in her hands. "It needs to come off."

"A couple inches?"

I shake my head. "All of it."

She laughs nervously. "To your shoulders, maybe?"

"All of it," I repeat.

Her eyes widen in alarm. "Oh, you don't mean that. Your hair is beautiful!" She disappears from behind me and reappears with a supervisor. They stand there conferring for a few minutes in hushed tones. Half the salon is staring at me. I wonder how many of them saw the San Diego news last night, and how many think I'm just an overly hormonal teenage girl.

"Sometimes people think they want a dramatic cut, but they don't really," the supervisor starts cautiously.

I don't let her finish. I'm beyond tired of people telling me what I want. "Do you guys do haircuts here? Or should I go somewhere else?"

She tugs at a lock of her own bleached-blond hair. "I'd hate for you to regret this. If you want a different look, you could try—"

Shears lie across the counter in front of me, and I reach for them. Before anyone can stop me, I grab a thick handful of hair and chop the whole thing off above my ear. Gasps run through the salon, and I meet the tattooed girl's shocked eyes in the mirror.

"Fix it," I tell her. So she does.

CHAPTER SIXTEEN

Bronwyn
Friday, October 12, 7:45 p.m.

Four days after we're featured on the local news, the story goes national on *Mikhail Powers Investigates.*

I knew it was coming, since Mikhail's producers had tried to reach my family all week. We never responded, thanks to basic common sense and also Robin's legal advice. Nate didn't either, and Addy said she and Cooper both refused to talk as well. So the show will be airing in fifteen minutes without commentary from any of the people actually involved.

Unless one of us is lying. Which is always a possibility.

The local coverage was bad enough. Maybe it was my imagination, but I'm pretty sure Dad winced every time I was referred to as "the daughter of prominent Latino business leader Javier Rojas." And he left the room when one station reported his nationality as Chilean instead of Colombian. The whole thing made me wish, for the hundredth time since this started, that I'd just taken that D in chemistry.

Maeve and I are sprawled on my bed watching the minutes on my alarm clock tick by until my debut as a national disgrace. Or rather, *I* am, and she's combing through the 4chan links she found through Simon's admin site.

"Check this out," she says, angling her laptop toward me.

The long discussion thread covers a school shooting that happened last spring a few counties over. A sophomore boy concealed a handgun in his jacket and opened fire in the hallway after the first bell. Seven students and a teacher died before the boy turned the gun on himself. I have to read a few of the comments more than once before I realize the thread isn't condemning the boy, but celebrating him. It's a bunch of sickos cheering on what he did.

"Maeve." I burrow my head in my arms, not wanting to read any more. "What the hell is this?"

"Some forum Simon was all over a few months back."

I raise my head to stare at her. "*Simon* posted there? How do you know?"

"He used that AnarchiSK name from About That," Maeve replies.

I scan the thread, but it's too long to pick out individual names. "Are you sure it's Simon? Maybe other people use the same name."

"I've been spot-checking posts, and it's definitely Simon," she says. "He references places in Bayview, talks about clubs he was in at school, mentions his car a few times." Simon drove a

1970s Volkswagen Bug that he was freakishly proud of. Maeve leans against the cushions, chewing on her bottom lip. "There's a lot to go through, but I'm going to read the whole thing when I have time."

I can't think of anything I'd like to do less. "Why?"

"The thread's full of weird people with axes to grind," Maeve says. "Simon might've made some enemies there. Worth looking into, anyway." She takes her laptop back and adds, "I got that encrypted file of Cooper's at the library the other day, but I can't get it open. *Yet.*"

"Girls." My mother's voice is strained as she calls upstairs. "It's time."

That's right. My entire family is watching *Mikhail Powers Investigates* together. Which is a circle of hell even Dante never imagined.

Maeve shuts her laptop as I heave myself to my feet. There's a slight buzzing from inside my end table, and I open the drawer to pull out my Nate phone. *Enjoy the show,* his text says.

Not funny, I reply.

"Put that away," Maeve says with mock severity. "Now is *not the time.*"

We head downstairs to the living room, where Mom has already settled into an armchair with an exceptionally full glass of wine. Dad's in full Evening Executive mode, wearing his favorite casual fleece vest and surrounded by a half-dozen communication devices. A commercial for paper towels flashes across the television screen as Maeve and I sit side by side on the couch and wait for *Mikhail Powers Investigates* to start.

The show focuses on true crime and it's pretty sensationalistic, but more credible than similar shows because of Mikhail's hard-news background. He spent years as an anchor with one of the major networks, and brings a certain gravitas to the proceedings.

He always reads the beginning hook in his deep, authoritative voice while grainy police photos play across the screen.

A young mother disappears. A double life exposed. And one year later, a shocking arrest. Has justice finally been served?

A high-profile couple dead. A dedicated daughter suspected. Could her Facebook account hold the key to the killer's identity?

I know the formula, so it shouldn't be any surprise when it's applied to me.

A high school student's mysterious death. Four classmates with secrets to hide. When the police keep running into dead ends, what's next?

Dread starts spreading through me: my stomach aches, my lungs compress, even my mouth has a horrible taste. For almost two weeks I've been questioned and scrutinized, whispered about and judged. I've had to deflect questions about Simon's allegations with police and teachers, and watch their eyes harden as they read between the lines. I've waited for another shoe to drop; for the Tumblr to release a video of me accessing Mr. Camino's files, or for the police to file charges. But nothing's felt quite so raw and real as watching my class picture appear over Mikhail Powers's shoulder on national television.

There's footage of Mikhail and his team in Bayview, but he does most of his reporting from behind a sleek chrome desk in his Los Angeles studio. He has smooth dark skin and hair, expressive eyes, and the most perfectly fitted wardrobe I've ever seen. I have no doubt that if he'd managed to catch me alone, I'd have spilled all sorts of things I shouldn't.

"But who *are* the Bayview Four?" Mikhail asks, staring intently into the camera.

"You guys have a name," Maeve whispers, but not quietly enough that Mom doesn't hear.

"Maeve, there is *nothing* funny about this," she says tightly as the camera cuts to video of my parents' offices.

Oh no. They're starting with me.

Honor student Bronwyn Rojas comes from a high-achieving family traumatized by their youngest child's lingering illness. Did the pressure to measure up compel her to cheat and take Yale out of her reach forever? Followed by a spokesperson from Yale confirming that I have not, in fact, applied yet.

We all get our turn. Mikhail examines Addy's beauty pageant past, speaks with baseball analysts about the prevalence of high school juicing and its potential impact on Cooper's career, and digs through the particulars of Nate's drug bust and probation sentence.

"It's not fair," Maeve breathes into my ear. "They're not saying anything about how his dad's a drunk and his mom's dead. Where's the context?"

"He wouldn't want that, anyway," I whisper back.

I cringe my way through the show until an interview with a lawyer from Until Proven. Since none of our lawyers agreed to talk, Mikhail's team tapped Until Proven as subject-matter experts. The lawyer they speak with, Eli Kleinfelter, doesn't look even ten years older than me. He has wild curly hair, a sparse goatee, and intense dark eyes.

"Here's what I'd say, if I were their lawyer," he says, and I lean forward despite myself. "All the attention's on these four kids. They're getting dragged through the mud with no evidence tying them to any crime after weeks of investigation. But there was a fifth kid in the room, wasn't there? And he seems like the type who might've had more than four enemies. So you tell me. Who *else* had a motive? What story's *not* being told? That's where I'd be looking."

"Exactly," Maeve says, drawing out each syllable.

"And you can't assume Simon was the only person with access to the About That admin panel," Eli continues. "Anybody could've gotten into that before he died and either viewed or changed those posts."

I look at Maeve, but this time she doesn't say anything. Just stares at the screen with a half smile on her face.

I can't stop thinking about Eli's words for the rest of the night. Even when I'm on the phone with Nate, half watching *Battle Royale,* which is better than a lot of the movies Nate likes. But between *Mikhail Powers Investigates* and our trip to the mall on Monday—which I've been thinking about nonstop in those spare moments when I'm not thinking about going to jail—I can't concentrate. Too many other thoughts compete for brain space.

Nate was about to kiss me, wasn't he? And I wanted him to. So why didn't we?

Eli finally said it. Why isn't anyone looking at other suspects?

I wonder if Nate and I are officially friend-zoned now.

Mikhail Powers does serial investigations, so this will only get worse.

Nate and I would be horrible together anyway. Probably.

Did People *magazine seriously just email me?*

"What's going on in that big brain of yours, Bronwyn?" Nate finally asks.

Too much, and most of it I probably shouldn't share. "I want to talk to Eli Kleinfelter," I say. "Not about you," I add when Nate doesn't reply. "Just in general. I'm intrigued by how he thinks."

"You already have a lawyer. Think she'd want you getting a second opinion?"

I know she wouldn't. Robin is all about containment and defense. *Don't give anybody anything they can use against you.* "I don't want him to represent me or anything. I just want a conversation. Maybe I'll try to call him next week."

"You never shut off, do you?"

It doesn't sound like a compliment. "No," I admit, wondering if I've killed whatever weird attraction Nate might've once felt toward me.

Nate's silent as we watch Shogo fake Shuya's and Noriko's deaths. "This isn't bad," he finally says. "But you still owe me finishing *Ringu* in person."

Tiny electrical sparks zip through my bloodstream. *Attraction not dead, then? Maybe on life support.* "I know. That's logistically challenging, though. Especially now that we're notorious."

"There aren't any news vans here now."

I've thought about this. Maybe a few dozen times since he

181

first asked me. And while I don't understand much about what's going on between Nate and me, I do know this: whatever happens next won't involve me driving to his house in the middle of the night. I start to tell him all my excellent practical reasons, like how the Volvo's noisy engine will wake my parents, when he says, "I could come get you."

I blow out a sigh and stare at the ceiling. I'm no good at navigating these situations, probably because they've only ever happened in my head. "I feel weird going to your house at one in the morning, Nate. Like, it's . . . different from watching a movie. And I don't know you well enough to, um, not watch a movie with you." Oh God. This is why people shouldn't wait until their senior year of high school to date. My whole face burns, and as I wait for him to answer, I'm deeply thankful he can't see me.

"Bronwyn." Nate's voice isn't as mocking as I'd expected. "I'm not trying to *not-watch* a movie with you. I mean, sure, if you were into that, I wouldn't say no. Believe me. But the main reason I invited you over after midnight is that my house sucks during the day. For one thing, you can see it. Which I don't recommend. For another, my dad's around. I'd rather you not . . . you know. Trip over him."

My heart keeps missing beats. "I don't care about that."

"I do."

"Okay." I don't fully understand Nate's rules for managing his world, but for once I'm going to mind my own business and not give my opinion about what does and doesn't matter. "We'll figure something else out."

Cooper
Saturday, October 13, 4:35 p.m.

There's no good place to break up with someone, but at least their living room is private and they don't have to go anywhere afterward. So that's where I give Keely the news.

It's not because of what Nonny said. It's been coming for a while. Keely's great in a dozen different ways but not for me, and I can't drag her through all this knowing that.

Keely wants an explanation, and I don't have a good one. "If it's because of the investigation, I don't care!" she says tearfully. "I'm behind you no matter what."

"It's not that," I tell her. It's not *only* that, anyway.

"And I don't believe a word of that awful Tumblr."

"I know, Keely. I appreciate that, I really do." There was another post this morning, crowing about the media coverage:

The *Mikhail Powers Investigates* site has thousands of comments about the Bayview Four. (Kind of a dull name, by the way. Would've expected better from a top-ranked newsmagazine.) Some call for jail time. Some rail about how spoiled and entitled kids are today, and how this is another example of that.

It's a great story: four good-looking, high-profile students all being investigated for murder. And nobody's what they seem.

The pressure's on now, Bayview Police. Maybe you should be looking a little closer at Simon's old

entries. You might find some interesting hints about
the Bayview Four.

Just saying.

That last part made my blood run cold. Simon had never
written about me before, but I don't like the implication. Or
the sick, heavy feeling that something else is coming. And soon.

"Then why are you doing this?" Keely has her head in her
hands, tears running down her face. She's a pretty crier; nothing
red or splotchy about her. She peers at me with swimming dark
eyes. "Did Vanessa say something?"

"Did—what? Vanessa? What would *she* say?"

"She's being a bitch about me still talking to Addy and she
was going to tell you something you shouldn't even care about,
because it happened before we were dating." She looks at me
expectantly, and my blank expression seems to make her mad.
"Or maybe you *should* care, so you'd care about *something* related
to me. You're so holier-than-thou about how Jake is acting, Cooper, but at least he has emotions. He's not a robot. It's normal to
be jealous when the girl you care about is with someone else."

"I know."

Keely waits a beat before giving a sarcastic little laugh. "That's
it, huh? You're not even a little bit curious. You're not worried
about me, or protective of me. You just don't give a shit."

We're at the point where nothing I say will be right. "I'm
sorry, Keely."

"I hooked up with Nate," she says abruptly, eyes locked on
mine. And I have to admit, that surprises me. "At Luis's party
the last night of junior year. Simon was following me around all

night and I was sick of it. Nate showed up and I figured, what the hell. He's hot, right? Even if he *is* a total degenerate." She smirks at me, a trace of bitterness in her face. "We just kissed, mostly. That night. Then you asked me out a few weeks later." She gives me that intense look again, and I'm not sure what she's trying to get across.

"So you were with me and Nate at the same time?"

"Would that bother you?"

She wants something from me out of this conversation. I wish I could figure it out and let her have it, because I know I haven't been fair to her. Her dark eyes are fastened on mine, her cheeks flushed, her lips slightly parted. She really is beautiful, and if I told her I'd made a mistake, she'd take me back and I'd keep being the most envied guy at Bayview. "I guess I wouldn't like it—" I start, but she interrupts me with a half laugh, half sob.

"Oh my God, Cooper. Your *face.* You seriously could not care less. Well, for the record, I stopped doing anything with Nate as soon as you asked me out." She's crying again, and I feel like the world's biggest jerk. "You know, Simon would've given anything if I'd chosen him. You didn't even know it *was* a choice. People always pick you, don't they? They always picked me, too. Until you came along and made me feel invisible."

"Keely, I never meant—"

She's not listening to me anymore. "You've never cared, have you? You just wanted the right accessory for scouting season."

"That's not fair—"

"It's all a big lie, isn't it, Cooper? Me, your fastball—"

"I've *never* used steroids," I interrupt, suddenly angry.

Keely gives another strangled laugh. "Well, at least you're passionate about *something*."

"I'm gonna go." I stand abruptly, adrenaline coursing through me as I stalk out her door before I say something I shouldn't. I got tested after Simon's accusations came to light, and I was clean. And I was tested once over the summer as part of an extensive physical the UCSD sports medicine center did before putting together my training regimen. But that's it, and since plenty of steroids disappear from your system within weeks, I can't escape the taint entirely. I've told Coach Ruffalo there's no truth to the accusations, and so far he's sitting tight on contacting any colleges. We're part of the news cycle now, though, so things won't stay quiet for long.

And Keely's right—I've been a lot more worried about that than about our relationship. I owe her a better apology than the one I just half-assed. But I don't know how to give it.

CHAPTER SEVENTEEN

Addy
Monday, October 15, 12:15 p.m.

Sexism is alive and well in true-crime coverage, because Bronwyn and I aren't nearly as popular with the general public as Cooper and Nate. *Especially* Nate. All the tween girls posting about us on social media love him. They couldn't care less that he's a convicted drug dealer, because he's got dreamy eyes.

Same goes for school. Bronwyn and I are pariahs—other than her friends, her sister, and Janae, hardly anyone talks to us. They just whisper behind our backs. But Cooper's as golden as ever. And Nate—well, it's not like Nate was ever popular, exactly. He's never seemed to care what people think, though, and he still doesn't.

"Seriously, Addy, stop pulling that stuff up. I don't want to see it."

Bronwyn rolls her eyes at me, but she doesn't really look

mad. I guess we're almost friends now, or as friendly as you can get when you're not one hundred percent sure the other person isn't framing you for murder.

She won't play along with my obsessive need to track our news stories, though. And I don't show her everything, especially not the horrible commenters tossing racial slurs at her family. That's an extra layer of suck she doesn't need. Instead, I show Janae one of the more positive articles I've found. "Look. The most-shared article on *BuzzFeed* is Cooper leaving the gym."

Janae looks awful. She's lost more weight since I first ran into her in the bathroom, and she's jumpier than ever. I'm not sure why she eats lunch with us, since most of the time she doesn't say a word. But she glances gamely at my phone. "It's a good picture of him, I guess."

Kate shoots me a severe look. "Would you put that away?" I do, but in my head I'm giving her the finger the whole time. Yumiko's all right, but Kate almost makes me miss Vanessa.

No. That's a complete and utter lie. I *hate* Vanessa. Hate how she's mean-girled her way into the center of my former group and how she's glommed on to Jake like they're a couple. Even though I don't see much interest on his part. Chopping my hair off was like giving up on Jake, since he wouldn't have noticed me three years ago without it. But just because I've abandoned hope doesn't mean I've stopped paying attention.

After lunch I head for earth science, settling myself on a bench next to a lab partner who barely glances in my direction. "Don't get too comfortable," Ms. Mara warns. "We're mixing things up today. You've all been with your partners for a while, so let's rotate." She gives us complicated directions—some people move left, others right, and the rest of us stay still—and I don't pay much attention to the process until I wind up next to TJ.

His nose looks a lot better, but I doubt it'll ever be straight again. He gives me a sheepish half smile as he pulls the tray of rocks in front of us closer. "Sorry. This is probably your worst nightmare, right?"

Don't flatter yourself, TJ, I think. He's got nothing on my nightmares. All those months of angsty guilt about sleeping with him in his beach house seem like they happened in another lifetime. "It's fine."

We classify rocks in silence until TJ says, "I like your hair."

I snort. "Yeah, right." With the possible exception of Ashton, who's biased, *nobody* likes my hair. My mother is appalled. My former friends laughed openly when they saw me the next day. Even Keely smirked. She's moved right on to Luis, like if she can't have Cooper, she'll settle for his catcher instead. Luis dumped Olivia for her, but nobody blinked an eye about *that*.

"I'm serious. You can finally see your face. You look like a blond Emma Watson."

That's false. But nice of him to say, I guess. I hold a rock between my thumb and forefinger and squint at it. "What do you think? Igneous or sedimentary?"

TJ shrugs. "I can't tell the difference."

I take a guess and sort the rock into the igneous pile. "TJ, if I can manage to care about rocks, I'm pretty sure you can put in more of an effort."

He blinks at me in surprise, then grins. "*There* you are."

"What?"

Everyone seems absorbed in their rocks, but he lowers his

voice anyway. "You were really funny when we—um, that first time we hung out. On the beach. But whenever I saw you after that you were so . . . passive. Always agreeing with whatever Jake said."

I glower at the tray in front of me. "That's a rude thing to say."

TJ's voice is mild. "Sorry. But I could never figure out why you'd fade into the background that way. You were a lot of fun." He catches my glare and adds hastily, "Not like *that*. Or, well, yes, like that, but also . . . You know what? Never mind. I'll stop talking now."

"Great idea," I mutter, scooping up a handful of rocks and dumping them in front of him. "Sort these, would you?"

It's not that TJ's "fade into the background" comment stings. I know it's true. I can't wrap my head around the rest, though. Nobody's ever said I'm funny before. Or fun. I always figured TJ was still talking to me because he wouldn't mind getting me alone again. I never thought he might've actually enjoyed hanging out during the nonphysical part of the day.

We finish the rest of the class in silence except to agree or disagree on rock classification, and when the bell rings I grab my backpack and head for the hall without a backward look.

Until the voice behind me stops me like I've slammed into an invisible wall. "Addy."

My shoulders tense as I turn. I haven't tried talking to Jake since he blew me off at his locker, and I'm afraid of what he's going to say to me now.

"How've you been?" he asks.

I almost laugh. "Oh, you know. *Not good.*"

I can't read Jake's expression. He doesn't look mad, but he's not smiling either. He seems different somehow. Older? Not exactly, but . . . less boyish, maybe. He's been staring right through me for almost two weeks, and I don't understand why I'm suddenly visible again. "Things must be getting intense," he says. "Cooper's totally clammed up. Do you—" He hesitates, shifting his backpack from one shoulder to the other. "Do you want to talk sometime?"

My throat feels like I swallowed something sharp. *Do I?* Jake waits for an answer, and I mentally shake myself. Of course I do. That's all I've wanted since this happened. "Yes."

"Okay. Maybe this afternoon? I'll text you." He holds my gaze, still not smiling, and adds, "God, I can't get used to your hair. You don't even look like yourself."

I'm about to say *I know* when I remember TJ's words. *You were so . . . passive. Always agreeing with whatever Jake said.* "Well, I am," I say instead, and take off down the hall before he can break eye contact first.

Nate
Monday, October 15, 3:15 p.m.

Bronwyn settles herself on the rock next to me, smoothing her skirt over her knees and looking over the treetops in front of us. "I've never been to Marshall's Peak before," she says.

I'm not surprised. Marshall's Peak—which isn't really a peak, more of a rocky outcropping overlooking the woods we cut through on our way out of school—is Bayview's so-called scenic area. It's also a popular spot for drinking, drugs, and hookups, although not at three o'clock on a Monday afternoon. I'm pretty sure Bronwyn has no clue what happens here on weekends. "Hope reality lives up to the hype," I say.

She smiles. "It beats getting ambushed by Mikhail Powers's crew." We had another sneak-out-the-back routine when they showed up at the front of school today. I'm surprised they haven't wised up to staking out the woods yet. Driving to the mall again seemed like a bad idea given how high our profile's risen over the past week, so here we are.

Bronwyn's eyes are down, watching a line of ants carry a leaf across the rock next to us. She licks her lips like she's nervous, and I shift a little closer. Most of my time with her is spent on the phone, and I can't tell what she's thinking in person.

"I called Eli Kleinfelter," she says. "From Until Proven."

Oh. *That's* what she's thinking. I shift back. "Okay."

"It was an interesting conversation," she says. "He was nice about hearing from me, didn't seem surprised at all. He promised he wouldn't tell anybody I'd called him."

For all her brains, Bronwyn can be like a little kid sometimes. "What's that worth?" I ask. "He's not your lawyer. He can talk to Mikhail Powers about you if he wants more airtime."

"He won't," Bronwyn says calmly, like she's got it all figured out. "Anyway, I didn't tell him anything. We didn't talk about me at all. I just asked him what he thought of the investigation so far."

"And?"

"Well, he repeated some of what he said on TV. That he was surprised there wasn't more talk about Simon. Eli thought anyone who'd run the kind of app Simon did, for as long as he did, would've made plenty of enemies who'd love to use the four of us as scapegoats. He said he'd check into some of the most damaging stories and the kids they covered. And he'd look into Simon generally. Like Maeve's doing with the 4chan stuff."

"The best defense is a good offense?" I ask.

"Right. He also said our lawyers aren't doing enough to pick apart the theory that nobody else could've poisoned Simon. Mr. Avery, for one." A note of pride creeps into her voice. "Eli said the exact same thing I did, that Mr. Avery had the best opportunity of anyone to plant the phones and doctor the cups. But other than questioning him a few times, the police are mostly leaving him alone."

I shrug. "What's his motive?"

"Technophobia," Bronwyn says, and glares at me when I laugh. "It's a *thing*. Anyway, that was just one idea. Eli also mentioned the car accident as a time when everybody was distracted and someone could've slipped into the room."

I frown at her. "We weren't at the window that long. We would've heard the door open."

"Would we? Maybe not. His point is, it's possible. And he said something else interesting." Bronwyn picks up a small rock and juggles it meditatively in her hand. "He said he'd look into the car accident. That the timing was suspect."

"Meaning?"

"Well, it goes back to his earlier point that someone could've opened the door while we watched the cars. Someone who knew it was going to happen."

"He thinks the car accident was *planned*?" I stare at her, and she avoids my gaze as she heaves the rock over the trees beneath us. "So you're suggesting somebody engineered a fender bender in the parking lot so they could distract us, slip into detention, and dump peanut oil into Simon's cup? That they couldn't possibly have known he had if they weren't already in the room? Then leave Simon's cup lying around, because they're stupid?"

"It's not stupid if they're trying to frame us," Bronwyn points out. "But it would be stupid for one of us to leave it there, instead of finding a way to get rid of it. Chances were good nobody would have searched us right after."

"It still doesn't explain how anybody outside the room would know Simon had a cup of water in the first place."

"Well, it's like the Tumblr post said. Simon was always drinking water, wasn't he? They could have been outside the door, watching through the window. That's what Eli says, anyway."

"Oh, well, if *Eli* says so." I'm not sure why this guy's a legal god in Bronwyn's eyes. He can't be more than twenty-five. "Sounds like he's full of dipshit theories."

I'm getting ready for an argument, but Bronwyn doesn't take the bait. "Maybe," she says, tracing her fingers over the rock between us. "But I've been thinking about this a lot lately and . . . I don't think it was anyone in that room, Nate. I really don't. I've gotten to know Addy a little bit this week"—she raises a palm at my skeptical look—"and I'm not saying I'm suddenly an Addy expert or anything, but I honestly can't picture her doing anything to Simon."

"What about Cooper? That guy's definitely hiding something."

"Cooper's not a killer." Bronwyn sounds positive, and for some reason that pisses me off.

"You know this how? Because you guys are so close? Face it, Bronwyn, none of us really know each other. Hell, *you* could've done it. You're smart enough to plan something this messed up and get away with it."

I'm kidding, but Bronwyn goes rigid. "How can you say that?" Her cheeks get red, giving her that flushed look that always unsettles me. *She'll surprise you one day with how pretty she is.* My mother used to say that about Bronwyn.

My mother was wrong, though. There's nothing surprising about it.

"Eli said it himself, right?" I say. "Anything's possible. Maybe you brought me here to shove me down the hill and break my neck."

"You brought *me* here," Bronwyn points out. Her eyes widen, and I laugh.

"Oh, come on. You don't actually think— Bronwyn, we're barely on an incline. Pushing you off this rock isn't much of an evil plan if all you'd do is twist your ankle."

"That's not funny," Bronwyn says, but a smile twitches at her lips. The afternoon sun's making her glow, putting glints of gold in her dark hair, and for a second I almost can't breathe.

Jesus. This girl.

I stand and hold out my hand. She gives me a skeptical look, but takes it and lets me pull her to her feet. I put my other hand in the air. "Bronwyn Rojas, I solemnly swear not to murder you today or at any point in the future. Deal?"

"You're ridiculous," she mutters, going even redder.

"It concerns me you're avoiding a promise not to murder me."

She rolls her eyes. "Do you say that to all the girls you bring here?"

Huh. Maybe she knows Marshall's Peak's reputation after all.

I move closer until there's only a couple of inches between us. "You're still not answering my question."

Bronwyn leans forward and brings her lips to my ear. She's so close I can feel her heart beating when she whispers, "I promise not to murder you."

"That's hot." I mean it as a joke, but my voice comes out like a growl and when her lips part I kiss her before she can laugh. A shock of energy shoots through me as I cup her face in my hands, my fingers grasping her cheeks and the line of her jaw. It must be the adrenaline that's making my heart pound so fast. The whole nobody-else-could-possibly-understand-this bond. Or maybe it's her soft lips and green apple–scented hair, and the way she winds her arms around my neck like she can't stand to let go. Either way I keep kissing her as long as she lets me, and when she steps away I try to pull her back because it wasn't enough.

"Nate, my phone," she says, and for the first time I notice a persistent, jangly text tone. "It's my sister."

"She can wait," I say, tangling a hand in her hair and kissing along her jawline to her neck. She shivers against me and makes a little noise in her throat. Which I like.

"It's just . . ." She runs her fingertips across the back of my neck. "She wouldn't keep texting if it weren't important."

Maeve's our excuse—she and Bronwyn are supposed to be at Yumiko's house together—and I reluctantly step back so Bronwyn can reach down and dig her phone out of her backpack.

She looks at the screen and draws in a quick, sharp breath. "Oh God. My mom's trying to reach me too. Robin says the police want me to come to the station. To, quote, *follow up on a couple of things.'* Unquote."

"Probably the same bullshit." I manage to sound calm even though it's not how I feel.

"Did they call you?" she asks. She looks like she hopes they did, and hates herself for it.

I didn't hear my phone, but pull it out of my pocket to check anyway. "No."

She nods and starts firing off texts. "Should I have Maeve pick me up here?"

"Have her meet us at my house. It's halfway between here and the station." As soon as I say it I kind of regret it—I still don't want Bronwyn anywhere near my house when it's light out—but it's the most convenient option. And we don't have to go inside.

Bronwyn bites her lip. "What if reporters are there?"

"They won't be. They've figured out no one's ever around." She still looks worried, so I add, "Look, we can park at my neighbor's and walk over. If anyone's there, I'll take you some-place else. But trust me, it'll be fine."

Bronwyn texts Maeve my address and we walk to the edge of the woods where I left my bike. I help her with the helmet and she climbs behind me, wrapping her arms around my waist as I start the engine.

I drive slowly down narrow, twisty side roads until we reach my street. My neighbor's rusted Chevrolet sits in her driveway, in the exact same spot it's been for the past five years. I park next to it, wait for Bronwyn to dismount, and take her hand as we make our way through the neighbor's yard to mine. As we get closer I see our house through Bronwyn's eyes, and wish I'd bothered to mow the lawn at some point in the last year.

Suddenly she stops in her tracks and lets out a gasp, but she's not looking at our knee-length grass. "Nate, there's someone at your door."

I stop too and scan the street for a news van. There isn't one, just a beat-up Kia parked in front of our house. Maybe they're getting better at camouflage. "Stay here," I tell Bronwyn, but she comes with me as I get closer to my driveway for a better look at whoever's at the door.

It's not a reporter.

My throat goes dry and my head starts to throb. The woman pressing the bell turns around, and her mouth falls open a little when she sees me. Bronwyn goes still beside me, her hand dropping from mine. I keep walking without her.

I'm surprised how normal my voice sounds when I speak. "What's up, Mom?"

CHAPTER EIGHTEEN

Bronwyn
Monday, October 15, 4:10 p.m.

Maeve pulls into the driveway seconds after Mrs. Macauley turns around. I stand rigid, my hands clenched at my sides and my heart pounding, staring at the woman I thought was dead.

"Bronwyn?" Maeve lowers her window and sticks her head out of the car. "You ready? Mom and Robin are already there. Dad's trying to get off work, but he's got a board meeting. I had to do some maneuvering about why you weren't answering your phone. You're sick to your stomach, okay?"

"That's accurate," I mutter. Nate's back is to me. His mother is talking, staring at him with ravenous eyes, but I can't hear anything she's saying.

"Huh?" Maeve follows my gaze. "Who's that?"

"I'll tell you in the car," I say, tearing my eyes away from Nate. "Let's go."

I climb into the passenger seat of our Volvo, where the heat is blasting because Maeve's always cold. She backs out of the driveway in her careful, just-got-my-license way, talking the whole time. "Mom's doing that whole Mom thing, where she's pretending not to be freaked out but she totally is," she says, and I'm half listening. "I guess the police aren't giving much information. We don't even know if anyone else is going to be there. Is Nate coming, do you know?"

I snap back to attention. "No." For once I'm glad Maeve likes to maintain broiler-oven temperatures while driving, because it's keeping the cold inching up my spine at bay. "He's not coming."

Maeve approaches a stop sign and brakes jerkily, glancing over at me. "What's the matter?"

I close my eyes and lean against the headrest. "That was Nate's mother."

"What was?"

"The woman at the door just now. At Nate's house. It was his mother."

"But . . ." Maeve trails off, and I can tell by the sound of the blinker that she's about to make a turn and needs to concentrate. When the car straightens again she says, "But she's dead."

"Apparently not."

"I don't—but that's—" Maeve sputters for a few seconds. I keep my eyes closed. "So . . . what's the deal? Did he not *know* she was alive? Or did he lie about it?"

"We didn't exactly have time to discuss it," I say.

But that's the million-dollar question. I remember hearing three years ago through the grapevine that Nate's mother had died in a car accident. We lost my mom's brother the same way, and I felt a lot of empathy for Nate, but I'd never asked him about it back then. I did over the past few weeks, though. Nate didn't like to talk about it. All he said was he hadn't heard anything about his mother since she flaked on taking him to Oregon, until he got news that she'd died. He never mentioned a funeral. Or much of anything, really.

"Well." Maeve's voice is encouraging. "Maybe it's some kind of miracle. Like it was all a horrible misunderstanding and everybody thought she was dead but really she . . . had amnesia. Or was in a coma."

"Right," I snort. "And maybe Nate has an evil twin who's behind it all. Because we're living in a telenovela." I think about Nate's face before he walked away from me. He didn't seem shocked. Or happy. He looked . . . stoic. He reminded me of my father every time Maeve had a relapse. As though an illness he'd been dreading had come back, and he was just going to have to deal with it now.

"We're here," Maeve says, pulling to a careful stop. I open my eyes.

"You're in the handicapped space," I tell her.

"I'm not staying, just dropping you off. Good luck." She reaches over and squeezes my hand. "I'm sure it'll be fine. All of it."

I walk slowly inside and give my name to the woman behind the glass partition in the lobby, who directs me to a conference room down the hall. When I enter, my mother, Robin, and Detective Mendoza are all already seated at a small round table. My heart sinks at the absence of Addy or Cooper, and at the sight of a laptop in front of Detective Mendoza.

Mom gives me a worried look. "How's your stomach, honey?"

"Not great," I say truthfully, slipping into a chair beside her and dropping my backpack on the floor.

"Bronwyn isn't well," Robin says with a cool look toward Detective Mendoza. She's in a sharp navy suit and a long, multi-strand necklace. "This should be a discussion between you and me, Rick. I can loop Bronwyn and her parents in as needed."

Detective Mendoza presses a key on the laptop. "We won't keep you long. Always better to talk face to face, in my opinion. Bronwyn, are you aware Simon used to have a companion website for About That, where he'd write longer posts?"

Robin interrupts before I can speak. "Rick, I'm not letting Bronwyn answer any questions until you tell me why she's here. If you have something to show or tell us, please get to that first."

"I do," Detective Mendoza says, rotating the laptop so it faces me. "One of your classmates alerted us to a post that ran eighteen months ago, Bronwyn. Does this look familiar?"

My mother moves her chair next to me as Robin leans over my shoulder. I focus my eyes on the screen, but I already know what I'm about to read. I've worried for weeks that it might come up.

So maybe I should have said something. But it's too late now.

News flash: LV's end-of-the-year party isn't a charity event. Just so we're clear. You'd be excused for thinking so, though, with frosh attendance at an all-time high.

Regular readers (and if you're not one, what the hell is wrong with you?) know I try to cut the kids some slack. Children are our future and all that. But let me do a little PSA for one new (and fleeting, I'm gonna guess) arrival to the social scene: MR, who doesn't seem to realize SC is out of her league.

He's not in the market for a puppy, kid. Stop with the following. It's pathetic.

And, guys, don't give me that poor-little-thing-had-cancer crap. Not anymore. M can put on her big-girl panties like anyone else and learn a few basic rules:

1. Varsity basketball players with cheerleader girlfriends are OFF THE MARKET. I shouldn't have to explain this, but apparently I do.
2. Two beers are too many when you're a lightweight, because it leads to:
3. The worst display of awkward kitchen table dancing I've ever seen. Seriously, M. Never again.
4. If that one beer makes you throw up, try not to do it in your hosts' washing machine. That's just rude.

Let's card at the door from now on, okay, LV? At first it's funny, but then it's just sad.

I stay still in my chair and try to keep my face impassive. I remember that post like it was yesterday: how Maeve, who'd been giddy from her first crush and her first party, even though neither had gone exactly as planned, folded into herself after she read Simon's post and refused to go out again. I remember all the impotent rage I'd felt, that Simon was so casually cruel, just because he could be. Because he had a willing audience that ate it up.

And I hated him for it.

I can't look at my mother, who has no idea any of this happened, so I focus on Robin. If she's surprised or concerned, she doesn't show it. "All right. I've read it. Tell me what you think the significance of this is, Rick."

"I'd like to hear that from Bronwyn."

"No." Robin's voice cracks like a velvet whip, soft but unyielding. "Explain why we're here."

"This post appears to be written about Bronwyn's sister, Maeve."

"What makes you think that?" Robin asks.

My mother chokes out a furious, disbelieving laugh, and I finally sneak a look at her. Her face is bright red, her eyes burning. Her voice shakes when she speaks. "Is this for real? You bring us here to show us this horrible post written by a—I have to say, a boy who quite clearly had *issues*—and for what? What are you hoping to accomplish, exactly?"

Detective Mendoza tilts his head in her direction. "I'm sure this is difficult to read, Mrs. Rojas. But between the initials and the cancer diagnosis, it's obvious Simon was writing about your younger daughter. There's no other current or past student at Bayview High who fits that profile." He turns toward me. "This must have been humiliating for your sister, Bronwyn. And from what other kids at school have told us recently, she's never really participated in social activities since then. Did that make you resent Simon?"

My mother opens her mouth to speak, but Robin puts a hand on her arm and cuts her off. "Bronwyn has no comment."

Detective Mendoza's eyes gleam, and he looks as though he can barely restrain himself from grinning. "Oh, but she does. Or she did, anyway. Simon unpublished the blog more than a year ago, but all the posts and comments are still recorded on the back end." He pulls the laptop back and presses a few keys, then spins it toward us with a new window open. "You have to give your email address to leave a comment. This is yours, right, Bronwyn?"

"Anybody can leave another person's email address," Robin says quickly. Then she leans over my shoulder again, and reads what I wrote at the end of sophomore year.

Fuck off and die, Simon.

Addy
Monday, October 15, 4:15 p.m.

The road from my house to Jake's is a pretty smooth ride until I turn onto Clarendon Street. It's a major intersection, and I have to get to the far left without the help of a bike lane. When I first started riding again I used to head for the sidewalk and cross with the light, but now I whiz across three lanes of traffic like a pro.

I cruise into Jake's driveway and push the kickstand down as I dismount, pulling off my helmet and looping it across my handlebars. I run a hand through my hair as I approach the house, but it's a pointless gesture. I've gotten used to the cut and sometimes I even like it, but short of growing it a foot and a half overnight, there's nothing I can do to improve it in Jake's eyes.

I ring the doorbell and step back, uncertainty humming through my veins. I don't know why I'm here or what I'm hoping for.

The door clicks and Jake pulls it open. He looks the same as ever—tousle-haired and blue-eyed, in a perfectly fitted T-shirt that shows off his football season workouts to great effect. "Hey. Come in."

I instinctively turn toward the basement, but that's not where we're headed. Instead, Jake leads me into the formal living room, where I've spent less than an hour total since I started dating Jake more than three years ago. I lower myself onto his parents' leather sofa and my still-sweaty legs stick to it almost immediately. Who decided leather furniture was a good idea?

When he sits down across from me, his mouth sets in such a hard line that I can tell this won't be a reconciliation conversation. I wait for crushing disappointment to hit, but it doesn't.

"So you ride a bike now?" he asks.

Of all the conversations we could have, I'm not sure why he's starting with this one. "I don't have a car," I remind him. *And you used to drive me everywhere.*

He leans forward with his elbows on his knees—such a familiar gesture that I almost expect him to start chatting about football season like he would have a month ago. "How's the investigation going? Cooper never talks about it anymore. You guys still all under the gun, or what?"

I don't want to talk about the investigation. The police have questioned me a couple of times over the past week, always finding new ways to ask me about the missing EpiPens in the nurse's office. My lawyer tells me the repetitive questioning means the investigation's going nowhere, not that I'm their main suspect. It's none of Jake's business, though, so I tell him a stupid, made-up story about how the four of us saw Detective Wheeler eating an entire plateful of doughnuts in an interrogation room.

Jake rolls his eyes when I'm done. "So basically, they're getting nowhere."

"Bronwyn's sister thinks people should be looking at Simon more," I say.

"Why Simon? He's dead, for crying out loud."

"Because it might turn up suspects the police haven't thought of yet. Other people who had a reason for wanting Simon out of the picture."

Jake blows out an annoyed sigh and flings an arm across the back of his chair. "Blame the victim, you mean? What happened to Simon wasn't his fault. If people didn't pull such sneaky, bullshit moves, About That wouldn't even have existed." He narrows his eyes at me. "You know that better than anyone."

"Still doesn't make him a great guy," I counter, with a stubbornness that surprises me. "About That hurt a lot of people. I don't understand why he kept it up for so long. Did he like people being afraid of him? I mean, you were friends with him growing up, right? Was he always that way? Is that why you stopped hanging out?"

"Are you doing Bronwyn's investigative work for her now?"

Is he *sneering* at me? "I'm as curious as she is. Simon's kind of a central figure in my life now."

He snorts. "I didn't invite you here to argue with me."

I stare at him, searching for something familiar in his face. "I'm not arguing. We're having a conversation." But even as I say it, I try to remember the last time I talked to Jake and didn't agree one hundred percent with whatever he said. I can't come up with a thing. I reach up and play with the back of my earring, pulling it until it almost comes off and then sliding it on again. It's a nervous habit I've developed now that I don't have hair to wind around my fingers. "So why *did* you invite me here?"

His lip curls as his eyes flick away from me. "Leftover concern, I guess. Plus, I deserve to know what's happening. I keep getting calls from reporters and I'm sick of it."

He sounds like he's waiting for an apology. But I've already given enough of those. "So am I." He doesn't say anything, and as silence falls I'm acutely aware of how loud the clock over his fireplace is. I count sixty-three ticks before I ask, "Will you ever be able to forgive me?"

I'm not even sure what kind of forgiveness I want anymore. It's hard to imagine going back to being Jake's girlfriend. But it would be nice if he stopped hating me.

His nostrils flare and his mouth pulls into a bitter twist. "How could I? You cheated on me and lied about it, Addy. You're not who I thought you were."

I'm starting to think that's a good thing. "I'm not going to make excuses, Jake. I screwed up, but not because I didn't care about you. I guess I never thought I was worthy of you. Then I proved it."

His cold gaze doesn't waver. "Don't play the poor-me card, Addy. You knew what you were doing."

"Okay." All of a sudden I feel like I did when Detective Wheeler first interrogated me: *I don't have to talk to you.* Jake might be getting satisfaction from picking at the scab of our relationship, but I'm not. I stand up, my skin making a faint peeling sound as it unsticks from the sofa. I'm sure I've left two thigh-shaped imprints behind. Gross, but who cares anymore. "I guess I'll see you around."

I let myself out and climb onto my bike, putting on my helmet. As soon as it's clipped tight I push up the kickstand and I'm pedaling hard down Jake's driveway. Once my heart finds a comfortable pounding rhythm, I remember how it almost beat out of my chest when I confessed to cheating on Jake. I'd never felt so trapped in my life. I thought I'd feel the same way in his living room today, waiting for him to tell me again I'm not good enough.

But I didn't, and I don't. For the first time in a long time, I feel free.

Cooper
Monday, October 15, 4:20 p.m.

My life isn't mine anymore. It's been taken over by a media circus. There aren't reporters in front of my house every day, but it's a common-enough occurrence that my stomach hurts whenever I get close to home.

I try not to go online more than I have to. I used to dream

about my name being a trending search on Google, but for pitching a no-hitter in the World Series. Not for possibly killing a guy with peanut oil.

Everyone says, *Just keep your head down.* I've been trying, but once you're under a microscope nothing slips by people. Last Friday at school I got out of my car the same time Addy got out of her sister's, the breeze ruffling her short hair. We were both wearing sunglasses, a pointless attempt at blending in, and gave each other our usual tight-lipped, still-can't-believe-this-is-happening smile. We hadn't gone more than a few steps before we saw Nate stride over to Bronwyn's car and open the door, being all exaggeratedly polite about it. He smirked as she got out, and she gave him a look that made Addy and me exchange glances behind our shades. The four of us ended up almost in a line, walking toward the back entrance.

The whole thing barely took a minute—just enough time for one of our classmates to record a phone video that wound up on TMZ that night. They ran it in slo-mo with the song "Kids" by MGMT playing in the background, like we're some kind of hip high school murder club without a care in the world. The thing went viral within a day.

That might be the weirdest thing about all this. Plenty of people hate us and want us in jail, but there are just as many— if not more—who love us. All of a sudden I have a Facebook fan page with over fifty thousand likes. Mostly girls, according to my brother.

The attention slows sometimes, but it never really stops. I thought I'd avoided it tonight when I left my house to meet Luis at the gym, but as soon as I arrive a pretty, dark-haired woman with a face full of makeup hurries toward me. My heart sinks because I'm familiar with her type. I've been followed again.

"Cooper, do you have a few minutes? Liz Rosen with Channel Seven News. I'd love your perspective on all this. A lot of people are rooting for you!"

I don't answer, brushing past her through the gym's entrance. She clicks after me in her high heels, a cameraman trailing in her wake, but the guy at the front desk stops them both. I've been going there for years and they've been pretty cool through all this. I disappear down the hall while he argues with her that no, she can't buy a membership on the spot.

Luis and I bench-press for a while, but I'm preoccupied with what's waiting outside for me when we're done. We don't talk about it, but in the locker room afterward he says, "Give me your shirt and keys."

"What?"

"I'll be you, head out of here in your cap and sunglasses. They won't know the difference. Take my car and get the hell out of here. Go home, go out, whatever. We can swap cars again at school tomorrow."

I'm about to tell him that'll never work. His hair's a lot darker than mine, and he's at least a shade tanner. Then again, with a long-sleeved shirt and a cap on, it might not matter. Worth a shot, anyway.

So I hover in the hallway as Luis strides out the front door in my clothes to the bright lights of cameras. My baseball cap sits low on his forehead and his hand shields his face as he climbs into my Jeep. He peels out of the parking lot and a couple of vans follow.

I put on Luis's hat and sunglasses, then get into his Honda and fling my gym bag across the seat. It takes a few tries to start the engine, but once it roars I pull out of the parking lot and take back roads until I'm on the freeway toward San Diego. When I'm downtown I circle for half an hour, still paranoid someone's following me. Eventually I make my way to the North Park neighborhood, pulling in front of an old factory that was renovated into condos last year.

The neighborhood's trendy, with lots of well-dressed kids a little older than me filling the sidewalk. A pretty girl in a flowered dress almost doubles over laughing at something the guy next to her says. She clutches his arm as they pass Luis's car without looking my way, and I feel a bone-deep sense of loss. I was like them a few weeks ago, and now I'm . . . not.

I shouldn't be here. What if someone recognizes me?

I pull a key out of my gym bag and wait for a break in the sidewalk crowds. I'm out of Luis's car and in the front door so fast, I don't think anyone could've seen me. I duck into the elevator and take it to the top floor, letting out a sigh of relief when it doesn't stop once. The hallway echoes with empty silence; all the hipsters who live here must be out for the afternoon.

Except one, I hope.

When I knock, I only half expect an answer. I never called or texted to say I was coming. But the door cracks open, and a pair of startled green eyes meet mine.

"*Hey.*" Kris steps aside to let me in. "What are you doing here?"

"Had to get out of my house." I close the door behind me and take off my hat and sunglasses, tossing them on an entry table. I feel silly, like a kid who's been caught playing spy. Except people *are* following me. Just not right this second. "Plus, I guess we should talk about the whole Simon thing, huh?"

"Later." Kris hesitates a fraction of a second, then leans forward and pulls me roughly toward him, pressing his lips against mine. I close my eyes and the world around me fades, like it always does, when I slide my hands into his hair and kiss him back.

PART THREE

TRUTH OR DARE

CHAPTER NINETEEN

Nate
Monday, October 15, 4:30 p.m.

My mother's upstairs, trying to have a conversation with my father. Good luck with that. I'm on our couch with my burner phone in hand, wondering what I can text to Bronwyn to keep her from hating me. Not sure *Sorry I lied about my mom being dead* is going to cut it.

It's not like I wanted her dead. But I thought she probably was, or would be soon. And it was easier than saying, or thinking, the truth. *She's a coke addict who ran off to some commune in Oregon and hasn't talked to me since.* So when people started asking where my mother was, I lied. By the time it hit me how fucked up a response that was, it was too late to take it back.

Nobody's ever really cared, anyway. Most of the people I know don't pay attention to what I say or do, as long as I keep the drugs coming. Except Officer Lopez, and now Bronwyn.

I thought about telling her, a few times late at night while we were talking. But I could never figure out how to start the conversation. I still can't.

I put my phone away.

The stairs creak as my mother comes down, brushing her hands on the front of her pants. "Your father's not in any shape to talk right now."

"Shocking," I mutter.

She looks both older and younger than she used to. Her hair's a lot grayer and shorter, but her face isn't so ragged and drawn. She's heavier, which I guess is good. Means she's eating, anyway. She crosses over to Stan's terrarium and gives me a small, nervous smile. "Nice to see Stan's still around."

"Not much has changed since we last saw you," I say, putting my feet on the coffee table in front of me. "Same bored lizard, same drunk dad, same falling-apart house. Except now I'm being investigated for murder. Maybe you heard about that?"

"Nathaniel." My mother sits in the armchair and clasps her hands in front of her. Her nails are as bitten off as ever. "I—I don't even know where to start. I've been sober for almost three months and I've wanted to contact you every single second. But I was so afraid I wasn't strong enough yet and I'd let you down again. Then I saw the news. I've been coming by the last few days, but you're never home."

I gesture at the cracked walls and sagging ceiling. "Would you be?"

Her face crumples. "I'm sorry, Nathaniel. I hoped . . . I hoped your father would step up."

You hoped. *Solid parenting plan.* "At least he's here." It's a low blow, and not a ringing endorsement since the guy barely moves, but I feel entitled to it.

My mother nods her head jerkily while cracking her knuckles. God, I forgot she did that. It's fucking annoying. "I know. I have no right to criticize. I don't expect you to forgive me. Or believe you'll get anything better than what you're used to from me. But I'm finally on meds that work and don't make me sick with anxiety. It's the only reason I could finish rehab this time. I have a whole team of doctors in Oregon who've been helping me stay sober."

"Must be nice. To have a team."

"It's more than I deserve, I know." Her downcast eyes and humble tone are pissing me off. But I'm pretty sure anything she did would piss me off right now.

I get to my feet. "This has been great, but I need to be somewhere. You can let yourself out, right? Unless you want to hang with Dad. Sometimes he wakes up around ten."

Oh crap. Now she's crying. "I'm sorry, Nathaniel. You deserve so much better than the two of us. My God, just look at you—I can't believe how handsome you've gotten. And you're smarter than both your parents put together. You always were. You should be living in one of those big houses in Bayview Hills, not taking care of this dump on your own."

"Whatever, Mom. It's all good. Nice to see you. Send me a postcard from Oregon sometime."

"Nathaniel, please." She stands and tugs at my arm. Her hands look twenty years older than the rest of her—soft and wrinkled, covered with brown spots and scars. "I want to do something to help you. Anything. I'm staying in the Motel Six on Bay Road. Could I take you out to dinner tomorrow? Once you've had some time to process all this?"

Process this. Christ. What kind of rehab-speak is she spewing? "I don't know. Leave a number, I'll call you. Maybe."

"Okay." She's nodding like a puppet again and I'm going to lose it if I don't get away from her soon. "Nathaniel, was that Bronwyn Rojas I saw earlier?"

"Yeah," I say, and she smiles. "Why?"

"It's just . . . well, if that's who you're with, we can't have messed you up too badly."

"I'm not *with* Bronwyn. We're murder cosuspects, remember?" I say, and let the door slam behind me. Which is self-defeating, because when it comes off its hinges, *again,* I'm the one who'll have to fix it.

Once I'm outside, I don't know where to go. I get on my bike and head for downtown San Diego, then change my mind and get on I-15 North. And just keep riding, stopping after an hour to fill up my tank. I pull out my burner phone while I'm doing it and check messages. Nothing. I should call Bronwyn, see how things went at the police station. She's gotta be fine, though. She has that expensive lawyer, along with parents who are like guard dogs between her and people trying to mess with her. And anyway, what the hell would I say?

I put my phone away.

I ride for almost three hours until I hit wide desert roads dotted with scrubby bushes. Even though it's getting late, it's hotter here near the Mojave Desert, and I stop to take off my jacket as I cruise closer to Joshua Tree. The only vacation I ever went on with my parents was a camping trip here when I was nine years old. I spent the whole time waiting for something bad to happen: for our ancient car to break down, for my mother to start screaming or crying, for my dad to go still and silent like he always did when we got to be too much for him to take.

It was almost normal, though. They were as tense with each other as ever, but kept the arguing to a minimum. My mother was on good behavior, maybe because she had a thing for those short, twisted trees that were everywhere. "The first seven years of the Joshua tree's life, it's just a vertical stem. No branches," she told me while we were hiking. "It takes years before it blooms. And every branching stem stops growing after it blossoms, so you've got this complex system of dead areas and new growth."

I used to think about that, sometimes, when I wondered what parts of her might still be alive.

It's past midnight by the time I get back to Bayview. I thought about getting on I-15 and riding through the night, as far as I could go until I dropped from exhaustion. Let my parents have whatever fucked-up reunion they're about to get into on their own. Let the Bayview Police come find me if they ever want to talk to me again. But that's what my mother would do. So in the end I came back, checked my phones, and followed up on the only text I had: a party at Chad Posner's house.

When I get there Posner's nowhere to be found. I end up in his kitchen, nursing a beer and listening to two girls go on and on about a TV show I've never seen. It's boring and doesn't take my mind off my mother's sudden reappearance, or Bronwyn's police summons.

One of the girls starts to giggle. "I know you," she says,

poking me in the side. She giggles harder and flattens her palm against my stomach. "You were on *Mikhail Powers Investigates,* weren't you? One of the kids who maybe killed that guy?" She's half-drunk and staggers as she leans closer. She looks like a lot of the girls I meet at Posner's parties: pretty in a forgettable way.

"Oh my God, Mallory," her friend says. "That's so rude."

"Not me," I say. "I just look like him."

"Liar." Mallory tries to poke me again, but I step out of reach. "Well, I don't think you did it. Neither does Brianna. Right, Bri?" Her friend nods. "We think it was the girl with the glasses. She looks like a stuck-up bitch."

My hand tightens around my beer bottle. "I told you, that's not me. So you can drop it."

"Shhorry," Mallory slurs, tilting her head and shaking bangs out of her eyes. "Don't be such a grouch. I bet I can cheer you up." She slides a hand into her pocket and pulls out a crumpled baggie filled with tiny squares. "Wanna go upstairs with us and trip for a while?"

I hesitate. I'd do almost anything to get out of my head right now. It's the Macauley family way. And everybody already thinks I'm that guy.

Almost everybody. "Can't," I say, pulling out my burner phone and starting to shoulder my way through the crowd. It buzzes before I get outside. When I look at the screen and see Bronwyn's number—even though she's the only one who ever calls me on this phone—I feel a massive sense of relief. Like I've been freezing and someone wrapped a blanket around me.

"Hey," Bronwyn says when I pick up. Her voice is far away, quiet. "Can we talk?"

Bronwyn
Tuesday, October 16, 12:30 a.m.

I'm nervous about sneaking Nate into the house. My parents are already furious with me for not telling them about Simon's blog post—both now and back when it actually happened. We got out of the police station without much trouble, though. Robin gave this haughty speech that was all, *Stop wasting our time with meaningless speculation that you can't prove, and that wouldn't be actionable even if you did.*

I guess she was right, because here I am. Although I'm grounded until, as my mother says, I stop "undermining my future by not being transparent."

"You couldn't have hacked into Simon's old blog while you were at it?" I muttered to Maeve before she went to bed.

She looked genuinely chagrined. "He took it down so long ago! I didn't think it even existed anymore. And I never knew you wrote that comment. It wasn't posted." She shook her head at me with a sort of exasperated fondness. "You were always more upset about that than I was, Bronwyn."

Maybe she's right. It occurred to me, as I lay in my dark room debating whether I should call Nate, that I've spent years thinking Maeve was a lot more fragile than she actually is.

Now I'm downstairs in our media room, and when I get

a text from Nate that he's at the house, I open the basement door and stick my head outside. "Over here," I call softly, and a shadowy figure comes around the corner next to our bulkhead. I retreat back into the basement, leaving the door open for Nate to follow me.

He comes in wearing a leather jacket over a torn, rumpled T-shirt, his hair falling sweaty across his forehead from the helmet. I don't say anything until I've led him into the media room and closed the door behind us. My parents are three floors away and asleep, but the added bonus of a soundproof room can't be overstated at a time like this.

"So." I sit in one corner of the couch, knees bent and arms crossed over my legs like a barrier. Nate takes off his jacket and tosses it on the floor, lowering himself on the opposite end. When he meets my eyes, his are clouded with so much misery that I almost forget to be upset.

"How'd it go at the police station?" he asks.

"Fine. But that's not what I want to talk about."

He drops his eyes. "I know." Silence stretches between us and I want to fill it with a dozen questions, but I don't. "You must think I'm an asshole," he says finally, still staring at the floor. "And a liar."

"Why didn't you tell me?"

Nate exhales a slow breath and shakes his head. "I wanted to. I thought about it. I didn't know how to start. Thing is—it was this lie I told because it was easier than the truth. And because I half believed it, anyway. I didn't think she'd ever come back. Then once you say something like that, how do you unsay it? You look like a fucking psycho at that point." He raises his eyes again, locking on mine with sudden intensity. "I'm not, though. I haven't lied to you about anything else. I'm not dealing drugs anymore, and I didn't do anything to Simon. I don't blame you if you don't believe me, but I swear to God it's true."

Another long silence descends while I try to gather my thoughts. I should be angrier, probably. I should demand proof of his trustworthiness, even though I have no idea what that would look like. I should ask lots of pointed questions designed to ferret out whatever other lies he's told me.

But the thing is, I do believe him. I won't pretend I know Nate inside and out after a few weeks, but I know what it's like to tell yourself a lie so often that it becomes the truth. I did it, and I haven't had to muddle through life almost completely on my own.

And I've never thought he had it in him to kill Simon.

"Tell me about your mom. For real, okay?" I ask. And he does. We talk for over an hour, but after the first fifteen minutes or so, we're mainly covering old ground. I start feeling stiff from sitting so long, and lift my arms over my head in a stretch.

"Tired?" Nate asks, moving closer.

I wonder if he's noticed that I've been staring at his mouth for the past ten minutes. "Not really."

He reaches out and pulls my legs over his lap, tracing a circle on my left knee with his thumb. My legs tremble, and I press them together to make it stop. His eyes flick toward mine, then down. "My mother thought you were my girlfriend."

Maybe if I do something with my hands I can manage to hold still. I reach up and tangle my fingers into the hair on the nape of his neck, smoothing the soft waves against his warm skin. "Well. I mean. Is that out of the question?"

Oh God. I actually said it. What if it is?

Nate's hand moves down my leg, almost absently. Like he has no idea he's turning my entire body into jelly. "You want a drug-dealing murder suspect who lied about his not-dead mother as your boyfriend?"

"Former drug dealer," I correct. "And I'm not in a position to judge."

He looks up with a half smile, but his eyes are wary. "I don't know how to be with somebody like you, Bronwyn." He must see my face fall, because he quickly adds, "I'm not saying I don't want to. I'm saying I think I'd screw it up. I've only ever been . . . you know. Casual about this kind of thing."

I don't know. I pull my hands back and twist them in my lap, watching my pulse jump under the thin skin of my wrist. "Are you casual now? With somebody else?"

"No," Nate says. "I was. When you and I first started talking. But not since then."

"Well." I'm quiet for a few seconds, weighing whether I'm about to make a giant mistake. Probably, but I plow ahead anyway. "I'd like to try. If you want to. Not because we're thrown together in this weird situation and I think you're hot, although I do. But because you're smart, and funny, and you do the right thing more often than you give yourself credit for. I like your horrible taste in movies and the way you never sugarcoat anything and the fact that you have an actual lizard. I'd be proud to be your girlfriend, even in a nonofficial capacity while we're, you know, being investigated for murder. Plus, I can't go more than a few minutes without wanting to kiss you, so—there's that."

Nate doesn't reply at first, and I worry I've blown it. Maybe that was too much information. But he's still running his hand down my leg, and finally he says, "You're doing better than me. I never stop thinking about kissing you."

He takes off my glasses and folds them, putting them on the side table next to the couch. His hand on my face is featherlight as he leans in close and pulls my mouth toward his. I hold my breath as our lips connect, and the soft pressure sends a warm ache humming through my veins. It's sweet and tender, different from the hot, needy kiss at Marshall's Peak. But it still makes me dizzy. I'm shaking all over and press my hands against his chest to try to get that under control, feeling a hard plane of muscle through his thin shirt. *Not helping.*

My lips part in a sigh that turns into a small moan when Nate slides his tongue to meet mine. Our kisses grow deeper and more intense, our bodies so tangled I can't tell where mine stops and his starts. I feel like I'm falling, floating, flying. All at once. We kiss until my lips are sore and my skin sparks like I've been lit by a fuse.

Nate's hands are surprisingly PG. He touches my hair and face a lot, and eventually he slides a hand under my shirt and runs it over my back and oh God, I might have whimpered. His fingers dip into the waistband of my shorts and a shiver goes through me, but he stops there. The insecure side of me wonders if he's not as attracted to me as I am to him, or as he is to other girls. Except . . . I've been pressed against him for half an hour and I *know* that's not it.

He pulls back and looks at me, his thick dark lashes sweeping low. *God,* his eyes. They're ridiculous. "I keep picturing your father walking in," he murmurs. "He kinda scares me." I sigh because, truth be told, that's been in the back of my mind too. Even though there's barely a five percent chance, it's still too much.

Nate runs a finger over my lips. "Your mouth is so red. We should take a break before I do permanent damage. Plus, I need to, um, calm down a little." He kisses my cheek and reaches for his jacket on the floor.

My heart drops. "Are you leaving?"

"No." He takes his phone out of his pocket and pulls up Netflix, then hands me my glasses. "We can finally finish watching *Ringu*."

"Damn it. I thought you'd forgotten about that." My disappointment's fake this time, though.

"Come on, this is perfect." Nate stretches on the couch and I curl next to him with my head on his shoulder as he props his iPhone in the crook of his arm. "We'll use my phone instead of that sixty-inch monster on your wall. You can't be scared of anything on such a tiny screen."

Honestly, I don't care what we do. I just want to stay wrapped around him for as long as possible, fighting sleep and forgetting about the rest of the world.

CHAPTER TWENTY

Cooper
Tuesday, October 16, 5:45 p.m.

"Pass the milk, would you, Cooperstown?" Pop jerks his chin at me during dinner, his eyes drifting toward the muted television in our living room, where college football scores scroll along the bottom of the screen. "So what'd you do with your night off?" He thinks it's hilarious that Luis posed as me after the gym yesterday.

I hand over the carton and picture myself answering his question honestly. *Hung out with Kris, the guy I'm in love with. Yeah, Pop, I said guy. No, Pop, I'm not kidding. He's a premed freshman at UCSD who does modeling on the side. Total catch. You'd like him.*

And then Pop's head explodes. That's how it always ends in my imagination.

"Just drove around for a while," I say instead.

I'm not ashamed of Kris. I'm *not*. But it's complicated.

Thing is, I didn't realize I could feel that way about a guy till I met him. I mean, yeah, I *suspected*. Since I was eleven or so. But I buried those thoughts as far down as I could because I'm a Southern jock shooting for an MLB career and that's not how we're supposed to be wired.

I really did believe that for most of my life. I've always had a girlfriend. But it was never hard to hold off till marriage like I was raised. I only recently understood that was more of an excuse than a deeply held moral belief.

I've been lying to Keely for months, but I did tell her the truth about Kris. I met him through baseball, although he doesn't play. He's friends with another guy I made the exhibition rounds with, who invited us both to his birthday party. And he *is* German.

I just left out the part about being in love with him.

I can't admit that to anybody yet. That it's not a phase, or experimentation, or distraction from pressure. Nonny was right. My stomach does flips when Kris calls or texts me. Every single time. And when I'm with him I feel like a real person, not the robot Keely called me: programmed to perform as expected.

But Cooper-and-Kris only exists in the bubble of his apartment. Moving it anyplace else scares the hell out of me. For one thing, it's hard enough making it in baseball when you're a regular guy. The number of openly gay players who are part of a major league team stands at exactly one. And he's still in the minors.

For another thing: Pop. My whole brain seizes when I imagine his reaction. He's the kind of good old boy who calls gay people "fags" and thinks we spend all our time hitting on straight guys. The one time we saw a news story about the gay baseball player, he snorted in disgust and said, *Normal guys shouldn't have to deal with that crap in the locker room.*

If I tell him about Kris and me, seventeen years of being the perfect son would be gone in an instant. He'd never look at me the same. The way he's looking at me now, even though I'm a murder suspect who's been accused of using steroids. *That* he can handle.

"Testing tomorrow," he reminds me. I have to get tested for steroids every damn week now. In the meantime I keep pitching, and no, my fastball hasn't gotten any slower. Because I haven't been lying. I didn't cheat. I strategically improved.

It was Pop's idea. He wanted me to hold back a little junior year, not give my all, so there'd be more excitement around me during showcase season. And there was. People like Josh Langley noticed me. But now, of course, it looks suspicious. *Thanks, Pop.*

At least he feels guilty about it.

I was sure, when the police got ready to show me the unpublished About That posts last month, that I was going to read something about Kris and me. I'd barely known Simon, only talked with him one-on-one a few times. But anytime I got near him I'd worry about him learning my secret. Last spring at junior prom he'd been drunk off his ass, and when I ran into him in the bathroom he flung an arm around me and pulled me so close I practically had a panic attack. I was sure that Simon—who'd never had a girlfriend as far as I knew—realized I was gay and was putting the moves on me.

I freaked out so bad, I had Vanessa disinvite him to her after-prom party. And Vanessa, who never passes up a chance to exclude somebody, was happy to do it. I let it stand even after I saw Simon hitting on Keely later with the kind of intensity you can't fake.

I hadn't let myself think about that since Simon died; how the last time I'd talked to him, I acted like a jerk because I couldn't deal with who I was.

And the worst part is, even after all this—I still can't.

Nate
Tuesday, October 16, 6:00 p.m.

When I get to Glenn's Diner half an hour after I'm supposed to meet my mother, her Kia is parked right out front. Score one for the new and improved version, I guess. I wouldn't have been at all surprised if she didn't show.

I thought about doing the same. A lot. But pretending she doesn't exist hasn't worked out all that well.

I park my bike a few spaces away from her car, feeling the first drops of rain hit my shoulders before I enter the restaurant. The hostess looks up with a polite, quizzical expression. "I'm meeting somebody. Macauley," I say.

She nods and points to a corner booth. "Right over there."

I can tell my mother's already been there for a while. Her

soda's almost empty and she's torn her straw wrapper to shreds. When I slide into the seat across from her, I pick up a menu and scan it carefully to avoid her eyes. "You order?"

"Oh, no. I was waiting for you." I can practically feel her willing me to look up. I wish I weren't here. "Do you want a hamburger, Nathaniel? You used to love Glenn's hamburgers."

I did, and I do, but now I want to order anything else. "It's Nate, okay?" I snap my menu shut and stare at the gray drizzle pelting the window. "Nobody calls me that anymore."

"Nate," she says, but my name sounds strange coming from her. One of those words you say over and over until it loses meaning. A waitress comes by and I order a Coke and a club sandwich I don't want. My burner phone buzzes in my pocket and I pull it out to a text from Bronwyn. *Hope it's going ok.* I feel a jolt of warmth, but put the phone back without answering. I don't have the words to tell Bronwyn what it's like to have lunch with a ghost.

"Nate." My mother clears her throat around my name. It still sounds wrong. "How is . . . How are you doing in school? Do you still like science?"

Christ. *Do you still like science?* I've been in remedial classes since ninth grade, but how would she know? Progress reports come home, I fake my father's signature, and they go back. Nobody ever questions them. "Can you pay for this?" I ask, gesturing around the table. Like the belligerent asshole I've turned into in the past five minutes. "Because I can't. So if you're expecting that you should tell me before the food comes."

Her face sags, and I feel a pointless stab of triumph. "Nath— Nate. I would never . . . well. Why should you believe me?" She pulls out a wallet and puts a couple of twenties on the table, and I feel like shit until I think about the bills I keep tossing into the trash instead of paying. Now that I'm not earning anything, my father's disability check barely covers the mortgage, utilities, and his alcohol.

"How do you have money when you've been in rehab for months?"

The waitress returns with a glass of Coke for me, and my mother waits until she leaves to answer. "One of the doctors at Pine Valley—that's the facility I've been in—connected me with a medical transcription company. I can work anywhere, and it's very steady." She brushes her hand against mine and I jerk away. "I can help you and your father out, Nate. I will. I wanted to ask you—if you have a lawyer, for the investigation? We could look into that."

Somehow, I manage not to laugh. Whatever she's making, it's not enough to pay a lawyer. "I'm good."

She keeps trying, asking about school, Simon, probation, my dad. It almost gets to me, because she's different than I remember. Calmer and more even-tempered. But then she asks, "How's Bronwyn handling all this?"

Nope. Every time I think about Bronwyn my body reacts like I'm back on the couch in her media room—heart pounding, blood rushing, skin tingling. I'm not about to turn the one good thing that's come out of this mess into yet another awkward conversation with my mother. Which means we've pretty much run out of things to say. Thank God the food's arrived so we can stop trying to pretend the last three years never happened. Even though my sandwich tastes like nothing, like dust, it's better than that.

My mother doesn't take the hint. She keeps bringing up Oregon and her doctors and *Mikhail Powers Investigates* until I feel as if I'm about to choke. I pull at the neck of my T-shirt like that'll help me breathe, but it doesn't. I can't sit here listening to her promises and hoping it'll all work out. That she'll stay sober, stay employed, stay sane. Just stay.

"I have to go," I say abruptly, dropping my half-eaten sandwich onto my plate. I get up, banging my knee against the edge of the table so hard I wince, and walk out without looking at her. I know she won't come after me. That's not how she operates.

When I get outside I'm confused at first because I can't see my bike. It's wedged between a couple of huge Range Rovers that weren't there before. I make my way toward it, then suddenly a guy who's way overdressed for Glenn's Diner steps in front of me with a blinding smile. I recognize him right away but look through him as if I don't.

"Nate Macauley? Mikhail Powers. You're a hard man to find, you know that? Thrilled to make your acquaintance. We're working on our follow-up broadcast to the Simon Kelleher investigation and I'd love your take. How about I buy you a coffee inside and we talk for a few minutes?"

I climb onto my bike and strap on my helmet like I didn't hear him. I get ready to back up, but a couple of producer types block my way. "How about you tell your people to move?"

His smile's as wide as ever. "I'm not your enemy, Nate. The

court of public opinion matters in a case like this. What do you say we get them on your side?"

My mother appears in the parking lot, her mouth falling open when she sees who's next to me. I slowly reverse my bike until the people in my way move and I've got a clear path. If she wants to help me, she can talk to him.

CHAPTER TWENTY-ONE

Bronwyn
Wednesday, October 17, 12:25 p.m.

At lunch on Wednesday, Addy and I are talking about nail polish. She's a font of information on the subject. "With short nails like yours, you want something pale, almost nude," she says, examining my hands with a professional air. "But, like, super glossy."

"I don't really wear nail polish," I tell her.

"Well, you're getting fancier, aren't you? For *whatever reason*." She arches a brow at my careful blow-dry, and my cheeks heat as Maeve laughs. "You might want to give it a try."

It's a mundane, innocuous conversation compared to yesterday's lunch, when we caught up on my police visit, Nate's mother, and the fact that Addy got called to the station separately to answer questions about the missing EpiPens again. Yesterday we were murder suspects with complicated personal lives, but today we're just being girls.

Until a shrill voice from a few tables over pierces the conversation. "It's like I told them," Vanessa Merriman says. "Which person's rumor is *definitely* true? And which person's totally fallen apart since Simon died? That's your murderer."

"What's she on about now?" Addy mutters, nibbling like a squirrel at an oversized crouton.

Janae, who doesn't talk much when she sits with us, darts a look at Addy and says, "You haven't heard? Mikhail Powers's crew is out front. A bunch of kids are giving interviews."

My stomach drops, and Addy shoves her tray away. "Oh, great. That's all I need, Vanessa on TV yakking about how guilty I am."

"Nobody really thinks it was you," Janae says. She nods toward me. "Or you. Or . . ." She watches as Cooper heads for Vanessa's table with a tray balanced in one hand, then spots us and changes course, seating himself at the edge of ours. He does that sometimes; sits with Addy for a few minutes at the beginning of lunch. Long enough to signal he's not abandoning her like the rest of her friends, but not so long that Jake gets pissed. I can't decide whether it's sweet or cowardly.

"What's up, guys?" he asks, starting to peel an orange. He's dressed in a sage button-down that brightens his hazel eyes, and he's got a baseball-cap tan from the sun hitting his cheeks more than anything else. Somehow, instead of making him look uneven, it only adds to the Cooper Clay glow.

I used to think Cooper was the handsomest guy at school. He still might be, but lately there's something almost Ken doll–like about him—a little plastic and conventional. Or maybe my tastes have changed. "Have you given your Mikhail Powers interview yet?" I joke.

Before he can answer, a voice speaks over my shoulder. "You should. Go ahead and be the murder club everybody thinks you guys are. Ridding Bayview High of its asshats." Leah Jackson perches on the table next to Cooper. She doesn't notice Janae, who turns brick red and stiffens in her chair.

"Hello, Leah," Cooper says patiently. As though he's heard it before. Which I guess he did, at Simon's memorial service.

Leah scans the table, her eyes landing on me. "You ever gonna admit you cheated?" Her tone's conversational and her expression is almost friendly, but I still freeze.

"Hypocritical, Leah." Maeve's voice rings out, surprising me. When I turn, her eyes are blazing. "You can't complain about Simon in one breath and repeat his rumor in the next."

Leah gives Maeve a small salute. "Touché, Rojas the younger."

But Maeve's just getting warmed up. "I'm sick of the conversation never changing. Why doesn't anybody talk about how awful About That made this school sometimes?" She looks directly at Leah, her eyes challenging. "Why don't *you*? They're right outside, you know. Dying for a new angle. You could give it to them."

Leah recoils. "I'm not talking to the media about that."

"Why not?" Maeve asks. I've never seen her like this; she's almost fierce as she stares Leah down. "You didn't do anything wrong. Simon did. He did it for years, and now everybody's sainting him for it. Don't you have a problem with that?"

Leah stares right back, and I can't make out the expression

that crosses her face. It's almost . . . triumphant? "Obviously I do."

"So do something about it," Maeve says.

Leah stands abruptly, pushing her hair over her shoulder. The movement lifts her sleeve and exposes a crescent-shaped scar on her wrist. "Maybe I will." She stalks out the door with long strides.

Cooper blinks after her. "Dang, Maeve. Remind me not to get on your bad side." Maeve wrinkles her nose, and I remember the file with Cooper's name on it she still hasn't managed to decrypt.

"*Leah's* not on my bad side," she mutters, tapping furiously on her phone.

I'm almost afraid to ask. "What are you doing?"

"Sending Simon's 4chan threads to *Mikhail Powers Investigates*," she says. "They're journalists, right? They should look into it."

"What?" Janae bursts out. "What are you talking about?"

"Simon was all over these discussion threads full of creepy people cheering on school shootings and stuff like that," Maeve says. "I've been reading them for days. Other people started them, but he jumped right in and said all kinds of awful things. He didn't even care when that boy killed all those people in Orange County." She's still tapping away when Janae's hand shoots out and locks around her wrist, almost knocking her phone from her hand.

"How would you know that?" she hisses, and Maeve finally snaps out of the zone to realize she might've said too much.

"Let her go," I say. When Janae doesn't, I reach out and pry her fingers off Maeve's wrist. They're icy cold. Janae pushes her chair back with a loud scrape, and when she gets to her feet she's shaking all over.

"None of you knew anything about him," she says in a choked voice, and stomps away just like Leah did. Except she's probably not about to give Mikhail Powers a sound bite. Maeve and I exchange glances as I drum my fingers on the table. I can't figure Janae out. Most days, I'm not sure why she sits with us when we must be a constant reminder of Simon.

Unless it's to hear conversations like the one we just had.

"I gotta go," Cooper says abruptly, as though he's used up his allotted non-Jake time. He lifts his tray, where the bulk of his lunch lies untouched, and smoothly makes his way to his usual table.

So our crew is back to being all girls, and stays that way for the rest of lunch. The only other guy who'd sit with us never bothers making an appearance in the cafeteria. But I pass Nate in the hallway afterward, and all the questions bubbling in my brain about Simon, Leah, and Janae disappear when he gives me a fleeting grin.

Because God, it's beautiful when that boy smiles.

Addy
Friday, October 19, 11:12 a.m.

It's hot on the track, and I shouldn't feel like running very hard. It's only gym class, after all. But my arms and legs pump with unexpected energy as my lungs fill and expand, as if all my recent bike riding has given me reserves that need a release. Sweat beads my forehead and pastes my T-shirt to my back.

I feel a jolt of pride as I pass Luis—who, granted, is barely trying—and Olivia, who's on the track team. Jake's ahead of me and the idea of catching him seems ridiculous because obviously Jake is much faster than me, and bigger and stronger too, and there's no way I can gain on him except I am. He's not a speck anymore; he's close, and if I shift lanes and keep this pace going I can almost, probably, definitely—

My legs fly out from under me. The coppery taste of blood fills my mouth as I bite into my lip and my palms slam hard against the ground. Tiny stones shred my skin, embedding in raw flesh and exploding into dozens of tiny cuts. My knees are in agony and I know before I see thick red dots on the ground that my skin's burst open on both of them.

"Oh no!" Vanessa's voice rings with fake concern. "Poor thing! Her legs gave out."

They didn't. While my eyes were on Jake, someone's foot hooked my ankle and brought me down. I have a pretty good idea whose, but can't say anything because I'm too busy trying to suck air into my lungs.

"Addy, are you okay?" Vanessa keeps her fake voice on as she kneels next to me, until she's right next to my ear and whispers, "Serves you right, slut."

I'd love to answer her, but I still can't breathe.

When our gym teacher arrives Vanessa backs off, and by the time I have enough air to talk she's gone. The gym teacher inspects my knees, turns my hands over, clucks at the damage. "You need the nurse's office. Get those cuts cleaned up and some antibiotics on you." She scans the crowd that's gathered around me and calls, "Miss Vargas! Help her out."

I guess I should be grateful it's not Vanessa or Jake. But I've barely seen Janae since Bronwyn's sister called Simon out a couple of days ago. As I limp toward school Janae doesn't look at me until we're almost at the entrance. "What happened?" she asks as she opens the door.

By now I have enough breath to laugh. "Vanessa's version of slut-shaming." I turn left instead of right at the stairwell, heading for the locker room.

"You're supposed to go to the nurse's," Janae says, and I flutter my hand at her. I haven't darkened the nurse's doorstep in weeks, and anyway, my cuts are painful but superficial. All I really need is a shower. I limp to a stall and peel off my clothes, stepping under the warm spray and watching brown-and-red water swirl down the drain. I stay in the shower until the water's clear and when I step out, a towel wrapped around me, Janae's there holding a pack of Band-Aids.

"I got these for you. Your knees need them."

"Thanks." I lower myself onto a bench and press flesh-colored strips across my knees, which sure enough are getting slick with blood again. My palms sting and they're scraped pink and raw, but there's nowhere I can put a Band-Aid that will make a difference.

Janae sits as far away as possible from me on the bench. I put three Band-Aids on my left knee and two on my right. "Vanessa's a bitch," she says quietly.

"Yeah," I agree, standing and taking a cautious step. My legs hold up, so I head for my locker and pull out my clothes. "But I'm getting what I deserve, right? That's what everybody thinks.

I guess it's what Simon would've wanted. Everything out in the open for people to judge. No secrets."

"Simon . . ." Janae's got that strangled sound to her voice again. "He's not . . . He wasn't like they said. I mean, yes, he went overboard with About That, and he wrote some awful things. But the past couple years have been rough. He tried so hard to be part of things and he never could. I don't think . . ." She stumbles over her words. "When Simon was himself, he wouldn't have wanted this for you."

She sounds really sad about it. But I can't bring myself to care about Simon now. I finish dressing and look at the clock. There's still twenty minutes left in gym class, and I don't want to be here when Vanessa and her minions descend. "Thanks for the Band-Aids. Tell them I'm still at the nurse's, okay? I'm going to the library till next period."

"Okay," Janae says. She's slumped on the bench, looking hollowed out and exhausted, and as I head for the door she abruptly calls out, "Do you want to hang out this afternoon?"

I turn to her in surprise. I hadn't thought we were at that point in our . . . acquaintance, I guess. *Friendship* still seems like a strong word. "Um, yeah. Sure."

"My mom's having her book club, so . . . maybe I could come to your house?"

"All right," I say, picturing my own mother's reaction to Janae after being used to a house full of pretty-perky Keelys and Olivias. The thought brightens me up, and we make plans for Janae to stop by after school. On a whim I text an invitation to Bronwyn, but I forgot she's grounded. Plus, she has piano lessons. Spontaneous downtime isn't really her thing.

* * *

I've barely stowed my bike under the porch after school when Janae arrives dragging her oversized backpack like she came to study. We make excruciating small talk with my mother, whose eyes keep roving from Janae's multiple piercings to her scuffed combat boots, until I bring her upstairs to watch TV.

"Do you like that new Netflix show?" I ask, aiming the remote at my television and sprawling across my bed so Janae can take the armchair. "The superhero one?"

She sits gingerly, like she's afraid the pink plaid will swallow her whole. "Yeah, okay," she says, lowering her backpack next to her and looking at all the framed photographs on my wall. "You're really into flowers, huh?"

"Not exactly. My sister has a new camera I was playing around with, and . . . I took a lot of old pictures down recently." They're shoved beneath my shoe boxes now: a dozen memories of me and Jake from the past three years, and almost as many with my friends. I hesitated over one—me, Keely, Olivia, and Vanessa at the beach last summer, wearing giant sun hats and goofy grins with a brilliant blue sky behind us. It had been a rare, fun girls' day out, but after today I'm more glad than ever that I banished Vanessa's stupid smirk to the closet.

Janae fiddles with the strap to her backpack. "You must miss how things were before," she says in a low voice.

I keep my eyes trained on the screen while I consider her comment. "Yes and no," I say finally. "I miss how easy school used to be. But I guess nobody I hung out with ever really cared about me, right? Or things would have been different." I shift restlessly on the bed and add, "I'm not gonna pretend it's anything like what you're dealing with. Losing Simon that way."

Janae flushes and doesn't answer, and I wish I hadn't brought it up. I can't figure out how to interact with her. Are we friends, or just a couple of people without better options? We stare silently at the television until Janae clears her throat and says, "Could I have something to drink?"

"Sure." It's almost a relief to escape the silence that's settled between us, until I run into my mother in the kitchen and have a terse, ten-minute-long conversation about *the kind of friends you have now.* When I finally get back upstairs, two glasses of lemonade in hand, Janae's got her backpack on and she's halfway out the door.

"I don't feel well suddenly," she mumbles.

Great. Even my unsuitable friends don't want to hang out with me.

I text Bronwyn in frustration, not expecting an answer since she's probably in the middle of Chopin or something. I'm surprised when she messages me back right away, and even more surprised at what she writes.

Be careful. I don't trust her.

CHAPTER TWENTY-TWO

Cooper
Sunday, October 21, 5:25 p.m.

We've almost finished dinner when Pop's phone rings. He looks at the number and picks up immediately, the lines around his mouth deepening. "This is Kevin. Yeah. What, tonight? Is that really necessary?" He waits a beat. "All right. We'll see you there." He hangs up and blows out an irritated sigh. "We gotta meet your lawyer at the police station in half an hour. Detective Chang wants to talk to you again." He holds up a hand when I open my mouth. "I don't know what about."

I swallow hard. I haven't been questioned in a while, and I'd been hoping the whole thing was fading away. I want to text Addy and see if she's getting brought in too, but I'm under strict orders not to put anything about the investigation in writing. Calling Addy's not a great idea, either. So I finish my dinner in silence and drive to the station with Pop.

My lawyer, Mary, is already talking with Detective Chang when we get inside. He beckons us toward the interrogation room, which is nothing like you see on TV. No big pane of glass with a two-way mirror behind it. Just a drab little room with a conference table and a bunch of folding chairs. "Hello, Cooper. Mr. Clay. Thanks for coming." I'm about to brush past him through the door when he puts a hand on my arm. "You sure you want your father here?"

I'm about to ask *Why wouldn't I?* but before I can speak, Pop starts blustering about how it's his God-given right to be present during questioning. He has this speech perfected and once he winds up, he needs to finish.

"Of course," Detective Chang says politely. "It's mainly a privacy issue for Cooper."

The way he says that makes me nervous, and I look to Mary for help. "It should be fine to start with just me in the room, Kevin," she says. "I'll bring you in if needed." Mary's okay. She's in her fifties, no-nonsense, and can handle both the police and my father. So in the end it's me, Detective Chang, and Mary seating ourselves around the table.

My heart's already pounding when Detective Chang pulls out a laptop. "You've always been vocal about Simon's accusation not being true, Cooper. And there's been no drop in your baseball performance. Which is inconsistent with the reputation of Simon's app. It wasn't known for posting lies."

I try to keep my expression neutral, even though I've been thinking the same thing. I was more relieved than mad when Detective Chang first showed me Simon's site, because a lie was better than the truth. But why would Simon lie about me?

"So we dug a little deeper. Turns out we missed something in our initial analysis of Simon's files. There was a second entry for you that was encrypted and replaced with the steroids accusation. It took a while to get that file figured out, but the original is here." He turns the screen so it's facing Mary and me. We lean forward together to read it.

Everybody wants a piece of Bayview southpaw CC and he's finally been tempted. He's stepping out on the beauteous KS with a hot German underwear model. What guy wouldn't, right? Except the new love interest models boxers and briefs, not bras and thongs. Sorry, K, but you can't compete when you play for the wrong team.

Every part of me feels frozen except my eyes, which can't stop blinking. This is what I was afraid I'd see weeks ago.

"Cooper." Mary's voice is even. "There's no need to react to this. Do you have a question, Detective Chang?"

"Yes. Is the rumor Simon planned to print true, Cooper?"

Mary speaks before I can. "There's nothing criminal in this accusation. Cooper doesn't need to address it."

"Mary, you know that's not the case. We have an interesting situation here. Four students with four entries they want to keep quiet. One gets deleted and replaced with a fake. Do you know what that looks like?"

"Shoddy rumormongering?" Mary asks.

"Like someone accessed Simon's files to get rid of this particular entry. And made sure Simon wouldn't be around to correct it."

"I need a few minutes with my client," Mary says.

I feel sick. I've imagined breaking the news about Kris to my parents in dozens of ways, but none as flat-out horrible as this.

"Of course. You should know we'll be requesting a warrant to search more of the Clays' home, beyond Cooper's computer and cell phone records. Given this new information, he's a more significant person of interest than he was previously."

Mary has a hand on my arm. She doesn't want me to talk. She doesn't have to worry. I couldn't if I tried.

Disclosing information about sexual orientation violates constitutional rights to privacy. That's what Mary says, and she's threatened to involve the American Civil Liberties Union if the police make Simon's post about me public. Which would fall into the category of Too Little, Way Too Late.

Detective Chang dances around it. They have no intention of invading my privacy. But they have to investigate. It would help if I told them everything. Our definitions of *everything* are different. His includes me confessing that I killed Simon, deleted my About That entry, and replaced it with a fake one about steroids.

Which makes no sense. Wouldn't I have taken myself out of the equation entirely? Or come up with something less career-threatening? Like cheating on Keely with another girl. That might've killed two birds with one stone, so to speak.

"This changes nothing," Mary keeps saying. "You have no more proof than you ever did that Cooper touched Simon's site.

Don't you dare disclose sensitive information in the name of your *investigation.*"

The thing is, though, it doesn't matter. It's getting out. This case has been full of leaks from the beginning. And I can't waltz out of here after being interrogated for an hour and tell my father nothing's changed.

When Detective Chang leaves, he makes it clear they'll be digging deep into my life over the next few days. They want Kris's number. Mary tells me I don't have to provide it, but Detective Chang reminds her they'll subpoena my cell phone and get it anyway. They want to talk to Keely, too. Mary keeps threatening the ACLU, and Detective Chang keeps telling her, mild as skim milk, that they need to understand my actions in the weeks leading up to the murder.

But we all know what's really happening. They'll make my life miserable until I cave from the pressure.

I sit with Mary in the interrogation room after Detective Chang leaves, thankful there's no two-way mirror as I bury my head in my hands. Life as I knew it is over, and pretty soon nobody will look at me the same way. I was going to tell eventually, but—in a few years, maybe? When I was a star pitcher and untouchable. Not now. Not like *this.*

"Cooper." Mary puts a hand on my shoulder. "Your father will be wondering why we're still in here. You need to talk to him."

"I can't," I say automatically. *Cain't.*

"Your father loves you," she says quietly.

I almost laugh. Pop loves *Cooperstown.* He loves when I strike out the side and get attention from flashy scouts, and when my name scrolls across the bottom of ESPN. But me?

He doesn't even know me.

There's a knock on the door before I can reply. Pop pokes his head in and snaps his fingers. "We done in here? I wanna get home."

"All set," I say.

"The hell was that all about?" he demands of Mary.

"You and Cooper need to talk," she says. Pop's jaw tenses. *What the hell are we paying you for?* is written all over his face. "We can discuss next steps after that."

"Fantastic," Pop mutters. I stand and squeeze myself through the narrow gap between the table and the wall, ducking past Mary and into the hallway. We walk in silence, one in front of the other, until we pass through the double glass doors and Mary murmurs a good-bye. "Night," Pop says, tersely leading the way to our car at the far end of the parking lot.

Everything in me clenches and twists as I buckle myself next to him in the Jeep. How do I start? What do I say? Do I tell him now, or wait till we're home and I can tell Mom and Nonny and . . . Oh God. *Lucas?*

"What was all that about?" Pop asks. "What took so long?"

"There's new evidence," I say woodenly.

"Yeah? What's that?"

I can't. I can't. Not just the two of us in this car. "Let's wait till we're home."

"This serious, Coop?" Pop glances at me as he passes a slow-moving Volkswagen. "You in trouble?"

My palms start sweating. "Let's wait," I repeat.

I need to tell Kris what's happening, but I don't dare text him. I should go to his apartment and explain in person. Another conversation that'll kill some part of me. Kris has been out since junior high. His parents are both artists and it was never a big deal. They were pretty much like, *Yeah, we knew. What took you so long?* He's never pressured me, but sneaking around isn't how he wants to live.

I stare out the window, my fingers tapping on the door handle for the rest of the ride home. Pop pulls into the driveway and our house looms in front of me: solid, familiar, and the last place I want to be right now.

We head inside, Pop tossing his keys onto the hallway table and catching sight of my mother in the living room. She and Nonny are sitting next to each other on the couch as though they've been waiting for us. "Where's Lucas?" I ask, following Pop into the room.

"Downstairs playing Xbox." Mom mutes the television as Nonny cocks her head to one side and fastens her eyes on me. "Everything okay?"

"Cooper's being all mysterious." Pop's glance at me is half-shrewd, half-dismissive. He doesn't know whether to take my obvious freaking out seriously or not. "You tell us, Cooperstown. What's all the fuss about? They got some actual evidence this time?"

"They think they do." I clear my throat and push my hands into my khakis. "I mean, they do. Have new information."

Everybody's quiet, absorbing that, until they notice I'm not in any hurry to continue. "What kind of new information?" Mom prompts.

"There was an entry on Simon's site that was encrypted before the police got there. I guess it's what he originally meant to post about me. Nothin' to do with steroids." There goes my accent again.

Pop never lost his, and doesn't notice when mine fades in and out. "I knew it!" he says triumphantly. "They clear you, then?"

I'm mute, my mind blank. Nonny leans forward, hands gripping her skull-topped cane. "Cooper, what was Simon going to post about you?"

"Well." A couple of words is all it'll take to make everything in my life Before and After. The air leaves my lungs. I can't look at my mother, and I sure as hell can't look at my father. So I focus on Nonny. "Simon. Somehow. Found out. That." *God.* I've run out of filler words. Nonny taps her cane on the floor like she wants to help me along. "I'm gay."

Pop laughs. Actually laughs, a relieved kind of guffaw, and slaps me on the shoulder. "Jesus, Coop. Had me going there for a minute. Seriously, what's up?"

"Kevin." Nonny grits the word through her teeth. "Cooper is *not joking.*"

"Course he is," Pop says, still laughing. I watch his face, because I'm pretty sure it's the last time he'll look at me the way he always has. "Right?" His eyes slide over to mine, casual and confident, but when he sees my face his smile dims. *There it is.* "Right, Coop?"

"Wrong," I tell him.

CHAPTER TWENTY-THREE

Addy
Monday, October 22, 8:45 a.m.

Police cars line the front of Bayview High again. And Cooper's stumbling through the hall like he hasn't slept in days. It doesn't occur to me the two might be related until he pulls me aside before first bell. "Can we talk?"

I peer at him more closely, unease gnawing at my stomach. I've never seen Cooper's eyes look bloodshot before. "Yeah, sure." I think he means here in the hallway, but to my surprise he leads me out the back staircase into the parking lot, where we lean against the wall next to the door. Which means I'll be late for homeroom, I guess, but my attendance record is already so bad another tardy won't make a difference. "What's up?"

Cooper runs a hand through his sandy hair until it sticks straight up, which is not a thing I ever imagined Cooper's hair could do until just now. "I think the police are here because of me. To ask questions about me. I just—wanted to tell somebody why before everything goes to hell."

"Okay." I put a hand on his forearm, and tense in surprise when I feel it shaking. "Cooper, what's wrong?"

"So the thing is . . ." He pauses, swallowing hard.

He looks like he's about to confess something. For a second Simon flashes through my mind: his collapse in detention and his red, gasping face as he struggled to breathe. I can't help but flinch. Then I meet Cooper's eyes—filmy with tears, but as kind as ever—and I know that can't be it. "The thing is what, Cooper? It's all right. You can tell me."

Cooper stares at me, taking in the whole picture—messy hair that's spiking oddly because I didn't take the time to blow-dry it, so-so skin from all the stress, faded T-shirt featuring some band Ashton used to like, because we're seriously behind on laundry—before he replies, "I'm gay."

"Oh." It doesn't register at first, and then it does. *"Ohhh."* The whole not-into-Keely thing suddenly makes sense. It seems like I should say more than that, so I add, "Cool." Inadequate response, I guess, but sincere. Because Cooper's pretty great except the way he's always been a little remote. This explains *a lot*.

"Simon found out I'm seeing someone. A guy. He was gonna post it on About That with everyone else's entries. It got switched out and replaced with a fake entry about me using steroids. I didn't switch it," he adds hastily. "But they think I did. So they're looking into me hard-core now, which means the whole school will know pretty soon. I guess I wanted to . . . tell somebody myself."

"Cooper, no one will care—" I start, but he shakes his head.

"They will. You know they will," he says. I drop my eyes, because I can't deny it. "I've been hiding my head under a rock about this whole investigation," he continues, his voice hoarse. "Hopin' they'd chalk it up to an accident because there's no real proof about anything. Now I keep thinking about what Maeve said about Simon the other day—how much weird stuff was going on around him. You think there's anything to that?"

"Bronwyn does," I say. "She wants the four of us to get together and compare notes. She says Nate will." Cooper nods distractedly, and it occurs to me that since he's still in Jake's bubble most of the time, he's not fully up to speed on everything that's been going on. "Did you hear about Nate's mom, by the way? How she's, um, not dead after all?"

I didn't think Cooper could get any paler, but he manages. "What?"

"Kind of a long story, but—yeah. Turns out she was a drug addict living in some kind of commune, but she's back now. And sober, supposedly. Oh, and Bronwyn got called into the police station because of a creepy post Simon wrote about her sister sophomore year. Bronwyn told him to drop dead in the comments section, so . . . you know. That looks kinda bad now."

"The hell?" By the incredulous look on Cooper's face, I've managed to distract him from his problems. Then the late bell rings, and his shoulders sag. "We'd better go. But, yeah. If you guys get together, I'm in."

* * *

The Bayview Police set themselves up in a conference room with a school liaison again, and start interviewing students one by one. At first things are kind of quiet, and when we get through the day without any rumors I'm hopeful that Cooper was wrong about his secret getting out. But by midmorning on Tuesday, the whispers start. I don't know if it's the kind of questions the police were asking, or who they were talking to, or just a good old-fashioned leak, but before lunch my ex-friend Olivia—who hasn't spoken to me since Jake punched TJ—runs up to my locker and grabs my arm with a look of pure glee.

"Oh my God. Did you hear about Cooper?" Her eyes pop with excitement as she lowers her voice to a piercing whisper. "Everyone's saying he's *gay*."

I pull away. If Olivia thinks I'm grateful to be included in the gossip mill, she's wrong. "Who cares?" I say flatly.

"Well, *Keely* does," Olivia giggles, tossing her hair over her shoulder. "No wonder he wouldn't sleep with her! Are you headed to lunch now?"

"Yeah. With Bronwyn. See you." I slam my locker shut and spin on my heel before she can say anything else.

In the cafeteria, I collect my food and head for our usual table. Bronwyn looks pretty in a sweater-dress and boots, her hair loose around her shoulders. Her cheeks are so pink I wonder if she's wearing makeup for a change, but if she is it's really natural. She keeps looking at the door.

"Expecting someone?" I ask.

She turns redder. "Maybe."

I have a pretty good idea who she's waiting for. Probably

not Cooper, although the rest of the room seems to be. When he steps into the cafeteria everything goes quiet, and then a low whispering buzz runs through the room.

"Cooper Clay is Cooper GAY!" somebody calls out in a high, falsetto voice, and Cooper freezes in the door as something flies through the air and hits him across the chest. I recognize the blue packaging immediately: Trojan condoms. Jake's brand. Along with half the school, I guess. But it did come from the direction of my old table.

"Doin' the butt, hey, pretty," somebody else sings, and laughter runs through the room. Some of it's mean but a lot of it's shocked and nervous. Most people look like they don't know what to do. I'm struck silent because Cooper's face is the worst thing I've ever seen and I want, so badly, for this to not be happening.

"Oh, for fuck's sake." It's Nate. He's in the entrance next to Cooper, which surprises me since I've never seen him in the cafeteria before. The rest of the room is equally taken aback, quieting enough that his contemptuous voice cuts across the whispers as he surveys the scene in front of him. "You losers seriously give a crap about this? Get a life."

A girl's voice calls out "Boyfriend!" disguised with a fake cough. Vanessa smirks as everyone around her dissolves into the kind of laughter that's been directed my way over the past month: half-guilty, half-gleeful, and all *Thank God this is happening to you and not me.* The only exceptions are Keely, who's biting her lip and staring at the floor, and Luis, who's half standing with his forearms braced on the table. One of the lunch ladies hovers in the doorway between the kitchen and the cafeteria, seemingly torn between letting things play out and getting a teacher to intervene.

Nate zeroes in on Vanessa's smug face without a trace of self-consciousness. "Really? *You've* got something to say? I don't even know your name and you tried to stick your hand down my pants the last time we were at a party." More laughter, but this time it's not at Cooper's expense. "In fact, if there's a guy at Bayview you haven't tried that with, I'd love to meet him."

Vanessa's mouth hangs open as a hand shoots up from the middle of the cafeteria. "Me," calls a boy sitting at the computer-nerd table. His friends all laugh nervously as the pulsing attention of the room—seriously, it's like a wave moving from one target to the next—focuses on them. Nate gives him a thumbs-up and looks back at Vanessa.

"There you go. Try to make that happen and shut the hell up." He crosses to our table and dumps his backpack next to Bronwyn. She stands up, winds her arms around his neck, and kisses him like they're alone while the entire cafeteria erupts into gasps and catcalls. I stare as much as everyone else. I mean, I kind of guessed, but this is pretty public. I'm not sure if Bronwyn's trying to distract everyone from Cooper or if she couldn't help herself. Maybe both.

Either way, Cooper's effectively been forgotten. He's motionless at the entrance until I grab his arm. "Come sit. The whole murder club at one table. They can stare at all of us together."

Cooper follows me, not bothering to get any food. We settle ourselves at the table and awkward silence descends until someone else approaches: Luis with his tray in hand, lowering himself into the last empty chair at our table.

"That was bullshit," he fumes, looking at the empty space in front of Cooper. "Aren't you gonna eat?"

"I'm not hungry," Cooper says shortly.

"You should eat something." Luis grabs the only untouched food item on his tray and holds it out. "Here, have a banana."

Everyone freezes for a second; then we all burst out laughing at the same time. Including Cooper, who rests his chin in his palm and massages his temple with his other hand.

"I'll pass," he says.

I've never seen Luis so red. "Why couldn't it have been apple day?" he mutters, and Cooper gives him a tired smile.

You find out who your real friends are when stuff like this happens. Turns out I didn't have any, but I'm glad Cooper does.

CHAPTER TWENTY-FOUR

Nate
Thursday, October 25, 12:20 a.m.

I ease my motorcycle into the cul-de-sac at the end of Bayview Estates and kill the motor, staying still for a minute to check for any hint that someone's nearby. It's quiet, so I climb off and give a hand to Bronwyn so she can do the same.

The neighborhood is still a half-finished construction area with no streetlights, so Bronwyn and I walk in darkness to house number 5. When we get there I try the front door, but it's locked. We circle to the back of the house and I jiggle each window until I find one that opens. It's low enough to the ground that I haul myself in easily. "Go back out front; I'll let you in," I say in a low voice.

"I think I can do it too," Bronwyn says, preparing to pull herself up. She doesn't have the arm strength, though, and I have to lean over and help her. The window's not big enough for two, and when I let go and step back to give her room, she scrambles the rest of the way and lands on the floor with a thud.

"Graceful," I say as she gets to her feet and brushes off her jeans.

"Shut up," she mutters, looking around. "Should we unlock the front for Addy and Cooper?"

We're in an empty, under-construction house after midnight for a meeting of the Bayview Four. It's like a bad spy movie, but there's no way all of us could get together anywhere else without drawing too much attention. Even my don't-give-a-crap neighbors are suddenly in my business now that Mikhail Powers's team keeps cruising down our street.

Plus, Bronwyn's still grounded.

"Yeah," I say, and we feel our way through a half-built kitchen and into a living room with a huge bay window. The moonlight streams bright across the door, and I twist its dead bolt open. "What time did you tell them?"

"Twelve-thirty," she says, pressing a button on her Apple watch.

"What time is it?"

"Twelve-twenty-five."

"Good. We have five minutes." I slide my hand along the side of her face and back her up against the wall, pulling her lips to mine. She leans into me and wraps her arms around my neck, opening her mouth with a soft sigh. My hands travel down the curve of her waist to her hips, finding a strip of bare skin under the hem of her shirt. Bronwyn has this unbelievable stealth body under all her conservative clothes, although I've barely gotten to see any of it.

"Nate," she whispers after a few minutes, in that breathless voice that drives me wild. "You were going to tell me how things went with your mom."

Yeah. I guess I was. I saw my mother again this afternoon and it was . . . all right. She showed up on time and sober. She backed off asking questions and gave me money for bills. But I spent the whole time taking bets with myself on how long it'd last. Current odds say two weeks.

Before I can answer, though, the door creaks and we're not alone anymore. A small figure slips inside and shuts the door behind her. The moonlight's bright enough that I can see Addy clearly, including the unexpected dark streaks in her hair. "Oh, good, I'm not the first one," she whispers, then puts her hands on her hips as she glares at Bronwyn and me. "Are you two making out? Seriously?"

"Did you dye your hair?" Bronwyn counters, pulling away from me. "What color is that?" She reaches a hand out and examines Addy's bangs. "Purple? I like it. Why the change?"

"I can't keep up with the maintenance requirements of short hair," Addy grumbles, dropping a bike helmet on the floor. "It doesn't look as bad with color mixed in." She cocks her head at me and adds, "I don't need your commentary if you disagree, by the way."

I hold up my hands. "Wasn't going to say a word, Addy."

"When did you even start knowing my name," she deadpans.

I grin at her. "You've gotten kinda feisty since you lost all the hair. And the boyfriend."

She rolls her eyes. "Where are we doing this? Living room?"

"Yeah, but back corner. Away from the window," Bronwyn

says, picking her way through construction supplies and sitting cross-legged in front of a stone fireplace. I sprawl next to her and wait for Addy to follow, but she's still poised near the door.

"I think I hear something," she says, peering through the peephole. She opens the door a crack and steps aside to let Cooper in. Addy leads him toward the fireplace but nearly goes flying when she trips on an extension cord. "*Ow!* Damn it, that was loud. Sorry." She settles herself next to Bronwyn, and Cooper sits beside her.

"How are things?" Bronwyn asks Cooper.

He rubs a hand over his face. "Oh, you know. Livin' the nightmare. My father won't talk to me, I'm getting torn apart online, and none of the teams that were scouting me will return Coach Ruffalo's calls. Other than that I'm great."

"I'm so sorry," Bronwyn says, and Addy grabs his hand and folds it in both of hers.

He heaves a sigh but doesn't pull away. "It is what it is, I guess. Let's just get to why we're here, huh?"

Bronwyn clears her throat. "Well. Mainly to . . . compare notes? Eli kept talking about looking for patterns and connections, which makes a lot of sense. I thought maybe we could go through some of the things we know. And don't know." She frowns and starts ticking things off on her fingers. "Simon was about to post some pretty shocking things about all of us. Somebody got us into that room together with the fake cell phones. Simon was poisoned while we were there. Lots of people besides us had reasons to be mad at Simon. He was mixed up in all kinds of creepy 4chan stuff. Who knows what kind of people he pissed off."

"Janae said he hated being an outsider and he was really up-set nothing more ever happened with Keely," Addy says, looking at Cooper. "Do you remember that? He started hitting on her during junior prom, and she caved at a party a couple weeks later and hooked up with him for, like, five minutes. He thought it was actually going somewhere."

Cooper hunches his shoulders like he's remembering something he'd rather not. "Right. Huh. I guess that's a pattern. Or a connection, or whatever. With me and Nate, I mean."

I don't get it. "What?"

He meets my eyes. "When I broke up with Keely, she told me she'd hooked up with you at a party to get rid of Simon. And I asked her out a couple weeks after."

"You and *Keely*?" Addy stares at me. "She never said!"

"It was just a couple times." Honestly, I'd forgotten all about it.

"And you're good friends with Keely. Or you were," Bronwyn says to Addy. She doesn't seem fazed at the idea of Keely and me getting together, and I have to appreciate how she doesn't lose focus. "But I have nothing to do with her. So . . . I don't know. Does that mean something, or doesn't it?"

"I don't see how it could," Cooper says. "Nobody except Simon cared what happened between him and Keely."

"*Keely* might have," Bronwyn points out.

Cooper stifles a laugh. "You can't think Keely had anything to do with this!"

"We're freewheeling here," Bronwyn says, leaning forward and propping her chin in her hand. "She's a common thread."

"Yeah, but Keely has zero motive for anything. Shouldn't we

be talking about people who hated Simon? Besides you," Cooper adds, and Bronwyn goes rigid. "I mean, for that blog post he wrote about your sister. Addy told me about it. That was low, really low. I never saw it the first time around. I'd have said something if I did."

"Well, I didn't *kill* him for it," Bronwyn says tightly.

"I'm not *saying*—" Cooper starts, but Addy interrupts.

"Let's stay on track. What about Leah, or even Aiden Wu? You can't tell me they wouldn't have liked revenge."

Bronwyn swallows and lowers her eyes. "I wonder about Leah too. She's been . . . Well, I have a connection to her I haven't told you guys about. She and I were partners in a Model UN competition, and by mistake we told Simon a wrong deadline that got him disqualified. He started torturing Leah on About That right after."

Bronwyn's told me this, actually. It's been eating at her for a while. But it's news to Cooper and Addy, who starts bobbing her head. "So Leah's got a reason to hate Simon *and* be mad at you." Then she frowns. "But what about the rest of us? Why drag us along?"

I shrug. "Maybe we were just the secrets Simon had on hand. Collateral damage."

Bronwyn sighs. "I don't know. Leah's hotheaded, but not exactly sneaky. I'm more confused about Janae's deal." She turns toward Addy. "One of the strangest things about the Tumblr is how many details it got right. You'd almost have to be one of us to know that stuff—or spend a lot of time with us. Don't you think it's weird that Janae hangs out with us even though we're accused of killing her best friend?"

"Well, to be fair, I *did* invite her," Addy says. "But she's been awfully skittish lately. And did you guys notice she and Simon weren't together as much as usual right before he died? I keep wondering if something happened between them." She leans back and chews on her bottom lip. "I suppose if anybody would've known what secrets Simon was about to spill and how to use them, it'd be Janae. I just . . . I don't know, you guys. I'm not sure Janae's got it in her to do something like this."

"Maybe Simon rejected her and she . . . killed him?" Cooper looks doubtful before he finishes the sentence. "Don't see how, though. She wasn't there."

Bronwyn shrugs. "We don't know that for sure. When I talked to Eli, he kept saying somebody could've planned the car accident as a distraction to slip into the room. If you take that as a possibility, anyone could've done it."

I made fun of Bronwyn when she first brought that up, but—I don't know. I wish I could remember more about that day, could say for sure whether it's even possible. The whole thing's turned into a blur.

"One of the cars was a red Camaro," Cooper recalls. "Looked ancient. I don't remember ever seeing it in the parking lot before. Or since. Which *is* weird when you think about it."

"Oh, come on," Addy scoffs. "That's so far-fetched. Sounds like a lawyer with a guilty client grasping at straws. Someone new was probably just picking up a kid that day."

"Maybe," Cooper says. "I dunno. Luis's brother works in a repair place downtown. Maybe I'll ask him if a car like that came through, or if he can check with some other shops." He holds up a hand at Addy's raised brows. "Hey, *you're* not the police's favorite new person of interest, okay? I'm desperate here."

We're not getting anywhere with this conversation. But I'm struck by a couple of things as I listen to them talk. One: I like all of them more than I thought I would. Bronwyn's obviously been the biggest surprise, and *like* doesn't cover it. But Addy's turned into kind of a badass, and Cooper's not as one-dimensional as I thought.

And two: I don't think any of them did it.

Bronwyn
Friday, October 26, 8:00 p.m.

Friday night my entire family settles in to watch *Mikhail Powers Investigates*. I'm feeling more dread than usual, between bracing myself for Simon's blog post about Maeve and worrying that something about Nate and me will make it into the broadcast. I never should have kissed him at school. Although in my defense he was unbelievably hot at that particular moment.

Anyway. We're all nervous. Maeve curls next to me as Mikhail's theme music plays and photos of Bayview flash across the screen.

A murder investigation turns witch hunt. When police tactics include revealing personal information in the name of evidence collection, have they gone too far?

Wait. What?

The camera zooms in on Mikhail, and he is *pissed*. I sit up straighter as he stares into the camera and says, "Things in Bayview, California, turned ugly this week when a closeted student involved in the investigation was outed after a round of police questioning, causing a media firestorm that should concern every American who cares about privacy rights."

And then I remember. Mikhail Powers is gay. He came out when I was in junior high and it was a big deal because it happened after some photos of him kissing a guy circulated online. It wasn't his choice. And from the way he's covering the story now, he's still bitter.

Because suddenly the Bayview Police are the bad guys. They have no evidence, they've disrupted our lives, and they've violated Cooper's constitutional rights. They're on the defensive as a police spokesperson claims they were careful in their questioning and no leaks came from the department. But the ACLU wants to get involved now. And there's Eli Kleinfelter from Until Proven again, talking about how poorly this case has been handled from the beginning, with the four of us made into scapegoats while nobody even asks who else might've wanted Simon Kelleher dead.

"Has everybody forgotten about the teacher?" he asks, leaning forward from behind an overflowing desk. "He's the only person who was in that room who's being treated as a witness instead of a suspect, even though he had more opportunity than anyone. That can't be discounted."

Maeve leans her head next to mine and whispers, "You should be working for Until Proven, Bronwyn."

Mikhail switches to the next segment: *Will the real Simon Kelleher please stand up?* Simon's class picture flashes across the screen as people reminisce about his good grades and nice family and all the clubs he belonged to. Then Leah Jackson pops up on-screen, standing on Bayview High's front lawn. I turn to Maeve, eyes wide, and she looks equally shocked.

"She did it," she murmurs. "She actually did it."

Leah's interview is followed by segments with other kids hurt by Simon's gossip, including Aiden Wu and a girl whose parents kicked her out when news spread about her being pregnant. Maeve's hand finds mine as Mikhail drops his last bombshell—a screen capture of the 4chan discussion threads, with Simon's worst posts about the Orange County school shooting highlighted:

Look, I support the notion of violently disrupting schools in theory, but this kid showed a depressing lack of imagination. I mean, it was fine, I guess. It got the job done. But it was so prosaic. Haven't we seen this a hundred times now? Kid shoots up school, shoots up self, film at eleven. Raise the stakes, for God's sake. Do something original.

A grenade, maybe. Samurai swords? Surprise me when you take out a bunch of asshole lemmings. That's all I'm asking.

I think back to Maeve texting away that day Janae got so upset with her at lunch. "So you really did send that to the show?" I whisper.

"I really did," she whispers back. "I didn't know they'd use them, though. Nobody ever got back to me."

By the time the broadcast finishes, the Bayview Police are the real villains, followed closely by Simon. Addy, Nate, and I are innocent bystanders caught in a cross fire we don't deserve, and Cooper's a saint. The whole thing's a stunning reversal.

I'm not sure you could call it journalism, but *Mikhail Powers Investigates* definitely has an impact over the next few days. Somebody starts a Change.org petition to drop the investigation that collects almost twenty thousand signatures. The MLB and local colleges get heat about whether they discriminate against gay players. The tone of the media coverage shifts, with more questions being raised about the police's handling of the case than about us. And when I return to school on Monday, people actually talk to me again. Even Evan Neiman, who's been acting like we've never met, sidles up to me at the last bell and asks if I'm going to Mathlete practice.

Maybe my life won't ever be fully normal again, but by the end of the week I start to hope it'll be less criminal.

Friday night I'm on the phone with Nate as usual, reading him the latest Tumblr post. Even that seems like it's about to give up:

Being accused of murder is turning into a monumental drag. I mean, sure, the TV coverage is interesting. And it makes me feel good that the smoke screen I put in place is working—people still have no clue who's responsible for killing Simon.

Nate cuts me off after the first paragraph. "Sorry, but we have more important things to discuss. Answer this honestly: If I'm no longer a murder suspect, will you still find me attractive?"

"You'll still be on probation for drug dealing," I point out. "That's pretty hot."

"Ah, but that's up in December," Nate replies. "By the new year I could be a model citizen. Your parents might even let me take you out on an actual date. If you wanted to go."

If I wanted to go. "Nate, I've been waiting to go on a date with you since fifth grade," I tell him. I like that he wonders what we'll be like outside this weird bubble. Maybe if we're both thinking about it, there's a possibility we'll figure it out.

He tells me about his latest visit with his mother, who really seems to be trying. We watch a movie together—his choice, unfortunately—and I fall asleep to his voice criticizing the shoddy camerawork. When I wake up Saturday morning, I notice my phone has only a few minutes left. I'll have to ask him for another one. Which will be phone number four, I think.

Maybe we can use our actual phones one of these days.

I stay in bed a little later than usual, right up till the time I need to get moving if Maeve and I are going to do our usual running-slash-library routine. I've just finished lacing up my sneakers and am rooting around in my dresser for my Nano when a tentative knock sounds on my bedroom door.

"Come in," I say, unearthing a small blue device from a pile of headbands. "Is that you, Maeve? Are you the reason this is only ten percent charged?" I turn around to see my sister so white-faced and trembling that I almost drop my Nano.

Anytime Maeve looks sick, I'm seized with the horrible fear she's had a relapse. "Do you feel all right?" I ask anxiously.

"I'm fine." The words come out as a gasp. "But you need to see something. Come downstairs, okay?"

"What's going on?"

"Just . . . come." Maeve's voice is so brittle that my heart thumps painfully. She clutches the banister all the way downstairs. I'm about to ask if something's wrong with Mom or Dad when she leads me into the living room and points mutely at the television.

Where I see Nate in handcuffs, being led away from his house, with the words *Arrest in the Simon Kelleher Murder Case* scrolling on the bottom of the screen.

CHAPTER TWENTY-FIVE

Bronwyn
Saturday, November 3, 10:17 a.m.

This time I *do* drop my Nano.

It slips from my hand and thuds softly onto our rug as I watch one of the police officers flanking Nate open the cruiser door and push him, not very gently, into the backseat. The scene cuts to a reporter standing outdoors, brushing windswept dark hair out of her face. "Bayview Police refused to comment, other than to say that new evidence provides probable cause to charge Nate Macauley, the only one of the Bayview Four with a criminal record, with Simon Kelleher's murder. We'll continue to provide updates as the story unfolds. I'm Liz Rosen, reporting for Channel Seven News."

Maeve stands next to me, the remote in her hand. I pluck at her sleeve. "Can you rewind to the beginning, please?"

She does, and I study Nate's face in the looping video. His

expression is blank, almost bored, as though he's been talked into going to a party that doesn't interest him.

I know that look. It's the same one he got when I mentioned Until Proven at the mall. He's shutting down and putting up defenses. There's no trace of the boy I know from the phone, or our motorcycle rides, or my media room. Or the one I remember from grade school, his St. Pius tie askew and his shirt untucked, leading his sobbing mother down the hallway with a fierce look that dared any of us to laugh.

I still believe that Nate's the real one. Whatever the police think, or found, doesn't change that.

My parents aren't home. I grab my phone and call my lawyer, Robin, who doesn't answer. I leave her such a long, rambling message that her voice mail cuts me off, and I hang up feeling helpless. Robin's my only hope for getting information, but she won't consider this an emergency. It's a problem for Nate's future lawyer, not her.

That thought makes me even more panicked. What's an overworked public defender who's never met Nate going to be able to do? My eyes dart around the room and meet Maeve's troubled gaze.

"Do you think he might have—"

"No," I say forcefully. "Come on, Maeve, you've seen how screwed up this investigation is. They thought *I* did it for a while. They're wrong. I'm positive they're wrong."

"I wonder what they found, though," Maeve says. "You'd think they'd be pretty careful after all the bad press they got this week."

I don't answer. For once in my life I have no idea what to

do. My brain's empty of everything except a churning anxiety. Channel 7 has given up pretending they know anything new, and they're replaying snippets about the investigation to date. There's footage from *Mikhail Powers Investigates*. Addy in her pixie haircut, giving whoever's filming her a defiant finger. A Bayview Police Department spokesperson. Eli Kleinfelter.

Of course.

I grab my phone and search for Eli's name. He gave me his cell the last time we spoke and told me to call anytime. I hope he meant it.

He answers on the first ring. "Eli Kleinfelter."

"Eli? It's Bronwyn Rojas. From—"

"Of course. Hi, Bronwyn. I take it you're watching the news. What do you make of it?"

"They're wrong." I stare at the television while Maeve stares at me. Dread's creeping through me like a fast-growing vine, squeezing my heart and lungs so it's hard to breathe. "Eli, Nate needs a better lawyer than whatever random public defender they'll assign him. He needs somebody who gives a crap and knows what they're doing. I think, um, well—basically I think he needs you. Would you consider taking his case?"

Eli doesn't answer straightaway, and when he does his voice is cautious. "Bronwyn, you know I'm interested in this case, and I sympathize with all of you. You've gotten a shit deal and I'm sure this arrest is more of the same. But I've got an impossible workload as it is—"

"Please," I interrupt, and words tumble out of me. I tell Eli about Nate's parents and how he's practically raised himself since he was in fifth grade. I tell him every awful, heart-wrenching

story Nate's ever told me, or that I witnessed or guessed. Nate would hate it, but I've never believed anything more strongly than I believe he needs Eli to stay out of jail.

"All right, all right," Eli says finally. "I get it. I really do. Are either of these parents in any shape to talk? I'll make time for a consult and give them some ideas for resources. That's all I can do."

It's not enough, but it's something. "Yes!" I say with brazen fake confidence. Nate talked to his mother two days ago and she was holding on, but I have no idea what effect today's news might have on her. "I'll talk to Nate's mom. When can we meet?"

"Ten tomorrow, our offices."

Maeve's still watching me when I hang up. "Bronwyn, what are you doing?"

I snatch the keys to the Volvo from the kitchen island. "I need to find Mrs. Macauley."

Maeve bites her lip. "Bronwyn, you can't—"

Run this like it's student council? She's right. I need help. "Will you come? Please?"

She debates for half a minute, her amber eyes steady on mine. "All right."

My phone almost slips out of my sweaty palm as we head for the car. I must've gotten a dozen calls and texts while I was talking with Eli. My parents, my friends, and a bunch of numbers I don't recognize that probably belong to reporters. I have four messages from Addy, all some variation of *Did you see?* and *WTF?*

"Are we telling Mom and Dad about this?" Maeve asks as I back out of the driveway.

"What 'this'? Nate's arrest?"

"I'm pretty sure they're in the loop on that. This . . . legal coordination you're doing."

"Do you disapprove?"

"Not *disapprove*, exactly. But you're flying off the handle before you even know what the police found. It could be cut-and-dried. I know you really like him, but . . . isn't it possible he did this?"

"No," I say shortly. "And yes. I'll tell Mom and Dad. I'm not doing anything wrong. Just trying to help a friend." My voice sticks on the last word, and we drive in silence until we reach Motel 6.

I'm relieved when the front desk clerk tells me Mrs. Macauley's still checked in, but she doesn't answer the phone in her room. Which is a good sign—hopefully she's wherever Nate is. I leave a note with my phone number and try not to overdo the underlines and capital letters. Maeve takes over driving responsibilities on the ride home while I call Addy.

"What the hell?" she says when she picks up, and the vise gripping my chest loosens at the disbelief in her voice. "First they think it's all of us. Then it's musical chairs till they finally land on Nate, I guess."

"Anything new?" I ask. "I've been away from screens for half an hour."

But there's nothing. The police are being tight-lipped about whatever they found. Addy's lawyer doesn't have a clue what's happening. "You want to hang out tonight?" she asks. "You must be going nuts. My mom and her boyfriend have plans, so Ashton and I are making pizza. Bring Maeve; we'll have a sister night."

"Maybe. If things aren't too out of control," I say gratefully.

Maeve turns into our street, and my heart sinks when I spy the line of white news vans in front of our house. It looks like Univision and Telemundo have joined the fray, which is seriously going to piss off my dad. He can never get them to cover anything positive about his company, but *this* they show up for.

We pull into the driveway behind my parents' cars, and as soon as I open my door a half-dozen microphones are in my face. I push past them and meet Maeve in front of the car, grabbing her hand as we weave through the cameras and the flashing lights. Most of the reporters shout some variation of "Bronwyn, do you think Nate killed Simon?" but one calls out, "Bronwyn, is it true you and Nate are romantically involved?"

I *really* hope my parents weren't asked the same question.

Maeve and I slam the door behind us and duck past the windows into our kitchen. Mom is sitting at the island with a coffee cup between both hands, her face tight with worry. Dad's voice rises in heated conversation from behind his closed office door.

"Bronwyn, we need to talk," Mom says, and Maeve floats away upstairs.

I sit across from my mother at the kitchen island and meet her tired eyes with a pang. *My fault.* "Obviously you saw the news," she says. "Your father's talking to Robin about what, if anything, this means for you. In the meantime, we got a lot of questions when we walked past that zoo out there. Some about you and Nate." I can tell she's trying hard to keep her voice neutral. "We might have made it difficult for you to talk about whatever . . . relationships you have with the other kids. Because from our perspective the best way to keep you safe was to keep you separate. So maybe you didn't think you could confide in us, but I need you to be straight with me now that Nate's been arrested. Is there something I should know?"

At first all I can think is *What's the least amount of information I can provide and still make you understand I need to help Nate?* But then she reaches out and squeezes my hand, and it hits me with a stab of guilt how I never used to keep things from her until I cheated in chemistry. And look how *that* turned out.

So I tell her almost everything. Not about bringing Nate to our house or meeting him at Bayview Estates, because I'm pretty sure that'll send us down a bad path. But I explain the late-night phone calls, the escape-from-school motorcycle rides, and, yeah, the kissing.

My mother is trying *so* hard not to freak out. I give her a lot of credit.

"So you're . . . serious about him?" She almost chokes on the words.

She doesn't want the real answer. Robin's answer-a-different-question-than-the-one-you're-trying-to-deflect strategy would work well now. "Mom, I understand this is a bizarre situation and I don't really know Nate. But I don't believe he'd hurt Simon. And he doesn't have anybody looking out for him. He needs a good lawyer, so that's what I'm trying to help with." My phone buzzes with a number I don't recognize, and I grimace as I realize I need to answer in case it's Mrs. Macauley. "Hi, this is Bronwyn."

"Bronwyn, so glad you picked up! This is Lisa Jacoby with the *Los Angeles Ti*—"

I hang up and face my mother again. "I'm sorry I haven't

been straight with you after everything you've done for me. But please let me connect Mrs. Macauley and Eli. Okay?"

My mother massages her temple. "Bronwyn, I'm not sure you understand how cavalier you've been. You ignored Robin's advice and you're lucky it didn't blow up in your face. It still might. But . . . no, I won't stop you from talking with Nate's mother. This case is messed up enough that everyone involved needs decent counsel."

I throw my arms around her and, God, it feels good to just hug my mom for a minute.

She sighs when I let go. "Let me talk to your father. I don't think a conversation between you two would be productive right now."

I couldn't agree more. I'm on my way upstairs when my phone rings again, and my heart leaps when I see a 503 area code. I can't keep the hope out of my voice when I pick up. "Hi, this is Bronwyn."

"Bronwyn, hello." The voice is low and strained, but clear. "It's Ellen Macauley. Nate's mother. You left me a note."

Oh, thank God thank God thank God. She didn't hightail it to Oregon in a drug-induced haze. "Yes. Yes, I did."

Cooper
Saturday, November 3, 3:15 p.m.

It's hard to evaluate exhibition games anymore, but overall this one went pretty well. My fastball hit ninety-four, I struck out the side twice, and only a few guys heckled me from the stands.

They were wearing tutus and baseball caps, though, so they stood out a little more than your average gay basher before security escorted them out.

A couple of college scouts showed up, and the guy from Cal State even bothered to talk to me afterward. Coach Ruffalo started hearing from teams again, but it strikes me as more of a PR play than genuine interest. Only Cal State is still talking scholarship, even though I'm pitching better than ever. That's life as an outed murder suspect, I guess. Pop doesn't wait for me outside the locker room anymore. He heads straight for the car when I'm done and starts the engine so we can make a quick exit.

Reporters are another story. They're dying to talk to me. I brace myself when a camera lights up as I leave the locker room, waiting for the woman with the microphone to cycle through the usual half-dozen questions. But she catches me by surprise.

"Cooper, what do you think about Nate Macauley's arrest?"

"Huh?" I stop short, too shocked to brush past her, and Luis almost bumps into me.

"You haven't heard?" The reporter grins like I handed her a winning lottery ticket. "Nate Macauley's been arrested for Simon Kelleher's murder, and the Bayview Police are saying you're no longer a person of interest. Can you tell me how that feels?"

"Um . . ." *Nope. I can't.* Or won't. Same difference. "Excuse me."

"The hell?" Luis mutters once we're past the camera gauntlet. He pulls out his phone and swipes wildly as I spot my father's car. "Damn, she wasn't lying. *Dude.*" He stares at me with wide eyes. "You're off the hook."

Weird, but that hadn't even occurred to me till he said it.

We're giving Luis a ride home, which is good since it cuts down the time Pop and I need to spend alone. Luis and I drop our bags in the backseat, and I climb into the passenger seat while Luis settles himself into the back. Pop's fiddling with the radio, trying to find a news station. "They arrested that Macauley kid," he says with grim satisfaction. "I'll tell you what, they're gonna have a pack of lawsuits on their hands when this is done. Starting with me."

He slides his eyes to my left as I sit. That's Pop's new thing: he looks *near* me. He hasn't met my eyes once since I told him about Kris.

"Well, you had to figure it was Nate," Luis says calmly. Throws Nate right under the bus, like he hadn't been sitting with the guy at lunch all last week.

I don't know what to think. If I'd had to point a finger at someone when this all started, it would've been Nate. Even though he'd acted genuinely desperate when he was searching for Simon's EpiPen. He was the person I knew the least, and he was already a criminal, so . . . it wasn't much of a stretch.

But when the entire Bayview High cafeteria was ready to take me down like a pack of hyenas, Nate was the only person who said anything. I never thanked him, but I've thought a lot about how much worse school would've gotten if he'd brushed past me and let things snowball.

My phone's filled with text messages, but the only ones I care about are a string from Kris. Other than a quick visit to warn Kris about the police and apologize for the oncoming media onslaught, I've barely seen him in the past couple of weeks. Even though people know about us, we haven't had a chance to be normal.

I'm still not sure what that would even look like. I wish I could find out.

Omg saw the news
This is good right??
Call when you can

I text him back while half listening to Pop and Luis talk. After we drop Luis off silence settles between me and my father, dense as fog. I'm the first to break it. "So how'd I do?"

"Good. Looked good." Bare-minimum response, as usual lately.

I try again. "I talked to the scout from Cal State."

He snorts. "*Cal State.* Not even top ten."

"Right," I acknowledge.

We catch sight of the news vans when we're halfway down our street. "Goddamn it," Pop mutters. "Here we go again. Hope this was worth it."

"What was worth it?"

He pulls around a news van, throws the gearshift into park, and yanks the key out of the ignition. "Your *choice.*"

Anger flares inside me—at both his words and how he spits them out without even looking at me. "None of this is a choice," I say, but the noise outside swallows my words as he opens the door.

The reporter gauntlet is thinner than usual, so I'm guessing most of them are at Bronwyn's. I follow Pop inside, where he immediately heads for the living room and turns on the TV. I'm supposed to do postgame stretching now, but my father hasn't bothered to remind me about my routine for a while.

Nonny's in the kitchen, making buttered toast with brown sugar on top. "How was the game, darlin'?"

"Fantastic," I say heavily, collapsing into a chair. I pick up a stray quarter and spin it into a silvery blur across the kitchen table. "I pitched great, but nobody cares."

"Now, now." She sits across from me with her toast and offers me a slice, but I push it back toward her. "Give it time. Do you remember what I told you in the hospital?" I shake my head. "Things'll get worse before they get better. Well, they surely did get worse, and now there's nowhere to go but up." She takes a bite and I keep spinning the quarter until she swallows. "You should bring that boy of yours by sometime for dinner, Cooper. It's about time we met him."

I try to picture my father making conversation with Kris over chicken casserole. "Pop would hate that."

"Well, he'll have to get used to it, won't he?"

Before I can answer her, my phone buzzes with a text from a number I don't recognize. *It's Bronwyn. I got your number from Addy. Can I call you?*

Sure.

My phone rings within seconds. "Hi, Cooper. You've heard about Nate?"

"Yeah." I'm not sure what else to say, but Bronwyn doesn't give me a chance.

"I'm trying to set up a meeting with Nate's mom and Eli Kleinfelter from Until Proven. I'm hoping he'll take Nate's case.

I was wondering, did you get a chance to ask Luis's brother about that red Camaro from the parking lot accident?"

"Luis called him last week about it. He was gonna look into it, but I haven't heard back yet."

"Would you mind checking in with him?" Bronwyn asks.

I hesitate. Even though I haven't processed everything yet, there's this little ball of relief growing inside me. Because yesterday I was the police's number one guy. And today I'm not. I'd be lying if I said it didn't feel good.

But this is Nate. Who's not a friend, exactly. Or at all, I guess. But he's not nothing.

"Yeah, okay," I tell Bronwyn.

CHAPTER TWENTY-SIX

Bronwyn
Sunday, November 4, 10:00 a.m.

We're quite the crew at the Until Proven offices Sunday morning: me, Mrs. Macauley, and my mom. Who was willing to let me go, but not unsupervised.

The small, sparsely furnished space is overflowing, with each desk holding at least two people. Everyone's either talking urgently on the phone or pounding away on a computer. Sometimes both. "Busy for a Sunday," I comment as Eli leads us into a tiny room crammed with a small table and chairs.

Eli's hair seems to have grown three inches since he was on *Mikhail Powers Investigates,* all of it upward. He runs a hand through the mad scientist curls and sends them even higher. "Is it Sunday already?"

There aren't enough chairs, so I sit on the floor. "Sorry," Eli says. "We can make this quick. First off, Mrs. Macauley, I'm sorry about your son's arrest. I understand he's been remanded to a juvenile detention center instead of an adult facility, which is good news. As I told Bronwyn, there's not much I can do given my current workload. But if you're willing to share whatever information you have, I'll do what I can to provide suggestions and maybe a referral."

Mrs. Macauley looks exhausted, but like she's made an effort to dress up a little in navy pants and a lumpy gray cardigan. My own mother is her usual effortless chic in leggings, tall boots, a cashmere sweater-coat, and a subtly patterned infinity scarf. The two of them couldn't be more different, and Mrs. Macauley tugs at the frayed hem of her sweater as though she knows it.

"Well. Here's what I've been told," she says. "The school received a call that Nate had drugs in his locker—"

"From whom?" Eli asks, scribbling on a yellow notepad.

"They wouldn't say. I think it was anonymous. But they went ahead and removed his lock Friday after school to check. They didn't find any drugs. But they did find a bag with Simon's water bottle and EpiPen. And all the EpiPens from the nurse's office that went missing the day he died." I run my fingers along the rough fiber of the rug, thinking of all the times Addy's been questioned about those pens. Cooper, too. They've been hanging over our heads for weeks. There's no way, even if Nate were actually guilty of something, that he'd be dumb enough to leave them sitting in his locker.

"Ah." Eli's voice comes out like a sigh, but his head stays bent over his legal pad.

"So the police got involved, and they got a warrant to search the house Saturday morning," Mrs. Macauley continues. "And they found a computer in Nate's closet with this . . . journal, I guess they're calling it. All those Tumblr posts that have been popping up everywhere since Simon died."

I raise my eyes and catch my mother staring at me, a kind of disturbed pity crawling across her face. I hold her gaze and shake my head. I don't believe any of it.

"Ah," Eli says again. This time he does look up, but his face remains calm and neutral. "Any fingerprints?"

"No," Mrs. Macauley says, and I exhale quietly.

"What does Nate say about all this?" Eli asks.

"That he has no idea how any of these things got into his locker or the house," Mrs. Macauley says.

"Okay," Eli says. "And Nate's locker hadn't been searched before this?"

"I don't know," Mrs. Macauley admits, and Eli looks at me.

"It was," I recall. "Nate says he was searched the first day they questioned us. His locker and his house. The police came with dogs and everything, looking for drugs. They didn't find any," I add hastily, with a sideways glance at my mother before I turn back to Eli. "But nobody found Simon's things or a computer then."

"Is your house typically locked?" Eli asks Mrs. Macauley.

"It's never locked," she replies. "I don't think the door even *has* a lock anymore."

"Huh," Eli mutters, scribbling on his pad again.

"There's something else," Mrs. Macauley says, and her voice wavers. "The district attorney wants Nate moved to a regular prison. They're saying he's too dangerous to be in a juvenile center."

A chasm cracks open in my chest as Eli sits bolt upright. It's the first time he's dropped his impartial lawyer mask and shown some emotion, and the horror on his face terrifies me. "Oh no. No, no, no. That would be a fucking disaster. Excuse my language. What's his lawyer doing to stop that?"

"We haven't met him yet." Mrs. Macauley sounds near tears. "Someone's been appointed, but they haven't been in touch."

Eli drops his pen with a frustrated grunt. "Possession of Simon's things isn't great. Not great at all. People have been convicted on less. But the way they got this evidence . . . I don't like it. Anonymous tips, things that weren't there before conveniently showing up now. In places that aren't hard to access. Combination locks are easy to pick. And if the DA's talking about sending Nate to federal prison at age seventeen . . . any lawyer worth a damn should be blocking the hell out of that." He rubs a hand across his face and scowls at me. "Damn it, Bronwyn. This is your fault."

Everything Eli's been saying has been making me more and more sick, except this. Now I'm just confused. "What did *I* do?" I protest.

"You brought this case to my attention and now I have to take it. And I *do not* have time. But whatever. That's assuming you're open to a change in counsel, Mrs. Macauley?"

Oh, thank God. The relief surging through me makes me limp and almost dizzy. Mrs. Macauley nods vigorously, and Eli sighs.

"I can help," I say eagerly. "We've been looking into—" I'm

about to tell Eli about the red Camaro, but he holds his hand out with a forbidding expression.

"Stop right there, Bronwyn. If I'm going to represent Nate, I can't speak with other represented people in this case. It could get me disbarred and put you at risk of implication. In fact, I need you and your mother to leave so I can work out some details with Mrs. Macauley."

"But . . ." I look helplessly at my mother, who's nodding and getting to her feet, securing her handbag over her shoulder with an air of finality.

"He's right, Bronwyn. You need to leave things with Mr. Kleinfelter and Mrs. Macauley now." Her expression softens as she meets Mrs. Macauley's eyes. "I wish you the best of luck with all this."

"Thank you," Mrs. Macauley says. "And thank *you*, Bronwyn."

I should feel good. Mission accomplished. But I don't. Eli doesn't know half of what we do, and now how am I supposed to tell him?

Addy
Monday, November 5, 6:30 p.m.

By Monday things have gotten oddly normal. Well, *new*-normal. Newmal? Anyway, my point is, when I sit down to dinner with my mother and Ashton, the driveway is free of news vans and my lawyer doesn't call once.

Mom deposits a couple of heated-up Trader Joe's dinners in

front of Ashton and me, then sits between us with a cloudy glass of yellow-brown beverage. "I'm not eating," she announces, even though we didn't ask. "I'm cleansing."

Ashton wrinkles her nose. "Ugh, Mom. That's not that lemonade with the maple syrup and cayenne pepper, is it? That's so gross."

"You can't argue with results," Mom says, taking a long sip. She presses a napkin to her overly plumped lips, and I take in her stiff blond hair, red lacquered nails, and the skintight dress she put on for a typical Monday. Is that me in twenty-five years? The thought makes me even less hungry than I was a minute ago.

Ashton turns on the news and we watch coverage of Nate's arrest, including an interview with Eli Kleinfelter. "Handsome boy," Mom notes when Nate's mug shot appears on the screen. "Shame he turned out to be a murderer."

I push my half-eaten tray away. There's no point in suggesting that the police might be wrong. Mom's just happy the lawyer bills are almost over.

The doorbell rings, and Ashton folds her napkin next to her plate. "I'll see who it is." She calls my name a few seconds later, and my mother shoots me a surprised look. Nobody's come to the door in weeks unless they wanted to interview me, and my sister always chases those away. Mom follows me into the living room as Ashton pulls the door open to let TJ enter.

"Hey." I blink at him in surprise. "What are you doing here?"

"Your history book ended up in my backpack after earth

science. This is yours, right?" TJ hands a thick gray textbook to me. We've been lab partners since the first rock sorting, and it's usually a bright spot in my day.

"Oh. Yeah, thanks. But you could've given it to me tomorrow."

"We have that quiz, though."

"Right." No point in telling him I've pretty much given up on academics for the semester.

Mom's staring at TJ like he's dessert, and he meets her eyes with a polite smile. "Hi, I'm TJ Forrester. I go to school with Addy." She simpers and shakes his hand, taking in his dimples and football jacket. He's almost a dark-skinned, crooked-nosed version of Jake. His name doesn't register with her, but Ashton exhales a soft breath behind me.

I've got to get TJ out of here before Mom puts two and two together. "Well, thanks again. I'd better go study. See you tomorrow."

"Do you want to study together for a while?" TJ asks.

I hesitate. I like TJ, I really do. But spending time together outside school isn't a step I'm ready to take. "I can't, because of . . . other stuff." I practically shove him out the door, and when I turn back inside, Mom's face is a mixture of pity and irritation.

"What's wrong with you?" she hisses. "Being so rude to a handsome boy like that! It's not as if they're beating down your door anymore." Her eyes flicker over my purple-streaked hair. "Given the way you've let yourself go, you should consider yourself lucky he wanted to spend time with you at all."

"God, Mom—" Ashton says, but I interrupt her.

"I'm not looking for another boyfriend, Mom."

She stares at me like I've sprouted wings and started speaking Chinese. "Why on earth not? It's been ages since you and Jake broke up."

"I spent more than three years with Jake. I could use some downtime." I say it mostly to argue, but as soon as the words come out of my mouth I know they're true. My mother started dating when she was fourteen, like me, and hasn't stopped since. Even when it means going out with an immature man-boy who's too cowardly to bring her home to his parents.

I don't want to be that afraid to be alone.

"Don't be ridiculous. That's the last thing you need. Have a few dates with a boy like TJ, even if you're not interested, and other boys at school might see you as desirable again. You don't want to end up on a shelf, Adelaide. Some sad single girl who spends all her time with that odd group of friends you've got now. If you'd wash that nonsense out of your hair, grow it a little, and wear makeup again, you could do *much* better than that."

"I don't need a guy to be happy, Mom."

"Of course you do," she snaps. "You've been miserable for the past month."

"Because I was being investigated for murder," I remind her. "Not because I'm *single*." It's not one hundred percent true, since the main source of my misery was Jake. But it was him I wanted to be with. Not just anyone.

My mother shakes her head. "You keep telling yourself that, Adelaide, but you're hardly college material. Now's the time to find a decent boy with a good future who's willing to take care of y—"

"Mom, she's *seventeen*," Ashton interrupts. "You can put this script on hold for at least ten years. Or forever. It's not like the whole relationship thing has worked out well for either of us."

"Speak for yourself, Ashton," Mom says haughtily. "Justin and I are ecstatically happy."

Ashton opens her mouth to say more, but my phone rings and I hold up my finger as Bronwyn's name appears. "Hey. What's up?" I say.

"Hi." Her voice sounds thick, as if she's been crying. "So, I was thinking about Nate's case and I wanted your help with something. Could you stop by for a little while tonight? I'm going to ask Cooper, too."

It beats being insulted by my mother. "Sure. Text me your address."

I scrape my half-eaten dinner into the garbage disposal and grab my helmet, calling good-bye to Ashton as I head out the door. It's a perfect late-fall night, and the trees lining our street sway in a light breeze as I pedal past. Bronwyn's house is only about a mile from mine, but it's a completely different neighborhood; there's nothing cookie-cutter about these houses. I coast into the driveway of her huge gray Victorian, eyeing the vibrant flowers and wraparound porch with a stab of envy. It's gorgeous, but it's not just that. It looks like a *home*.

When I ring the doorbell Bronwyn answers with a muted "Hey." Her eyes droop with exhaustion and her hair's come half out of its ponytail. It occurs to me that we've all had our turn getting crushed by this experience: me when Jake dumped me and all my friends turned against me; Cooper when he was outed, mocked, and pursued by the police; and now Bronwyn when the guy she loves is in jail for murder.

Not that she's ever said she loves Nate. It's pretty obvious, though.

"Come on in," Bronwyn says, pulling the door open. "Cooper's here. We're downstairs."

She leads me into a spacious room with overstuffed sofas and a large flat-screen television mounted on the wall. Cooper is already sprawled in an armchair, and Maeve's sitting cross-legged in another with her laptop on the armrest between them. Bronwyn and I sink into a sofa and I ask, "How's Nate? Have you seen him?"

Wrong question, I guess. Bronwyn swallows once, then twice, trying to keep herself together. "He doesn't want me to. His mom says he's . . . okay. Considering. Juvenile detention's horrible but at least it's not prison." Yet. We all know Eli's locked in a battle to keep Nate where he is. "Anyway. Thanks for coming. I guess I just . . ." Her eyes fill with tears, and Cooper and I exchange a worried glance before she blinks them back. "You know, I was so glad when we all finally got together and started talking about this. I felt a lot less alone. And now I guess I'm asking for your help. I want to finish what we started. Keep putting our heads together to make sense of this."

"I haven't heard anything from Luis about the car," Cooper says.

"I wasn't actually thinking about that right now, but please keep checking, okay? I was more hoping we could all take another look at those Tumblr posts. I have to admit, I started ignoring them because they were freaking me out. But now the police say Nate wrote them, and I thought we should read through and note anything that's surprising, or doesn't fit with how we remember things, or just strikes us as weird." She pulls her ponytail over her shoulder as she opens her laptop. "Do you mind?"

"Now?" Cooper asks.

Maeve angles her screen so Cooper can see it. "No time like the present."

Bronwyn's next to me, and we start from the bottom of the Tumblr posts. *I got the idea for killing Simon while watching Dateline.* Nate's never struck me as a newsmagazine show fan, but I doubt that's the kind of insight Bronwyn's looking for. We sit in silence for a while, reading. Boredom creeps in and I realize I've been skimming, so I go back and try to read more thoroughly. *Blah blah, I'm so smart, nobody knows it's me, the police don't have a clue.* And so on.

"Hang on. This didn't happen." Cooper's reading more carefully than I am. "Have you gotten to this yet? The one dated October twentieth, about Detective Wheeler and the doughnuts?"

I raise my head like a cat pricking up its ears at a distant sound. "Um," Bronwyn says, her eyes scanning the screen. "Oh yeah. That's a weird little aside, isn't it? We were never all at the police station at once. Well, maybe right after the funeral, but we didn't see or talk to each other. Usually when whoever's writing these throws in specific details, they're accurate."

"What are you guys looking at?" I ask.

Bronwyn increases the page size and points. "There. Second to last line."

This investigation is turning into such a cliché, the four of us even caught Detective Wheeler eating a pile of doughnuts in the interrogation room.

A cold wave washes over me as the words enter my brain and nest there, pushing everything else out. Cooper and Bronwyn are right: that didn't happen.

But I told Jake it did.

CHAPTER TWENTY-SEVEN

Bronwyn
Tuesday, November 6, 7:30 p.m.

I'm not supposed to talk to Eli. So last night I texted Mrs. Macauley a link to the Tumblr post that Addy, Cooper, and I read together, and told her what was weird about it. Then I waited. A frustratingly long time, until I got a text back from her after school.

Thank you. I've informed Eli, but he asks that you don't involve yourself further.

That's all. I wanted to throw my phone across the room. I'll admit it; I spent most of last night fantasizing that Addy's bombshell would get Nate out of jail immediately. While I realize that was ridiculously naïve, I still think it deserves more than a brush-off.

Even though I can't wrap my brain around what it means. Because—*Jake Riordan?* If I had to pick the most random possible person to be involved in this, it still wouldn't have been him. And involved how, exactly? Did he write the whole Tumblr, or just that one post? Did he frame Nate? Did he kill Simon?

Cooper shot that down almost immediately. "He couldn't have," he said Monday night. "Jake was at football practice when Addy called him."

"He might have left," I insisted. So Cooper called Luis to confirm. "Luis says no," Cooper reported. "Jake was leading passing drills the whole time."

I'm not sure we can hinge an entire investigation on Luis's memory, though. That boy's killed a lot of brain cells over the years. He didn't even question why Cooper was asking.

Now I'm in my room with Maeve and Addy, putting dozens of colored Post-its on the wall that summarize everything we know. It's very *Law & Order*, except none of it makes sense.

Someone planted phones in our backpacks
Simon was poisoned during detention
Bronwyn, Nate, Cooper, Addy & Mr. Avery were in the room
The car accident distracted us
Jake wrote at least one Tumblr post
Jake and Simon were friends once
Leah hates Simon
Aiden Wu hates Simon
Simon had a thing for Keely
Simon had a violence-loving alter ego online
Simon was depressed
Janae seems depressed
Janae & Simon stopped being friends?

My mother's voice floats up the stairs. "Bronwyn, Cooper's here."

Mom already loves Cooper. So much that she doesn't protest all of us getting together again, even though Robin's legal advice is to still keep our distance from one another.

"Hey," Cooper says, not the least bit breathless from bounding up our stairs. "I can't stay long, but I got some good news. Luis thinks he might've found that car. His brother called a buddy at a repair place in Eastland and they had a red Camaro come through with fender damage a few days after Simon died. I got you the license plate and a phone number." He searches through his backpack and hands me a torn envelope with numbers scrawled across the back. "I guess you can pass that along to Eli, huh? Maybe there's something there."

"Thanks," I say gratefully.

Cooper runs his eyes over my wall. "This helping?"

Addy sits back on her haunches with a frustrated noise. "Not really. It's just a collection of random facts. Simon this, Janae that, Leah this, Jake that . . ."

Cooper frowns and crosses his arms, leaning forward for a better look at the wall. "I don't get the Jake part, at all. I can't believe he'd actually sit around and write that damn Tumblr. I think he just . . . blabbed to the wrong person or something." He taps a finger on the Post-it with all our names on it. "And I keep wondering: Why *us*? Why'd we get dragged into this? Are we just collateral damage, like Nate said? Or is there some specific reason we're part of this?"

I tilt my head at him, curious. "Like what?"

Cooper shrugs. "I don't know. Take you and Leah. It's a

small thing, but what if something like that started a domino effect? Or me and . . ." He scans the wall and settles on a Post-it. "Aiden Wu, maybe. He got outed for cross-dressing, and I was hiding the fact I'm gay."

"But that entry was changed," I remind him.

"I know. And that's weird too, isn't it? Why get rid of a perfectly good piece of gossip that's true, and replace it with one that's not? I can't shake the feeling that this is *personal*, y'know? The way that Tumblr kept everything going, egging people on about us. I wish I understood why."

Addy tugs on one of her earrings. Her hand trembles, and when she speaks, her voice does too. "Things were pretty personal between me and Jake, I guess. And maybe he was jealous of you, Cooper. But Bronwyn and Nate . . . why would he involve them?"

Collateral damage. We've all been affected, but Nate's gotten the worst of it by far. If Jake's to blame, that doesn't make sense. But then again, none of this does.

"I should go," Cooper says. "I'm meeting Luis."

I manage a smile. "Not Kris?"

Cooper's return smile is a little strained. "We're still figuring things out. Anyway, let me know if the car stuff is helpful."

He leaves and Maeve gets up, crossing over to the spot near my bed that Cooper just vacated. She shuffles Post-its on the wall, putting four of them into a square:

Jake wrote at least one Tumblr post
Leah hates Simon
Aiden Wu hates Simon
Janae seems depressed

"These are the most connected people. They've either got reason to hate Simon, or we already know they're involved in some way. Some are pretty unlikely"—she taps on Aiden's name—"and some have big red flags against them." She points to Jake and Janae. "But nothing's clear-cut. What are we missing?"

We all stare at the Post-its in silence.

You can learn a lot about a person when you have his license plate and phone number. His address, for example. And his name, and where he goes to school. So if you wanted to, you could hang out in the parking lot of his school before it started and wait for his red Camaro to arrive. Theoretically.

Or actually.

I meant to turn the numbers Cooper gave me over to Mrs. Macauley so she could pass them along to Eli. But I kept thinking about her terse text: *I've informed Eli, but he asks that you don't involve yourself further.* Would Eli even take me seriously? He's the one who first mentioned the car accident as suspicious, but he's spending all his time trying to keep Nate in the juvenile detention center. He might consider this nothing but a pesky distraction.

Anyway, I'm just scoping things out. That's what I tell myself as I enter Eastland High's parking lot. They start classes forty minutes before we do, so I can still get back to Bayview in plenty of time for the first bell. It's stuffy in the car, and I lower both front-seat windows as I pull into an empty spot and turn the car off.

Thing is, I need to be doing stuff. If I don't, I think about Nate too much. About where he is, what he's going through, and the fact that he won't talk to me. I mean, I understand he has limited communication options. Obviously. But they're not nonexistent. I asked Mrs. Macauley if I could visit, and she told me Nate didn't want me there.

Which stings. She thinks he wants to protect me, but I'm not so sure. He's pretty used to people giving up on him, and maybe he's decided to do it to me first.

A flash of red catches my eye, and an ancient Camaro with a shiny fender parks a few spaces away from me. A short dark-haired boy gets out and hauls a backpack from the passenger seat, looping one strap over his shoulder.

I don't intend to say anything. But he glances my way as he walks by my window and before I can stop myself I blurt out, "Hey."

He pauses, curious brown eyes meeting mine. "Hey. I know you. You're the girl from the Bayview investigation. Bronte, right?"

"Bronwyn." Since I've already blown my cover, might as well go all in.

"What are you doing here?" He's dressed like he's waiting for a '90s grunge comeback, in a flannel shirt over a Pearl Jam T-shirt.

"Um . . ." My eyes skitter to his car. I should just ask, right? That's what I came for. But now that I'm actually talking to this boy the whole thing seems ridiculous. What am I supposed to say? *Hey, what's the deal with your oddly timed car accident at a school you don't go to?* "Waiting for somebody."

He wrinkles his brow at me. "You know people here?"

"Yeah." *Sort of. I know about your recent car repair, anyway.*

"Everybody's been talking about you guys. Weird case, huh? The kid who died—he was kind of weird, right? I mean, who even has an app like that? And all that stuff they said on *Mikhail Powers*. Random."

He seems . . . nervous. My brain chants *ask ask ask* but my mouth won't obey.

"Well. See ya." He starts to move past my car.

"Wait!" My voice unsticks and he pauses. "Can I talk to you for a second?"

"We just *were* talking."

"Right, but . . . I have an actual question for you. The thing is, when I said I was waiting for somebody? I meant you."

He's definitely nervous. "Why would you be waiting for me? You don't even know me."

"Because of your car," I say. "I saw you get into an accident in our parking lot that day. The day Simon died."

He pales and blinks at me. "How do you—why do you think that was me?"

"I saw your license plate," I lie. No need to sell out Luis's brother. "The thing is . . . the timing was weird, you know? And now someone's been arrested for something I'm sure he didn't do and I wondered . . . did you happen to see anything or anyone strange that day? It would help—" My voice catches and tears prick my eyes. I blink them back and try to focus. "Anything you could tell me would help."

He hesitates and steps back, looking toward the stream of kids funneling into the school. I wait for him to back away and join them, but instead he crosses to the other side of my car,

306

opens the passenger door, and climbs inside. I press a button to raise the windows and turn to face him.

"So." He runs a hand through his hair. "This is weird. I'm Sam, by the way. Sam Barron."

"Bronwyn Rojas. But I guess you know that already."

"Yeah. I've been watching the news and wondering if I should say something. But I didn't know if it meant anything. I still don't." He gives me a quick sideways glance, as though checking for signs of alarm. "We didn't do anything wrong. Like, illegal. As far as I know."

My spine tingles as I sit up straighter. "Who's 'we'?"

"Me and my buddy. We had the accident on purpose. A guy paid us a thousand bucks each to do it. Said it was a prank. I mean, wouldn't you? The fender barely cost five hundred to fix. The rest was pure profit."

"Someone . . ." It's warm in the car with the windows up, and my hands gripping the steering wheel are slick with sweat. I should turn the air conditioning on, but I can't move. "Who? Do you know his name?"

"I didn't, but—"

"Did he have brown hair and blue eyes?" I blurt out.

"Yeah."

Jake. He must've gotten away from Luis at some point after all. "Was he— Wait, I have a picture in here somewhere," I say, fumbling through my backpack for my phone. I'm sure I took a picture of the homecoming court in September.

"I don't need a picture," Sam says. "I know who he is."

"Really? Like, you know his name?" My heart's beating so

fast I can see my chest moving. "Are you sure he gave you a real name?"

"He didn't give me any name. I figured it out later when I saw the news."

I remember those first few stories, with Jake's class picture next to Addy's. A lot of people thought it wasn't fair to show him, but I'm glad they did. I have the homecoming picture pulled up now, and I hand it to Sam. "Him, right? Jake Riordan?"

He blinks at my phone, shakes his head, and hands it back. "No. That's not him. It was someone a lot more . . . closely involved with the whole thing."

My heart's about to explode. If it wasn't Jake, there's only one other boy with dark hair and blue eyes involved in the investigation. *Closely* involved, no less. And that's Nate.

No. No. Please, God, no.

"Who?" My voice isn't even a whisper.

Sam blows out a sigh and leans against the headrest. He's quiet for the longest seconds of my life until he says, "It was Simon Kelleher."

CHAPTER TWENTY-EIGHT

Cooper
Wednesday, November 7, 7:40 p.m.

These murder club meetings are becoming a regular thing. We need a new name, though.

This time we're at a coffee shop in downtown San Diego, crammed into a back table because our numbers keep expanding. Kris came with me, and Ashton with Addy. Bronwyn's got all her Post-it notes on a bunch of manila folders, including the newest one: *Simon paid two kids to stage a car accident.* She says Sam Barron promised to call Eli and let him know. How that'll help Nate, I have no idea.

"Why'd you pick this place, Bronwyn?" Addy asks. "Kind of out of the way."

Bronwyn clears her throat and makes a big production of rearranging her Post-it notes. "No reason. So, anyway." She

309

shoots a businesslike look around the table. "Thanks for coming. Maeve and I keep going over this stuff and it never makes any sense. We thought a meeting of the minds might help."

Maeve and Ashton return from the counter, balancing our orders on a couple of recyclable trays. They hand drinks around, and I watch Kris methodically open five packets of sugar and dump them into his latte. "What?" he asks, catching my expression. He's in a green polo shirt that brings out his eyes, and he looks really, really good. That still seems like the kind of thing I'm not supposed to notice.

"You like sugar, huh?" It's a dumb thing to say. What I mean is, *I have no idea how you take your coffee because this is the first time we've been out in public together.* Kris presses his lips together, which shouldn't be attractive but is. I feel awkward and jittery and accidentally bump his knee under the table.

"Nothing wrong with that," Addy says, tipping her cup against Kris's. The liquid inside hers is so pale it barely resembles coffee.

Kris and I have been spending more time together, but it doesn't feel natural yet. Maybe I'd gotten used to the sneaking around, or maybe I haven't come to terms with the fact that I'm dating a guy. I found myself keeping my distance from Kris when we walked from my car to the coffee shop, because I didn't want people guessing what we are to each other.

I hate that part of me. But it's there.

Bronwyn has some kind of steaming tea that looks too hot to drink. She pushes it aside and props one of the manila folders against the wall. "Here's all the stuff we know about Simon: He was going to post rumors about us. He paid two kids to stage a car accident. He was depressed. He had a creepy online persona.

He and Janae seemed on the outs. He had a thing for Keely. He used to be friends with Jake. Am I missing anything?"

"He deleted my original About That entry," I say.

"Not necessarily," Bronwyn corrects. "Your entry was deleted. We don't know by whom."

Fair enough, I guess.

"And here's what we know about Jake," Bronwyn continues. "He wrote at least one of the Tumblr posts, or helped somebody else write it. He wasn't in the school building when Simon died, according to Luis. He—"

"Is a complete control freak," Ashton interrupts. Addy opens her mouth in protest, but Ashton cuts her off. "He *is*, Addy. He ran every part of your life for three years. Then as soon as you did something he didn't like, he blew up." Bronwyn scribbles *Jake is a control freak* on a Post-it with an apologetic glance at Addy.

"It's a data point," Bronwyn says. "Now, what if—"

The front door bangs and she goes bright red. "What a coincidence." I follow her gaze and see a young guy with wild hair and a scruffy beard enter the coffee shop. He looks familiar, but I can't place him. He spots Bronwyn with an exasperated expression that turns alarmed when he takes in Addy and me.

He holds a hand in front of his face. "I don't see you. Any of you." Then he catches sight of Ashton and does a classic double take, almost tripping over his feet. "Oh, hi. You must be Addy's sister."

Ashton blinks, confused, looking between him and Bronwyn. "Do I know you?"

"This is Eli Kleinfelter," Bronwyn says. "He's with Until Proven. Their offices are upstairs. He's, um, Nate's lawyer."

"Who cannot talk to you," Eli says, like he just remembered. He gives Ashton a lingering look, but turns away and heads for the counter. Ashton shrugs and blows on her coffee. I'm sure she's used to having that effect on guys.

Addy's eyes are round as she watches Eli's retreating back. "God, Bronwyn. I can't believe you stalked Nate's lawyer."

Bronwyn looks almost as embarrassed as she should be, taking the envelope I'd given her out of her backpack. "I wanted to see if Sam Barron ever got in touch, and pass along his information if he hadn't. I thought if I ran into Eli casually, he might talk to me. Guess not." She darts a hopeful look at Ashton. "I bet he'd talk to *you,* though."

Addy locks her hands on her hips and juts her chin in outrage. "You can't pimp out my sister!"

Ashton smiles wryly and holds out her hand for the envelope. "As long as it's for a good cause. What am I supposed to say?"

"Tell him he was right—that the car accident at Bayview the day Simon died was staged. The envelope has contact information for the boy Simon paid to do it."

Ashton heads for the counter, and we all sip our drinks in silence. When she returns a minute later, the envelope's still in her hand. "Sam called him," she confirms. "He said he's looking into it, he appreciates the information, and you should mind your fucking business. That's a direct quote."

Bronwyn looks relieved and not at all insulted. "Thank you. That's good news. So, where were we?"

"Simon and Jake," Maeve says, propping her chin in one hand as she gazes at the two manila folders. "They're connected. But how?"

"Excuse me," Kris says mildly, and everyone looks at him like they'd forgotten he was at the table. Which they probably had. He's been quiet since we got here.

Maeve tries to make up for it by giving him an encouraging smile. "Yeah?"

"I wonder," Kris says. His English is unaccented and almost perfect, with just a little formality that hints he's from someplace else. "There has always been so much focus on who was in the room. That's why the police originally targeted the four of you. Because it would be almost impossible for anyone who wasn't in the room to kill Simon. Right?"

"Right," I say.

"So." Kris removes two Post-its from one of the folders. "If the killer wasn't Cooper, or Bronwyn, or Addy, or Nate—and nobody thinks the teacher who was there could have had anything to do with it—who does that leave?" He layers one Post-it on top of the other on the wall next to the table, then sits back and looks at us with polite attentiveness.

Simon was poisoned during detention
Simon was depressed

We're all silent for a long minute, until Bronwyn exhales a small gasp. "I'm the omniscient narrator," she says.

"What?" Addy asks.

"That's what Simon said before he died. I said there wasn't any such thing in teen movies, and he said there was in life. Then he drained his drink in one gulp." Bronwyn turns and calls *"Eli!"* but the door's already closing behind Nate's lawyer.

"So you're saying . . ." Ashton stares around the table until her eyes land on Kris. "You think Simon committed *suicide*?" Kris nods. "But why? Why like *that*?"

"Let's go back to what we know," Bronwyn says. Her voice is almost clinical, but her face is flushed brick red. "Simon was one of those people who thought he should be at the center of everything, but wasn't. And he was obsessed with the idea of making some kind of huge, violent splash at school. He fantasized about it all the time on those 4chan threads. What if this was his version of a school shooting? Kill himself and take a bunch of students down with him, but in an unexpected way. Like framing them for murder." She turns to her sister. "What did Simon say on 4chan, Maeve? *Do something original. Surprise me when you take out a bunch of lemming assholes.*"

Maeve nods. "Exact quote, I think."

I think about how Simon died—choking, panicked, trying to catch his breath. If he really did it to himself, I wish more than ever we'd found his damn EpiPen. "I think he regretted it at the end," I say, the weight of the words settling heavy on my heart. "He looked like he wanted help. If he could've gotten medication in time, maybe a close call like that would've jolted him into being a different kind of guy."

Kris's hand squeezes mine under the table. Bronwyn and Addy both look like they're back in the room where Simon died, horrified and stunned. They know I'm right. Silence descends and I think we might be done until Maeve looks over at the Post-it wall and sucks in her cheeks.

"But how does Jake fit in?" she asks.

Kris hesitates and clears his throat, like he's waiting for

314

permission to speak. When nobody protests he says, "If Jake isn't Simon's killer, he must be his accomplice. Someone had to keep things going after Simon died."

He meets Bronwyn's eyes, and some kind of understanding passes between them. They're the brains of this operation. The rest of us are just trying to keep up. Kris's hand pulled away from mine while he was talking, and I take it back.

"Simon found out about Addy and TJ," Bronwyn says. "Maybe that's how he approached Jake in the first place to get his help. Jake would've wanted revenge, because he—"

A chair scrapes noisily beside me as Addy pushes herself away from the table. "Stop," she says in a choked voice, her purple-streaked hair falling into her eyes. "Jake wouldn't . . . He couldn't . . ."

"I think we've had enough for one night," Ashton says firmly, getting to her feet. "You guys keep going, but we need to get home."

"Sorry, Addy," Bronwyn says with a chagrined expression. "I got carried away."

Addy waves a hand. "It's fine," she says unsteadily. "I just . . . can't right now." Ashton links arms with her until they get to the door; then she pulls it open and lets Addy slip through ahead of her.

Maeve watches them, her chin in her hands. "She has a point. The whole thing sounds impossible, doesn't it? And even if we're right, we can't prove anything." She looks hopefully at Kris, as though she's willing him to work more Post-it magic.

Kris shrugs and taps the colored square closest to him. "Perhaps there's one person remaining who knows something useful."

Bronwyn and Maeve leave around nine, and Kris and I don't stay much longer. We gather up the table debris that's left and deposit it in the trash can next to the exit. We're both quiet, coming off one of the weirdest dates in history.

"Well," Kris says, pushing through the door and pausing on the sidewalk to wait for me. "That was interesting." Before he can say anything else I grab him and press him against the coffee shop wall, my fingers digging into his hair and my tongue sliding between his teeth in a deep, wanting kiss. He makes a sound like a surprised growl and pulls me hard against his chest. When another couple exits through the door and we break apart, he looks dazed.

He straightens his shirt and runs a hand over his hair. "Thought you'd forgotten how to do that."

"I'm sorry." My voice thickens with the need to kiss him again. "It's not that I didn't want to. It's just—"

"I know." Kris laces his fingers in mine and holds our hands up like a question. "Yes?"

"Yes," I say, and we start down the sidewalk together.

Nate
Wednesday, November 7, 11:30 p.m.

So here's how you deal with being locked up.

You keep your mouth shut. Don't talk about your life or why you're there. Nobody cares unless they want to use it against you.

You don't take shit from anyone. Ever. Juvenile detention's not *Oz*, but people will still fuck with you if they think you're weak.

You make friends. I use the term loosely. You identify the least shitty people you can find and associate with them. Moving around in a pack is useful.

You don't break rules, but you look the other way when someone else does.

You work out and watch television. A lot.

You stay under the guards' radar as much as possible. Including the overly friendly woman who keeps offering to let you make calls from her office.

You don't complain about how slowly time passes. When you've been arrested for a capital offense and you're four months away from your eighteenth birthday, days that crawl by are your friends.

You come up with new ways to answer your lawyer's endless questions. *Yeah, I leave my locker open sometimes. No, Simon's never been to my house. Yeah, we saw each other outside of school sometimes. The last time? Probably when I was selling him weed. Sorry, we're not supposed to talk about that, are we?*

You don't think about what's outside. Or who. Especially if she's better off forgetting you exist.

CHAPTER TWENTY-NINE

Addy
Thursday, November 8, 7:00 p.m.

I keep reading through the About This Tumblr as if it's going to change. But it never does. Ashton's words loop through my head: *Jake's a complete control freak.* She's not wrong. But does that mean the rest of it has to be right? Maybe Jake told somebody else what I said, and they wrote it. Or maybe it's all just a coincidence.

Except. A memory surfaces from the morning of Simon's death, so seemingly insignificant that it hadn't crossed my mind till now: Jake pulling my backpack off my shoulder with an easy grin as we walked down the hallway together. *That's too heavy for you, baby. I've got it.* He'd never done that before, but I didn't question him. Why would I?

And a phone that wasn't mine got pulled from my backpack a few hours later.

I'm not sure what's worse—that Jake might be part of something so awful, that I drove him to it, or that he's been putting on an act for weeks.

"His choice, Addy," Ashton reminds me. "Plenty of people get cheated on and don't lose their minds. Take me, for example. I threw a vase at Charlie's head and moved on. That's a normal reaction. Whatever's going on here isn't your fault."

That might be true. But it doesn't *feel* true.

So I'm supposed to talk to Janae, who hasn't been in school all week. I tried texting her a few times after school and again after dinner, but she never responded. Finally, I decided to find her address in the school directory and just show up. When I told Bronwyn she offered to come along, but I thought it'd go better with only me. Janae never warmed up to Bronwyn all that much.

Cooper insists on driving me even though I tell him he'll need to wait in the car. There's no way Janae'll open up about anything if he's around. "That's fine," he says as he pulls across the street from Janae's faux-Tudor house. "Text me if things turn weird."

"Will do," I say, giving him a salute as I close the door and cross the street. There aren't any cars in Janae's driveway, but lights are burning throughout the house. I ring the doorbell four times with no answer, glancing back at Cooper with a shrug after the last one. I'm about to give up when the door cracks and one of Janae's black-rimmed eyes stares out at me. "What are you doing here?" she asks.

"Checking on you. You haven't been around and you're not answering my texts. Are you all right?"

"Fine." Janae tries to close the door, but I stick my foot in it to stop her.

"Can I come in?" I ask.

She hesitates but releases the door and steps back, allowing me to push it forward and enter. When I get a good look at her, I almost gasp. She's thinner than ever, and angry red hives cover her face and neck. She scratches at them self-consciously. "What? I'm not feeling well. Obviously."

I peer down the hallway. "Anyone else home?"

"No. My parents are out to dinner. Look, um, no offense, but do you have some reason for being here?"

Bronwyn coached me on what to say. I'm supposed to start with small, subtle questions about where Janae's been all week and how she's feeling. To follow up on the thread of Simon's depression and encourage her to tell me more. As a last resort, I can maybe talk about what Nate's facing as the DA's office tries to send him to an honest-to-God prison.

I don't do any of that. Instead I step forward and hug her, cradling her scrawny body as though she's a little kid who needs comforting. She feels like one, all weightless bones and fragile limbs. She stiffens, then slumps against me and starts to cry.

"Oh my God," she says in a thick, raspy voice. "It's all fucked up. Everything's so massively fucked up."

"Come on." I lead her to the living room sofa, where we sit and she cries some more. Her head digs awkwardly into my shoulder while I pat her hair. It's stiff with product, her mouse-brown roots blending into shiny blue-black dye.

"Simon did this to himself, didn't he?" I ask carefully. She pulls away and buries her head in her hands, rocking back and forth.

"How did you know?" she chokes out.

God. It's true. I didn't fully believe it till now.

I'm not supposed to tell her everything. I'm actually not supposed to tell her *anything,* but I do. I can't think how else to have this conversation. When I finish she rises and goes upstairs without a word. I wait for a couple of minutes, curling one hand on my lap and using the other to tug at my earring. Is she calling somebody? Getting a gun to blow my head off? Slitting her wrists to join Simon?

Just when I think I might have to go after her, Janae thuds down the stairs holding a thin sheaf of papers she thrusts toward me. "Simon's manifesto," she says with a sour twist of her mouth. "It's supposed to be sent to the police a year from now, after all your lives are completely screwed. So everyone would know he pulled it off."

The papers tremble in my hand as I read:

> *Here's the first thing you need to know: I hate my life and everything in it.*
>
> *So I decided to get the hell out. But not go quietly.*
>
> *I thought a lot about how to do this. I could buy a gun, like pretty much any asshole in America. Bar the doors one morning and take out as many Bayview lemmings as I have bullets for before turning the last one on myself.*

And I'd have a lot of bullets.

But that's been done to death. It doesn't have the same impact anymore.

I want to be more creative. More unique. I want my suicide to be talked about for years. I want imposters to try to imitate me. And fail, because the planning this takes is beyond your average depressed loser with a death wish.

You've been watching it unfold for a year now. If it's gone the way I hope, you have no clue what actually happened.

I look up from the papers. "Why?" I ask, bile rising in my throat. "How did Simon get to this point?"

"He'd been depressed for a while," Janae says, kneading the fabric of her black skirt between her hands. The stacks of studded bracelets she wears on both arms rattle with the movement. "Simon always felt like he should get a lot more respect and attention than he did, you know? But he got really bitter about it this year. He started spending all his time online with a bunch of creepers, fantasizing about getting revenge on everyone who made him miserable. It got to the point where I don't think he even knew what was real anymore. Whenever something bad happened, he blew it way out of proportion."

Words are tumbling out of her now. "He started talking about killing himself and taking people with him, but, like, *creatively.* He got obsessed with the idea of using the app to frame everyone he hated. He knew Bronwyn cheated and it pissed him off. She practically had valedictorian sewn up anyway, but

322

she made it impossible for him to catch up. He thought she'd screwed him out of going to the Model UN finals too. And he couldn't stand Nate because of what happened with Keely. Simon had thought he had a shot with her, and then Nate stole her away without even trying or actually giving a fuck."

My heart contracts. God, poor Nate. What a stupid, pointless reason to end up in jail. "What about Cooper? Did Simon involve him because of Keely too?"

Janae snorts out a bitter laugh. "Mr. Nice Guy? Cooper got Simon blacklisted from Vanessa's after-prom party. Even though Simon was on the court and everything. He was *so* humiliated that he was not only not invited, but actually not even allowed to go. *Everyone* was going to be there, he said."

"*Cooper* did?" I blink. That's news to me. Cooper hadn't mentioned it, and I never even noticed Simon wasn't there.

Which I guess was part of the problem.

Janae bobs her head. "Yeah. I don't know why, but he did. So those three were Simon's targets, and he had his gossip all lined up. I still thought it was just talk, though. A way to blow off steam. Maybe it would've been, if I could have convinced him to get offline and stop obsessing. But then Jake found out something Simon didn't want anyone to know and it just—that was the final straw."

Oh no. Every second that went by without a mention of Jake's name made me hope he wasn't involved, after all. "What do you mean?" I pull at my earring so hard, I'm in danger of tearing a lobe.

Janae picks at her chipped nail polish, sending gray flakes across her skirt. "Simon rigged the votes so he'd be on the junior prom court." My hand freezes at my ear and my eyes go wide. Janae huffs out a humorless little laugh. "I know. Stupid, right? Simon was weird like that. He'd make fun of people for being lemmings, but he still wanted the same things they did. And he wanted them to look up to him. So he did it, and he was gloating about it at the pool last summer, saying how easy it was and how he'd mess with homecoming too. And Jake overheard us."

I can immediately picture Jake's reaction, so Janae's next words don't surprise me. "He laughed his head off. Simon freaked. He couldn't stand the thought of Jake telling people, and everyone at school knowing he'd done something so pathetic. Like, he'd spent years spilling everybody's secrets, and now he was gonna get humiliated with one of his own." She cringes. "Can you imagine? The creator of About That getting exposed as such a wannabe? It sent him over the edge."

"The edge?" I echo.

"Yeah. Simon decided to stop talking about his crazy plan and actually *do* it. He already knew about you and TJ, but he'd been sitting on that till school started again. So he used it to shut Jake up and bring him in. Because Simon needed somebody to keep things going after he died, and I wouldn't do it."

I don't know whether to believe her or not. "You wouldn't?"

"No, I wouldn't." Janae doesn't meet my eyes. "Not for *your* sake. I didn't care about any of you. For Simon's sake. But he wouldn't listen to me, and then all of a sudden he didn't need me. He knew what Jake was like, that he'd lose it when he found out about you and TJ. Simon told Jake he could plant everything on you so you'd take the fall and wind up in jail. And Jake was totally on board. He even came up with the idea of sending you to the nurse's office that day for Tylenol so you'd look more guilty."

White noise buzzes through my brain. "The perfect revenge for cheating on a perfect boyfriend." I'm not sure I've said it out loud until Janae nods.

"Right, and no one would ever guess since Simon and Jake weren't even friends. For Simon, there was the added bonus that he didn't care if Jake screwed up and got caught. He was almost hoping he would. He'd hated Jake for years."

Janae's voice rises like she's warming up for the kind of bitch session she and Simon probably used to have all the time. "The way Jake just dropped Simon freshman year. Started hanging out with Cooper like they'd always been best friends, as if Simon didn't exist anymore. Like he didn't *matter*."

Saliva swims at the back of my throat. I'm going to throw up. No, pass out. Maybe both. Either would be better than sitting here listening to this. All that time after Simon died, when Jake comforted me, made me drive to a party with TJ like nothing happened, *slept* with me—he knew. He knew I'd cheated and he was just biding his time. Waiting to punish me.

That might be the worst part. How *normal* he acted the whole time.

Somehow, I find my voice. "But he . . . But *Nate* was framed. Did Jake change his mind?"

It hurts how much I want that to be true.

Janae doesn't answer right away. The room's silent except for her ragged breathing. "No," she says finally. "The thing is . . . it all unfolded almost exactly the way Simon planned. He and Jake snuck those phones into your backpacks that morning, and Mr.

Avery found them and gave you detention, just like Simon said he would. He made it easy for the police to investigate by keeping the About That admin site wide open. He wrote an outline of the Tumblr journal, and told Jake to post updates from public computers with details about what was really happening. It was like watching some out-of-control reality TV show where you keep thinking producers are gonna step in and say, *Enough*. But nobody did. It made me sick. I kept telling Jake he needed to stop before it went too far."

My gut twists. "And Jake wouldn't?"

Janae sniffs. "No. He got really into the whole thing once Simon died. Total power trip watching you guys get hauled into the station, seeing the school scrambling and everybody freaking out about the Tumblr. He liked having that control." She stops for a second and glances at me. "I guess you'd know about that."

Yeah, I guess I would. But I could do without the reminder right now. "*You* could've stopped it, Janae," I say, my voice rising as anger starts to overtake my shock. "You should've told somebody what was going on."

"I *couldn't,*" Janae says, hunching her shoulders. "One time when we were meeting with Simon, Jake recorded us on his phone. I was trying to talk sense into Simon, but the way Jake edited things made it sound like it was practically my idea. He said he'd give the recording to the police and pin everything on me if I didn't help."

She takes a deep, shuddering breath. "I was supposed to plant all the evidence on you. You remember that day I came to your house? I had the computer with me then. But I couldn't do it. After that, Jake kept harassing me and I panicked. I just dumped everything on Nate." She chokes out a sob. "It was easy. Nate doesn't lock anything. And I called in the tip about him instead of you."

"Why?" My voice is tiny, and my hands are shaking so badly that Simon's manifesto makes a rattling sound. "Why didn't you stick to the plan?"

Janae starts rocking back and forth again. "You were nice to me. Hundreds of people in that stupid school and *nobody*, except you, ever thought about if I missed Simon. I did. I *do*. I totally get how fucked up he was, but—he was my only friend." She starts crying hard again, her thin shoulders shaking. "Until you. I know we're not really friends and you probably hate me now, but . . . I couldn't do that to you."

I don't know how to respond. And if I keep thinking about Jake, I'm going to lose it. My mind latches on to one small piece of this messed-up puzzle that doesn't make sense. "What about Cooper's entry? Why would Simon write the truth and then replace it with a lie?"

"That was Jake," Janae says, swiping at her eyes. "He made Simon change it. He said he was doing Cooper a favor, but . . . I don't know. I think it was more he didn't want anyone to know his best friend was gay. And he seemed pretty jealous of all the attention Cooper was getting for baseball."

My head's spinning. I should be asking more questions, but I can think of only one. "Now what? Are you . . . I mean, you can't let Nate get convicted, Janae. You're going to tell someone, right? You have to tell someone."

Janae passes a hand over her face. "I know. I've been sick about it all week. But the thing is, I don't have anything except this printout. Jake has the video version on Simon's hard drive, along with all the backup files that show he'd planned the whole thing for months."

I brandish Simon's manifesto like a shield. "This is good enough. This, and your word, is *plenty*."

"What would even happen to me?" Janae mutters under her breath. "I'm, like, aiding and abetting, right? Or obstructing justice? *I* could wind up in jail. And Jake has that recording hanging over my head. He's already pissed at me. I've been too afraid of him to go to school. He keeps stopping by and—" The doorbell chimes, and she freezes as my phone rings out with a text. "Oh God, Addy, that's probably him. He only ever comes by when my parents' car isn't in the driveway."

My phone blares with a message from Cooper. *Jake's here. What's going on?* I grab hold of Janae's arm. "Listen. Let's do to him exactly what he did to you. Talk to him about all this, and we'll record it. Do you have your phone on you?"

Janae pulls it out of her pocket as the doorbell rings again. "It won't do any good. He always makes me give it to him before we talk."

"Okay. We'll use mine." I look into the darkened dining room across from us. "I'll hide in there while you talk to him."

"I don't think I can," Janae whispers, and I give her arm a hard shake.

"You have to. You need to make this right, Janae. It's gone way too far." My hands are trembling, but I manage to send a quick text to Cooper—*It's fine, just wait*—and get to my feet, pulling Janae with me and shoving her toward the door. "Answer it." I stumble into the dining room and sink to my knees, opening my phone's Voice Recorder app and pressing Play. I put it as close as I dare to the entryway between the dining room and the living room, and scoot against the wall next to a china cabinet.

At first, the blood rushing in my ears blocks out every other sound, but when it starts to recede I hear Jake's voice: ". . . haven't you been at school?"

"I don't feel well," Janae says.

"Really." Jake's voice drips with contempt. "Me either, but I still show up. Which you need to do too. Business as usual, you know?"

I have to strain to hear Janae. "Don't you think this has gone on long enough, Jake? I mean, Nate's in *jail*. I realize that's the plan and all, but now that it's happening it's pretty messed up." I'm not sure the phone's going to be able to pick her up, but there's not much I can do about it. I can't exactly stage-direct her from the dining room.

"I knew you were freaking out." Jake's voice carries easily. "No, we fucking *can't*, Janae. That'd put us both at risk. Anyway, sending Nate to jail was *your* choice, wasn't it? That should've been Addy, which is why I'm here, by the way. You fucked that up and need to turn it around. I have some ideas."

Janae's voice gets a little stronger. "Simon was *sick*, Jake. Killing yourself and framing other people for murder is crazy. I want out. I won't tell anybody you're involved, but I want us to—I don't know—put out an anonymous note that says it was a hoax or something. We have to make it stop."

Jake snorts. "Not your call, Janae. Don't forget what I have on hand. I can put everything on your doorstep and walk away. There's nothing to tie me to any of this."

Wrong, asshole, I think. Then time seems to stop as a text message from Cooper crosses my phone with a loud blare of Rihanna's "Only Girl." *You ok?*

I forgot the all-important step of silencing my phone before using it as a spy device.

"What the hell? *Addy?*" Jake roars. I don't even think, just take off out of the dining room and through Janae's kitchen, thanking God that she has a back door I can burst through. Heavy footsteps pound behind me, so instead of going for Cooper's car I run straight into the dense woods behind Janae's house. I fly through the underbrush in a panic, dodging bushes and overgrown roots until my foot hooks under something and I tumble to the ground. It's like the gym track all over again—knees torn, breath gone, palms raw—except this time my ankle's twisted also.

I hear branches crashing behind me, farther away than I would have thought but heading straight to me. I get to my feet, wincing, and weigh my options. One thing's sure after everything I heard in the living room—Jake's not leaving these woods till he finds me. I don't know if I can hide, and I sure as hell can't run. I take a deep breath, scream *"Help!"* at the top of my lungs, and take off again, trying to zigzag away from where I think Jake is while still getting closer to Janae's house.

But, oh God, my ankle hurts so badly. I'm barely dragging myself forward, and the noises behind me get louder until a hand catches my arm and yanks me back. I manage to scream once more before Jake clamps his other hand over my mouth.

"You little bitch," he says hoarsely. "You brought this on yourself, you know that?" I sink my teeth into Jake's palm and he lets out an animal sound of pain, dropping his hand and lifting it just as quickly to strike me across the face.

I stagger, my face aching, but manage to stay upright and twist in an attempt to connect my knee to his groin and my nails to his eye. Jake grunts again when I make contact, stumbling enough that I break free and spin away. My ankle buckles and his hand locks around my arm, tight as a vise. He pulls me toward him and grips me hard by the shoulders. For one bizarre second I think he's going to kiss me.

Instead he shoves me to the ground, kneels down, and slams my head on a rock. My skull explodes with pain and my vision goes red around the edges, then black. Something presses across my neck and I'm choking. I can't see anything, but I can hear. "You should be in jail instead of Nate, Addy," Jake snarls as I claw at his hands. "But this works too."

A girl's panicked voice pierces the pain in my head. "Jake, stop! Leave her alone!"

The awful pressure releases and I gasp for air. I hear Jake's voice, low and angry, then a shriek and a thud. I should get up, *right now.* I reach my hands out, feeling grass and dirt beneath my fingers as I scramble to find an anchor. I just need to pull myself off the ground. And get these starbursts out of my eyes. One thing at a time.

Hands are at my throat again, squeezing. I lash out with my legs, willing them to work the way they do on my bike, but they feel like spaghetti. I blink, blink, blink some more, until I can finally see. Except now I wish I couldn't. Jake's eyes flash silver in the moonlight, filled with a cold fury. *How did I not see this coming?*

I can't budge his hands no matter how hard I try.

Then I can breathe again as Jake flies backward, and I wonder dimly how and why he did that. Sounds fill the air as I roll onto my side, gasping to fill my empty lungs. Seconds or minutes pass, it's hard to tell, until a hand presses my shoulder and I blink into a different pair of eyes. Kind, concerned. And scared as shitless as I am.

"Cooper," I rasp. He pulls me into a sitting position and I let my head fall against his chest, feeling his heart hammering against my cheek as the distant wail of sirens draws closer.

CHAPTER THIRTY

Nate
Friday, November 9, 3:40 p.m.

I know something's different by how the guard looks at me when he calls my name. Not as much like a piece of dirt he wants to grind under his shoe as usual. "Bring your things," he says. I don't have much, but I take my time shoving everything into a plastic bag before I follow him down the long gray corridor to the warden's office.

Eli hovers in the doorway with his hands in his pockets, giving me that intense stare of his times a hundred. "Welcome to the rest of your life, Nate." When I don't react, he adds, "You're free. You're out. This whole thing was a hoax that's been blown wide open. So get out of that jumpsuit and into civilian clothes, and let's get you the hell out of here."

At this point I'm used to doing what I'm told, so that's all I do. Nothing else registers, even when Eli shows me news stories about Jake's arrest, until he tells me Addy's in the hospital with a concussion and a fractured skull. "Good news is, it's a hairline fracture with no underlying brain injury. She'll make a full recovery."

Addy, that airhead homecoming princess turned badass ninja investigator, in the hospital with a cracked skull because she tried to help me. Possibly only alive because of Janae, who got a busted jaw for her trouble, and Cooper, who's suddenly some kind of superhero the media's fawning over. I'd be happy for him if the whole thing didn't make me sick.

There's a lot of paperwork when you get out of jail for a crime you didn't commit. *Law & Order* never shows how many forms you have to fill out before you rejoin the world. The first thing I see when I step blinking into bright sunshine is a dozen cameras whirring to life. Of course. This whole thing's a neverending movie, and I've gone from villain to hero in a matter of hours even though I haven't done a single thing to make a difference since I got here.

My mother's outside, which I guess is a pleasant surprise. I'm never *not* prepared for her to disappear. And Bronwyn, even though I specifically said I didn't want her anywhere near this place. Guess nobody thought I was serious about that. Before I can react her arms are around me and my face is buried in her green-apple hair.

Jesus. This girl. For a few seconds I breathe her in and everything's all right.

Except it's not.

"Nate, how does it feel to be free? Do you have any comment about Jake? What's your next step?" Eli shoots sound bites at all the microphones in my face as we make our way to his car. He's the man of the hour, but I don't see what he did to earn it. The charges were dropped because Bronwyn kept unraveling threads and tracked down a witness. Because Cooper's boyfriend connected dots nobody else saw. Because Addy put herself in the line of fire. And because Cooper saved the day before Jake could shut her up.

I'm the only one in the murder club who didn't contribute a goddamn thing. All I did was be the guy who's easy to frame.

Eli inches his car past all the media vans until we're on the highway and the juvenile detention center fades to a speck in the distance. He's rattling on about too many things to follow: how he's working with Officer Lopez to get my drug charges dropped; how if I want to make a statement through the media he'd recommend Mikhail Powers; how I need a strategy for re-integrating into school. I stare out the window, my hand a dead weight in Bronwyn's. When I finally hear Eli's voice asking if I have any questions, I can tell he's been repeating himself for a while.

"Did someone feed Stan?" I ask. My father sure as shit didn't.

"I did," Bronwyn says. When I don't respond, she squeezes my hand and adds, "Nate, are you all right?"

She tries to catch my eye, but I can't do it. She wants me to be happy and I can't do that either. The impossibility of Bronwyn hits me like a punch to the gut: everything she wants is good and right and logical and I can't do any of it. She'll always be that girl in front of me in the scavenger hunt, her shining hair hypnotizing me so much I almost forget how uselessly I'm trailing behind her.

"I just want to go home and sleep." I'm still not looking at Bronwyn, but out of the corner of my eye I can see her face fall, and for some reason that's perversely satisfying. I'm disappointing her right on schedule. Finally, something makes sense.

Cooper
Saturday, November 17, 9:30 a.m.

It's pretty surreal to come downstairs for breakfast Saturday morning to my grandmother reading an issue of *People* with me on the cover.

I didn't pose for it. It's a shot of Kris and me leaving the police station after giving our statements. Kris looks fantastic, and I look like I just woke up after a night of heavy drinking. It's obvious which of us is the model.

Funny how this accidental-fame thing works. First people supported me even though I'd been accused of cheating and murder. Then they hated me because of who I turned out to be. Now they love me again because I was in the right place at the right time and managed to flatten Jake with a well-aimed punch.

And because of the halo effect of being with Kris, I guess. Eli's giving him full credit for figuring out what really happened, so he's the new breakout star of this whole mess. The fact that he's trying to avoid the media machine only makes them want him more.

Lucas sits across from Nonny, spooning Cocoa Puffs into his mouth while scrolling through his iPad. "Your Facebook fan page has a hundred thousand likes now," he reports, flicking a strand of hair out of his face like it's an annoying bug. This is good news for Lucas, who took it personally when most of my so-called fans deserted the page after the police outed me.

Nonny sniffs and flings the magazine across the table. "Awful. One boy's dead, another ruined his life and almost ruined yours, and people still treat this like it's a TV show. Thank God for short attention spans. Something else'll come along soon and you can get back to normal."

Whatever that is.

It's been about a week since Jake was arrested. So far he's being charged with assault, obstruction of justice, evidence tampering, and a whole bunch of other things I can't keep track of. He's got his own lawyer now, and he's in the same detention center where Nate was being held. Which I guess is poetic justice, but it doesn't feel good. I still can't reconcile the guy I pulled off Addy with the kid who'd been my friend since ninth grade. His lawyer's talking about undue influence from Simon, and maybe that explains it. Or maybe Ashton was right and Jake's been a control freak all along.

Janae's cooperating with the police and it looks like she'll get a plea bargain in exchange for her testimony. She and Addy are thick as thieves now. I have mixed feelings about Janae and the way she let things get this far. But I'm not as innocent as I'd thought, either. While Addy was zonked out on painkillers in the hospital she told me everything, including how my stupid, panicked slight at junior prom made Simon hate me enough to frame me for murder.

I have to figure out a way to live with that, and it won't be by not forgiving other people's mistakes.

"You meetin' Kris later?" Nonny asks.

"Yup," I say. Lucas keeps eating cereal without blinking an eye. Turns out he couldn't care less that his older brother has a boyfriend. Although he does seem to miss Keely.

Who I'm also seeing today, before Kris and I get together. Partly because I owe her an apology, and partly because she's been sucked into this mess too, even though the police tried to keep her name out of Simon's confession. It wasn't part of the public record, but people at school knew enough to guess. I texted her earlier in the week to see how she was doing, and she texted back an apology for not being more supportive when the story about me and Kris broke. Which was pretty big of her, considering all the lies I told.

We went back and forth for a while after that. She was pretty broken up about the part she played in everything, even though she had no idea what was happening. I'm one of the few people in town who can understand how that feels.

Maybe we can manage to be friends after all this. I'd like that.

Pop comes into the kitchen with his laptop, jiggling it like there's a present inside. "You check your email?"

"Not this morning."

"Josh Langley's touching base. Wants to know what you're thinking about college versus the draft. And the UCLA offer came through. Still nothin' from LSU, though." Pop won't be happy until all the top-five college baseball teams make me a scholarship offer. Louisiana State is the lone holdout, which annoys him since they're ranked number one. "Anyway, Josh wants to talk next week. You up for it?"

"Sure," I say, even though I've already decided I'm not going right into the draft. The more I think about my baseball future, the more I want college ball to be the next step. I have the rest of my life to play baseball, but only a few years to go to college.

And my first choice is Cal State. Since they're the only school that didn't back away from me when I was down.

But it'll make Pop happy to talk with Josh Langley. We've gotten back on tentative father-son footing since the good baseball news started pouring in. He still doesn't talk to me about Kris, and clams up when anyone else mentions him. He doesn't bolt out of the room anymore, though. And he's looking me in the eye again.

It's a start.

Addy
Saturday, November 17, 2:15 p.m.

I can't ride my bike because of the skull fracture and my sprained ankle, so Ashton drives me to my follow-up doctor's appointment. Everything's healing the way it should, although I still get instant headaches if I move my head too fast.

The emotional stuff will take longer. Half the time I feel like Jake died, and the other half I want to kill him. I can admit, now, that Ashton and TJ weren't wrong about how things were between Jake and me. He ran everything, and I let him. But I never would have believed he could be capable of what he did in the woods. My heart feels like my skull did right after Jake attacked me—as though it's been split in two with a dull ax.

I don't know how to feel about Simon, either. Sometimes I get really sad when I think about how he planned to ruin four people because he thought we'd taken away from him things that everybody wants: to be successful, to have friends, to be loved. To be *seen*.

But most of the time I just wish I'd never met him.

Nate visited me in the hospital and I've seen him a few times since I've been out. I'm worried about him. He's not one to open up, but he said enough that I could tell getting arrested made him feel pretty useless. I've been trying to convince him otherwise, but I don't think it's sinking in. I wish he'd listen, because if anyone knows how badly you can screw up your life when you decide you're not good enough, it's me.

TJ's texted a few times since I was discharged a couple of days ago. He kept dropping hints about asking me out, so I finally had to tell him it's not happening. There's no way I can hook up with the person who helped me set off this whole chain reaction. It's too bad, because there might've been potential if we'd gone about things differently. But I'm starting to realize there are some things you can't undo, no matter how good your intentions are.

It's all right, though. I don't agree with my mother that TJ was my last, best hope to avoid premature spinsterhood. She's not the expert she thinks she is on relationships.

I'd rather take my cues from Ashton, who's getting a kick out of Eli's sudden infatuation. He tracked her down after things settled with Nate and asked her out. She told him she's not ready to date yet, so he keeps interrupting his insane workload to take her on elaborate, carefully planned not-dates. Which, she has to admit, she's enjoying.

"I'm not sure I can take him seriously, though," she tells me as I hobble to the car on crutches after my checkup. "I mean, the hair alone."

"I like the hair. It has character. Plus, it looks soft, like a cloud."

Ashton grins and brushes a stray lock of mine off my forehead. "I like *yours*. Grow it a little more and we'll be twins."

That's my secret plan. I've been coveting Ashton's hair all along.

"I have something to show you," she says as she pulls away from the hospital. "Some good news."

"Really? What?" Sometimes it's hard to remember what good news feels like.

Ashton shakes her head and smiles. "It's a show, not a tell."

She pulls up in front of a new apartment building in the closest thing Bayview has to a trendy neighborhood. Ashton matches my slow pace as we step into a bright atrium, and guides me to a bench in the lobby. "Wait here," she says, propping my crutches next to the bench. She disappears around the corner, and when she returns ten minutes later she leads me to an elevator and we head for the third floor.

Ashton fits a key into a door marked 302 and pushes it open to a large apartment with soaring, loftlike ceilings. It's all windows and exposed brick and polished wood floors, and I love it instantly. "What do you think?" she asks.

I lean my crutches against the wall and hop into the open

kitchen, admiring the mosaic tile backsplash. Who knew Bayview had something like this? "It's beautiful. Are you, um, thinking of renting it?" I try to sound enthusiastic and not terrified of Ashton leaving me alone with Mom. Ashton hasn't been home all that long, but I've gotten kind of attached to having her there.

"I already did," she says with a grin, spinning around a little on the hardwood floors. "Charlie and I got an offer on the condo while you were in the hospital. It still has to close, but once it does, we'll make a pretty good profit. He's agreed to take on all his student loans as part of the divorce settlement. My design work's still slow, but I'll have enough of a cushion that it won't be a stretch. And Bayview's so much more affordable than San Diego. This apartment downtown would cost three times as much."

"That's fantastic!" I hope I'm doing a good job of acting excited. I *am* excited for her, truly. I'll just miss her. "You'd better have a spare room so I can visit."

"I do have a spare room," Ashton says. "I don't want you to visit, though."

I stare at her. I can't have heard her correctly. I thought we'd been getting along great these past couple of months.

She laughs at my expression. "I want you to *live* here, silly. You need to get out of that house as much as I do. Mom said it's okay. She's in that decline phase with Justin where she thinks lots of private couple time will fix their problems. Plus, you'll be eighteen in a few months and can live wherever you want then anyway."

I grab her in a hug before she can finish, and she suffers it for a few seconds before ducking away. We still haven't mastered the art of non-awkward sisterly affection. "Go ahead, check out your room. It's over there."

I limp into a sun-splashed room with a huge window overlooking a bike path behind the building. Built-in bookshelves line the wall, and exposed beams in the ceiling frame an amazing light fixture with a dozen Edison bulbs in different shapes and sizes. I love everything about it. Ashton leans against the doorway and smiles at me.

"Fresh start for both of us, huh?"

It finally feels like that might be true.

Bronwyn
Sunday, November 18, 10:45 a.m.

The day after Nate was released, I gave my one and only interview to the media. I didn't mean to. But Mikhail Powers himself ambushed me outside my house, and as I expected when I first saw the full force of his charm turned on our case, I couldn't resist him.

"Bronwyn Rojas. The girl most likely." He was dressed in a crisp navy suit and subtly patterned tie, gold cuff links glinting as he held out his hand with a warm smile. I almost didn't notice the camera behind him. "I've been wanting to talk to you for weeks. You never gave up on your friend, did you? I admire that. I've admired you throughout this entire case."

"Thanks," I said weakly. It was a transparent attempt to butter me up and it totally worked.

"I would love your take on everything. Can you spare a few

minutes to tell us what this ordeal has been like for you, and how you feel now that it's over?"

I shouldn't have. Robin and my family had held our last legal meeting that morning, and her parting advice was to keep a low profile. She was right, as usual. But there was something I'd wanted to get off my chest that I hadn't been allowed to say before.

"Just one thing." I looked into the camera while Mikhail smiled encouragingly. "I did cheat in my chemistry class, and I'm sorry. Not only because it got me into this mess, but because it was an awful thing to do. My parents raised me to be honest and work hard, like they do, and I let them down. It wasn't fair to them, or my teachers, or the colleges I wanted to apply to. And it wasn't fair to Simon." My voice started shaking then, and I couldn't blink back the tears any longer. "If I'd known . . . If I'd thought . . . I won't ever stop being sorry for what I did. I'll never do anything like that again. That's all I want to say."

I doubt that's what Mikhail was hoping for, but he used it anyway for his final Bayview report. Rumor has it he's submitting the series for Emmy consideration.

My parents keep telling me I can't blame myself for what Simon did. Just like I keep telling Cooper and Addy the same thing. And I'd tell Nate, if he'd let me, but I've barely heard from him since he got out of juvenile detention. He talks to Addy more than me now. I mean, he *should* talk to Addy, who is obviously a rock star. But still.

He finally agreed to let me stop by and catch up, but I don't feel my usual excited anticipation as I ring his doorbell.

Something's changed since he was arrested. I almost don't expect him to be home, but he opens the creaking door and steps aside.

Nate's house looks better than it did when I was feeding Stan. His mother's staying here and she's added all sorts of new touches like curtains, throw pillows, and framed pictures. The only time Nate spoke to me at any length after he got home, he said his mother had convinced his father to try a stint at rehab. Nate didn't hold out much hope for it, but I'm sure having his father out of the house temporarily is a relief.

Nate flops into an armchair in the living room as I make my way over to Stan and peer into his cage, glad for the distraction. He lifts one of his front legs in my direction, and I laugh in surprise. "Did Stan just *wave* at me?"

"Yeah. He does that, like, once a year. It's his only move." Nate meets my eyes with a grin, and for a second things are normal between us. Then his smile fades and he looks down. "So. I don't actually have a lot of time. Officer Lopez wants to hook me up with a weekend job at some construction company in Eastland. I have to be there in twenty minutes."

"That's great." I swallow hard. Why is it so hard to talk to him now? It was the easiest thing in the world a few weeks ago. "I just—I guess I wanted to say, um, I know you went through something awful and I understand if you don't want to talk about it, but I'm here if you do. And I still . . . care about you. As much as ever. So. That's all, I guess."

It's an awkward start, made worse by the fact that he won't look at me during my sad little speech. When he finally does, his eyes are flat.

"I've been meaning to talk to you about that. First, thanks for everything you did. Seriously, I owe you one. I probably won't ever be able to repay you. But it's time to get back to normal, right? And we're not each other's normal." He averts his eyes again, and it's killing me. If he'd look at me for more than ten seconds I'm positive he wouldn't say this.

"No, we're not." I'm surprised at how steady my voice is. "But that's never mattered to me, and I didn't think it mattered to you. My feelings haven't changed, Nate. I still want to be with you."

I've never said anything that matters so much in such a straightforward way, and at first I'm glad I didn't wimp out. But Nate looks like he couldn't care less. And while I'm not fazed by external obstacles thrown my way—*Disapproving parents? No problem! Jail time? I'll get you out!*—his indifference makes me wilt.

"I don't see the point. We've got separate lives, and nothing in common now that the investigation's wrapped up. You need to get ready for the Ivy League, and I—" He lets out a humorless snort. "I'll be doing whatever the opposite of that is."

I want to throw my arms around him and kiss him until he stops talking like this. But his face is closed off, as though his mind's already a thousand miles away, waiting for his body to catch up. Like he only let me come here out of a sense of obligation. And I can't stand it.

"If that's how you feel."

He nods so fast that whatever tiny flicker of hope I might've been nursing disappears. "Yup. Good luck with everything, Bronwyn. Thanks again."

He stands up like he's going to walk me to the door, but I can't take fake politeness right now. "Don't bother," I say, stalking past him with my eyes on the floor. I let myself out and walk stiffly to my car, willing myself not to run, and fumble through my bag with shaking hands until I find my keys.

I drive home with dry, unblinking eyes and make it all the way to my room before I lose it. Maeve knocks softly and enters without waiting for an invitation, curling up next to me and stroking my hair while I sob into a pillow like my heart just broke. Which I guess it did.

"I'm sorry," she says. She knew where I was headed, and I don't need to tell her how it went. "He's being a jerk."

She doesn't say anything else until I wear myself out and sit up, rubbing my eyes. I'd forgotten how tired full-body crying can make you. "Sorry I can't make this better," Maeve says, reaching into her pocket and pulling out her phone. "But I have something to show you that might cheer you up. Lots of reaction on Twitter to your statement on *Mikhail Powers Investigates*. All positive, by the way."

"Maeve, I don't care about *Twitter*," I say wearily. I haven't been on there since this whole mess started. Even with my profile set to private, I couldn't deal with the onslaught of opinions.

"I know. But you should see this." She hands me her phone and points to a post on my timeline from Yale University:

To err is human @BronwynRojas. We look forward to receiving your application.

EPILOGUE

Bronwyn
Friday, February 15, 6:50 p.m.

I'm sort of seeing Evan Neiman now. It snuck up on me. First we were together a lot in big groups, then smaller ones, and a few weeks ago he drove me home after a bunch of us hate-watched *The Bachelor* at Yumiko's house. When we got to my driveway, he leaned over and kissed me.

It was . . . nice. He's a good kisser. I found myself analyzing the kiss in almost clinical detail while it was happening, mentally congratulating him on a stellar technique while noting the absence of any heat or magnetic pull between us. My heart didn't pound as I kissed him back, and my limbs didn't shake. It was a good kiss with a nice boy. The kind I'd always wanted.

Now things are almost exactly how I thought they'd be when I first imagined dating Evan. We make a solid couple. I have an automatic date for the spring break dance, which is nice. But

I'm planning my post-Bayview life on a parallel track that has nothing to do with him. We're an until-graduation couple, at best.

I applied to Yale, but not early action. I'll find out next month along with everyone else whether I got in or not. It doesn't seem like the be-all, end-all of my future anymore, though. I've been interning for Eli on the weekends, and I'm starting to see the appeal of staying local and keeping up with Until Proven.

Everything's pretty fluid, and I'm trying to be okay with that. I think a lot about Simon and about what the media called his "aggrieved entitlement"—the belief he was owed something he didn't get, and everyone should pay because of it. It's almost impossible to understand, except by that corner of my brain that pushed me to cheat for validation I hadn't earned. I don't ever want to be that person again.

The only time I see Nate is at school. He's there more often than he used to be, and I guess he's doing all right. I don't know for sure, though, because we don't talk anymore. At all. He wasn't kidding about going back to separate lives.

Sometimes I almost catch him looking at me, but it's probably wishful thinking.

He's still on my mind constantly, and it sucks. I'd hoped starting up with Evan might curb the Nate loop in my head, but it's made things worse. So I try not to think about Evan unless I'm actually with him, which means I sometimes overlook things that I shouldn't as Evan's sort-of girlfriend. Like tonight.

I have a piano solo with the San Diego Symphony. It's part of their High School Spotlight concert series, something I've applied for since I was a freshman without ever getting an invitation. Last month, I finally did. It's probably due to residual notoriety, although I like to think the audition video I submitted of "Variations on the Canon" helped. I've improved a lot since the fall.

"Are you nervous?" Maeve asks as we head downstairs. She's dressed for the concert in a burgundy velvet dress that has a Renaissance feel, her hair in a loose braid threaded with small jeweled pins. She recently got the part of Lady Guinevere in the drama club's upcoming *King Arthur,* and she's gone a little overboard getting in character. It suits her, though. I'm more conservative in a scoop-necked jacquard dress with a subtle gray-and-black tonal-dot pattern that nips in at the waist and flares out above my knees.

"A little," I reply, but she's only half listening. Her fingers fly across her phone, probably arranging yet another weekend rehearsal with the boy who plays Lancelot in *King Arthur.* Who she insists is just a friend. *Right.*

I have my own phone out, texting last-minute directions to Kate, Yumiko, and Addy. Cooper's bringing Kris, although they're having dinner with his parents first, so they might be late. With Kris's parents, that is. Cooper's dad is slowly coming around, but he's not at that stage yet. Yumiko texts *Should we look for Evan?* and at that point I remember I never invited him.

It's fine, though. It's not a big deal. It was in the newspaper, and I'm sure he would have mentioned it if he'd seen it and wanted to come.

* * *

We're at Copley Symphony Hall, in front of a capacity crowd. When it's my turn to play I walk onto a huge stage that dwarfs the piano at its center. The crowd's silent except the occasional cough, and my heels click loudly on the polished floor. I smooth my dress beneath me before taking a seat on the ebony bench. I've never performed in front of this many people, but I'm not as nervous as I thought I'd be.

I flex my fingers and wait for a signal from backstage. When I start, I can tell right away it's going to be the best I've ever played. Every note flows, but it's not only that. When I reach the crescendo and the soft notes that follow, I pour every ounce of emotion from the past few months into the keys beneath my fingers. I feel each note like a heartbeat. And I know the audience does too.

Loud applause echoes through the room when I finish. I stand and incline my head, absorbing the crowd's approval until the stage manager beckons me and I walk into the wings. Backstage I collect flowers my parents left for me, holding them close while I listen to the rest of the performers.

Afterward I catch up with my friends in the foyer. Kate and Yumiko give me a smaller bouquet of flowers, which I add to the ones already in my hands. Addy is pink-cheeked and smiling, wearing her new track team jacket over a black dress like the world's unlikeliest jock. Her hair's in a choppy bob that's almost exactly like her sister's except the color. She decided to go full-on purple instead of back to blond, and it suits her.

"That was so good!" she says gleefully, pulling me into a hug. "They should have let you play *all* the songs."

To my surprise, Ashton and Eli come up behind her. Ashton mentioned she'd be here, but I didn't think Eli would leave the office so early. I guess I should have known better. They're an official couple now, and Eli somehow manages to find time for whatever Ashton wants to do. He's wearing that moony grin he always has around her, and I doubt he heard a note I played. "Not bad, Bronwyn," he says.

"I got you on video," Cooper says, brandishing his phone. "I'll text it once I make a few edits."

Kris, who looks dashing in a sports jacket and dark jeans, rolls his eyes. "Cooper finally learned how to use iMovie, and now there's no stopping him. Trust me. I have tried." Cooper grins unrepentantly and puts his phone away, slipping his hand into Kris's.

Addy keeps craning her neck to look around the crowded foyer, so much that I wonder if she brought a date. "Expecting someone?" I ask.

"What? No," she says with a breezy wave. "Just checking things out. Beautiful building."

Addy has the world's worst poker face. I follow her eyes but can't catch a glimpse of any potential mystery guy. She doesn't seem disappointed, though.

People keep stopping to talk, so it takes half an hour before Maeve, my parents, and I work our way outside. My father squints at the twinkling stars above us. "I had to park pretty far away. You three don't want to walk there in heels. Wait here and I'll bring the car."

"All right," my mother says, kissing his cheek. I clutch my

flowers and look at all the well-dressed people surrounding us, laughing and murmuring as they spill onto the sidewalks. A line of sleek cars pulls forward, and I watch them even though it's too soon for my father to be among them. A Lexus. A Range Rover. A Jaguar.

A motorcycle.

My heart pounds as the bike's lights dim and its rider removes his helmet. Nate climbs off, skirting past an older couple, and advances toward me with his eyes locked on mine.

I can't breathe.

Maeve tugs on my mother's arm. "We should go closer to the parking lot so Dad sees us." My eyes are on Nate, so I hear rather than see Mom's deep sigh. But she moves away with Maeve, and I'm alone on the sidewalk when Nate reaches me.

"Hey." He looks at me with those dreamy, dark-fringed eyes, and resentment surges through my veins. I don't want to see his stupid eyes, his stupid mouth, and every other part of his stupid face that's made me miserable for the past three months. I had one night, finally, where I got to lose myself in something besides my pathetic love life. Now he's ruined it.

But I'm not going to give him the satisfaction of knowing that. "Hi, Nate." I'm surprised at my calm, neutral voice. You'd never guess how desperately my heart's trying to escape my rib cage. "How've you been?"

"Okay," he says, shoving his hands into his pockets. He looks almost—awkward? It's a novel stance for him. "My dad's back in rehab. But they say that's positive. That he's giving it another shot."

"That's great. I hope it works out." I don't sound like I mean it, even though I do. The longer he stands there, the harder it is to act natural. "How's your mom?"

"Good. Working. She moved everything from Oregon, so—I guess she'll be here for a while. That's the plan, anyway." He runs a hand through his hair and shoots me another half-lidded glance. The kind he used to give right before he kissed me. "I saw your solo. I was wrong, that night at your house when I first heard you. *That*, tonight, was the best thing I've ever heard."

I squeeze the stems of my flowers so hard that thorns from the roses prick me. "Why?"

"Why what?"

"Why did you come? I mean—" I lift my chin toward the crowd. "It's not really your thing, is it?"

"No," Nate admits. "But this is a big deal for you, right? I wanted to see it."

"Why?" I repeat. I want to ask more, but I can't. My throat closes and I'm horrified as my eyes prickle and fill. I concentrate on breathing and press my hands against the thorns, willing the mild pain to distract me. Okay. There we go. Tears receding. Disaster averted.

In the seconds I've been pulling myself together, Nate's stepped closer. I don't know where to look because there's no part of him that doesn't undo me.

"Bronwyn." Nate rubs the back of his neck and swallows hard, and I realize he's as nervous as I am. "I've been an idiot. Being arrested messed with my head. I thought you'd be better off without me in your life so I just . . . made that happen. I'm sorry."

I drop my eyes to his sneakers, which seem like the safest spot. I don't trust myself to speak.

"The thing is . . . I never really had anybody, you know? I'm not saying that so you'll feel bad for me. Just to try and explain. I don't—I didn't—get how stuff like this works. That you can't pretend you don't give a crap and it's done." Nate shifts his weight from one foot to the other, which I notice since my eyes remain fastened on the ground. "I've been talking to Addy about this, because"—he laughs a little—"she won't let it go. I asked her if she thought you'd be mad if I tried to talk to you and she said it didn't matter. That I owe you an explanation anyway. She's right. As usual."

Addy. That meddler. No wonder she'd been bobbleheading all over Symphony Hall.

I clear my throat to try to dislodge the lump, but it's no good. I'll have to talk around it. "You weren't just my boyfriend, Nate. You were my *friend*. Or I thought you were. And then you stopped talking to me like we were nothing." I have to bite hard on the inside of my cheek to keep from tearing up again.

"I know. It was— God, I can't even explain it, Bronwyn. You were the best thing that ever happened to me, and it freaked me out. I thought I'd ruin you. Or you'd ruin me. That's how things tend to go in the Macauley house. But you're not like that." He exhales sharply and his voice dips lower. "You're not like anybody. I've known that since we were kids, and I just—I fucked up. I finally had my chance with you and I fucked it all up."

He waits a beat for me to say something, but I can't yet. "I'm sorry," he says, shifting again. "I shouldn't have come. I sprang this on you out of nowhere. I didn't mean to ruin your big night."

The crowd is thinning, the night air cooling. My father will be here soon. I finally look up, and it's every bit as unnerving as I thought it would be. "You really hurt me, Nate. You can't just ride here on your motorcycle with . . . all *this*"—I gesture around his face—"and expect everything to be okay. It's not."

"I know." Nate's eyes search mine. "But I was hoping . . . I mean, what you were saying before. How we were friends. I wanted to ask you—it's probably stupid, after all this, but you know Porter Cinema, on Clarendon? The one that plays older stuff? They've got the second Divergent movie there. I was, um, wondering if you want to go sometime."

Long pause. My thoughts are a tangled mess, but I'm sure of one thing—if I tell him no, it'll be out of pride and self-preservation. Not because it's what I want. "As friends?"

"As whatever you want. I mean, yeah. Friends would be great."

"You hate those movies," I remind him.

"I really do." He sounds regretful, and I almost crack a smile. "I like you more, though. I miss you like crazy." I furrow my brow at him and he quickly adds, "As a friend." We stare at each other for a few seconds until his jaw twitches. "Okay. Since I'm being honest here, more than a friend. But I get that's not where your head is. I'd still like to take you to a shitty movie and hang out with you for a couple hours. If you'll let me."

My cheeks burn, and the corners of my mouth keep trying to turn upward. My face is a fickle traitor. Nate sees it and brightens, but when I don't say anything he pulls at the neck of his T-shirt and drops his head like I've already turned him down. "Well. Just think about it, okay?"

I take a deep breath. Being dumped by Nate was heartbreaking, and the idea of opening myself up to that kind of hurt again is scary. But I put myself on the line for him once, when I told him how I felt about him. And again, when I helped get him out of jail. He's worth at least a third time. "If you'll admit that *Insurgent* is a cinematic tour de force and you're dying to see it, I'll consider your proposal."

Nate snaps his head up and gives me a smile like the sun coming out. "*Insurgent* is a cinematic tour de force and I'm dying to see it."

Happiness starts bubbling through me, making it hard to keep a straight face. I manage, though, because I'm not going to make things *that* easy on him. Nate can sit through the entire series before we leave the friend zone. "That was fast," I say. "I expected more resistance."

"I already wasted too much time."

I give a small nod. "All right, then. I'll call you."

Nate's smile fades a little. "We never exchanged numbers, though, did we?"

"Still have your burner phone?" I ask. Mine's been charging in my closet for three months. Just in case.

His face lights up again. "Yeah. I do."

The gentle but insistent honk of a horn penetrates my brain. Dad's BMW idles directly behind us, and Mom lowers the passenger window to peer outside. If I had to use one word to describe her expression it would be *resigned*. "There's my ride," I tell Nate.

He reaches for my hand and squeezes it quickly before letting go, and I swear to God, actual sparks shoot across my skin. "Thanks for not telling me to get lost. I'll wait to hear from you, okay? Whenever you're ready."

"Okay." I move past him toward my parents' car and feel him turn to watch me. I finally let myself smile, and now that I've started, I can't stop. That's okay, though. I catch his reflection in the backseat window, and he can't either.

RESOURCES

Although *One of Us Is Lying* is a work of fiction, its characters experience many of the same issues and challenges that teens, young adults, and their families deal with every day in the real world. If you or someone you care about needs information, help, or someone to talk to, the list below provides a starting point for resources and support.

Food Allergy Research & Education® (FARE)
FARE's mission is to improve the quality of life and the health of individuals with food allergies, and to provide hope through the promise of new treatments. foodallergy.org

The National Domestic Violence Hotline
This free, confidential hotline is available 24/7 for anyone experiencing domestic violence or questioning unhealthy

aspects of their relationship.
1-800-799-SAFE (7233)
thehotline.org

National Suicide Prevention Lifeline
The Lifeline provides free and confidential emotional support 24/7 to people in suicidal crisis or emotional distress.
1-800-273-TALK (8255)
suicidepreventionlifeline.org

PACER Center's Teens Against Bullying
A website coordinated by the National Bullying Prevention Center created to help teens learn about bullying, how to respond to it, and how to stop it.
pacerteensagainstbullying.org

SAMHSA's National Helpline
A free, confidential, 24/7 treatment referral and information service for individuals and families facing mental and/or substance use disorders.
1-800-662-HELP (4357)
samhsa.gov/find-help/national-helpline

ACKNOWLEDGMENTS

So many people helped me along the journey from idea to publication, and I will be forever grateful to all of them. First, a profound thank-you to Rosemary Stimola and Allison Remcheck, without whom this book wouldn't exist. Thank you for taking a chance on me, and for your brilliant advice and unwavering support.

To Krista Marino, thank you for being an incredible editor and for your deep understanding of my story and its characters. Your insightful feedback and guidance strengthened this book in ways I didn't realize were possible. To all the team at Random House/Delacorte Press, I'm honored to be counted among your authors.

Writers are so much better when they're part of a community. To Erin Hahn, my first critique partner, thank you for being an honest critic, a tireless cheerleader, and a good friend. Thank you Jen Fulmer, Meredith Ireland, Lana Kondryuk, Kathrine Zahm, Amelinda Berube, and Ann Marjory K for your thoughtful reads and words of wisdom. Every one of you made this book better.

Thank you, Amy Capelin, Alex Webb, Bastian Schlueck, and Kathrin Nehm for bringing *One of Us Is Lying* to audiences around the world.

Thank you to my sister, Lynne, at whose kitchen table I sat and announced, "I'm finally going to write a book." You've read every word I've written since, and believed in me when all this seemed like a pipe dream. Thank you, Luis Fernando, Gabriela, Carolina, and Erik for your love and support, and for putting up with my laptop at family gatherings. Thank you, Jay and April, who are part of every sibling story I write, and Julie for always checking in on book progress.

Deep gratitude to my mom and dad for instilling in me a love of reading and the discipline required for writing. And to my second-grade teacher, the late Karen Hermann Pugh, who was the first to ever call me a storyteller. I wish I could have thanked you in person.

All the love in the world to my kind, smart, and funny son, Jack. I am proud of you always.

And finally, to my readers—thank you from the bottom of my heart for choosing to spend your time with this book. I couldn't be happier to share it with you.

Maeve

Cooper's hand cups the remote, pointing it toward a frozen television screen. "So we're really doing this?"

"We have to, right?" Bronwyn says. "Everybody else is going to watch it. We might as well know what they're talking about." My sister sits across from me in our basement media room, curled up against her boyfriend in a corner of the overstuffed sofa. Nate's arm is around her shoulder, his hand absently playing with a lock of her hair. He looks, as usual, like he couldn't care less what Mikhail Powers has to say, but even he has to be a little bit curious. "Plus, we need to see Addy's interview."

Nate shakes his head. "Still can't believe you agreed to talk to that guy."

Addy makes a face. "I *had* to. They were totally going to use the 'washed-up beauty queen' angle with me, just because I'm not in college like the rest of you. It's sexist."

"Also false," Bronwyn says, leaning her head on Nate's shoulder. She's been at Yale for less than three months, but it's been a rocky road for those two already. Lots of long-distance arguments, and even a brief breakup that lasted until this afternoon, when Nate asked me not to pick her up at the airport for Thanksgiving break so he could. I haven't had a chance to talk with Bronwyn alone since then, but I'm assuming it went well since she's practically on his lap now.

Still. I have a feeling it's going to be a long year for them.

"There's nothing wrong with taking time off," Bronwyn continues.

"Agreed," I say, and my sister narrows her eyes. She doesn't mean for *me*. She's been sending me college brochures ever since she left for Yale, and she's deeply disappointed every time she asks for an update and learns they're still stacked, unopened, in a corner of my room.

"I'm a *junior*," I keep reminding her. Bronwyn and I are only a year apart in age, but I'm two years behind her in school because I was in and out of hospitals for half my childhood. Homework wasn't exactly a priority when I was battling leukemia.

"That's the perfect time to be thinking about your future," Bronwyn always says back. I can tell from the look she's giving me now that we are very obviously going to have a Discussion about this as soon as she manages to peel herself away from Nate.

Cooper's boyfriend, Kris, grabs a handful of popcorn from the bowl between them. "It's very common to take a gap year in Europe," he says before popping a kernel in his mouth. "I would have done it myself if I hadn't moved here."

"Don't pretend you've ever been tempted to slack, Mr. Pre-Med," Addy says, pushing a lock of purple hair out of her eye. "No one's buying it."

Cooper is still holding the remote control in midair. He clears his throat loudly, scanning the room with an air of barely suppressed impatience. "Y'all are the most easily distracted bunch of people I've ever known. The question remains: Are we watching this damn thing or not?"

"Well, we have it queued up. We have popcorn." Addy shakes the plastic bowl in her lap. "Might as well."

Cooper presses a button and lowers his arm. The screen unfreezes, and a well-dressed man behind a chrome desk flashes dazzling white teeth. "Good evening, and thank you for joining this special Thanksgiving edition of *Mikhail Powers Investigates*. I'm Mikhail Powers, and tonight I'll be following up on one of our top investigations of last year. Welcome to 'The Bayview Four: Where Are They Now?'"

Four quick videos flash on the screen. Handsome, square-jawed Cooper, winding up to hurl a blistering fastball. Addy, her vibrant purple hair framing delicate pixie features, striding down a sun-dappled street. My sister, rocking a sexy nerd look in her glasses and a loose ponytail, clutching an armload of books as she exits a red brick building. And Nate astride a parked motorcycle, pulling off his helmet to reveal that bad-angel face and dangerous smirk.

No wonder the media was obsessed with them last year. Even in candid shots, they're all ridiculously camera-ready.

There aren't any pictures of Kris or me, thank God. We're honorary members only of the Bayview Four, although I'm sure we'll be mentioned at some point. Kris ups the romance factor, and I'm here for pathos. The sad little sister who nearly died of cancer, sending Bronwyn down a relentless path of overachievement to compensate. It's a story that's been repeated so many times, I've come to believe it myself. I'm a prop in my sister's intensely dramatic life, background to her center stage. Nothing I do or say on my own will ever be as interesting.

When the camera returns to Mikhail Powers, he's wearing an expression of deep gravitas. "Last fall, the world watched a sensational, disturbing mystery unfold as Simon Kelleher, a high school senior in Bayview, California, took his own life and framed four fellow students for his death," he says. "While our Emmy Award–winning coverage explored that case in depth, including the personal and cultural factors that led to such an unfathomable tragedy, today's special focuses on how the four affected students have moved on—or not."

"Hey!" Addy sits up straighter, frowning. "He better not be talking about me."

New images flash—of a baseball stadium, downtown Bayview, and a leafy college campus—as Mikhail Powers summarizes in a few sentences what he'll spend the next hour discussing.

"Cooper Clay accepted a full baseball scholarship at California State University, Fullerton, where he's now training for a season that opens next February. Cooper continues to receive interest from major league teams, but has been candid with his concerns about how receptive they'll be to an openly gay player.

"After retaking the chemistry course she cheated on and immersing herself in extra credit classes and community service activities, Bronwyn Rojas was granted admission to Yale University. She is currently a freshman majoring in political science and has expressed interest in a law career.

"Adelaide Prentiss was a key witness in the conviction of her former boyfriend, Jake Riordan, on attempted murder charges earlier this fall. While Riordan awaits sentencing, Addy has deferred college to embark on a journey of self-discovery and is currently working at a friend's family's restaurant."

Addy, who'd been leaning forward in her chair with a furrowed brow, relaxes and plucks a kernel of popcorn from her bowl. "That could've been a lot worse," she says.

Mikhail continues. "All criminal charges against Nate

Macauley, including drug charges made prior to his false arrest for Simon Kelleher's murder, have been dropped. Nate now works for a local company, Myers Construction, while taking business classes at community college. According to sources, he and Bronwyn Rojas remain romantically involved." I glance at my sister, who looks uncomfortable. Nate *hates* when the media talks about the two of them, but he just gives her a half smile. I'd suspect Bronwyn of being the "source," because she's never been able to resist a call from Mikhail Powers, if she and Nate hadn't gotten back together mere hours ago.

And then Mikhail's face freezes, his mouth open. We all look at Cooper, who's raised the remote again to pause the program.

"I changed my mind," he says. "I lived this. I'm *still* livin' it. I don't need to watch it."

"Thank Christ," Nate says. He rubs the hand that's not tangled in Bronwyn's hair over his jaw. "Co-signed." He and Cooper exchange glances, and it strikes me that while the two of them have the least in common of anybody in the room—and would probably never hang out with just each other—they almost always agree.

Addy shrugs. "I'm gonna watch it eventually," she says. "I can't not. But it doesn't have to be now, when Bronwyn just got back. It's been ages since we all did something together. You guys want to go to Glenn's Diner instead?"

Bronwyn looks torn. She deals in information and likes having all the facts; it's going to bug her that there are people walking around Bayview who have seen the Mikhail Powers special before she has. But I'm pretty sure she doesn't want her relationship with Nate analyzed on-screen while she's sitting next to him, either. "All right," she says, her eyes lingering so long on the frozen television that I know we'll be watching it before the night is over.

Good. Maybe it'll distract her from the Time to Get Your Life on Track conversation that's headed my way otherwise.

There are two units of time: regular time, and time spent waiting for your sister while she's preparing to separate for an afternoon from the boyfriend she hasn't seen for months. The latter must move backward, because I'm pretty sure I've been parked in the driveway of the rambling old house where Nate rents a room since yesterday.

Okay, slight exaggeration. But I've been waiting almost twenty minutes. Bronwyn and I are going to be late for lunch with Eli Kleinfelter, which would be a bigger problem if I really believed Eli was going to take a break to eat with us. Even on Black Friday, when the rest of the country is either shopping or sleeping off yesterday's turkey, he's at work.

Bronwyn finally emerges, buttoning her light jacket against the brisk breeze as she crosses the driveway toward our Volvo. Nate picked her up at ten o'clock this morning so they could go to the San Diego Museum of Art, which has an exhibit on German Expressionism that Bronwyn's been dying to see.

That's the story she told our parents, anyway.

"Brush your hair, young lady," I say in mock severity as she slides into the passenger seat. "That's the worst case of bedhead I've ever seen."

Bronwyn turns bright red, glancing into the sun visor mirror as she buckles her seat belt. "It's windy out," she says defensively.

"Mm-hmm." I turn the keys in the ignition. "How were the Germans?"

Her mouth twitches. "Expressive," she says, and we both start laughing as I pull out of the driveway. Bronwyn only brought her phone with her, so she digs a brush out of my bag and pulls it through her tangled hair.

"So everything's good with Nate again?" I ask. Understatement of the year, apparently. It couldn't be more obvious how they spent the last two hours. And twenty minutes.

"Better than good," she says happily. "The breakup was a blip. We just had to adjust to this whole long-distance thing." I meet her eyes before shifting into drive, and can almost see her force herself not to gush. If I'm aware of how opposite our lives sometimes seem, she's even more so. "Do you ever think you might want to get back together with Knox?"

"No. We're better off as friends."

Bronwyn makes a little sound in her throat like she's not sure whether to believe me, but it's the truth. Knox Myers and I were in a play together last spring and started going out over the summer. He was my first boyfriend, and we were both so inexperienced that it took us way too long to realize we weren't actually attracted to one another. One of these days, I hope, I'll find the kind of chemistry my sister has with Nate. But Knox definitely wasn't it. I'm just glad we got through the awkwardness and managed to stay friends. I need as many as I can get now that Bronwyn has abandoned me for Yale.

"Will he be at Until Proven today?" Bronwyn asks.

"No," I say, amused. Knox interns at Eli's nonprofit legal firm, taking the spot Bronwyn vacated when she left Bayview, but he wouldn't be there over a holiday even if he weren't visiting his grandparents in Kansas. "Not everyone is as much of a workaholic as you and Eli."

Traffic is light, and we pull into an empty space in front of Eli's office building less than twenty minutes later. The coffee shop in the lobby is open, serving a sparse line of customers. I always get a little chill when we pass that coffee shop, because it's where we finally figured out what happened with Simon last year.

But it holds happier memories, too. I poke Bronwyn in the arm en route to the elevator. "Remember how moony Eli got the first time he saw Ashton?"

Bronwyn laughs. "Oh my God, yes. He almost tripped over his own feet." She lowers her voice to imitate Eli's. "*Oh, hi, you must be Addy's sister.* So smooth. And Ashton's all, *I'm sorry, have we met?*"

"Who would've thought they'd still be going strong a year later?" I say as we step into the elevator and I press the up button. Eli and Ashton are two of my favorite people on their own, and somehow they're even better together.

The elevator stops on the third floor. The doors slide open, and we're greeted by a pungent smell. Bronwyn wrinkles her nose and looks over at me. "Ugh, what is that?"

"One of those hair clubs for men moved in," I say, inclining my head toward the door as we pass.

"Glad that happened after I left," she mutters.

The Until Proven office is a lot less crowded than usual, with only a handful of people scattered across the maze of desks. I spot Eli leaning against his, chatting with a young woman with long braids pulled into a ponytail. His face lights up with a big grin when he spies my sister, and he immediately starts across the room toward us.

"Bronwyn, hey! Welcome back," he says, engulfing her in a hug, then gives me one for good measure, even though I saw him last week. He looks the same as ever: wrinkled button-down shirt with rolled-up sleeves, a cloud of curly hair that defies gravity, and bright dark eyes behind glasses. "Great to see you guys. Let me introduce you to someone." He gestures toward the woman he was just talking to, who approaches us with a wide smile. "This is Bethany Okonjo, our new paralegal. Bethany, this is my former intern extraordinaire Bronwyn Rojas, and her tech wizard sister, Maeve." It's nice of him to give me an honorific, I guess, even if I've let my computer skills get rusty since I used them to track Simon last year.

Bethany shakes our hands in turn with a quick, firm grip. "Great to meet you both. I've heard a lot about you."

"I'm almost ready for lunch," Eli says, surprising me. I was 90 percent sure he'd blow us off. "I just need five minutes for a quick call with Bethany's professor. We have a big case brewing, and I might bring her on as a consultant."

"Eli, it's fine," Bethany protests. "You have plans. We can talk to my professor another time."

"We don't mind," I say. "We're not in a rush."

"If you're sure," Bethany says doubtfully, but Bronwyn and I both wave her off.

"Five minutes, I promise," Eli says as he and Bethany head for a conference room. "If that. We're just laying the groundwork for a longer discussion next week."

"We'll see him in half an hour," Bronwyn predicts, settling herself into the chair behind his desk.

I pull an empty chair beside her and sit down with a loud sniff, rooting through my bag for a tissue. I've had a lingering cold for more than a week, and I suck in a frustrated breath when I come up empty. "You don't happen to have a Kleenex, do you?" I ask Bronwyn.

"No. I don't have anything. I left in a hurry this morning."

"*Yeah,* you did," I tease, kicking her foot.

She makes a face at me. "Try the top left drawer. That's where Eli usually keeps them."

I pull it open, but no luck. It's nearly empty, except . . .

"Bronwyn." I kick her again, pulling the drawer until it's fully extended, and lower my voice to a near-whisper. "Is that what I think it is?"

She leans across me, eyes widening as she spots the small black velvet box. *"No,"* she breathes. "But yes! I think." We've both watched enough jewelry store commercials to recognize an engagement ring box when we see it.

I can feel a grin start to take over my face. "Should we look inside?" I ask.

"Of course not. That would be a violation of Eli's privacy." Bronwyn shoots me a lofty look and adjusts her glasses. "We're better than that."

"Right," I agree. "Much better." We both look up at the glass-walled conference room near the office entrance, where Eli and Bethany are hunched over a phone in the middle of the table. "Anyway, it might just be cuff links or something."

"Sure," Bronwyn says. "Because Eli wears those all the time." We're silent for a few beats, staring into the drawer.

"I really want to look," I finally say in a low voice.

"Me too," she admits, and I reach over to grab the box.

"Just a tiny peek," I promise, lifting the lid.

We both gasp when we see what's inside. It's an engagement ring, I'm almost sure, but not the standard diamond-and-platinum dazzler you see all over Bayview. The stone has a gorgeous brown hue, and it's set in a simple matte gold bezel dotted with tiny gemstones of the same color. "It's so pretty!" Bronwyn exclaims, taking the box from me and turning it so the jewels sparkle under the office lights.

"Is that a diamond?" I ask.

"I think so." Bronwyn squints at it. "A raw one."

"What does that mean?"

"It's not shaped or polished," Bronwyn says. "More organic. Not processed."

I blink at her, startled. Is she checking out engagement rings already? I didn't think that was in the five-year plan she laid out for herself when she graduated high school. The ten-year one, maybe. "How do you know this stuff?"

She shrugs. "We're studying the gem industry in my econ class. Knowing Eli, this diamond is probably conflict-free."

"You've got that right," says a voice. Bronwyn gasps, slams the box closed, and throws it back into the drawer like a three-year-old caught stealing cookies.

Eli stands in front of us, arms crossed. Bethany is nowhere in sight. I don't have to look at my sister to know her face is as red as mine. "Sorry," we murmur in unison, eyes down.

"You two are unbelievable," Eli complains. "I can't leave you alone for five minutes."

"But, um, congratulations?" I offer in a small voice.

"She hasn't said yes yet." Eli holds up a hand when I open my mouth to protest. "Save the reassurances, please. Ashton's been down this road before. She's cautious. So if you could keep this to yourselves, I'd appreciate it." He narrows his eyes as we both nod vigorously. "Including Addy. It's up to Ashton what she chooses to share."

"Okay," Bronwyn says. "When are you going to ask her?"

"None of your business," Eli says shortly. Then he swallows visibly.

I feel a prickle of excitement. Eli and Ashton's first official date—when she finally agreed that's what they were doing, and not just hanging out as friends—was *last* Black Friday. It sticks in my mind because they debuted as an actual couple at Café Contigo in downtown Bayview, where half the town congregates for Thanksgiving break. Cooper's best friend Luis's family owns the restaurant, and Addy is a waitress there now. Bronwyn and I will be heading over after dinner, along with most of our friends.

"Tonight, because it's your one-year anniversary!" I exclaim before I can stop myself.

"Oh my God, yes! That must be it!" Bronwyn yelps. We high-five, our moment of shame entirely forgotten.

"*Enough,*" Eli says in a threatening voice, but we can't take him seriously when he's blushing that hard. "Come on. Get away from that desk right now if you still expect me to take you to lunch."

I flash him my most angelic smile as I get to my feet. "Our treat," I say sweetly. "It's the least we can do."

Café Contigo is packed by nine o'clock that night. It's an Argentinean café with bright blue walls and a tin ceiling, the day's specials written across a large blackboard with colorful chalk. Mr. Santos, Luis's father, helped us pull a bunch of tables together, and now it's a Bayview High reunion on one side of the room. I'm sitting between Luis and Cooper, who have been reliving last year's state baseball championship for the last fifteen minutes in excruciating detail.

"I miss Kris," I sigh to no one in particular. He's visiting family tonight, so can't distract Cooper from nonstop sports talk.

Luis nudges my shoulder with his. "You want us to talk about that infield fly call again? I've never seen you look so interested."

I hold up my fork. "I'd rather gouge my eyes out with this."

Luis frowns. "That makes no sense. You could still hear us."

"It's the principle," I say, as he adds, "Besides, your eyes are too pretty for that."

I feel my cheeks get warm as Cooper loudly asks, "Weren't you going to bring us more empanadas, Luis?"

"I was," Luis says good-naturedly.

He gets up to head for the kitchen, and I raise my brows at Cooper. "Am I imagining things, or did you just chase Luis off like you're my *dad*?"

Cooper smiles sheepishly. "Sorry. I love the guy, but he's such a dog. Besides, he knows you're not available."

I pause, wondering if reminding Cooper that I am, in fact, available as of last month would make it sound like I'm interested in Luis. And whether that's true. Before I can decide, Bronwyn's arm shoots across the table and grabs my wrist.

"Maeve," she hisses. *"Look."*

I follow her gaze to see Eli walking into Café Contigo alone. He sits down heavily at the only empty table in the place and folds his hands in front of him, head bowed. "Oh no," I say, lowering my voice to a frantic whisper. "You don't think . . ."

"What?" Cooper asks, following our gaze.

"Nothing," Bronwyn and I say together.

Nate, leaning forward from his seat next to Bronwyn, narrows his eyes. "That's the most something-sounding *nothing* I've ever heard," he says. He catches sight of Eli and adds, "What's wrong with Eli? He looks like someone just told him he's not allowed to work weekends anymore."

"Nothing," Bronwyn and I repeat. My stomach is legitimately full of lead for Eli, but I'm hoping it's not as bad as it looks. Maybe he chickened out, or maybe Ashton just said she needs more time. Surely she couldn't have flat-out broken up with him, right?

Addy, who had been deep in conversation with her friend Keely on Cooper's other side, twists to face us. "What are you guys talking about?" she asks.

Nate smirks. "Nothing, apparently."

"That's right," I say, just as Eli looks up and meets my eye. He lifts his shoulders in a deep sigh, then winks.

The door flies open, and Ashton bursts through in a gorgeous red dress, her pretty face glowing. "Addy!" she calls out. "Addy, come here!" She grabs Eli's hand and tugs him to his feet as Addy rises from her chair with a confused expression.

"What's up?" she asks, squeezing behind Cooper and me.

Bronwyn is still holding my wrist. She shakes it, eyes popping behind her glasses. Nate glances between us. "Is this still nothing?" he asks.

"Just wait," Bronwyn says as Ashton holds out her left hand to an approaching Addy. Addy grabs hold of it and screams, then flings her arms around Ashton and Eli in turn. My sister and I are grinning like fools, but we don't say a word until Addy turns in the general direction of our table and yells, "They're engaged!" She drags Ashton our way and Eli follows as people get up and start crowding to see the ring. I rise and skirt around them, plucking at Eli's sleeve.

"What was with the hangdog face?" I say in his ear.

He grins. "Ashton got a call from her mom right when we got here. She shooed me inside, so I figured I'd take the opportunity to mess with you guys."

"I almost had a heart attack," I admit.

"Serves you right for going through my stuff," he says, but he lets me hug him before I crane my neck to get a better look at the ring. It's even prettier out of the box, and you can tell from the way Ashton can't stop staring at it that it's exactly what she would have picked if she'd designed it herself. Cooper shakes Eli's hand, and Bronwyn beams while she leans into Nate and listens to Ashton's excited chatter about possible wedding dates.

It hits me, then, what a difference a year makes. When we were here last Black Friday, everyone was subdued and quiet, still traumatized from what happened with Simon. Now it looks as though things in Bayview are, finally, exactly as they should be.

I'm sure they'll stay that way. What could possibly go wrong?

THE MYSTERY ISN'T OVER YET—
DON'T MISS THE SEQUEL!

Turn the page to start reading.

Friday, March 6

REPORTER: (standing at the edge of a winding street with a large white stucco building behind her): Good morning, this is Liz Rosen with Channel Seven News, reporting live from Bayview High, where students are reeling from the loss of one of their classmates yesterday. It's the second tragic teenage death in the past eighteen months for this small town, and the mood outside the school is one of shocked déjà vu.

(Cut to two girls, one wiping tears, the other stone-faced)

CRYING GIRL: It's just . . . it's just really sad. Like, sometimes it feels as though Bayview is cursed, you know? First Simon, and now this.

STOIC GIRL: This isn't anything like what happened with Simon.

REPORTER (angling her microphone toward the crying girl): Were you and the deceased student close?

CRYING GIRL: Not like, *close* close. Or at all close. I mean, I'm just a freshman.

REPORTER (turning toward the other girl): And how about you?

STOIC GIRL: I don't think we're supposed to be talking to you.

Ten Weeks Earlier

Reddit, Vengeance Is Mine subforum
Thread started by Bayview2020

Hey.
Is this the same group Simon Kelleher used to
post with?—Bayview2020

Greetings.
One and the same.—Darkestmind

Why'd you move? And why are there hardly
any posts?—Bayview2020

Too many gawkers and reporters on the
old site.

And we have new security measures. Lesson
learned from our friend Simon.
Who I'm guessing you know, based on your
user name?—Darkestmind

Everyone knows Simon. Well. Knew him.
It's not like we were friends, though.
—Bayview2020

Okay. So what brings you here?—Darkestmind

I don't know. Just stumbled across it.
—Bayview2020

Bullshit. This is a forum dedicated to revenge,
and it's not easy to find.
You're here for a reason.
What is it? Or should I say who?—Darkestmind

Who.
Somebody did something horrible.
It wrecked my life and so many others.
Meanwhile NOTHING happened to them.
And I can't do anything about it.—Bayview2020

Same, same.
We have a lot in common.
It sucks when the person who ruined your life
gets to walk around like always.

As if what they did doesn't matter.
I beg to disagree with your conclusion,
though.
There's always something you can do.
—Darkestmind

Phoebe
Tuesday, February 18

The logical part of my brain knows my mother isn't playing with dolls. But it's early, I'm tired, and I'm not wearing my contacts yet. So instead of squinting harder, I lean against the kitchen counter and ask, "What's with the dolls?"

"They're wedding cake toppers," Mom says, yanking one away from my twelve-year-old brother, Owen, and handing it to me. I look down to see a white-clad bride with her legs wrapped around the groom's waist. Some underappreciated artist has managed to pack a lot of lust into their tiny plastic faces.

"Classy," I say. I should have guessed it was wedding related. Last week the kitchen table was covered with stationery samples, and before that it was do-it-yourself floral centerpieces.

"That's the only one like that," she says with a hint of defensiveness. "I suppose you have to account for all kinds of tastes. Could you put it in the box?" She juts her chin toward a cardboard box half-full of foam peanuts on the counter.

I drop the happy couple inside and pull a glass from the cabinet next to our sink, filling it from the tap and finishing the whole thing in two long, greedy gulps. "Cake toppers, huh?" I ask. "Do people still use those?"

"They're just samples from Golden Rings," Mom says. Ever since she joined the local wedding planners' organization, boxes full of stuff like this show up at our apartment every couple of weeks. Mom takes pictures, makes notes of what she likes, and then packs it back up to send along to the next wedding planner in the group. "Some of them are cute, though." She holds up one of a bride and groom waltzing in silhouette. "What do you think?"

There's an open box of Eggo waffles on the counter. I pull out the last two and pop them into the toaster. "I think plastic people on top of a cake isn't really Ashton and Eli's style. Aren't they trying to keep things simple?"

"Sometimes you don't know what you want until you see it," Mom says brightly. "Part of my job is opening their eyes to what's out there."

Poor Ashton. Addy's older sister has been a dream neighbor ever since we moved into the apartment across from them last summer—giving takeout recommendations, showing us which washing machines never eat your quarters, and sharing concert tickets from her job as a graphic designer with the California Center for the Arts. She had no idea what she was getting into when she agreed to help Mom launch a side business in wedding planning by coordinating "a few details" of her upcoming wedding to Eli Kleinfelter.

Mom's gone a little overboard. She wants to make a good impression, especially since Eli is something of a local celebrity. He's the lawyer who defended Nate Macauley when Nate was framed for killing Simon Kelleher, and now he's always being interviewed about some big case or another. The press loves the fact that he's marrying the sister of one of the Bayview Four, so they reference his upcoming wedding a lot. That means free publicity for Mom, including a mention in the *San Diego Tribune* and an in-depth profile last December in the *Bayview Blade*. Which has turned into a total gossip rag since covering the Simon story, so of course they took the most dramatic angle possible: "After Heartbreaking Loss, Area Widow Launches a Business Based on Joy."

We all could've done without *that* reminder.

Still, Mom has put more energy into this wedding than just about anything else over the past few years, so I should be grateful for Ashton and Eli's endless patience.

"Your waffles are burning," Owen says placidly, stuffing a forkful of syrup-soaked squares into his mouth.

"Shit!" I yank my Eggos out with a whimper of pain as my fingers graze hot metal. "Mom, can we please buy a new toaster? This one has gotten completely useless. It goes from zero to scalding in thirty seconds."

Mom's eyebrows pull together with the worried look she always gets when any of us talk about spending money. "I noticed that. But we should probably try cleaning it before we replace it. There must be ten years' worth of bread crumbs built up in there."

"I'll do it," Owen volunteers, pushing his glasses up on his nose. "And if that doesn't work, I'll take it apart. I bet I can fix it."

I smile absently at him. "No doubt, brainiac. I should've thought of that first."

"I don't want you playing around with anything electrical, Owen," Mom objects.

He looks affronted. "It wouldn't be *playing*."

A door clicks as my older sister, Emma, leaves our bedroom and heads for the kitchen. That's something I'll never get used to about apartment living—how being on a single floor makes you acutely aware of where everyone is, all the time. There's nowhere to hide. Nothing like our old house, where not only did we all have our own bedrooms, but we had a family room, an office that eventually turned into a game room for Owen, and Dad's basement workroom.

Plus, we had Dad.

My throat tightens as Emma runs her eyes over the piles of formally clad plastic people on our kitchen table. "Do people still use cake toppers?"

"Your sister asked the exact same thing," Mom says. She's always doing that—pointing out threads of similarity between Emma and me, as though acknowledging them will somehow knit us back into the tight sisterly unit we were as kids.

Emma makes a *hmm* noise, and I stay focused on my waffle as she steps closer. "Could you move?" she asks politely. "I need the blender."

I shift to one side as Owen picks up a cake topper featuring a bride with dark red hair. "This one looks like you, Emma," he says.

All of us Lawton kids are some version of redhead—Emma's hair is a deep auburn, mine is a coppery bronze, and Owen's strawberry blond—but it was our father who really stood out in a crowd, with hair so orange that his high school nickname was Cheeto. One time when we were at the Bayview Mall food court, Dad went to the bathroom and came back to see an older couple surreptitiously checking out my dark-haired, olive-skinned mother and her three pale, redheaded kids. Dad plopped down next to Mom and put an arm around her shoulders, flashing a grin at the couple. "See, *now* we make sense," he said.

And now, three years after he died? We don't.

If I had to pinpoint Emma's least favorite part of the day . . . I'd be hard-pressed, because there doesn't seem to be a lot that Emma enjoys lately. But having to pick my friend Jules up on the way to school easily ranks in the top three.

"Oh my God," Jules says breathlessly when she climbs into the backseat of our ten-year-old Corolla, shoving her backpack ahead of her. I turn in my seat, and she whips off her sunglasses to fasten me with a death stare. "Phoebe. I cannot *stand* you."

"What? Why?" I ask, confused. I shift in my seat, smoothing my skirt when it rides up on my thighs. After years of trial and error I've finally found the wardrobe that works best for my body type: a short, flouncy skirt, preferably in a bold pattern; a brightly colored V-neck or scoop-neck top; and some kind of stack-heeled bootie.

"Seat belt, please," Emma says.

Jules clips her belt, still glaring at me. "You know why."

"I seriously do not," I protest. Emma pulls away from the curb in front of Jules's modest split-level house, which is just one street away from where we used to live. Our old neighborhood isn't Bayview's wealthiest by a long shot, but the young couple Mom sold our house to was still thrilled to get a starter home here.

Jules's green eyes, striking against her brown skin and dark hair, pop for dramatic effect. "Nate Macauley was at Café Contigo last night and you didn't text me!"

"Oh well . . ." I turn up the radio so my mumbled response will get lost in Taylor Swift's latest. Jules has always had a thing for Nate—she's a total sucker for the dark, handsome bad-boy type—but she never considered him boyfriend material until Bronwyn Rojas did. Now she circles like a vulture every time they break up. Which has caused divided loyalties since I started working at Café Contigo and became friendly with Addy, who, obviously, is firmly on Team Bronwyn.

"And he *never* goes out," Jules moans. "That was such a missed opportunity. Major friend failure, Phoebe Jeebies. Not cool." She pulls out a tube of wine-colored lip gloss and leans forward so she can see herself in the rear view mirror as she applies a fresh coat. "How did he seem? Do you think he's over Bronwyn?"

"I mean. It's hard to tell," I say. "He didn't really talk to anyone except Maeve and Addy. Mostly Addy."

Jules smacks her lips together, an expression of mild panic crossing her face. "Oh my God. Do you think *they're* together now?"

"No. Definitely not. They're friends. Not everyone finds him irresistible, Jules."

Jules drops the lip gloss back into her bag and leans her head against the window with a sigh. "Says you. He's so hot, I could die."

Emma pauses at a red light and rubs her eyes, then reaches for the volume button on the radio. "I need to turn this down," she says. "My head is pounding."

"Are you getting sick?" I ask.

"Just tired. My tutoring session with Sean Murdock went too long last night."

"No surprise there," I mutter. If you're searching for signs of intelligent life in the Bayview High junior class, Sean Murdock isn't where you'll find it. But his parents have money, and they'll happily throw it at Emma for the chance that either her work ethic or her grades might rub off on Sean.

"I should hire you, Emma," Jules says. "Chemistry is going to be a nightmare this semester unless I get some help. Or pull a Bronwyn Rojas and steal the tests."

"Bronwyn made up that class," I remind her, and Jules kicks my seat.

"Don't defend her," she says sulkily. "She's ruining my love life."

"If you're serious about tutoring, I have a slot free this weekend," Emma says.

"Chemistry on the *weekend*?" Jules sounds scandalized. "No thank you."

"Okay then." My sister exhales a light sigh, like she shouldn't have expected anything different. "Not serious."

Emma's only a year older than Jules and me, but most of the time she seems more Ashton Prentiss's age than ours. Emma doesn't act seventeen; she acts like she's in her midtwenties and stressing her way through graduate school instead of senior AP classes. Even now, when her college applications are all in and she's just waiting to hear back, she can't relax.

We drive the rest of the way in silence, until my phone chimes when Emma pulls into the parking lot. I look down to a text. *Bleachers?*

I shouldn't. But even as my brain reminds me that I've already gotten two late warnings this month, my fingers type *OK.* I put my phone in my pocket and have the passenger door halfway open before Emma's even shifted into Park. She raises her eyebrows as I climb out.

"I have to go to the football field real quick," I say, hiking my backpack over my shoulder and resting my hand on the car door.

"What for? You don't want to be late again," Emma says, narrowing her light brown eyes at me. They're exactly like Dad's, and—along with the reddish hair—the only trait she and I share. Emma is tall and thin, I'm short and curvy. Her hair is stick-straight and doesn't quite reach her shoulders, mine is long and curly. She freckles in the sun, and I tan. We're both February-pale now, though, and I can feel my cheeks redden as I look down at the ground.

"It's, um, for homework," I mumble.

Jules grins as she climbs out of the car. "Is that what we're calling it now?"

I turn on my heel and beat a hasty retreat, but I can still feel the weight of Emma's disapproval settling over my shoulders like a cloak. Emma has always been the serious one, but when we were younger it didn't matter. We were so close that we used to have entire conversations without talking. Mom would joke that we must be telepaths, but it wasn't that. We just knew one another so well that we could read every expression as clearly as a word.

We were close with Owen too, despite the age difference. Dad used to call us the Three Amigos, and every childhood photo shows us posed exactly the same way: Emma and me on either side of Owen, our arms around one another, grinning widely. We look inseparable, and I thought we were. It never occurred to me that Dad was the glue keeping us together.

The pulling apart was so subtle that I didn't notice it right away. Emma withdrew first, burying herself in schoolwork. "It's her way of grieving," Mom said, so I let her be, even though *my* way of grieving would have been to do it together. I compensated by throwing myself into every social activity I could find—especially once boys started getting interested in me—while Owen retreated into the comforting fantasy world of video games. Before I'd realized it, those had become our lanes, and we stayed in them. Our card last Christmas featured the three of us standing beside the tree, arranged by height, hands clasped in front of us with stiff smiles. Dad would've been so disappointed by that picture.

And by me shortly after we took it, for what happened at Jules's Christmas party. It's one thing to treat your older sister like a polite stranger, and quite another thing to . . . do what I did. I used to feel a wistful kind of loneliness when I thought about Emma, but now I just feel guilt. And relief that she can't read my feelings on my face anymore.

"Hey!" I'm so caught up in my thoughts that I would've walked right into a pole under the bleachers if a hand hadn't reached out and stopped me. Then it pulls me forward so quickly that my phone slides out of my pocket and makes a faint bouncing noise on the grass.

"Shit," I say, but Brandon Weber's lips are pressed against mine before I can get anything else out. I shimmy my shoulders until my backpack joins my phone on the ground. Brandon tugs at the hem of my shirt, and since this is one hundred percent what I came for, I help him along by untucking it.

Brandon's hands move up and across my bare skin, pushing aside the lace of my bra, and he groans against my mouth. "God, you're so sexy."

He is, too. Brandon quarterbacks the football team, and the *Bayview Blade* likes to call him "the next Cooper Clay" because he's good enough that colleges are already starting to scout him. I don't think that's an accurate comparison, though. For one thing, Cooper has next-level talent, and for another, he's a sweetheart. Brandon, on the other hand, is basically an asshole.

The boy can kiss, though. All the tension flows out of me as he pushes me against the pole behind us, replaced with a heady spark of anticipation. I wrap one arm around his neck, trying to pull him down to my height, while my other hand teases at the waistband of his jeans. Then my foot sends something skidding across the ground, and the sound of my text tone distracts me.

"My phone," I say, pulling away. "We're going to smash it if I don't pick it up."

"I'll buy you a new one," Brandon says, his tongue in my ear. Which I don't like—*why* do guys think that's hot?—so I shove at him until he lets go. His front pocket dings loudly, and I smirk at the bulge there as I retrieve my phone.

"Is that a text, or are you just happy to see me?" I say, brushing off my screen. Then I glance down and catch my breath. "Ugh, are you kidding me? This again?"

"What?" Brandon asks, pulling out his own phone.

"Unknown number, and guess what it says?" I put on an affected voice. "*Still missing About That? I know I do. Let's play a new game.* I can't believe somebody would pull this crap after Principal Gupta's warning."

Brandon's eyes flick over his screen. "I got the same thing. You see the link?"

"Yeah. Don't click it! It's probably a virus or—"

"Too late," Brandon laughs. He squints at his phone while I take him in: over six feet tall with dirty-blond hair, blue-green eyes, and the kind of full lips a girl would kill for. He's so pretty, he looks like he could fly off with a harp any second. And nobody knows it more than he does. "Jesus, this is a freaking book," he complains.

"Let me see." I grab his phone, because no way am I following that link with mine. I angle the screen away from the sun until I can see it clearly. I'm looking at a website with a bad replica of the About That logo, and a big block of text beneath it. *"Pay attention, Bayview High. I'm only going to explain the rules once,"* I read. *"Here's how we play Truth or Dare. I'll send a prompt to one person only—and you can't tell ANYONE if it's you. Don't spoil the element of surprise. It makes me cranky, and I'm not nearly as nice when I'm cranky. You get 24 hours to text your choice back. Pick Truth, and I'll reveal one of your secrets. Pick Dare, and I'll give you a challenge. Either way, we'll have a little fun and relieve the monotony of our tedious existence."*

Brandon runs a hand through his thick, tawny hair. "Speak for yourself, loser."

"Come on Bayview, you know you've missed this." I scowl when I finish. "Do you think this went to everyone at school? People better not say anything if they want to keep their phones." Last fall, after Principal Gupta shut down the latest Simon copycat, she told us she was instituting a zero-tolerance policy: if she saw even a hint of another About That, she'd ban phones at school permanently. And expel anyone caught trying to bring one in.

We've all been model citizens since then, at least when it comes to online gossip. Nobody can imagine getting through a school day—never mind *years*—without their phones.

"No one cares. It's old news," Brandon says dismissively.

He pockets his phone and wraps an arm around my waist, pulling me close. "So where were we?"

I'm still holding my own phone, pressed against his chest now, and it chimes in my hand before I can answer. When I pull my head back to look at the screen, there's another message from an unknown contact. But this time, there's no simultaneous text tone from Brandon's pocket.

Phoebe Lawton, you're up first! Text back your choice: Should I reveal a Truth, or will you take a Dare?

MORE FROM KAREN M. McMANUS!

"A must-read YA thriller if you love *Riverdale* and *Sharp Objects*." —*Bustle*

Turn the page for a special preview!

CHAPTER ONE

ELLERY

FRIDAY, AUGUST 30

If I believed in omens, this would be a bad one.

There's only one suitcase left on the baggage carousel. It's bright pink, covered with Hello Kitty stickers, and definitely not mine.

My brother, Ezra, watches it pass us for the fourth time, leaning on the handle of his own oversized suitcase. The crowd around the carousel is nearly gone, except for a couple arguing about who was supposed to keep track of their rental car reservation. "Maybe you should take it," Ezra suggests. "Seems like whoever owns it wasn't on our flight, and I bet they have an interesting wardrobe. A lot of polka dots, probably. And glitter." His phone chimes, and he pulls it out of his pocket. "Nana's outside."

"I can't believe this," I mutter, kicking the toe of my sneaker against the carousel's metal side. "My entire life was in that suitcase."

It's a slight exaggeration. My *actual* entire life was in La Puente, California, until about eight hours ago. Other than a few boxes shipped to Vermont last week, the suitcase contains what's left.

"I guess we should report it." Ezra scans the baggage claim area, running a hand over his close-cropped hair. He used to have thick dark curls like mine, hanging in his eyes, and I still can't get used to the cut he got over the summer. He tilts his suitcase and pivots toward the information desk. "Over here, probably."

The skinny guy behind the desk looks like he could still be in high school, with a rash of red pimples dotting his cheeks and jawline. A gold name tag pinned crookedly to his blue vest reads "Andy." Andy's thin lips twist when I tell him about my suitcase, and he cranes his neck toward the Hello Kitty bag still making carousel laps. "Flight 5624 from Los Angeles? With a layover in Charlotte?" I nod. "You sure that's not yours?"

"Positive."

"Bummer. It'll turn up, though. You just gotta fill this out." He yanks open a drawer and pulls out a form, sliding it toward me. "There's a pen around here somewhere," he mutters, pawing half-heartedly through a stack of papers.

"I have one." I unzip the front of my backpack, pulling out a book that I place on the counter while I feel around for a pen. Ezra raises his brows when he sees the battered hardcover.

"Really, Ellery?" he asks. "You brought *In Cold Blood* on the plane? Why didn't you just ship it with the rest of your books?"

"It's valuable," I say defensively.

Ezra rolls his eyes. "You *know* that's not Truman Capote's actual signature. Sadie got fleeced."

"Whatever. It's the thought that counts," I mutter. Our mother bought me the "signed" first edition off eBay after she landed a role as Dead Body #2 on *Law & Order* four years ago. She gave Ezra a Sex Pistols album cover with a Sid Vicious autograph that was probably just as forged. We should've gotten a car with reliable brakes instead, but Sadie's never been great at long-term planning. "Anyway, you know what they say. When in Murderland . . ." I finally extract a pen and start scratching my name across the form.

"You headed for Echo Ridge, then?" Andy asks. I pause on the second *c* of my last name and he adds, "They don't call it that anymore, you know. And you're early. It doesn't open for another week."

"I know. I didn't mean the theme park. I meant the . . ." I trail off before saying *town* and shove *In Cold Blood* into my bag. "Never mind," I say, returning my attention to the form. "How long does it usually take to get your stuff back?"

"Shouldn't be more than a day." Andy's eyes drift between Ezra and me. "You guys look a lot alike. You twins?"

I nod and keep writing. Ezra, ever polite, answers, "We are."

"I was supposed to be a twin," Andy says. "The other one got absorbed in the womb, though." Ezra lets out a surprised little snort, and I bite back a laugh. This happens to my brother all the time; people overshare the strangest things with him. We might have almost the same face, but his is the one everyone trusts. "I always thought it would've been cool to have a twin.

You could pretend to be one another and mess with people." I look up, and Andy is squinting at us again. "Well. I guess you guys can't do that. You aren't the right kind of twins."

"Definitely not," Ezra says with a fixed smile.

I write faster and hand the completed form to Andy, who tears off the top sheets and gives me the yellow carbon. "So somebody will get in touch, right?" I ask.

"Yep," Andy says. "You don't hear from them tomorrow, call the number at the bottom. Have fun in Echo Ridge."

Ezra exhales loudly as we head for the revolving door, and I grin at him over my shoulder. "You make the nicest friends."

He shudders. "Now I can't stop thinking about it. *Absorbed.* How does that even happen? Did he . . . No. I'm not going to speculate. I don't want to know. What a weird thing to grow up with, though, huh? Knowing how easily you could've been the wrong twin."

We push through the door into a blast of stifling, exhaust-filled air that takes me by surprise. Even on the last day of August, I'd expected Vermont to be a lot cooler than California. I pull my hair off my neck while Ezra scrolls through his phone. "Nana says she's circling because she didn't want to park in a lot," he reports.

I raise my brows at him. "Nana's texting and driving?"

"Apparently."

I haven't seen my grandmother since she visited us in California ten years ago, but from what I can remember, that seems out of character.

We wait a few minutes, wilting in the heat, until a forest-green Subaru station wagon pulls up beside us. The passenger-side window rolls down, and Nana sticks her head out. She doesn't look much different than she does over Skype, although her thick gray bangs appear freshly cut. "Go on, get in," she calls, side-eyeing the traffic cop a few feet from us. "They won't let you idle for more than a minute." She pulls her head back in as Ezra wheels his solitary suitcase toward the trunk.

When we slide into the backseat Nana turns to face us, and so does a younger woman behind the steering wheel. "Ellery, Ezra, this is Melanie Kilduff. Her family lives down the street from us. I have terrible night vision, so Melanie was kind enough to drive. She used to babysit your mother when she was young. You've probably heard the name."

Ezra and I exchange wide-eyed glances. *Yes.* Yes, we have.

Sadie left Echo Ridge when she was eighteen, and she's only been back twice. The first time was the year before we were born, when our grandfather died from a heart attack. And the second time was five years ago, for Melanie's teenage daughter's funeral.

Ezra and I watched the *Dateline* special—"Mystery at Murderland"—at home while our neighbor stayed with us. I was transfixed by the story of Lacey Kilduff, the beautiful blond homecoming queen from my mother's hometown, found strangled in a Halloween theme park. Airport Andy was right; the park's owner changed its name from Murderland to Fright Farm a few months later. I'm not sure the case would have gotten as much national attention if the park hadn't had such an on-the-nose name.

Or if Lacey hadn't been the second pretty teenager from Echo Ridge—and from the same exact street, even—to make tragic headlines.

Sadie wouldn't answer any of our questions when she got back from Lacey's funeral. "I just want to forget about it," she said whenever we asked. Which is what she's been saying about Echo Ridge our entire lives.

Ironic, I guess, that we ended up here anyway.

"Nice to meet you," Ezra says to Melanie, while I somehow manage to choke on my own saliva. He pounds me on the back, harder than necessary.

Melanie is pretty in a faded sort of way, with pale blond hair pulled into a French braid, light blue eyes, and a sprinkling of freckles. She flashes a disarming, gap-toothed smile. "You as well. Sorry we're late, but we hit a surprising amount of traffic. How was your flight?"

Before Ezra can answer, a loud rap sounds on the roof of the Subaru, making Nana jump. "You need to keep moving," the traffic cop calls.

"Burlington is the *rudest* city," Nana huffs. She presses a button on the door to close her window as Melanie eases the car behind a taxi.

I fumble with my seat belt as I stare at the back of Melanie's head. I wasn't expecting to meet her like this. I figured I would eventually, since she and Nana are neighbors, but I thought it would be more of a wave while taking out the trash, not an hour-long drive as soon as I landed in Vermont.

"I was so sorry to hear about your mother," Melanie says as she exits the airport and pulls onto a narrow highway dotted with green signs. It's almost ten o'clock at night, and a small cluster of buildings in front of us glows with lit windows. "But I'm glad she's getting the help she needs. Sadie is such a strong woman. I'm sure you'll be back with her soon, but I hope you enjoy your time in Echo Ridge. It's a lovely little town. I know Nora is looking forward to showing you around."

There. *That's* how you navigate an awkward conversation. No need to lead with *Sorry your mom drove her car into a jewelry store while she was high on opioids and had to go to rehab for four months.* Just acknowledge the elephant in the room, sidestep, and segue into smoother conversational waters.

Welcome to Echo Ridge.

I fall asleep shortly after we hit the highway and don't stir until a loud noise jolts me awake. It sounds as though the car is being pelted from every direction with dozens of rocks. I turn toward Ezra, disoriented, but he looks equally confused. Nana twists in her seat, shouting to be heard over the roar. "Hail. Not uncommon this time of year. Although these are rather large."

"I'm going to pull over and let this pass," Melanie calls. She eases the car to the side of the road and shifts into park. The hail is hitting harder than ever, and I can't help but think that she's going to have hundreds of tiny dents in her car by the time it stops. One particularly large hailstone smacks right into the middle of the windshield, startling us all.

"How is it *hailing*?" I ask. "It was hot in Burlington."

"Hail forms in the cloud layer," Nana explains, gesturing toward the sky. "Temperatures are freezing there. The stones will melt quickly on the ground, though."

Her voice isn't warm, exactly—I'm not sure warmth is possible for her—but it's more animated than it's been all night.

Nana used to be a teacher, and she's obviously a lot more comfortable in that role than that of Custodial Grandparent. Not that I blame her. She's stuck with us during Sadie's sixteen weeks of court-ordered rehab, and vice versa. The judge insisted we live with family, which severely limited our options. Our father was a one-night stand—a stuntman, or so he claimed during the whopping two hours he and Sadie spent together after meeting at an LA club. We don't have aunts, uncles, or cousins. Not a single person, except for Nana, to take us in.

We sit in silence for a few minutes, watching hailstones bounce off the car hood, until the frequency tapers and finally stops altogether. Melanie pulls back onto the road, and I glance at the clock on the dashboard. It's nearly eleven; I slept for almost an hour. I nudge Ezra and ask, "We must almost be there, right?"

"Almost," Ezra says. He lowers his voice. "Place is hopping on a Friday night. We haven't passed a building for miles."

It's pitch black outside, and even after rubbing my eyes a few times I can't see much out the window except the shadowy blur of trees. I try, though, because I want to see the place Sadie couldn't wait to leave. "It's like living in a postcard," she used to say. "Pretty, shiny, and closed in. Everyone who lives in Echo Ridge acts like you'll vanish if you venture outside the border."

The car goes over a bump, and my seat belt digs into my neck as the impact jolts me to one side. Ezra yawns so hard that his jaw cracks. I'm sure that once I crashed he felt obligated to stay awake and make conversation, even though neither of us has slept properly for days.

"We're less than a mile from home." Nana's voice from the front seat startles us both. "We just passed the 'Welcome to Echo Ridge' sign, although it's so poorly lit that I don't suppose you even noticed."

She's right. I didn't, though I'd made a mental note to look for it. The sign was one of the few things Sadie ever talked about related to Echo Ridge, usually after a few glasses of wine. "'Population 4,935.' Never changed the entire eighteen years I lived there," she'd say with a smirk. "Apparently if you're going to bring someone in, you have to take someone out first."

"Here comes the overpass, Melanie." Nana's voice has a warning edge.

"I know," Melanie says. The road curves sharply as we pass beneath an arch of gray stone, and Melanie slows to a crawl. There are no streetlights along this stretch, and Melanie switches on the high beams.

"Nana is the worst backseat driver ever," Ezra whispers.

"Really?" I whisper back. "But Melanie's so careful."

"Unless we're at a red light, we're going too fast."

I snicker, just as my grandmother hollers, "Stop!" in such a commanding voice that both Ezra and I jump. For a split second, I think she has supersonic hearing and is annoyed at our snarking. Then Melanie slams on the brakes, stopping the car so abruptly that I'm pitched forward against my seat belt.

"What the—?" Ezra and I both ask at the same time, but Melanie and Nana have already unbuckled and scrambled out of the car. We exchange confused glances and follow suit. The ground is covered with puddles of half-melted hail, and I pick my way around them toward my grandmother. Nana is standing in front of Melanie's car, her gaze fixed on the patch of road bathed in bright headlights.

And on the still figure lying right in the middle of it. Covered in blood, with his neck bent at a horribly wrong angle and his eyes wide open, staring at nothing.

ABOUT THE AUTHOR

Karen M. McManus earned her BA in English from the College of the Holy Cross and her MA in journalism from Northeastern University. She is the #1 *New York Times* bestselling author of *One of Us Is Lying, Two Can Keep a Secret,* and *One of Us Is Next.* Her work has been published in more than forty countries.

karenmcmanus.com